THE ROAD HOME

Rose Tremain is a writer of novels, short stories and screenplays. She lives in Norfolk and London with the biographer Richard Holmes. Her books have been translated into numerous languages, and have won many prizes including the Whitbread Novel of the Year, the James Tait Black Memorial Prize, the Prix Femina Etranger, the Dylan Thomas Prize, the Angel Literary Award and the *Sunday Express* Book of the Year.

Restoration was shortlisted for the Booker Prize and made into a movie; *The Colour* was shortlisted for the Orange Prize and selected by the *Daily Mail* Reading Club. Rose Tremain's most recent collection, *The Darkness of Wallis Simpson*, was shortlisted for both the First National Short Story Award and the Frank O'Connor International Short Story Award. Three of her novels are currently in development as films.

ALSO BY ROSE TREMAIN

Novels

Sadler's Birthday
Letter to Sister Benedicta
The Cupboard
The Swimming Pool Season
Restoration
Sacred Country
The Way I Found Her
Music and Silence
The Colour

Short Story Collections

The Colonel's Daughter
The Garden of the Villa Mollini
Evangelista's Fan
The Darkness of Wallis Simpson

For Children

Journey to the Volcano

ROSE TREMAIN

The Road Home

VINTAGE BOOKS
London

Published by Vintage 2008

4 6 8 10 9 7 5 3

First published in Great Britain in 2007 by Chatto & Windus

Vintage
Random House, 20 Vauxhall Bridge Road,
London SW1V 2SA

www.vintage-books.co.uk

Addresses for companies within The Random House Group Limited
can be found at: www.randomhouse.co.uk/offices.htm

The Random House Group Limited Reg. No. 954009

A CIP catalogue record for this book
is available from the British Library

ISBN 9780099478461

The Random House Group Limited supports The Forest
Stewardship Council (FSC), the leading international forest
certification organisation. All our titles that are printed on
Greenpeace approved FSC certified paper carry the FSC logo.
Our paper procurement policy can be found at:
www.rbooks.co.uk/environment

Printed and bound in Great Britain by
CPI Cox & Wyman, Reading RG1 8EX

Chapter Titles

'How can we live, without our lives?'

John Steinbeck: *The Grapes of Wrath*

For Brenda and David Reid,
with fondest love

I

Significant Cigarettes

On the coach, Lev chose a seat near the back and he sat huddled against the window, staring out at the land he was leaving: at the fields of sunflowers scorched by the dry wind, at the pig farms, at the quarries and rivers and at the wild garlic growing green at the edge of the road.

Lev wore a leather jacket and jeans and a leather cap pulled low over his eyes and his handsome face was grey-toned from his smoking and in his hands he clutched an old red cotton handkerchief and a dented pack of Russian cigarettes. He would soon be forty-three.

After some miles, as the sun came up, Lev took out a cigarette and stuck it between his lips, and the woman sitting next to him, a plump, contained person with moles like splashes of mud on her face, said quickly: 'I'm sorry, but there is no smoking allowed on this bus.'

Lev knew this, had known it in advance, had tried to prepare himself mentally for the long agony of it. But even an unlit cigarette was a companion – something to hold on to, something that had promise in it – and all he could be bothered to do now was to nod, just to show the woman that he'd heard what she'd said, reassure her that he wasn't going to cause trouble; because there they would have to sit for fifty hours or more, side by side with their separate aches and dreams, like a married couple. They would hear each other's snores and sighs, smell the food and drink each had brought with them, note the degree to which each was fearful or unafraid, make short forays into conversation. And then later, when they finally arrived in London, they would probably separate with barely a word or a look, walk out into a rainy morning, each alone and beginning a new life. And Lev thought how all of this was odd but necessary and already told him things about the world he was travelling to, a world in which he would break his back working – if only that work could be found. He would hold himself apart from other people, find corners and shadows in which to sit and smoke, demonstrate that he didn't need to belong, that his heart remained in his own country.

There were two coach-drivers. These men would take turns to drive and to sleep. There was an on-board lavatory, so the only stops the bus would make would be for gas. At gas stations, the passengers would be able to clamber off, walk a few paces, see wild flowers on a verge, soiled paper among bushes, sun or rain on the road. They might stretch up their arms, put on dark glasses against the onrush of nature's light, look for a clover leaf, smoke and stare at the cars rushing by. Then they would be herded back onto the coach, resume their old attitudes, arm themselves for the next hundred miles, for the stink of another industrial zone, or the sudden gleam of a lake, for rain and sunset and the approach of darkness on silent marshes. There would be times when the journey would seem to have no end.

Sleeping upright was not something Lev was practised in. The old seemed to be able to do it, but forty-two was not yet old. Lev's father, Stefan, sometimes used to sleep upright, in summer, on a hard wooden chair in his lunch break at the Baryn sawmill, with the hot sun falling onto the slices of sausage wrapped in paper on his knee and onto his flask of tea. Both Stefan and Lev could sleep lying down on a mound of hay or on the mossy carpet of a forest. Often, Lev had slept on a rag rug beside his daughter's bed, when she was ill or afraid. And when his wife, Marina, was dying, he'd lain for five nights on an area of linoleum flooring no wider than his outstretched arm, between Marina's hospital bed and a curtain patterned with pink and purple daisies, and sleep had come and gone in a mystifying kind of way, painting strange pictures in Lev's brain that had never completely vanished.

Towards evening, after two stops for gas, the mole-flecked woman unwrapped a hard-boiled egg. She peeled it silently. The smell of the egg reminded Lev of the sulphur springs at Jor, where he'd taken Marina, just in case nature could cure what man had given up for lost. Marina had immersed her body obediently in the scummy water, lain there looking at a female stork returning to its high nest, and said to Lev: 'If only we were storks.'

'Why d'you say that?' Lev had asked.

'Because you never see a stork dying. It's as though they didn't die.'

If only we were storks.

On the woman's knee a clean cotton napkin was spread and her white hands smoothed it and she unwrapped rye bread and a twist of salt.

'My name is Lev,' said Lev.

'My name is Lydia,' said the woman. And they shook hands, Lev's hand holding the scrunched-up kerchief, and Lydia's hand rough with salt and smelling of egg, and then Lev asked: 'What are you planning to do in England?' and Lydia said: 'I have some interviews in London for jobs as a translator.'

'That sounds promising.'

'I hope so. I was a teacher of English at School 237 in Yarbl, so my language is very colloquial.'

Lev looked at Lydia. It wasn't difficult to imagine her standing in front of a class and writing words on a blackboard. He said: 'I wonder why you're leaving our country when you had a good job at School 237 in Yarbl?'

'Well,' said Lydia. 'I became very tired of the view from my window. Every day, summer and winter, I looked out at the school yard and the high fence and the apartment block beyond, and I began to imagine I would die seeing these things, and I didn't want this. I expect you understand what I mean?'

Lev took off his leather cap and ran his fingers through his thick grey hair. He saw Lydia turn to him for a moment and look very seriously into his eyes. He said: 'Yes, I understand.'

Then there was a silence, while Lydia ate her hard-boiled egg. She chewed very quietly. When she'd finished the egg, Lev said: 'My English isn't too bad. I took some classes in Baryn, but my teacher told me my pronunciation wasn't very good. May I say some words and you can tell me if I'm pronouncing them correctly?'

'Yes, of course,' said Lydia.

Lev said: 'Lovely. Sorry. I am legal. How much please. Thank you. May you help me.'

'May I help *you*,' corrected Lydia.

'May I help you,' repeated Lev.

'Go on,' said Lydia.

'Stork,' said Lev. 'Stork's nest. Rain. I am lost. I wish for an interpreter. Bee-and-bee.'

'Be-and-be?' said Lydia. 'No, no. You mean "to be, or not to be".'

'No,' said Lev. 'Bee-and-bee. Family hotel, quite cheap.'

'Oh, yes, I know. B & B.'

Lev could now see that darkness was falling outside the window and he thought how, in his village, darkness had always arrived in precisely the same way, from the same direction, above the same trees, whether early or late, whether in summer, winter or spring, for the whole of his life. This darkness – particular to that place, Auror – was how, in Lev's heart, darkness would always fall.

And so he told Lydia that he came from Auror, had worked in the Baryn sawmill until it closed two years ago, and since then he'd found no work at all and his family – his mother, his five-year-old daughter and he – had lived off the money his mother made selling jewellery manufactured from tin.

'Oh,' said Lydia. 'I think that's very resourceful, to make jewellery from tin.'

'Sure,' said Lev. 'But it isn't enough.'

Tucked into his boot was a small flask of vodka. He extracted the flask and took a long swig. Lydia kept eating her rye bread. Lev wiped his mouth with the red handkerchief and saw his face reflected in the coach window. He looked away. Since the death of Marina, he didn't like to catch sight of his own reflection, because what he always saw in it was his own guilt at still being alive.

'Why did the sawmill at Baryn close?' asked Lydia.

'They ran out of trees,' said Lev.

'Very bad,' said Lydia. 'What other work can you do?'

Lev drank again. Someone had told him that in England vodka was too expensive to drink. Immigrants made their own alcohol from potatoes and tap water, and when Lev thought about these industrious immigrants, he imagined them sitting by a coal fire

4

in a tall house, talking and laughing, with rain falling outside the window and red buses going past and a television flickering in a corner of the room. He sighed and said: 'I will do any work at all. My daughter Maya needs clothes, shoes, books, toys, everything. England is my hope.'

Towards ten o'clock, red blankets were given out to the coach passengers, some of whom were already sleeping. Lydia put away the remnants of her meal, covered her body with the blanket and switched on a fierce little light above her under the baggage rack and began reading a faded old paperback, printed in English. Lev saw that the title of her book was *The Power and the Glory*. His longing for a cigarette had grown steadily since he'd drunk the vodka and now it was acute. He could feel the yearning in his lungs and in his blood, and his hands grew fidgety and he felt a tremor in his legs. How long before the next gas stop? It could be four or five hours. Everyone on the bus would be asleep by then, except him and one of the two drivers. Only they would keep a lonely, exhausting vigil, the driver's body tensed to the moods and alarms of the dark, unravelling road; his own aching for the comfort of nicotine or oblivion – and getting neither.

He envied Lydia, immersed in her English book. Lev knew he had to distract himself with something. He'd brought with him a book of fables: improbable stories he'd once loved about women who turned into birds during the hours of darkness, and a troupe of wild boar that killed and roasted their hunters. But Lev was feeling too agitated to read such fantastical things. In desperation, he took from his wallet a brand new British twenty-pound note and reached up and switched on his own little reading light and began to examine the note. On one side, the frumpy Queen, E II R, with her diadem, her face grey on a purple ground, and on the other, a man, some personage from the past, with a dark drooping moustache and an angel blowing a trumpet above him and all the angel's radiance falling on him in vertical lines. 'The British venerate their history,' Lev had been told in his English class, 'chiefly because they have never been subjected to Occupation. Only intermittently do they see that some of their past deeds were not good.'

The indicated lifespan of the man on the note was 1857–1934.

He looked like a banker, but what had he done to be on a twenty-pound note in the twenty-first century? Lev stared at his determined jaw, squinted at his name written out in a scrawl beneath the wing collar, but couldn't read it. He thought that this was a person who would never have known any other system of being alive but Capitalism. He would have heard the names Hitler and Stalin, but not been afraid – would have had no need to be afraid of anything except a little loss of capital in what Americans called the Crash, when men in New York had jumped out of windows and off roofs. He would have died safely in his bed before London was bombed to ruins, before Europe was torn apart. Right to the end of his days, the angel's radiance had probably shone on this man's brow and on his fusty clothes, because it was known across the world: the English were *lucky*. Well, thought Lev, I'm going to their country now and I'm going to make them share it with me: their infernal luck. I've left Auror and that leaving of my home was hard and bitter, but my time is coming.

Lev was roused from his thoughts by the noise of Lydia's book falling to the floor of the bus, and he looked at her and saw that she'd gone to sleep, and he studied her face with its martyrdom of moles. He put her age at about thirty-nine. She appeared to sleep without travail. He imagined her sitting in some booth with earphones clamped to her mousy hair, buoyant and alert on a relentless tide of simultaneous translation. *May you help me please. No. May I help you*.

Lev decided, as the night progressed, to try to remember certain significant cigarettes of the past. He possessed a vibrant imagination. At the Baryn sawmill he'd been known, derogatorily, as a 'dreamer'. 'Life is not for dreaming, Lev,' his boss had warned. 'Dreaming leads to subversion.' But Lev knew that his nature was fragile, easily distracted, easily made joyful or melancholy by the strangest of small things, and that this condition had afflicted his boyhood and his adolescence and had, perhaps, prevented him from getting on as a man. Especially after Marina had gone. Because now her death was with him always, like a shadow on the X-ray of his spirit. Other men might have been able to chase this shadow away – with drink, or with young women or with the novelty of making money – but Lev hadn't even tried. He knew that forgetting Marina was something he was not yet capable of doing.

All around him on the coach, passengers were dozing. Some lay slumped towards the aisle, their arms hanging loosely down in an attitude of surrender. The air was filled with repetitive sighing. Lev pulled the peak of his cap further over his face and decided to remember what was always known by him and his mother, Ina, as 'the poinsettia miracle', because this was a story that led towards a good ending, towards a smoke as immaculate as love.

Ina was a woman who never allowed herself to care about anything, because, she often said, 'What's the point of it, when life takes everything away?' But there were a few things that gave her joy and one of these was the poinsettia. Scarlet-leafed and shaped like a fir, resembling a brilliant man-made artefact more than a living plant, poinsettias excited in Ina a sober admiration, for their unique strangeness, for their seeming permanence in a world of perpetually fading and dying things.

One Sunday morning some years ago, near to Ina's sixty-fifth birthday, Lev had got up very early and cycled twenty-four miles to Yarbl where flowers and plants were sold in an open-air market behind the railway station. It was an almost autumnal day, and on the silent figures setting out their stalls a tender light was falling. Lev smoked and watched from the railway buffet, where he drank coffee and vodka. Then he went out and began to look for poinsettias.

Most of the stuff sold in the Yarbl market was fledgling food: cabbage plants, sunflower seeds, sprouting potatoes, currant bushes, bilberry canes. But more and more people were indulging their half-forgotten taste for decorative, useless things and the sale of flowers was increasing as each year passed.

Poinsettias were always visible from a long way off. Lev walked slowly along, alert for red. The sun shone on his scuffed black shoes. His heart felt strangely light. His mother was going to be sixty-five years old and he would surprise and astonish her by planting a trough of poinsettias on her porch, and in the evenings she would sit and do her knitting and admire them, and neighbours would arrive and congratulate her – on the flowers and on the care her son had taken.

7

But there were no poinsettias in the market. Up and down, Lev trudged, staring bleakly at carrot fern, at onion sets, at plastic bags filled with pig manure and ash.

No poinsettias.

The great catastrophe of this now announced itself to Lev. So he began again, retracing his steps along the lines of stalls, stopping now and then to badger the stall-holders, recognising that this badgering was accusatory, suggestive of the notion that these people were *greys*, keeping the red plants out of sight under the trestles, waiting for buyers who offered American dollars or motor parts or drugs.

'I *need* poinsettias,' he heard himself say, like a man parched with thirst or a petulant only child.

'Sorry, comrade,' said the market traders. 'Only at Christmas.'

All he could do was pedal home to Auror. Behind his bicycle he dragged a home-made wooden trailer (built with offcuts poached from the Baryn lumber yard) and the wheels of this trailer squeaked mockingly as the miles passed. The emptiness of Ina's sixty-fifth birthday yawned before Lev like an abandoned mine.

Lev shifted quietly in his seat, trying not to disturb Lydia's sleep. He laid his head on the cool window glass. Then he remembered the sight that had greeted him, like a vision, in some lost village along the road: an old woman dressed in black, sitting silently on a chair in front of her house, with a baby sleeping in a plastic pram by her side. And at her feet a motley of possessions for sale: a gramophone, some scales and weights, an embroidered shawl, a pair of leather bellows. And a barrow of poinsettia plants, their leaves newly tinctured with red.

Lev had wobbled on the bike, wondering if he was dreaming. He put a foot down on the dusty road. 'Poinsettias, Grandma, are they?'

'Is that their name? I call them red flags.'

He bought them all. The trailer was crammed and heavy. His money was gone.

He hid them under sacks until it was dark, planted them out in Ina's trough under the stars and stood by them, watching the dawn come up, and when the sun reached them the red of their leaves intensified in a startling way, as when desert crocuses bloom after rain. And that was when Lev lit a cigarette. He sat down on the steps of Ina's porch and smoked and stared at the poinsettias, and the cigarette was like radiant amber in him and he smoked it right down to its last centimetre and then put it out, but still kept it pressed into his muddy hand.

Lev slept after all.

He woke when the coach stopped for gas, somewhere in Austria, he assumed, for the petrol station was large and bright and in an open bay to one side of it was parked a silent congregation of trucks, with German names written on them, lit by orange sodium light. *Freuhof. Bosch. Grunewald. Königstransporte . . .*

Lydia was awake and together she and Lev got off the bus and breathed the cool night air. Lydia pulled a cardigan round her shoulders. Lev looked for dawn in the sky, but could see no sign of it. He lit a cigarette. His hands trembled as he took it in and out of his mouth.

'It's going to be cold in England,' said Lydia. 'Are you prepared for that?'

Lev thought about his imaginary tall house, with the rain coming down and the television flickering and the red buses going past.

'I don't know,' he said.

'When the winter comes,' said Lydia, 'we're going to be shocked.'

'Our own winters are cold,' said Lev.

'Yes, but not for so long. In England, I've been told, some winters never quite depart.'

'You mean there's no summer?'

'There is summer. But you don't feel it in your blood.'

Other passengers from the coach were now wandering around the gas station. Some were making visits to the washrooms. Others just stood about, as Lev and Lydia were doing, shivering a little, onlookers unsure what they were looking at, arrivals who had not yet arrived, everybody in transit and uncertain what time their watches should be telling. Behind the area where the trucks were parked lay a deep, impenetrable darkness of trees.

Lev had a sudden desire to send a postcard from this place to his daughter Maya, to describe this night-limbo to her: the sodium sky, the trees unmoving, the glare of the pay-station, the people like people in an art gallery, helpless before the unexplained exhibits. But Maya was too young to understand any of this. She was only five. When morning came, she would take Ina's hand and walk to school. For her lunch, she would eat cold sausage and poppyseed bread. When she came home, Ina would give her goat's milk with cinnamon in a yellow glass and raisin cakes and rose-petal jam. She would do her homework at the kitchen table, then go out into the main street of Auror and look for her friends and they would play with the goats and chickens in the dust.

'I miss my daughter already,' Lev said to Lydia.

By the time the coach crossed the border between Germany and Holland, Lev had surrendered himself to it: to his own small space by the window; to the eternal hum of the air-conditioning; to the quiet presence of Lydia, who offered him eggs and dried fruit and pieces of chocolate; to the smell and voices of the other passengers; to the chemical odour of the on-board lavatory; to the feeling of moving slowly across wide distances, but moving always forwards and on.

Watching the flat fields and the shimmering poplars, the canals and windmills and villages and grazing animals of the Netherlands going past, Lev felt so peaceful and quiet that it was as if the bus had become his life and he would never be asked to stir from the inertia of this bus-life ever again. He began to wish Europe were larger, so that he could linger over its scenery for days and days to come, until something in him altered, until he got bored with hard-boiled eggs and the sight of cattle in green pastures and he rediscovered the will to arrive at his destination.

He knew his growing apathy was dangerous. He began to wish that his best friend, Rudi, was with him. Rudi never surrendered to anything, and he wouldn't have surrendered to the opium of the passing miles. Rudi fought a pitched battle with life through every waking hour. 'Life is just a *system*,' Rudi often reminded Lev. 'All that matters is cracking the system.' In his sleep, Rudi's body lay crouched, with his fists bunched in front of his chest, like a boxer's. When he woke, he sprang and kicked away the bedclothes. His wild dark hair gleamed with its own invincible shine. He loved vodka and cinema and football. He dreamed of owning what he called a 'serious car'. In the bus, Rudi would have sung songs and danced folk dances in the aisle and traded goods with other passengers. He would have *resisted*.

Like Lev, Rudi was a chain-smoker. Once, after the sawmill closed, they'd made a smoke-filled journey together to the distant city of Glic, in the deep, purple cold of winter, when the sun hung low among the bones of trees, and ice gleamed like a diamond coating on the railway lines and Rudi's pockets were stashed with *grey* money and in his suitcase lay eleven bottles of vodka, cradled in straw.

Rumours of an American car, a Chevrolet Phoenix, for sale in Glic had reached Rudi in Auror. Rudi lovingly described this car as a 'Tchevi'. He said it was blue with white and chrome trim and had only done two hundred and forty thousand miles and he was going to travel to Glic and see it, and if he could beat the owner down on the price, he was going to damn well buy it and drive it home. The fact that Rudi had never driven a car before didn't worry him at all. 'Why should it?' he said to Lev. 'I drove a heavy-lifting vehicle at the sawmill every day of my fucking life. Driving is driving. And with American cars you don't even have to worry about gears. You just slam the stick into the "D-for-drive" position and take off.'

The train was hot, with a fat heating pipe running directly under the seats. Lev and Rudi had a carriage to themselves. They piled their sheepskin coats and fur hats into the luggage rack and opened the vodka suitcase and played music on a tiny, shrieking radio, small as a rat. The hot vodka fug of the carriage was beautiful and wild. They soon felt as reckless as mercenaries. When the ticket collector came round, they embraced him on both cheeks.

At Glic, they stepped out into a snow blizzard, but their blood was still hot and so the snow seemed delectable to them, like the caress of a young girl's hand on their faces, and they stumbled through the streets laughing. But by then the night was coming down and Rudi announced: 'I'm not looking at the Tchevi in the fucking dark. I want to see it gleaming.' So they stopped at the first frugal guest-house they found and sated their hunger with bowls of goulash and dumplings and went to sleep in a narrow room that smelled of mothballs and linoleum polish, and never stirred till morning.

The sun was up in a clear blue sky when Lev and Rudi found their way to the Tchevi owner's building. The snow all around them was thick and clean. And there it was, parked alone on the dingy street, under a solitary linden tree, the full extraordinary length and bulk of it, an ancient sky-blue Chevrolet Phoenix with white fins and shining chrome trim; and Rudi fell to his knees. 'That's my girl,' he said. 'That's my baby!'

It had its imperfections. On the driver's door, one hinge had rusted away. The rubber windscreen-wiper blades had perished to almost nothing in successive cold winters. All four tyres were worn. The radio didn't work.

Lev watched Rudi hesitate. He walked round and round the car, trailing his hand over the bodywork, scooping snow from the roof, examining the wiper blades, kicking the tyres, opening and closing the defective door. Then he looked up and said: 'I'll take her.' After that, he began to haggle, but the owner understood how great was Rudi's longing for the car and refused to lower his price by more than a fraction. The Tchevi cost Rudi everything he had with him, including his sheepskin coat and his fur hat and five of the eight bottles of vodka remaining in the suitcase. The owner was a professor of mathematics.

'I wonder what you're thinking about?' asked a voice. And it was Lydia, pausing suddenly in her new task, which was knitting.

Lev stared at her. He thought it was a long time since anybody had asked him this. Or perhaps nobody had ever asked him, because Marina had always seemed to know what was in his mind and tried to accommodate what she found there.

'Well,' said Lev, 'I was thinking about my friend Rudi and the time when I went with him to Glic to buy an American car.'

'Oh,' said Lydia. 'He's rich, then, your friend Rudi?'

'No,' said Lev. 'Or never for long. But he likes to trade.'

'Trading is so bad,' said Lydia, with a sniff. 'We shall never make progress as long as there is *grey* trade. But tell me about the car. Did he get it?'

'Yes,' said Lev. 'He did. What are you knitting?'

'A sweater,' said Lydia. 'For the English winter. The English call this garment a "jumper".'

'A jumper?'

'Yes. There's another word for you. Tell me about Rudi and the car.'

Lev took out his vodka flask and drank. Then he told Lydia how, after Rudi had bought the Tchevi, he drove a couple of times round the empty streets of the apartment estate to practise being at the wheel, with the professor of mathematics watching from his doorway, wearing an astrakhan hat and an amused expression on his face.

Then Lev and Rudi set off home, with the sun gleaming down on the quiet, icy world and Rudi put on the car heater to maximum and said this was the nearest he would get to Paradise. The car engine made a low, grumbling sound, like the engine of a boat, and Rudi said this was the sound of America, musical and strong. In the glove-box, Lev found three bars of Swiss chocolate, gone pale with time, and they shared these between cigarettes, which they lit with the radiant car lighter, and Rudi said: 'Now I have my new vocation in Auror: taxi driver.'

Towards afternoon, still miles from their village, they stopped at a petrol station, which consisted of one rusty pump in a silent valley, and a freckled dog keeping watch. Rudi honked the horn and an elderly man limped out of a wooden hut, where sacks of coal were on sale, and he looked upon the Tchevi with fear, as though it might have been an army tank or a UFO, and the freckled dog stood up and began barking. Rudi got out, wearing only his trousers and boots and checked shirt, and when he slammed the driver's door behind him, the remaining hinge broke and the door fell off into the snow.

Rudi swore. He and the pump attendant gazed at this mishap, for which there didn't seem to be any immediate remedy, and even the dog fell into a nonplussed silence. Then Rudi lifted up the door and attempted to put it back on, but though it went on all right, it wouldn't stay on and had to be tied to the seat fixings with a frayed bit of rope, and Rudi said: 'That fucking professor! He knew this would happen. He's turned me over, good and sweet.'

Rudi stamped about in the snow, while the tank was filled with gas, because it was beginning to freeze again and Rudi had no coat or hat and the falling of the door had pricked his bubble of happiness. Lev got out and examined the broken hinges and said: 'It's just the hinges, Rudi. We can fix them, back home.'

'I know,' said Rudi, 'but is the fucking door going to stay on the car for the next hundred miles? That's my question.'

They drove on, brimming with petrol Lev had paid for, going west towards the sunset, and the sky was first deep orange, then smoky red, then purple, and lilac shadows flecked the snow-blanketed fields and Lev said: 'Sometimes this country can look quite beautiful,' and Rudi sighed and said: 'It looked beautiful this morning, but soon we'll be back in the dark.'

When the dark came on, ice formed on the windshield, but all the worn wiper blades would do was crunch over this ice, back and forth very slowly, making a moaning noise as they moved, and soon it became impossible to see the way ahead. Rudi drew the car to the side of the road and he and Lev stared at the patterns the ice had made and at the faint yellow glow the headlights cast on the filigree branches of the trees, and Lev saw that Rudi's hands were trembling.

'Now fucking what?' Rudi said.

Lev took off the woollen scarf he was wearing and put it round Rudi's neck. Then he got out and opened the trunk and took out one of the three remaining bottles of vodka from the straw and told Rudi to turn off the engine, and as the engine died the wiper blades made one last useless arc, then lay down, like two exhausted old people fallen end to end beside a skating rink. Lev wrenched open the vodka, took a long sip, then began pouring the alcohol very slowly onto the windscreen and watched it make clear runnels through the ice. As the frosting slowly vanished, Lev could just make out Rudi's wide face, very close to the windshield, like a child's face, gazing up in awe. And after that they drove on through the night, stopping to pour on more vodka from time to time and watching the illuminated needle of the petrol gauge falling and falling.

Lydia paused in her knitting. She held the 'jumper' up to her chest, to see how much further she had to go before casting off for the shoulder seam. She said: 'Now I'm interested in that journey. Did you reach your home?'

'Yes,' said Lev. 'By dawn we were there. We were pretty tired. Well, we were *very* tired. And the gas tank was almost empty. That car's so greedy it's going to bankrupt Rudi.'

Lydia smiled and shook her head. 'And the door?' she asked. 'Did you mend it?'

'Oh, sure.' said Lev. 'We soldered on new hinges from a baby's pram. It's fine. Except the driver's door opens violently now.'

'Violently? But Rudi still drives the Tchevi as a taxi, with this violent door?'

'Yes. In summer, he has all the windows open and you can ride along with the wind in your hair.'

'Oh, I wouldn't like that,' said Lydia, 'I spend a lot of time trying to protect my hair from the wind.'

Night was coming down again when the coach arrived at the Hook of Holland and waited in a long line to drive onto the ferry. No berths had been booked for the passengers of the bus; they were advised to find benches or deck-chairs in which to sleep and to avoid buying drinks from the ship's bar, which charged unfair prices. 'When the ferry arrives in England,' said one of the coach-drivers, 'we're only about two hours away from London and your destination, so try to sleep if you can.'

Once aboard the boat, Lev made his way to the top deck and looked down at the port, with its cranes and containers, its bulky sheds and offices and parking lots and its quayside, shimmery with oil. An almost invisible rain was falling. Gulls cried, as though to some long-lost island home, and Lev thought how hard it would be to live near the sea and hear this melancholy sound every day of your life.

The sea was calm and the ferry set off very silently, its big engines seemingly muffled by the dark. Lev leaned on the rail, smoking and staring at the Dutch port as it slipped away, and when the land was gone and the sky and the sea merged in blackness he remembered the dreams he'd had when Marina was dying, of being adrift on an ocean that had no limits and never broke on any human shore.

The briny smell of the sea made his cigarette taste bitter, so he ground it underfoot on the high deck, then lay down on a bench to sleep. He pulled his cap over his eyes and, to soothe himself, imagined the night falling on Auror, falling as it always fell over the fir-covered hills and the cluster of chimneys and the wooden steeple of the school-house. And there in this soft night lay Maya, under her goose-down quilt, with one arm thrown out sideways, as if showing some invisible visitor the small room she shared with her grandmother: its two beds, its rag rug, its chest of drawers painted green and yellow, its paraffin stove, and its square window, open to the cool air and the night dews and the cry of owls ...

It was a nice picture, but Lev couldn't get it to stabilise in his mind. The knowledge that when the Baryn sawmill closed Auror and half a dozen other villages like it were doomed kept obliterating the room and the sleeping girl and even the image of Ina, shuffling about in the dark before kneeling to say her prayers.

'Prayers are no fucking good,' Rudi had said, when the last tree was sawn up and shipped away and all the machinery went quiet. 'Now comes the reckoning, Lev. Only the resourceful will survive.'

2

The Diana Card

The coach pulled in to Victoria at nine in the morning and the tired passengers stepped off the bus into the unexpected brightness of a sunny day. They looked all around them at the shine on the buildings, at the gleaming rack of baggage carts, at the dark shadows their bodies cast on the London pavement, and tried to become accustomed to the glare. 'I dreamed of rain,' said Lev to Lydia.

It felt very warm. Lydia's half-finished jumper was stowed in her suitcase. Her winter coat was heavy on her arm.

'Goodbye, Lev,' she said, holding out her hand.

Lev leaned forward and put a kiss on each of Lydia's mole-splashed cheeks and said: 'May you help me. May I help you.' And they laughed and started to walk away – as Lev had known they would do – each to a separate future in the unknown city.

But Lev turned to watch Lydia, as she hurried towards a line of black taxis. When she opened the door of her cab, she looked back and waved, and Lev saw that there was a sadness in this wave of hers – or even a sudden, unexpected reproach. In answer to this, he touched the peak of his leather cap, in a gesture he knew was either too military or too old-fashioned, or both, and then Lydia's taxi drove away and he saw her looking determinedly straight ahead, like a gymnast trying to balance on a beam.

Now Lev picked up his bag and went in search of a washroom. He knew that he stank. He could detect an odd kind of seaweed stench under his checked shirt and he thought, Well, this is appropriate, I'm beached here now, under this unexpected sun, on this island ... He could hear planes roaring overhead and he thought, Half the continent is headed this way, but nobody imagined it like it is, with the heat rising and the sky so empty and blue.

He followed signs to the station toilets, then found himself barred from entering them by a turnstile. He put down his bag and watched what other people did. They put money into a slot and the turnstile moved, but the only money Lev had was a wad of twenty-pound notes – each one calculated by Rudi to last him a week, until he found work.

'Please may you help me?' said Lev to a smart, elderly man approaching the stile. But the man put in his coin, pushed at the turnstile with his groin and held his head high as he passed through, as though Lev hadn't even come within his sightline. Lev stared after him. Had he said the words incorrectly? The man didn't pause in his confident stride.

Lev waited. Rudi, he knew, would have vaulted over the barrier, without a second's pause, untroubled by what the consequences might be, but Lev felt that vaulting was beyond him right now. His legs lacked Rudi's inexhaustible spring. Rudi made his own laws and they were different from his and this would probably always be the case.

Standing there, Lev's longing to be clean increased steadily as the moments passed. He could feel stinging pains here and there on his skin, like sores. Sweat broke on his skull and ran down the back of his neck. He felt slightly sick. He took out a cigarette from an almost empty pack and lit it, and the men coming and going from the washroom stared at him, and those stares drew his attention at last to a *No Smoking* sign stuck onto the tiles a few feet from where he stood. He drew in a last sweet breath from the cigarette and ground it out under his feet and he saw then that his black shoes were stained with mud and thought, This is the mud of my country, the mud of all Europe, and I must find some rags and wipe it away ...

After some time, a young man, wearing overalls, unshaven and carrying a canvas bag of tools, approached the washroom turnstile and Lev decided that this man – because he was young and because the overalls and the work-bag marked him as a member of the once-honourable proletariat – might not pretend that he hadn't seen him, so he said as carefully as he could: 'May you help me, please?'

The man had long, untidy hair and the skin of his face was white with plaster-dust. 'Sure,' he said. 'What's up?'

Lev indicated the turnstile, holding up a twenty-pound note. The man smiled. Then he rummaged in the pocket of his overalls, found a coin, handed it to Lev and snatched the note away. Lev stared in dismay. 'No,' he said. 'No, please …'

But the young man turned, went through the barrier and began to walk into the washroom. Lev gaped. Not a single word of English would come to him now and he cursed loudly in his own language. Then he saw the man coming back towards him with a smile that made dark creases in the white dust of his face. He held the twenty-pound note out to Lev. 'Only joking,' he said. 'Just joking, mate.'

Lev stood in a toilet stall and removed his clothes. He took an old striped towel from his bag and wrapped it round his waist. He felt his sickness pass.

He went to one of the washbasins and ran hot water. From a seat by the entrance, the elderly Sikh washroom attendant stared at him with grave, unblinking eyes under his carefully wound turban.

Lev washed his face and hands, tugged out his razor and shaved the four-day stubble from his chin. Then, careful to keep the threadbare towel in place, he soaped his armpits and his groin, his stomach and the backs of his knees. The Sikh didn't move, only kept staring at Lev, as at some old motion picture he knew by heart, which still fascinated but no longer moved him. The feel of the warm water and the soap on Lev's body was so soothing he felt almost like crying. Reflected in the washroom mirrors, he could see men glancing at him, but nobody spoke and Lev soaped and scrubbed at his body until it was pink and tingling and the sea-stench was gone. He put on clean underpants, then washed his feet and stamped on the towel to dry them. He took socks and a clean shirt from his bag. He ran a comb through his thick grey hair. His eyes looked tired, his clean-shaven face, gaunt in the cold light of the washroom, but he felt human again: he felt ready.

Lev repacked his things and went towards the door. The Sikh

was still motionless on his hard plastic chair, but then Lev saw that near him was a saucer and that it contained a few coins – just a few, because people here were apparently in too much of a hurry to bother with a tip for an old man with bruised eyes – and Lev felt troubled that he had no coin to put in the saucer. After all the soap he'd used and the amount of water he'd splashed onto the floor, he owed the attendant some small consideration. He stopped and searched in his pockets and found a cheap plastic cigarette lighter he'd bought at the bus depot in Yarbl. He was about to put this in the saucer when he thought, No, this Sikh man has a job and a chair to sit on and I have nothing, which makes every single thing I own too precious to give away to him. Lev's thinking in relation to the tip he was refusing to give grew more sophisticated when he told himself that the Sikh appeared so unmoved by everything that went on around him that he would therefore certainly be unmoved by a paltry cigarette lighter. And so Lev walked away and out through the turnstile, heading for the sunshine and the street, and he imagined that the Sikh wouldn't even bother to turn his head to give him a reproachful stare.

Where the buses pulled in and drove out, Lev paused. Long ago – or it seemed long ago to him – when he'd booked his seat on the Trans-Euro bus, the young girl in the travel office had said to him: 'On your arrival in London, you may be approached by people with offers of work. If these people come to you, do not sign any contract. Ask them what work they are offering and how much they will pay and what place they will find for you to sleep in. Then you may accept, if the conditions appear right.'

In Lev's mind, these 'people' resembled the policemen of cities like Yarbl and Glic, heavy types with muscled forearms and healthy complexions and hand-guns slung about their anatomy in clever places. And now Lev began hoping they would appear, to take from him all responsibility for the next few days and hours of his life. He didn't really care what the 'work' was, as long as he had a wage and a routine and a bed to lie in. He was so tired that he felt almost like lying down where he was, in the warm sunshine, and just waiting until someone showed up, but then he thought that he didn't know how long a day was, a summer day in England, and how soon afternoon and evening would arrive, and he didn't want to find himself still on the street when it got dark.

People arrived and departed in buses, taxis and cars, but no one came near Lev. He began to walk, following the sun, very hungry suddenly, but devoid of a plan, even a plan for getting some food. He passed a coffee shop, and the smell of the good coffee was tempting, but though he hesitated on the pavement outside the place, he didn't dare go in, worrying that he wouldn't have the right denomination of money for the food and coffee he desired. Again, he thought how Rudi would have mocked this pathetic timidity and gone bounding in and found the right words and the right money to get what he wanted.

The street Lev was in was wide and noisy, with red buses swaying along close to the kerb and the stench of traffic spoiling the air. There was no breeze. On a high building he saw flags hanging limp against their poles and a woman with long hair and a gauzy dress standing at the pavement's edge, silent and still, as if a figure in a painting. Planes kept passing overhead, embroidering the sky with garlands of vapour.

Lev turned left off the crowded boulevard and into a street where trees had been planted and he stood in the shade of one of these trees and put down his bag, which felt heavy now, and lit a cigarette. He remembered that when he had started to smoke, all those years ago, he had discovered that smoking could mask hunger. And he'd remarked on this to his father, Stefan, and Stefan had replied: 'Of course it does. Didn't you know this till now? And it's much better to die from the smoke than to die of hunger.'

Lev leaned against the tree. It was a young plane tree. Its patterning of shade on the ground was delicate and precise, as though nature were designing wallpaper. Stefan had 'died from the smoke', or from the years and years of sawdust at the Baryn mill, died at fifty-nine, before Maya was born, long before Marina fell ill or the rumours of closure began to circulate in Baryn. And all he'd said at the end, in his frail voice, like the breaking voice of an adolescent boy, was: 'This is a rotten death, Lev. Don't go this way, if you can help it.'

A sudden spasm of choking assailed Lev. He threw away his cigarette and drank the last dregs of vodka from his flask. Then he sat down on the iron grating that circled the plane tree and closed his eyes. The feel of the tree on his spine was comforting, like a familiar chair, and his head fell sideways and he slept. One hand rested on his bag. The vodka flask lay on his thigh. Above him, a nesting sparrow came and went from the tree.

Lev woke when someone touched his shoulder. He stared blankly at a fleshy face inside a motorcycle helmet and at a bulging belly. He'd been dreaming about a potato field, about being lost in the enormity of the field, among its never-ending troughs and ridges.

'Wake up, sir. Police.'

The policeman's breath smelled stale, as though he too had been travelling without rest for days on end. Lev attempted to reach into his jacket pocket to produce his passport, but a wide hand seized his wrist and now gripped it with fearsome force.

'Steady on! No tricks, thank you kindly. Up you get!'

He pulled Lev roughly to his feet, then pinioned him against the tree, giving his ankle a nudge with his boot to force his legs apart.

The vodka flask clattered to the ground. On the policeman's hip, his radio made sudden, violent sounds, like the coughing of a dying man.

Lev felt the policeman's free hand move over his body: arms, torso, hips, groin, legs, ankles. He held himself as still as he could and made no protest. Some far-away part of his brain wondered if he were about to be arrested and sent back home and then he thought of all those unending miles to be covered and the shame of his arrival in Auror with nothing to show for the pain and disruption he'd caused.

The radio coughed again and Lev felt the iron grip on his arm relax. The policeman faced him square-on, standing so close to him that his fat belly nudged the buckle of Lev's belt.

'Asylum-seeker, are you?'

He uttered these words as though they disgusted him, as though they made him want to bring up some of the food that had soured his breath. And Lev recognised the words. At the travel office in Yarbl, the helpful young woman had said: 'Remember, you are legal, economic migrants, not "asylum-seekers", as the British call those who have been dispossessed. Our country is part of the EU now. You have the right to work in England. You must not let yourself be harassed.'

'I am legal,' said Lev.

'See your passport, please, sir.'

Lev's arms were still held high, against the tree. Slowly, he lowered them and reached into his pocket and produced his passport and the policeman snatched it away. Lev watched him look from the passport photograph to Lev's face and back again.

'All militiamen are dumb bastards,' Rudi had once said. 'Only stupid people want to fart around with handcuffs and two-way fucking radios.'

'All right,' said the policeman. 'Just arrived, then, have you?'

'Yes.'

'Look in your bag, please, sir?'

The policeman squatted down, his belt creaking, the tubular folds of his belly squashing themselves into an uncomfortable-looking huddle. He dragged open the zip of Lev's cheap canvas bag and removed the contents: the clothes Lev had taken off in the station lavatory, his grimy wash-bag, clean T-shirts and sweaters, a pair of new shoes, packs of Russian cigarettes, an alarm clock, two pairs of trousers, photographs of Marina and Maya, a money belt, an English dictionary and his book of fables, two bottles of vodka ...

Lev waited patiently. Hunger growled in his gut, which he knew was constipated from all the hard-boiled eggs Lydia had pressed on him. He stared at the fragility of his possessions, laid out on the pavement.

At last, the policeman repacked the bag and stood up. 'Have an address in London, do you? Place to stay? Hotel? Flat?'

'Bee-and-bee,' said Lev.

'You've got a B & B? Where?'

Lev shrugged.

'Where's your B & B, sir?'

'I dunno,' said Lev. 'I find one.'

A growling, urgent voice now came through on the radio. The policeman (whose rank Lev was unable to judge) jammed it to the side of his head and the voice laid a stream of incomprehensible words into his ear. Now Lev could see the police motorbike, flamboyantly striped with fluorescent decals, parked nose-on into the kerb, and he thought how Rudi would have been interested in the make and c.c. of the bike, but that he, Lev, was indifferent to it. He waited silently and heard for the first time the bird disturbing the leaves above his head. It felt hot, even in the shade of the tree. Lev had no idea whether it was still morning.

The policeman moved away, talking on his radio. From time to time he looked back at Lev, like the master of a dog without a lead, to make sure he hadn't wandered away. Then he returned and said: 'Right.'

He picked up Lev's bag and the empty vodka flask and shoved them towards him, together with his passport. He now reminded Lev of a bully at his school called Dmitri and Lev remembered that Dmitri-the-bully had died in a tram that had overturned in the Yarbl market, and that when he and Rudi had heard about his death, they'd laughed and stamped around, screaming with joy.

'On your way,' said the policeman. 'No sleeping in streets. This is anti-social behaviour and liable to a heavy fine. So get yourself sorted. Clean your fucking shoes. Get a haircut, and you may just have a chance.'

Lev remained where he was. Slowly, he returned his passport to his jacket pocket and watched the policeman heave his bulk onto the heavy bike and manoeuvre it out into the road. He kicked the engine into clamorous life and rode away, without glancing at Lev, as though Lev no longer had any existence in his mind.

Lev looked at his watch. It said 12.23, but he had no idea whether this was English time or only time in Auror, when the children in Maya's little school would be sitting on a bench and eating their lunch, which would consist of goat's milk and bread and pickled cucumber, with, sometimes in summer, wild strawberries from the hills above the village.

Reaching the river, Lev set down his bag and extracted one twenty-pound note from his wallet. He bought two hot dogs and a can of Coca-Cola from a stall and a hoard of change was put into his hand. He felt proud of this transaction.

He leaned on the embankment wall, and looked at London. The food felt rich and burning, the cola seemed to pinch at his teeth. Though the sky was blue, the river remained an opalescent grey-green and Lev wondered whether this was always true of city rivers – that they were incapable of reflecting the sky because of all the centuries of dark mud beneath. Travelling on the water, going in both directions, were cumbersome tourist boats, with carefree people clustered into seating on the top deck, taking photographs in the sun.

Lev's eye was held by these people. He envied them their ease and their summer shorts and the way the voices of the tour guides echoed out across the wavelets, naming the buildings in three or four different languages, so that those on the boats would never feel confused or lost. Lev noted, too, that this journey of theirs was finite – upriver a few miles, past the giant white wheel turning slowly on its too-fragile stem, then back to where they'd started from – whereas his own journey in England had barely begun; it was infinite, with no known ending or destination, and yet already, as the moments passed, confusion and worry were sending pains to his head.

At Lev's back, joggers kept passing, and the scuff and squeak of their trainers, their rapid breathing, were like a reproach to Lev, who stood without moving, bathing his teeth in cola, devoid of any plan, while these runners had purpose and strength and a tenacious little goal of self-improvement.

Lev finished the cola and lit a cigarette. He was sure his 'self' needed improving, too. For a long time now, he'd been moody, melancholy and short-tempered. Even with Maya. For days on end, he'd sat on Ina's porch without moving, or lain in an old grey hammock, smoking and staring at the sky. Many times he'd refused to play with his daughter, or help her with her reading, left everything to Ina. And this was unfair, he knew. Ina kept the family alive with her jewellery-making. She also cooked their meals and cleaned the house and hoed the vegetable patch and fed the animals – while Lev lay and looked at clouds. It was more than unfair; it was lamentable. But at last he'd been able to tell his mother he was going to make amends. By learning English and then by migrating to England, he was going to save them. Two years from now, he would be a man-of-the-world. He would own an expensive watch. He would put Ina and Maya aboard a tourist boat and show them the famous buildings. They would have no need of a tourist guide because he, Lev, would know the names of everything in London by heart ...

Reproaching himself for his laziness, his thoughtlessness towards Ina, Lev walked in the direction of a riverside stall selling souvenirs and cards. The stall was shaded by the pillars of a tall bridge and

Lev felt suddenly cold as he moved out of the sunlight. He stared at the flags, toys, models, mugs and linen towels, wondering what to buy for his mother. The stall-holder watched him lazily from his corner in the shadows. Lev knew that Ina would like the towels – the linen felt thick and hard-wearing – but the price on them was £5.99, so he moved away.

Slowly, he turned the rack of postcards, and scenes from life in London revolved obediently in front of him. Then he saw the thing he knew he would have to buy: it was a greetings card in the shape of Princess Diana's head. On her face was her famous, heartbreaking smile and in her blonde hair nestled a diamond tiara and the blue of her eyes was startling and sad.

Buying the Diana card exhausted Lev. As he slouched back into the sunshine, he felt spent, lame, at the end of what he could endure that day. He had to find a bed somewhere and lie down.

He made a decision and he knew it was reckless, but he felt incapable of doing anything else: he hailed a taxi. He was almost surprised when it stopped for him. The cabbie was small and old with stringy grey hair. He waited patiently for Lev to speak.

'Bee-and-bee, please,' said Lev.

'Eh?' said the cabbie.

'Please,' said Lev. 'I am very tired. May you take to Bee-and-bee.'

The cabbie scratched his head, dislodging the few ancient strands of hair that lay over his scalp. 'Nothing I know of round here. Only reliable ones I know are in Earls Court. That OK for you?'

'Sorry?' said Lev.

'Earls Court,' said the cabbie loudly. 'Off the Earls Court Road. All right?'

'Right,' said Lev. 'Take, please.'

He got into the cab and lay back on the wide, comfortable seat. He could see the cabbie staring at him in his driver's mirror: staring as he drove. Outside the taxi window, shimmered London, a show-city, with no memory of war. From time to time, Lev thought he recognised a building he'd seen in one of the slides shown to the English class in Yarbl, but he wasn't sure. All he could feel was the onrush of the English day, time hastened by the moving traffic and the hurrying people and the sun appearing and disappearing behind roofs and towers.

The landlady of the Champions Bed and Breakfast Hotel introduced herself to Lev as Sulima. She was about fifty. She wore a sari and her skin was the colour of olive-bread and her lips were glossy and crimson and her voice seemed sweet to Lev, courteous and slow.

He followed her along a clean, carpeted landing to Room 7 and she showed him in.

'My last room,' said Sulima. 'You are lucky. All rooms have shower and coffee-making facilities. There is your TV. This room is a little dark as it looks out onto the flats, but you will see that it is quiet. You will sleep very well.'

Lev nodded. His eye rested on the narrow bed with its wooden headboard and its two clean pillows.

Sulima smiled at him. 'How many nights do you wish to stay?' she asked.

Lev understood the question, but he didn't know what to answer. He set down his bag.

'One night?' said Sulima. 'Two nights?'

'How much is cost?' asked Lev.

'Twenty pounds for the room. Twenty-two pounds with breakfast.'

Twenty pounds. Twenty-two pounds ...

Lev sighed, damning Rudi for miscalculating the money question so disastrously. 'One night,' he said.

'You would like breakfast in the morning, sir?'

Lev hesitated. He wondered what breakfast would be and whether he would have the stomach to eat it. The hot dog still flamed inside him, as though his belly were filled with greasy gas.

'I don't know,' he said.

Sulima was switching on lights, placing the remote control of the TV on the bedside table, and Lev saw that she moved in an elegant and unobtrusive way. She smoothed the bed. 'Well, you can let me know about breakfast. Just phone Reception. You want an alarm call?'

'Sorry?' said Lev.

'Wake-up call?'

Lev shrugged. He had no idea what Sulima had just said, but she seemed to understand, through that smile of hers, what he was feeling, that he was beyond answering any more questions, that his human frame was about to fall. She handed Lev his key and went quietly away.

Now that he had a bed at last, Lev sat down on it and was able to put off for a while longer the sweet moment of closing his eyes. He took off his jacket and laid out the money remaining in his pocket and tried to count it, but his mind seemed set against doing any kind of sum. He just sat and stared at the unfamiliar coins until his eye suddenly rested on a piece of torn and crumpled paper he'd brought out from his pocket with the money. He didn't recognise it. He picked it up and unfolded it and saw a few words scrawled on it in his own language.

> *Dear Lev, I have enjoyed this journey. May I wish you luck. If you should ever need a translator, here is my number where I am staying with my friends in North London. I shall help you if I can. Sincerely yours, Lydia.*

Lev stared at the note. He wondered when Lydia had decided to write it – decided to put it into the pocket of his leather jacket! And he smiled fondly. It was the kind of secret thing a lover might do. Yet he suspected that nothing of this sort had been in Lydia's mind. She was simply an affectionate person, a little lonely perhaps, but moved by kindness, not by sex, and with a sensibility delicate enough to tell her that, in all probability, Lev would never telephone the number, never risk the small percentage of compromise such a phone call would entail. Yet Lev didn't throw away the piece of paper. He put it into his wallet and, as he did so, thought with tenderness of Lydia's knitting and of her dimpled white hands and the hard-boiled eggs she ate with such conspicuous care, so that no morsel of egg, no shard of shell was dropped onto her skirt or down onto the carpeted floor of the bus.

Lev moved slowly to the window of his room and looked out. The sun was obscured by the back of a high building and only a few feet from the window was a grimy flat roof, along which a pigeon was wandering.

'Pigeons,' Stefan had once said, 'carry the soul of the countryside into the city: the souls of trees and wood-sprites. The souls of the dead of the forest.'

'Who are the "dead of the forest"?' Lev had asked his father.

'Those who have suffered,' Stefan had replied. 'Doesn't the past of our country have *any* meaning for you?'

Lev had got up and walked away from this conversation. He'd hated it when Stefan put him down, as he'd so often chosen to do, and the old man's talk of 'wood-sprites' always infuriated and embarrassed him. He knew that Stefan hung 'spirit rags' in the trees behind Auror: he'd seen them dangling there, pathetic offerings to the dead. Lev had shown them to Rudi and said: 'Look at those. My father and his generation! I'm fed up with them. Their heads are in a complete fucking muddle.'

'True,' Rudi had answered, staring at the strips of cloth. 'History got them at an impressionable age.'

Lev now stared at the pigeon, at its wine-coloured legs, its little jerking head. Stefan was one of the 'dead of the forest' now, buried in an overgrown plot behind Auror, where firs and ash trees were seeding themselves anew. But Lev seldom visited him. He knew Ina went there and sometimes took Maya with her, and in summer they would return home with armfuls of wild marguerites, and Maya would tell Lev: 'We saw that place where Grandpappi is sleeping.' Lev had half intended to go before he left for England, to say a kind of goodbye to his father, but in the end he had stayed away. And it had been easy to stay away. It had been easy to dismiss such a visit as pointless, sentimental ritual. Yet, seeing the pigeon on the flat roof now, it was nevertheless Stefan who immediately came into Lev's mind, and at once he could see him clear as sunlight, sitting on his hard chair at Baryn, with his half-eaten heel of salami, tearing bread with his stained hands, dabbing at his droopy moustache with his kerchief. And he knew that Stefan was part of the reason he was here in London, that he'd had to defy in himself that longing of his father's to resist change, and he thought: I should feel grateful that the sawmill closed, or I'd be exactly where he was, immortal on a chair. I'd be enslaved to a lumber yard until I died, and to the same lunch each day and to the snow falling and drifting, year on year, falling and drifting in the same remote and backward places.

Now, the bed received his bones.

It was already afternoon. Lev lay unmoving, half covered by the sheet and blanket, in a sleep too heavy for dreams.

He emerged once from this torpor, just to stagger to the toilet and piss away the cola in a clean bowl that smelled of boiled sweets and to note that the sky was darkening over London and that a few lights had come on in the block of flats opposite. He ran water in the washbasin and drank and caught the sound of laughter along the passage.

The bed was as comfortable as any he'd ever slept in and he tried not to think about the cost of it, but only about his good fortune to be lying there, with the city settling down around him for its momentous night and the woman called Sulima sitting, quiet and contained, in the hall, keeping watch.

He put on a shaded bedside light and momentarily fell into the habitual pattern of wondering – as he had in Auror – how long the electricity would remain before some self-satisfied engineer in the Yarbl power station flicked a switch to divert it elsewhere. Maya once asked him, 'Why do the lights always go out, Pappa?' but Lev couldn't now remember what he'd replied. Something about there being too little light to go round? Something about the need to share? Who knows? But he did remember that, drunk one night, and thrown into the familiar, fumey darkness of Rudi's house, he'd heard himself say: 'Power cuts are deliberate. There's plenty of juice. They just like to spoil our evenings.'

Rudi's wife, Lora, wearing her night clothes, had come into the room where they drank. She was carrying the stub of a lit candle in a cracked saucer, and she put it down among the empty vodka bottles, and went away again, without a word, and Rudi said: 'Lora's a very nice woman. One day, she'll find a good husband.' And then they sat, laughing, either side of the flickering candle, laughing until their stomachs cramped, laughing a drunken, silent, inexplicable laugh, which felt as though it was going to have no end.

Lev closed his eyes again. The light behind his eyelids was the colour of chocolate and he knew that sleep would be like this, velvety and dark, and that it would last until morning.

3

'A Man May Travel Far, but His Heart May Be Slow to Catch Up'

Hello, Mamma, hello, Maya. Here is Princess Diana for you.
I am safe. Weather is quite hot. I am going to find a job today.
XXX Lev/Pappa.

Lev sat in Sulima's tidy dining room, drinking tea and writing his card. He was alone there. The tea was comforting and strong and he remembered how Rudi, who, as a young man, had been in prison for two months, had told him that, in the Institute of Correction in Yarbl, tea was the prime currency traded by the inmates, and he thought how in their youth – his and Rudi's – the world had still contained small corners of innocence, like air pockets in a ship that was going down. At the open window, net curtains swayed in a warm breeze. On the wall above him, near a gaudy picture of a tiger, the hands of a wall clock moved silently on. It was just after ten thirty-five.

Lev had showered and washed his hair. His body felt clean yet heavy, as though on the surface it was young but its sinews were those of an old man. He pictured this old man walking the hot London streets, trailing his heavy bag, trying to talk to strangers, pretending he was willing and strong, ready for any work, a person of many skills ...

Sulima appeared through the plaster arch that led to her hallway. 'You want more tea?' she asked pleasantly.

Sulima was wearing a different sari today, the colour of opals, the colour of the grey-green river. Between the sari bodice and its skirt, the bulge of her midriff was smooth and golden. She stood and looked at Lev and his Diana card and then she sat down opposite him and said: 'I try to help people who come from overseas. I was helped when I arrived here. I was given a job as a chambermaid in a hotel called The Avenues. Very hard work. Cleaning and cleaning. And everything just-so: pelmet top dusted, edge of the toilet paper folded under. You know?'

Lev had no idea what a pelmet top was, or why toilet paper might have to be folded, but he nodded just the same. Sulima moved away his breakfast plate. The sausage was half eaten, but the egg and bacon hadn't been touched. Lev pulled out his cigarettes, took the last one from the packet and lit it. Sulima passed him a glass ashtray.

'You have a wife and family?' she asked.

Lev took a pull on the cigarette, turned his head away from Sulima as he blew out the smoke. 'My wife died,' he said.

Sulima put a hand to her mouth, and Lev saw in this gesture the reaction of a much younger woman, of a child even, who'd been brought up to show repentance whenever she said something inappropriate or wrong. To help her out of her discomfort, he pointed at the picture of the tiger and said: 'My daughter, Maya. Age of five years. Loves animals.'

'Yes?' said Sulima.

'Yes. Says to me sometimes: "Pappa, this pig is sad, this goose is tired."'

'Yes? Really?'

'This tiger. She might say, "He is angry".'

Sulima stared at Lev. She blinked nervously and her smooth hands began to arrange and rearrange her hair. Outside in the street, Lev could hear the traffic grinding slowly by.

'For Maya,' he said, 'I must find work.'

Sulima cleared her throat and said: 'The Avenues Hotel exists no more. Alas, or I could send you there. It is a gym now. Everybody pedalling to save their hearts. But for work you should try in the Earls Court Road. Food outlets of every kind. Always in need of staff.'

'Yes?' said Lev.

'I think that is the first place you should try.'

'Court Road?'

'Earls Court Road. Out of this front door. Turn left, then right, then left. I am very sorry about your wife.'

So here he was now, lugging the bag, in the dirty, shimmering street. The thing he most longed to buy was a pair of dark glasses.

The words of the Yarbl teacher of English came to him as he walked: 'When you ask for work, try to be polite. Our people are a proud people. We do not grovel, but neither are we rude. So say, for instance, "Excuse me for troubling you. But do you have anything you could give me? I am legal."'

Do you have anything you could give me? These words were difficult to remember, let alone say. And Lev was finding it hard, each time he ventured into a shop or stood at a fast-food counter, to say anything at all. In a newsagents', a dimly lit old-fashioned place, he was filled with a sadness so sharp he could hardly breathe. So he said nothing, except to ask for Russian cigarettes, and the fat girl behind the counter picked her nose and stared at him like a lunatic.

'*Russian?*'

'Yes. Russian or Turkish.'

'Nah. You won't find them. Not round 'ere.'

In a pizza parlour that felt cool, with ceiling fans turning slowly among pinpoints of bright light, Lev waited near the door until a young waiter approached him. 'Smoking or non?'

Smoking or non.

'Do you have anything you could give me?' Lev said, managing the difficult phrase correctly this time. 'I am legal.'

'Sorry?' said the waiter.

'No, excuse me. I am looking for work. Excuse me to trouble you.'

'Oh right,' said the young man. 'Right. Well, hang on.'

Lev watched the waiter walk away and disappear behind a door marked *Staff Only*. The place was almost empty and other waiters stood aimlessly about, wearing white shirts and red bow-ties, staring at Lev. The noise of the ceiling fans reminded Lev of the old ice rink at Baryn, where he and Marina used to skate, holding onto the backs of chairs, and where the freezing air smelled of disinfectant.

When the young waiter returned, he said: 'Sorry. Uh ... the manager's popped out.'

'*Popped?*' said Lev.

'Yes. Out. But there's nothing at the moment. No jobs. Sorry.'

'OK,' said Lev.

The bag was beginning to bother him. Not just its heaviness, but the sight of it, containing as it did all that he'd brought with him of his former life. He imagined that somehow its contents were visible to all, and that his pitiful possessions would be derided. He had a further worry about it. Every time he set it down, the vodka bottles clanked together, and this was embarrassing, as though he were an inept *grey*, telling the world what he had to sell. He wished he'd asked Sulima if he could leave the bag at Champions B & B. But he was stuck with it now, as though it were part of his body.

He came to a skip parked in the gutter and noticed that among planks of wood, stained mattresses and piles of rubble a quantity of rusty metal had been thrown. Lev stopped and put down the bag and stared at the scrap metal and imagined what such a find would mean to Ina and how the tin would be hammered and beaten so fine it could be cut and shaped with small clippers, like fingernails. 'Rust is beautiful,' Ina often said. 'Rust does my work for me. Rust makes everything delicate in time.'

Lev leaned on the edge of the skip. Anxiety about Ina was something from which he'd always suffered, even as a child, noticing that, somehow – in a way that he couldn't describe precisely – his mother appeared ghostly, as though, in the race through life, she was an entrant nobody had seen and who crept in last, always last, with worry in her eyes. Lev often wished this wasn't so, but it *was* so. And now, for years, Ina had spent her days making jewellery for other women, women for whom one didn't have to feel any particular sorrow, women with confident smiles and fashion boots, women who smoked and laughed and defied the world. Ina had never defied the world. She sat in shadow in a wood cabin, lit by a paraffin lamp that whispered like a living and breathing thing, and her work-bench was covered with metal shavings and lengths of copper wire, and her hands were burned here and there by the hot-torch and the soldering irons and as time wound on her eyesight was becoming poor. Lev knew that nobody wanted to think about the day when that eyesight failed.

'But she will see Princess Diana,' Lev told himself now. He could imagine Ina propping up the card at the back of her work-bench and letting the white paraffin light illuminate the rose-blushed skin and the hesitant smile, then sitting back in her chair to gaze at these lost things and at the fascinating intricacy of the diamond tiara. And Maya would come into the cabin sometimes and stare at Diana, too. And once in a while – not often – the two of them might turn the card around to reread the words he'd written: *I am going to find a job today.*

Lev picked up his bag and heard the bottles clank. He cursed himself for day-dreaming. Day-dreaming may have been all right during the lunch hour at the Baryn lumber yard, but you couldn't day-dream and survive in cities like Glic or Jor, let alone in London. 'Cities are fucking circuses,' Rudi once remarked, 'and people like you and me are the dancing bears. So dance on, comrade, dance on, or feel the whip.'

The heat was rising again. You could feel it coming off the stained pavement, see it shimmering above the cars. Lev prided himself on being strong – a strong, lean-limbed man – but now he felt himself begin to stagger. Sweat ran down his forehead. The other people in the street started to look grotesque to him, fat and mocking and sick. He'd somehow naïvely imagined that most English people would look something like Alec Guinness in *Bridge on the River Kwai*, thin and quizzical, with startled eyes; or like Margaret Thatcher, hurrying along with purpose, like an indigo bird. But now, in this place, they appeared indolent and ugly and their heads were shaved or their hair was dyed and many of them sucked cans of cola as they walked, like anxious babies, and Lev thought that something catastrophic had happened to them – something nobody mentioned but which was there in their faces and in the clumsy, slouching way they moved.

Lev walked into a cool, brightly lit place called *Ahmed's Kebabs*. An Arab man was cleaning the tiled floor with bleach. Behind a counter, a grey cone of meat revolved on a perpendicular grill. A chill cabinet had been stocked with torn lettuce, chopped tomatoes and breads of different kinds. A large glass-fronted fridge was filled with cans of cold drinks.

Lev put down his bag and the Arab man turned and looked at him while he squeezed out his mop.

'Excuse me,' said Lev. 'Do you have anything to give me?'

The Arab man picked up the bucket and mop and took it

behind the counter. Then he turned and examined Lev. His eyes were worried and wild and his hair was glossy and disorderly, like Rudi's.

'Sit down,' he said.

Against the counter were lined up three chrome and plastic stools, so Lev hoisted himself onto one of these and rested his arms on the cool counter top. The Arab man set down a paper plate. He took a floury bread pocket from the chill cabinet, and filled it with some of the torn lettuce. Then he walked to the meat cone and deftly shaved off a few slices and put these into the pocket and set it down in front of Lev on the paper plate. Lev stared at it. The meat smelled of goat.

The Arab was at the drinks refrigerator now. He took out a green-coloured can, snapped open the ring pull and put it beside the plate with the bread and meat. 'Drink,' he said.

Lev thanked the man and slowly pulled the can towards him. With his other hand, he wiped the sweat off his forehead. Then he lifted the can to his mouth and drank, and the Arab man watched him intently. The water was fizzy and felt almost scratchy on Lev's tongue, but it was beautifully cool, so he kept drinking, and as he drank he remembered Marina begging for water that was cold and had no taste, then crying with rage and saying that hospital water was tepid and tasted of the sewer.

'I am Ahmed,' said the Arab man. 'Please eat. On the house.'

'Excuse me?' said Lev.

'You ask if there was anything I could give you. Well, I give you this food and water. Where you from? Eastern Europe somewhere, uhn? So eat. My kebab meat is very good. And for you it is free.'

Free.

Lev knew this word very well. His English teacher had explained to him that the West described itself as the 'Free World' and these words had fascinated him across months and months of time. But how was one supposed to imagine this freedom? In Lev's dreams, it had often become a black road, laid straight and true to a flat horizon where a few birds looped and turned against a white sky, but there was something austere and unforgiving about this land-scape, so he'd said to Rudi: 'I don't know what it really means,' and Rudi had replied: 'You don't *know*, Lev, because you've put no vehicles on the fucking road! Freedom is speed. Freedom is horsepower and torque. Freedom is four wheels under your arse.'

Lev thanked Ahmed again for the free food and water. He tried to eat the kebab thing, but gave up after one mouthful. He longed to smoke, but his last two packs of cigarettes were deep in his bag and he was too embarrassed to start searching for them.

'So,' said Ahmed, 'you want work? What work do you want?'

'Any work,' said Lev.

'Well,' said Ahmed. 'You are lucky. You came to the right place, because I am a Muslim.'

'Yes?' said Lev.

'The Koran teaches that deeds of unselfish kindness will be rewarded in Heaven. I've given you precious food, and for this unselfishness, I will find reward. But now I shall go further. I am going to give you work.'

Lev waited. He wasn't sure how much he'd understood. Ahmed asked him his name and what city he'd come from and Lev told him and Ahmed smiled and said: 'A man may travel far, but his heart may be slow to catch up.'

'Sorry?' said Lev.

'Take no notice. I like to invent proverbs.' Ahmed's smile turned into a wide grin, then into laughter, and the laughter echoed all around the tiled and empty surfaces and Lev thought, suddenly, He's playing games with me and the food and water will not be free. Then Ahmed disappeared through a plastic fly curtain, very like the one Ina hung from her door lintel in summer, all colours, but faded with sunshine and time, and Lev found himself alone. He went to his bag and, with hands that shook, rummaged about until he found the cigarettes, then tore open the packet and lit up, using the plastic lighter he'd almost given to the Sikh washroom attendant at the station. He inhaled deeply, loving that first pull, feeling the smoke begin to steady him as he went back to the plastic seat and waited. He sat very still, smoking with concentration. The goat meat kept turning on its automatic spit. In a mirrored surface near it, Lev could see the street behind him and the slow traffic and the heavy-bellied people slouching past.

A long time seemed to pass before Ahmed returned. Onto the counter top he put down a tall cardboard box containing an overflowing pile of black-and-white leaflets, on which the name,

Ahmed's Kebabs was written in twirly, backward-sloping script. Ahmed banged his fist down proudly onto the pile. 'Your work,' he said. 'Deliver leaflets. OK?'

'Yes?'

'Yes. All round this neighbourhood. Everything residential. Smart houses. Shabby houses. Flats. B & Bs. Every private door. Check the basements especially. Many kebab people live in basements. Don't bother with the hotels. Every leaflet you post in, I pay you 2p. Ten houses, 20p. A hundred houses, £2. Perhaps you are a godless man, Lev, but today Allah has smiled on you. Eh?'

There was the question of the bag.

Because it contained everything Lev owned, he didn't want to be parted from it, but he knew he wouldn't be able to walk from house to house encumbered by it. He considered hoisting it onto his back, sticking his arms through the two handles, but he saw how it would weigh him down, so Lev told himself calmly to trust Ahmed and leave the bag with him and not think about it, because the things it contained were valueless, except to him.

Before setting off, Lev forced himself to eat a few mouthfuls of the goat sandwich. Something would have to sustain him through the hours that lay ahead, when the heat of midday would arrive and he would be lost in this heat, lost in the labyrinth of grey streets. But he felt cheerful all the same. On this job, he wouldn't be required to speak or to understand other people speaking to him. He'd be alone again with his own familiar reveries.

Ahmed put half of the leaflets into a plastic carrier-bag and handed this to Lev. Lev was unable to judge how many leaflets were in the bag, but it was heavy and he could tell that the plastic was going to bite into his hands. He wished he had with him the little canvas satchel he used to carry to school long ago, when the school in Auror still had its iron bell, and eagles could be seen in the hills above. He found himself wondering what had become of the bell and what had become of the eagles, but knew the timing of these thoughts was somehow inappropriate and that they had to be banished. 'Most things disappear,' Lev heard Rudi say. 'Just make fucking sure some of them disappear into your own pocket.'

He walked out into the sunshine. He passed a flower stall filled with roses, lilies and cornflowers and the scent of these, in the heart of the city, surprised Lev, as though he'd imagined flowers only gave off any perfume when the air was silent.

He knew he should begin straight away delivering the leaflets, so he turned off the busy Earls Court Road and found himself in a street of tall houses, not unlike the one he'd imagined inhabited by the immigrants making vodka out of potatoes, except that there was a solid kind of grandeur about the buildings he hadn't quite anticipated. Some of them were smart, with newly painted railings round them and fat pillars shining white or cream in the hot day; others looked neglected, almost broken-down, with cracks in the window ledges and garbage bags dumped on the front steps, and Lev saw that this cohabitation of restored and dilapidated things was everywhere he looked and he found this consoling, as though, at last, he'd found some evidence of war damage in London that no one had been able to erase.

He took out a handful of Ahmed's leaflets and put them through the letter-box of the first house. Under *Ahmed's Kebabs* were written the words *Best Luxury Halal Meat; Best Prices In Your Area; Eat In Or Take Away; Friendly Service At All Times*, but only some of these words had any meaning for Lev. 'Best' he knew was an important concept, one seldom alluded to in his country, except by people like Rudi, who yearned to adorn himself with marvels, so that even his boots had to be worthy of admiration and his shaving balm possess powers of seduction over men and women alike. 'Friendly Service' Lev saw as a contradiction, remembering the few restaurants he'd ever visited in his country, in the days when Marina was alive and he'd wanted to show her how much he prized her by offering her a nice dinner. The waiters and waitresses had behaved like labour-camp guards, slamming down dishes of sinewy meat, sloshing out wine from dirty carafes, snatching their plates away before their meal was finished ...

'Why don't any of you smile?' Marina had once asked a surly waiter in a stained apron. And the boy – for he was a boy really and not yet a man – had looked at her, astonished.

'To smile at the customers wouldn't cost you anything,' Marina had continued gently, but the boy had looked away.

'You're wrong,' he said. 'To smile would cost us our dignity.'

And after he'd hurried back to the kitchen, stamp-stamp-stamp in his heavy shoes, carrying the plates and the glasses and the empty carafe on a tilting tray, Marina had taken Lev's hand and said: 'Now I feel pity for the boy. Before, I felt fury and now I feel pity and I was happier with the fury!'

Marina.

It was important not to start thinking about her now. It was essential to Lev's survival not to lose himself in dreams of her.

He descended some steps into a basement area and found, almost hidden under the pavement, a tiny garden planted with bay trees and lavender and big hydrangea bushes, struggling towards the light. A tabby cat lay curled on the low window-sill of the basement flat and barely opened an eye as Lev took out a few more leaflets and put them through the brightly painted yellow door. Next to the yellow door was a bell, with two names above: Kowalski and Shepard. Lev stood for a moment, looking at these names and at the yellow door and then at the garden, which had been made out of very few things but which was so beautiful in its small way that envy of these people, Kowalski and Shepard, stabbed at him suddenly with surprising force. He imagined them returning from their well-paid jobs, watering their plants, feeding the cat, ordering kebabs from Ahmed, buying wine or vodka, sitting close together at their table, eating and laughing and smoking, then going hand in hand into their bedroom as the night came down. And he thought: My life will never be like theirs. Never.

Lev walked on. The weight of the leaflets in the carrier-bag became lighter as he completed the first three streets and came into a quiet square, where children played on a rough lawn, safe behind railings, and where the air was scented with privet. He was in a trance of delivery now: walk up the front steps, grab the leaflets, hurl them through the letter-box, walk down the front steps, go down again into the basement, examine the number of names, select the right number of leaflets, throw them in, climb back into the sunlight of the street, pass on to the next house ... His legs ached a little, he wore his leather cap low, against the midday glare, but he wasn't unhappy with his task. Before long, he calculated that he'd earned £1.

Lev rested for a while, leaning on the gate that opened on the square garden, watching the children on some swings and their young mothers, dressed in tight little vests and jeans, lounging on the grass in the shade of a mulberry tree. He lit a cigarette and it tasted good, and the scent of privet seemed to be drawn with the smoke into his lungs, and there was something in this combination that made Lev feel alert and fearless, and he thought that when the night came he'd return here and sleep under the mulberry and watch the life that was going on in the houses all around him and in this way acquire a new vision of London – a secret vision. And this cheered him, that he'd chosen a place to sleep, somewhere free, somewhere secret, a place where he could keep watch ...

But now Lev saw that the young mothers had turned and were all staring at him and then whispering together. He looked down. He kept the cigarette cupped in his palm. One of the women got up and began marching towards him. He looked at her from under the peak of his cap. She was pale and pretty, with freckled arms, and she arrived very close to him, so that he could smell her sun lotion.

'This is a private garden,' she said.

'Yes?' said Lev.

'Yes. This is a garden for residents only. So can you ... go away, please?'

Lev looked beyond the young woman to her group of friends, and he saw that they'd called the children from the swings and had their arms round them and he understood that they thought him a criminal of the kind who was bullied and ostracised at the Yarbl Institute of Correction and of whom society didn't wish to speak.

'You are thinking ...' he began, then stopped. He ran short of words, but felt that, even if he'd known the words, he couldn't have brought himself to say them about himself. The freckled young woman stood confronting him with her hands on her hips. Lev wanted to say to her that he had a daughter, the age of the children in the garden, that even now Maya would be walking home from school with her small satchel and her worn shoes ...

'OK?' said the young woman. 'You're leaving now. Right?'

Lev shook his head, trying to show her that she'd read him wrong, that he was a good man, a loving father, but this shaking of his head alarmed the woman and she called to her friends: 'He's not going. Someone call the police.'

'No,' said Lev. 'No police ...'

'Then leave.'

'I am new,' said Lev. 'I am only looking my way through many streets.'

The woman sighed, as one of her friends joined her. 'Nutter,' she said. 'Foreign nutter. Probably harmless.'

'OK,' said the friend, approaching Lev. 'Pissez-off, right? *Comprendo?*'

By late afternoon, and with all the leaflets delivered, hunger and thirst began to torment Lev. He thought longingly of Lydia's hard-boiled eggs.

He knew he was lost now. He wished he'd left a trail of leaflets to guide him back the way he'd come. He stood and looked around him, staring left and right, left and right. Then he set off again, trying to remember what route he'd followed.

When at last he reached Ahmed's kebab shop, it was crowded with a group of Arab men, eating meat in the bread pouches and drinking coffee from paper cups. The smell of the goat meat now seemed almost perfumed and sweet to Lev and he made his way to Ahmed's counter and put down the empty bag.

'Leaflets gone,' he said.

Ahmed's back was turned to Lev. He was carving meat from the cone, sweat gleaming on his arms.

'What I hope, my friend,' Ahmed said after a moment, 'is that you put every one through a letter-box. I have had workers who dump my leaflets in the fucking trash and then ask me for money, and, although I am a very kind Muslim, that makes me hopping.'

Around him, the Arab men began laughing.

Were they laughing about 'hopping'? Lev recalled his English teacher saying, 'In a foreign language meaning sometimes arrives a little while after the words have been spoken.'

Ahmed began filling three bread pockets with meat and salad. He set these on the counter for his Arab friends and then moved away to his coffee machine. All Lev could glean by way of meaning was that Ahmed's mood had changed since the morning. He watched him serve the coffee and take money and put this into his sophisticated cash register, which had no ringing bell like cash registers in Lev's country, but made only a quiet little buzzing sound of appreciation as its drawer opened to receive the notes. Lev stared at the cash register. He saw Ahmed's wide hand poised above it and, after a moment's hesitation, the hand snatched out a green note and closed the drawer. Ahmed crossed over to where Lev stood. He put the note down on the counter.

'There you are,' he said. 'Five pounds. Two hundred leaflets. I'm being generous. OK? And I'm trusting you because I am a very kind man. You like a coffee?'

'Thank you,' said Lev. 'Thank you very much.'

Homelessness, hunger, these things just had to be borne for a while, Lev told himself. Thousands – even millions – of people in the world were hungry and had no proper place to sleep. It didn't necessarily mean they died or lost hope or went crazy.

But by this, the end of his first working day in London, Lev could see that it would be impossible to survive delivering leaflets for Ahmed. From a fruit stall, Lev had bought two bananas, and from a bread shop, a soft white roll, and from a post office, a stamp for his Princess Diana card and from a shop selling newspapers a pouch of tobacco, some cigarette papers and a bottle of water – and then his five pounds was gone.

He lugged his bag to the street where Kowalski and Shepard lived and, as the evening came on, went down into their basement and sat hidden in the space under the road, behind the bay trees and the hydrangea bushes. He discovered some flattened cardboard boxes tucked away in the furthest corner of his hiding-place and he laid these out and sat on them, and ate the bananas and the white roll and watched everything darken around him.

He was waiting for Kowalski and Shepard to come home. He could already imagine their voices, which would be youthful, and the light from their windows, which would be comforting and soft. And he thought that if they came out to water their trees and found him, he would be able to explain to them that he'd chosen their basement because of the plants and the yellow door and persuade them to let him stay there – just for this one night.

Yet part of him felt stupid, waiting there. Above him in the street, he could hear people laughing and car doors slamming and the click of women's high heels on the pavement. And he started to reassure himself that when Marina had been alive he, too, had had a proper kind of life – even if a poorer one than those lives going on around him in London – and he remembered how, on

Marina's thirtieth birthday, he had found at the Baryn market some scarlet shoes with three-inch heels and open toes, and Marina had put them on and dressed herself in a flouncy black skirt and a red shawl borrowed from Lora and they had eaten roast goose and drunk beer and vodka and danced a tango on Rudi's porch – Rudi and Lora, Marina and Lev – and felt crazy with happiness and desire. Even now, Lev could feel the beautiful weight of Marina's supple back bending against his arm, see the sexy kick of her feet in the red shoes, and hear her laughter floating away into the hills behind Auror. Such a night. Even Rudi never forgot it and would sometimes say to Lev: 'That night of Marina's birthday. Something happened to us, Lev. We were beyond mortal.'

Beyond mortal.

Now, all Lev could feel was the weight of his exhausted frame, sitting on the cardboard boxes, and the great and unimaginable weight of the city above. He tried to think about positive things: about his Diana card beginning its journey to Ina and Maya; about the kindness of women like Lydia and Sulima; about the money he was going to make, if he could only hang on and not lose heart ...

Still nobody came down to the basement flat. The cat had disappeared. The street lighting shaded orange the large blue hydrangea flowers. Lev tugged his bag towards him and took out a sweater knitted for him by his mother, folded it into a pillow and laid his head on it. He lit a cigarette and smoked silently, watching the smoke curl outwards from his hiding-place and touch the dark leaves of the bay trees before vanishing into the air. Then, before the cigarette was gone, Lev knew that he was falling ... falling helplessly into sleep. He had time to reach out, to extinguish the cigarette, and then he surrendered to the long fall.

Now, his dreaming mind conjured a memory. He was riding home on his bicycle to Auror from the Baryn lumber yard. Strapped to his back with a hank of rope were the offcuts of wood he'd taken from the yard and with which he planned to build a low trailer to run behind the bike. This trailer (for which he'd already drawn a simple design) was going to be the most useful thing he'd ever made. It would be the object that made possible the transportation of countless other objects, the need for which would inevitably become apparent with the passing of time. 'Because this is what life does,' Rudi had observed. 'It makes holes in front of your eyes that you have to fill with *things*.'

The offcuts lay at an angle across Lev's spine. The foreman at the Baryn sawmill, Vitali, had turned a blind eye to Lev's gathering of the pieces of wood – or almost blind. All he'd said to Lev was: 'You know there will have to be a small fine. Nothing severe. Some eggs would do well. Or a tin bracelet for my wife.'

The road to Auror was narrow and steep. It was late afternoon in early summer and Lev sweated as he pedalled and the rope bit into his shoulders and he prayed the tyres of the bicycle wouldn't burst under the weight of man and wood.

On the one level stretch of road, bordered by deep ditches, he saw a tractor coming towards him. The tractor was hitched to a loaded hay-cart and Lev noticed the bales shifting and tilting as the tractor came on. He told himself he should dismount and pull off the road, to let the load pass, but to dismount with the wood strapped to him was going to be difficult, so he decided it was better to keep on, straight and steady, because there was room on this bit of the road for a bicycle and a cart, and the tractor driver would see him soon enough and slow down.

But the tractor didn't slow down. On it came, with its roaring engine and its high wheels, and then it reached Lev and went by, but at the back of the cart, one bale was jutting out a few inches further than the others and this bale struck the wood strapped to Lev's back and he fell sideways off the bicycle and into the ditch.

For a moment, everything went dark. Then Lev saw light returning and stared up at the sky, which was crowded with the innocent pink clouds of a summer evening, and he tried to draw some strength from this sight, but the pain in his back and along his outstretched arms was fierce and he could feel the wood pressing into his bones and he thought that some kind of crucifixion was surely taking place. But for what was he being crucified? For not loving his father? For not clawing and tearing his way through life, like Rudi? For lying in a grey hammock when sadness got him down?

He didn't know. All he understood was that he had to try to rise up, to get free of his wooden cross, to resume his road.

4

Electric Blue

When Lev woke up, daylight pale as milk had crept into the basement area and a soft rain was falling. He lay without moving, watching the rain, refreshed by sleep, and thought that he'd never seen a rain quite like this, so gentle it seemed barely to fall, yet slowly laid its shine on the bay leaves and on the hydrangea flowers and on the grey stone of the yard.

Plumbed into the wall of Kowalski and Shepard's flat was a stand-pipe with a drain underneath it and a coil of garden hose looped over the head of the tap. Lev crawled out from his hiding-place, crept over to the tap and listened. A few cars went by in the street, but he knew that it was still early; no sound from inside the flat and no sign of the tabby cat. As modestly as he could, Lev pissed into the drain, then turned on the tap and rinsed his hands, splashed water on his face. Then he returned to his sleeping-place and lay down again with his head on Ina's sweater, which, he remembered, was known as a 'jumper' by the English, and he couldn't imagine how this word had come into being. He lit a cigarette.

He lay and smoked and listened for the opening of the yellow door. He wasn't afraid of the moment when he'd be discovered, only curious to see Kowalski and Shepard. He half wondered whether he'd ask them to let him stay there, in return for looking after their plants, but heard Rudi laugh derisively and say: 'Oh sure, Lev. They'll be delighted to have a complete fucking stranger using their wall as a toilet and messing up their coal-hole with his human form – all for a couple of minutes hosing down their pot plants. In fact, I think they'll believe this is really their lucky day!'

After a while, the silent rain ceased and the sun began shining on the wet leaves. The street was noisier than before and Lev felt the pulse of the city beat faster as people gathered themselves for the working day. He was certain now, that, whoever they were, Kowalski and Shepard weren't there; they'd left everything tidy, with the hose neatly coiled and the brass door-knocker shined up, but they were somewhere else.

Ahmed was raising the grille over the front of his kebab shop when Lev came walking along with his bag.

'Good,' said Ahmed, with one of his toothy smiles. 'My leaflet man. Ready for a new day?'

Lev asked Ahmed if he had a washroom he could use and Ahmed showed him through the fly curtain into a dark passage, piled up with cartons of cola and paper plates, and off the passage was a tiled lavatory with a washbasin and a plastic mirror. The room had no window and the floor, recently washed with disinfectant, had been spread with pages of newsprint to encourage it to dry. On one of the pages, near the basin, there was a photograph of a topless woman.

Lev shaved his face and washed his body. The presence of the near-naked woman troubled him. Since the death of Marina, he couldn't stand to think about sex. He had told Rudi one night: 'I could be a monk now. I wouldn't care.' And Rudi had said: 'Sure. I understand, comrade. But that will pass, because everything fucking passes. One day, you'll come alive again.'

That day still seemed far off. Lev stared down at the photograph. How could such a picture be in a national newspaper? The model had ridiculous breasts the size of pumpkins, and lips fat and wet and all she was wearing was a spangled G-string. He wished the girl was dead. He wished the person who'd photographed her was dead. He wished copulation had died out, as a thing to do, like collecting old postage stamps, like sticking up pictures of Communist leaders on your wall ...

Twenty-first-century man is a dog, he thought, a vile, raunchy dog, with its teeth bared and its cock purple and hard and strands of stinking drool falling from its greedy mouth ...

He ground his heel on the picture, to tear it. Took his towel from his bag and dried his body. He stared at his face in the plastic mirror and tried to see in it some glance or trait that he could admire, but in the ugly light of this toilet his face looked yellow and ghostly, barely human. There was no light in his eyes.

And he could feel it overwhelm him then – as it seemed to have to do from time to time – his sorrow for the death of Marina. Just thirty-six years, she'd lived. *Thirty-six years.* She was a beautiful woman with a voice that was full of laughter. She went to work every morning at the Procurator's Office of Public Works in Baryn, wearing a clean white blouse. In the evenings, she put on a striped pinafore and sang as she cooked supper. She rocked her child to sleep in her tiny bed, patient as a madonna. She danced the tango on a summer's night, wearing red shoes. She fashioned a rug from rags, over months and months of time. She made love like a crazy gypsy, with her dark hair falling around Lev's face. She was perfect and she was gone …

Lev knew this wasn't a good place in which to start crying.

He tried to act as Rudi would have acted, to start swearing or stamping his feet to stop any tears welling up, but they were choking him, they had to fall. Lev pressed his damp towel to his face and prayed the heartache would pass, like a brief storm, like a nightmare from which it's possible to wake. But it wouldn't pass and so he stood there weeping, and after a while – he didn't know how long – he heard Ahmed bang on the door.

'Lev,' Ahmed called softly. 'What's up with my leaflet man?'

'Nothing,' stammered Lev.

There was a moment's silence and then Ahmed said: 'When men cry, it is never for nothing – and that's not one of my proverbs. That's the truth.'

In the midst of his sorrow, Lev also felt foolish. 'I am sorry,' he said. 'I am sorry.'

'OK,' said Ahmed. 'I'm going to make you coffee. You take your time. Then you come out and drink the coffee. All right?'

Lev heard Ahmed go away. The offer of coffee moved him and he thought: Twenty-first-century man is a dog, but sometimes, like a faithful dog, he remembers the trick of showing affection.

*

One more day.

He told Ahmed he'd work one more day delivering leaflets, but after that he'd have to find a job that was better paid.

Ahmed said: 'I understand. My pay is shit. I know. I am a very small outfit with a very big fucking rent. But what job are you going to get?'

'I don't know,' said Lev.

'You go to the Job Centre, I'm telling you, my friend, they won't help you.'

'They won't help me?'

'No. Catch-22. You know what this means?'

'No.'

'Lose-lose, it means. American slang for lose-fucking-lose.'

'Yes?'

'To get any job, you must be on Benefit for one year. To get Benefit, you must have worked for one year in this country. Funny, eh? You see? Catch-22.'

Lev fumbled to roll a cigarette with the new tobacco he'd bought. His hands were still shaking from his outbreak of grief. He remembered the word 'Benefit' from his English classes, but knew that it had about it a complexity of meaning he'd never been able to unravel. He struggled to recall what his teacher had said as he watched Ahmed hack the torn remains of his meat cone from the spit, throw them into the trash bucket and start cleaning the grease from the spit mechanism. Lev completed rolling the thin cigarette and lit it, and the taste of the Virginia tobacco was unfamiliar, like the sugar-tainted breath of a stranger.

After a while, Ahmed wiped his hands on a stained dishcloth and turned back to Lev. 'Coffee good?' he said.

'Yes. Thank you, Ahmed. You are kind.'

'I'm a good Muslim, that's all. In Heaven, at least a few virgins will be mine.' Ahmed laughed.

Lev wondered whether, in his mind, these 'virgins' had breasts like pumpkins and oily lips. Then Ahmed searched around on a crowded shelf underneath the counter, pulled out a crumpled newspaper and put it down in front of Lev.

'*Evening Standard*,' said Ahmed, tracing the two black words with his thumb, 'London newspaper. You look in here, Lev. Look very carefully. Find the pages "ESJOBS". Also hundreds of rooms to let. Today you do my leaflets. Tomorrow you find a job right here in this paper. Job and a room. OK? Then you'll be right as rain.'

When his day reached its end and Ahmed had paid him another £5, Lev couldn't think of anywhere else to go except back to his hiding-place in Kowalski and Shepard's yard. This time, his supper was a loaf of brown bread and a packet of salami. Of the £5 he'd earned, only £2.24 remained. He hardly dared to think about the cost of everything. To quench his thirst, he drank water from the tap on the wall.

Night came and the flat remained dark. Lev sat in his hole under the pavement and smoked and brought out a flashlight from his bag and began to study the columns of jobs in the newspaper:

> *Hod carriers req Croydon; commissioning mangrs build serv mech or elec exp; dryliners and ceiling fixers Sydenham; LUL traffic marshal perm pos; plumber own tools Corgi reg . . .*

His brain yearned for rest. He lay down. He kept the torch alight and shone its narrow beam onto the hydrangea flowers and this electric blue reminded him of a time when he'd gone night-fishing with Rudi and they had made one of the strangest discoveries of their lives.

They'd driven in the Tchevi to Lake Essel, which was a cold, still lake miles from Auror, surrounded by firs and pines, where, Rudi had been told, you could stun fish with electric light and pick them out of the water with your hands. 'It's because,' Rudi had explained to Lev, 'that lake is so remote. Those fucking fish have never seen man-made light before, so they come to take a look and then – too late, brother! – they're killed by curiosity.'

Lake Essel was hard to find. The Tchevi squeaked and growled as Rudi drove it down this track and that, and the overhanging branches of trees thrashed at the car roof and the wheels spun in the ruts of sandy mud and fallen pine needles. Sometimes Lev and Rudi could see the lake in the distance, with the moon glancing down on it, but then the track would run out and there would be nowhere to turn, so the Tchevi had to roar backwards with its engine screaming and Lev told Rudi he could smell burning.

'Burning?' snorted Rudi. 'That's not fucking burning. That's protest! That's a beautiful engine telling you it doesn't appreciate being treated like a pickup truck. It's like a racehorse getting frisky when you ask it to pull a cart. You just have to master it.'

When they found the lake at last, Rudi parked the Tchevi right down on the shoreline, on a curve of sand, so that they could shine the headlights onto the water. 'The fish will never have seen lights that huge,' said Rudi. 'Every fucker in that water is going to swim over.' The back seat and the trunk of the car were loaded with plastic buckets and the plan was to fill these with live fish, then drive to Yarbl and sell them at the early-morning Saturday market. Live fish always sold better than dead ones and there were rumours that these were carp – considered a delicacy in this region. Rudi said: 'Even if they're not carp, we'll call them carp. Unless they're fucking eels. Then I guess we'll have to call them eels.'

Lev and Rudi got out and looked at the moon on the water and listened to the sounds of the night and the small wavelets breaking on the strip of beach. Then they built a fire and sat by it, drinking vodka and smoking and cooking dumplings, made by Ina, in a little black stew-pot hooked up to a curving branch. It was a summer night and moths came drifting to the fire and the moon fell out of sight behind the firs as Lev and Rudi ate the dumplings, which were floury and delicious. With their bellies full and the vodka and the cigarettes easing their minds, it was tempting to go on sitting there, talking about the world, and not bother to start catching carp. Only the thought of the money they could make at Yarbl made them turn their attention to their night mission.

They filled the buckets with lake water and set them in a line near the breaking waves. Then they turned on the headlights of the car. They took off their shoes and rolled up their trousers and stood knee deep in the freezing water, with their heads bent low, waiting for the carp to swim into the blazing beams of light.

'It's good the moon's gone down,' whispered Rudi, 'or they might get confused. Fish aren't that intelligent.'

Nothing happened for a while. Then they began to see peculiar flashes and shimmerings of blue light under the water. These came and went and came again and Lev and Rudi stared at them. 'What the fuck are they?' said Rudi. 'Is this lake full of aliens? Is that why no one comes here?'

But Lev soon saw what they were: they were the fish. Where the light touched them, their bodies gave off a neon-blue shine.

'Shit!' said Rudi. 'Why blue?'

'Perhaps they're Russian fish,' said Lev. 'Russian gay carp.'

'Blue' was the word Russians used to denote gay men, and Rudi sniggered, but now they both felt there was something troubling about the sight of this blueness. And the fish were small – they didn't look like carp: they looked like exotic creatures that belonged in an aquarium, and though a few of them were now swimming very close to Lev and Rudi's legs, neither wanted to try to pick them up.

After some useless minutes of staring, Rudi waded ashore and turned off the Tchevi's headlights to see what would happen, and what happened was that, in the darkness, the blue fish remained illuminated, like slow-flickering gas flames, irradiating the water all around them, and Lev thought he'd never seen anything as strange and surprising as this sight. He reached down and tried to seize one of the fish in his hand, but the fish jumped clean out of the water in a dazzling arc, like a blue shooting star, and now ten or twenty fish began to jump, making a neon fountain all around them, which after a while subsided and the blue began to fade and fade, until all that was visible to Lev and Rudi was the black surface of the lake.

They sat by the remains of their fire, drying their feet. Both of them wondered whether they'd had some kind of vision or waking dream, but after a while, Rudi said: 'It was real, that colour. There's got to be something wrong here. Radiation from somewhere. I reckon those fish are contaminated.'

'Well,' said Lev, 'they're too small to sell, anyway. Aren't they?'

'Nothing's too small to sell,' Rudi said, and Lev agreed. In Yarbl market you could sell hairpins, you could sell pine cones. So they sat there, looking at the buckets lined up, and thought of all the things they could call those small fish, like 'freshwater sardines' or 'Essel blue grayling', but then they remembered the dumplings they'd eaten, cooked in the contaminated lake water, and wondered whether they were already marked out for illness or death, and so they emptied the buckets in silence, piled them back into the car and drove home.

Since then, it had sometimes worried Lev that he might be slowly dying, without noticing anything much, from eating dumplings cooked beside Lake Essel, or even from accidentally touching the body of a leaping fish. Now, in Kowalski's yard, seeing a similar blue on the hydrangea petals, this worry returned to him: the peculiar worry and the beautiful memory, tangled together, pushing against each other, like wrestlers, neither giving way.

The night felt cold – far colder than the night before – and Lev had to take all his clothes out of his bag and spread them over his body, but even then he found it difficult to sleep.

'When you can't sleep, son, make a plan,' was something his father used to say. 'Then you won't have wasted those hours.' So Lev made a decision. The decision surprised him and yet he knew it was a sensible one: tomorrow he would call Lydia. She'd offered to help him and now he needed help, so he would accept. It was as simple as that. He'd make his way to wherever she was, in her friends' house. Together, he and she would read all the job advertisements in the newspaper and Lydia would decipher everything for him. She would know what a hod carrier was. She would call the telephone numbers printed on the ESJOBS pages to arrange interviews, and by nightfall he would have found work.

Although, at Lev's English class, students travelling to England had been advised to buy a mobile phone 'as soon as you can afford one', they'd also been taught how to use a public telephone and he had memorised these instructions, like a poem:

> *Detach receiver.*
> *Insert coin.*
> *Dial your number.*
> *Speak.*

It was still early in the morning. Lev heard a man's voice answer and felt sweat break out on his brow. 'Excuse me,' he said. 'May I talk to Lydia?'

'Who is it?' snapped the English voice.

'My name is Lev.'

'Olev?'

'Yes. Lev. May I talk with Lydia?'

He heard the man's voice calling her name and then Lydia came on the line.

'Lev?' she asked. 'Is that you from the bus?'

The sound of his own language made Lev want to laugh with joy. He apologised to Lydia for bothering her and she told him this was no bother, it was a pleasure, and he explained about the newspaper and the job descriptions he couldn't begin to understand.

'Ah,' said Lydia at once, 'you need a translator. Why don't you come to Muswell Hill this evening and we can remember our journey together?'

Lev asked where Muswell Hill was and Lydia told him that it was a nice area, where the houses and flats had gardens growing round them and where you heard foxes barking in the night and these foxes lived off domestic garbage and reared families in lairs dug cleverly under garden walls.

'Oh,' said Lev. 'I'm like a fox then. I've been sleeping in a lair under the road.'

This upset Lydia. She told Lev she would go and find a Tube map and instruct him how to get to Highgate, which was the nearest Underground stop to Muswell Hill. She said that when he arrived at the station and came out into the daylight, she would be waiting for him, and they would go back to the flat of her friends, who were called Larissa and Tom, and Lev could share a meal with them.

Lev dozed in his fox-hole for most of the day and the sun came and went and he rolled cigarettes and listened to the sounds of the street. A postman came down the basement steps and put some mail through Kowalski's letter-box, but hurried away without catching sight of Lev. When he felt hungry, he ate the remaining crust of the bread and the last two slices of the salami.

On the crowded Tube, Lev sat very still, clutching his bag. He let his eyes swivel round to take in the other passengers, and he thought how, in his own country, people mostly looked the same and were the same kind of size, but here in Britain there seemed to be a gathering of nations, and in this gathering, human flesh of every colour was being too well fed, so that even young African girls, who, a generation ago, would have been thin and stately, were overweight, with pregnant-seeming stomachs bulging out of tight clothes and big round faces and hands pudgy and ugly, with silver jewellery digging into their fat fingers. And there was a lot of food being eaten right there, on the Tube train. One of the African girls was sucking a lollipop. Children filled their mouths with crisps, cramming the food in, like babies, with their fat little palms. Two huge white men, sitting with their knees wide apart, as if to show off the insolent bulge of their private parts, were consuming hamburgers and onions out of cardboard boxes, and the smell of the onions was like that of something festering and Lev put his hand over his face. When the men got off the train, they left the half-empty cartons, stinking up the carriage, on a narrow shelf behind the seats. Lev felt sick. Everybody knew America was a fat country, but somehow news of England's decline into obesity hadn't travelled as far as Auror. There, in people's imaginations, English people were still pale and thin. They wore their belts tight.

At Embankment station, as Lev changed for the Northern Line, he passed a saxophonist, playing for coins in one of the long, airless corridors, and he noticed that this person was very thin, like him, and wondered whether he'd come from miles away and whether he slept there, in the Tube station, on a ragged-looking coat, and spent time watching the tourist boats on the river. He wondered, too, how much money he made. Because here everybody was hurrying, and though some people began, without noticing it, to walk in time to the jazz music, they didn't stop to throw down any change. But the guy just kept playing anyway. It was better than begging, Lev supposed. It was a way to pass the time.

The journey from Embankment to Highgate took so long it was as though Muswell Hill might be in a different city. Lev's bag grew heavy on his knee. He longed to see daylight again. He longed for a cigarette. The exhaustion in the eyes of his fellow passengers now began to convey itself to him. And he remembered how, in Yarbl or Glic, he'd felt this same tiredness, which was the tiredness that came from crowds, from the breath of others, from the town's harsh light, from being visible to so many eyes. And he realised that, since the close of the Baryn sawmill, he'd seen almost no one, only Maya and Ina, and Rudi and Lora occasionally, and that this invisible life had left him unprepared for the city and unaccustomed to its scrutiny.

Lydia was waiting for him, as promised, outside the Tube station.

She was wearing a summer dress, and the material of the dress was printed with scarlet flowers and her arms were bare and pale and she wore blue-tinted sunglasses against the vivid light. When she saw Lev she smiled, and as he approached her she held out her pale arms, as though Lev were a friend she'd known all her life.

She said that Tom and Larissa's flat wasn't far and as they walked along steep streets where the paving slabs were crooked and lumpy, where small gardens overflowed with abundant green and where the scent of privet and roses perfumed the air, she told Lev that Larissa came from their own country and was a teacher of yoga, and Tom was an English psychotherapist who made good money and was generous with everything he owned. 'As you see,' she added, 'Muswell Hill is a Paradise.'

The flat was on the ground floor of a tall house and it had a basement part, which was Tom's counselling room, that had its own entrance and waiting room and a toilet where the patients could prepare or recover. It looked out onto a neglected garden, where apple trees had clustered together and formed a deep shade and where a few cracked terracotta pots had been planted up with geraniums. Its main room was long and light, with a wood floor and Afghan rugs and worn leather sofas and an upright piano and a round table set for the evening meal. Lev looked at this room and thought that the colours in it and the proportions of it made it the most beautiful room he'd ever seen. He put his bag down and stood in the doorway, staring at it, and Lydia said: 'I know what you're thinking, Lev.'

Larissa came out of the kitchen and shook Lev's hand. She was a dark, graceful woman, with wild hair scrunched up on the top of her head and big eyes, like the eyes of a Greek movie star whose name Lev couldn't remember. Lev kissed her hand in an old-fashioned gesture he hadn't intended, then felt stupid and awkward as she took her hand away, yet he saw that she wasn't irritated, only amused. 'Welcome,' she said. 'Lydia has told me all about your journey and how it seemed quite short because of all your conversations.'

'Yes?' said Lev.

'Yes. Tom and I feel we know all about you. So, now, come and sit down. Has Lydia told you about her job?'

'No,' said Lev.

'Oh, tell him, Lydia!' said Larissa.

And Lev saw Lydia blush and start smoothing down the scarlet flowers on her dress, as though preparing for some entrance into a grand *soirée*.

'Well,' she said, 'I've just been so lucky, Lev, because Larissa and Tom know Pyotor Greszler, the well-known conductor from our country, who has just arrived here in London to rehearse with the London Philharmonic Orchestra, and everything about this job was lined up for me when I arrived.

'You see, Pyotor is quite old and his English is very bad and so I am his translator, between him and the orchestra. I tell the musicians everything Pyotor says and everything they say back to him. I am there all day, telling instructions and listening to their music. And I just could never have imagined any job so wonderful.'

Lydia put a kiss on Larissa's cheek and Larissa smiled and said: 'We're so happy for you, Lydia. We couldn't be more happy.' And then she turned to Lev and said: 'Pyotor telephoned me after the day Lydia began work and he was delighted with her. He said she was a very, very sensitive translator of musical mood and he really enjoyed having her there in the rehearsal room. Isn't that fantastic?'

'The only thing is,' said Lydia, 'I haven't had time, because of the hours I spend with Maestro Greszler, to look for somewhere else to stay and Tom and Larissa have been so kind, to let me stay here as long as I like. I think Fortune has smiled on me and I really don't know what I've done to deserve all this.'

Lev looked at Lydia's face, bathed in a wide, ecstatic smile, and he thought how, sometimes, life uncovers hidden marvels, like consignments of poinsettia flowers.

Lev was about to congratulate Lydia when Tom appeared in the room. He looked confused for a moment, as though he hadn't expected to see a stranger standing there, but Larissa said quickly: 'Tom, darling, this is Lev, Lydia's friend. You remember?'

Tom looked at Lev, and Lev saw that he was, in some ways, the embodiment of how he'd imagined all Englishmen to be: tall and lean-framed, with blue eyes and hair of no colour, edging towards grey, and clothes that were unremarkable. Tom shook Lev's hand and said: 'Welcome to London,' and this seemed odd to Lev, as though his first arrival had been a mistake and this was the real beginning to his new life, here in the 'Paradise' of Muswell Hill.

'Sir,' said Lev. 'Thank you.'

'Well,' said Larissa, brightly, 'let's have a drink, Tom.'

'Sure,' said Tom. 'Wine? Vodka? What would everybody like?'

'Lev likes vodka,' said Lydia, quickly.

'Larissa?'

'Yes, vodka. But open some white wine, too. I'm cooking sea bass.'

'OK,' said Tom, 'wine and vodka coming up.'

When Tom left the room to go to the kitchen, Lev asked Larissa if he could visit the lavatory. His bowels had begun, suddenly, to cramp. It was as if his lower intestine had been asleep for four days and now it had inconveniently woken up.

Larissa showed him to a bright little bathroom, where sea shells had been arranged in a line along the window-sill and where soft white towels hung on a wooden rail and the pull-cord to the light switch was made of plaited silk. Outside the bathroom window, Lev could smell the freshness of the garden.

He looked at his face in a shiny mirror cabinet and saw that there were smudges of soot or dirt on his cheeks and that his hair looked dusty and his shirt stained. He sat down on the toilet and relieved himself as quietly as he could. The idea that he was taking a shit in the flat of an English psychotherapist made him feel very mildly afraid. When he was done, he ran warm water in the washbasin and soaped his hands and face and took off his filthy shirt, which stank of sweat and of Ahmed's kebabs, and washed his armpits and dried himself on one of the soft white towels. He looked longingly at the bathtub. He found a clean shirt – his last one – in his bag, and put it on. It was a brown-and-white checked shirt he'd obtained in the Yarbl market, in exchange for a wood plane and some three-inch nails.

He felt restored.

When he emerged from the bathroom, he could smell the fish simmering. As he sat down on one of the leather sofas, a large glass of vodka was put into his hands. He asked whether he could smoke and Tom said: 'Yes, of course, of course,' and brought him an ashtray. He began the paraphernalia of rolling a cigarette and looked up to see Lydia smiling at him protectively as he arranged and rearranged his little line of tobacco on the Rizla paper.

The dinner astonished Lev: a tomato and pepper soup served with hot bread, then the sea bass cooked on a bed of fennel, with waxy new potatoes and a cucumber salad. Each mouthful surprised him afresh with its exquisite savour. He found himself staring at Larissa, at her face and then at her hands, wondering what knowledge she possessed to make food taste like this. Lev ate as slowly as he could, taking smaller and smaller mouthfuls. When his serving was gone, he wanted to start again with the scarlet soup. He thought that he'd be happy to eat this same meal every day for the rest of his life.

As the evening went on, darkness began to fall in the room and Larissa lit candles on the table. Lev looked out of the tall windows and saw the sky behind the apple trees fade to a luminous green.

The paradise of Muswell Hill.

It felt yet more marvellous to Lev because of the beautiful food and because, at last, he was comfortable in his own language again, but it wouldn't be his paradise for long. Later, when he'd gone through all the jobs in the paper with Lydia, he'd be out again in the street on his own. He knew he was miles and miles from Kowalski's yard, so where would he sleep? Would he ask to be found another B & B? Spend another twenty pounds for a clean bed and a shower?

He told himself he'd think about this later. If need be, he could sleep under the apple trees. Foxes might come in the night and sniff his dreaming form. He drank the white wine and felt it go to his head as Lydia kept talking excitedly about her job, about the genius of Pyotor Greszler and about her love of music, and Tom and Larissa proposed toasts to the future and the wine glasses were filled again and Tom got up to open another bottle. Then Lydia said: 'Enough about me. I am so selfish. Now, we must help Lev to find a good job. This is our mission.'

'Yes. I agree,' said Larissa. 'What work do you want to do, Lev?'

Lev said that he was only qualified in one kind of work, which was that of an engineer at a lumber yard. And then he found himself describing how the trees at Baryn had all been cut down and never replanted so, in the end, the sawmill had nothing to saw and all the machinery was silent now and rusting away as the seasons came and went.

'That is so typical of our country, isn't it, Larissa?' said Lydia. 'Nobody thinks about the future and nobody ever has and now the future is here and the people are leaving.'

'Well,' said Larissa, 'I left ages ago.' And she told the story of how, in 1992, Tom had come to an international conference of therapists at Glic and she had gone with a friend from her yoga class to a late-night bar and met Tom drinking there on his own and fallen in love with him in the space of one night.

While she told this story, Tom sipped his wine and smiled, and his blue eyes looked bright, in the candlelight, like the eyes of a child. And Lev thought, My life will never be like theirs. It will be humdrum and devoid of love. But he didn't want these people to see how he envied them, so he feigned great interest in Larissa's story of the meeting in the bar and Tom's courtship of her and the way they gave each other language lessons in bed. And the subject of his own want of a job floated away, as though nobody could bear to spoil the evening with anything so wretched – not even Lydia – and Lev thought, Well, never mind, the food is beautiful and the wine, and the light in the room is golden; I'll sleep under the apple trees and in the early morning Lydia and I can go through the jobs in the paper.

After supper, they sat on the leather sofas drinking coffee and Lev smoked and they talked about yoga. Larissa said: 'The practitioner of yoga lives in a state of what we call "alert passivity". That is, we are wide awake – not sleeping, as so many people in this country are emotionally and spiritually sleeping – and yet not questing perpetually after this or that thing. You understand? We're alive and waiting, and when you wait in this kind of way, ideas for your own endeavours and solutions to problems of all kinds come to you without difficulty.'

Lev liked this. He wished it could be true in his own case. But he felt obliged to say: 'I don't think many people are in the state of mind you describe, Larissa. I'll mention my friend Rudi, for example, who is most definitely "questing perpetually after this or that thing" every moment of his life!'

And everybody laughed and Lydia said: 'Oh, tell Tom and Larissa the story of the Tchevi, Lev.' So Lev began on the long drama of going with Rudi to buy the car and the door falling off into the snow and pouring vodka onto the windscreen to melt the ice. And as he talked, he began to embellish the story with new details, as if he were an actor improvising on a theme, and he felt the power of the tale – its disasters and its moments of hilarity, and the way it drove to a good ending – and when it was over, he saw that Tom and Larissa had been held by it so completely that, after it, no other conversation felt entertaining enough and the room fell silent. And this was very satisfying to Lev and he thought how moments of importance had, through all his forty-two years of life, so often belonged to other people, but that these last few minutes had belonged to him alone.

Soon after this, a church clock somewhere on the sloping streets of Muswell Hill chimed midnight and Larissa got up and began to gather the wine glasses and the coffee cups.

Lev stubbed out his cigarette. 'I must go,' he said. 'Thank you for the beautiful dinner.'

He saw Lydia look anxiously at Larissa. Larissa caught the look and turned to Tom. 'What I suggest,' she said, 'is that we make up a bed on the sofa for Lev. Don't you think, Tom? It's too late for him to find some place to sleep.'

'Yes,' said Tom brightly. 'Good idea.'

'Oh, yes!' blurted out Lydia, pressing her hands together. 'I was going to suggest it, but I didn't dare. I think a bed on the sofa is a good solution. Then, in the morning, I can do some translating for Lev.'

Lev's head now rested on clean pillows and his body was covered with a white sheet and a tartan rug. He kept the window open and the curtains drawn back, so that he could fall asleep looking out at the night. He heard planes pass.

Around three o'clock, he was woken by a posse of young men, shouting drunkenly in the street. He tried to make out what they were shouting about.

'Fuh'!'

'Yeh, fuh'!'

'Effing cun'!'

'Effing fucking cun'!'

Slowly, they moved on, kicking a can along the road. Lev heard the sound of vomiting.

The paradise of Muswell Hill.

Lev was wide awake now. He reached for his cigarette papers. He was wondering whether Lydia had heard the commotion when the door to the room opened and he saw her standing there in her dressing-gown.

'Lydia? What is it?'

'I'm sorry,' said Lydia. 'I couldn't sleep. I feel so bad.'

Lev sat up and switched on a light. Lydia's dressing-gown was quilted pink satin and her slippers were white and fluffy. Her face looked shiny.

'I feel so bad, Lev, that we didn't pay any attention to you.'

'What do you mean?' said Lev.

'We should have talked more about your work and tried to make plans for you. And when I heard those people shouting and swearing in the street, I remembered how horrible streets can be, and how you have been out there all the time and we just didn't try to help you at all last night.'

'You helped me,' said Lev. 'You gave me lovely food ...'

'I mean for the future,' said Lydia. 'I want you to have a future.'

Lydia crossed the room and came and sat on the floor by Lev's sofa. The street had gone quiet again and Lev could hear a night bird singing softly in one of the deep-shaded gardens. He began to roll his cigarette. Lydia touched his arm.

'I would like to try ...' she said. 'I would like to help you and be close to you, Lev,' she whispered.

Lev was glad he had a cigarette. He lit it quickly and inhaled.

Lydia's face was very near to his. 'I know you may not want this,' said Lydia. 'I know you are still mourning your wife. I respect this. But I was thinking, I have a good job now. I could help you—'

'That's a kind thought,' said Lev. 'So kind. And I'm pleased about your job with Maestro Greszler. But that's your new life, Lydia, and tomorrow I must follow your example and find mine.'

'I don't mean money,' said Lydia, flustered. 'I mean just helping each other a little. Spend time together ...'

'Yes,' said Lev. 'Sure. And I'll accept your help with the jobs in the paper.'

Lydia looked down. 'On the bus,' she said, 'I got so used to being with you. Side by side. It's ridiculous, I know. But I pretended to myself we were travelling together. And when I said goodbye to you ...'

'Lydia,' Lev said gently, 'we weren't travelling together.'

'I know. I know. This is really stupid of me.'

'No, it's not stupid, but ...'

Lydia put her hand round Lev's wrist. She held it tight. 'Can I touch your hair, Lev?' she whispered. 'You have beautiful hair. So thick and nice. May I just touch that?'

Lev looked down at Lydia's shiny face, with its splash of brown moles. There was something about her that had moved him from the beginning – the way she'd eaten those neatly packed hard-boiled eggs, the quietness of her voice – but the idea of being touched by her terrified him.

'Listen ...' he began.

'Just your hair,' said Lydia. 'That's all.'

'My hair's dusty,' said Lev.

'I don't mind.'

'Listen ...' he began again. But now Lydia reached up and put the back of her hand on Lev's head, just above his ear. Lev didn't move. Lydia's hand didn't move. The cigarette kept burning. Lev thought how, during the evening, he'd been close to feeling happy in this room, but now this happiness seemed shallow and compromised. He cursed himself for telephoning Lydia.

'Lev,' said Lydia, in a quiet little childlike voice, 'you know you're a very handsome man. It would be so sad if you decided to be alone always. Don't you remember how a kiss can feel? Do you?'

'Yes,' said Lev. 'I do. But now we must both go to sleep.'

As gently as he could, Lev reached up and took hold of Lydia's hand and placed it in her lap, and he watched her lower her eyes and stare at her own hand as though it were some unexpected gift he had put there.

'It's nearly morning,' said Lev. 'Can you hear the birds singing?'

'Well,' said Lydia, 'I am not particularly interested in birds.'

5

Two-point-five Metres of
Steel Draining Top

With Lydia's help, Lev found a job as a kitchen porter in a restaurant kitchen in Clerkenwell. It paid £5.30 an hour.

The chef-proprietor of the restaurant, *GK Ashe,* was Gregory (GK) Ashe. The restaurant manager, Damian, who interviewed Lev at three in the afternoon, said: 'GK Ashe is the next big thing in this city. Are you hearing me, Olev?'

'Yes,' said Lev.

Damian was a pale, middle-aged man with a shaven head. He was dressed smartly in an expensive suit and a shirt the colour of lemonade. He had the kind of smile that faded and died as soon as it touched his lips. Damian looked intently at Lev, his glance moving over the other man's body, frisking him with his brown, wide-awake eyes. Then he said: 'You're skinny. That's good. Mr Ashe likes his staff to be skinny. Because it's a sign they're nimble. And everybody in this kitchen has to be nimble. Nimble, fast and tireless. D'you understand what I'm saying?'

'Tireless?' said Lev. 'What is that?'

'Never tired. Never showing you're tired, even if you are. Because the shifts are long and you've got to be up for it. Nobody yawns here. OK? You just stifle it. Catch you yawning and you could get a bain-marie chucked at your head.'

'Bain-marie?' said Lev.

'And you never, *never* eat the food, right? If Mr Ashe sees you put so much as a slice of lemon rind in your gob, you'll be history. So don't do it. There's a staff meal at 5 p.m. It's light, because we don't want the workers' guts weighed down with protein, but you'll survive. And – if the service has gone exceptionally well – Mr Ashe is sometimes overcome with magnanimity at one in the morning and he makes crostini for us all. And we open a few beers. And we're like a family, then. You'll see.'

Damian smiled his fast-vanishing smile and Lev said: 'Family is good.'

'Yes, it is,' said Damian. 'It certainly is. I expect you've got a family at home, have you? That's what you boys do – I've seen it – send all your money home to some village, right?'

'For my mother and for my daughter.'

'Yes? Well, you're a kind-hearted bunch, I'll say that. Is your wife here in England with you?'

'No,' said Lev. 'My wife ... she died.'

'Right,' said Damian. 'Right. OK. Sorry. Now, come and see your sinks. Here they are. Two sinks and two-point-five metres of steel draining top. State-of-the-art hygiene area. Racks here for service platters and plates. Multi-programme dishwashers here for glassware. Jet-scourers. Temperature-controlled rinse-faucet. OK, Olev? You could wash up for a regiment in this facility.'

Lev stood at the sinks and looked at the length of steel-tiled wall behind them and at the clean-laundered linen tea towels hung up in a neat line on steel pegs. He wished Rudi were here to see all this and be awed. Heard him say: 'Jesus, Lev! Take a look at this ravishing shiny shit!'

Lev would start the following day, reporting for work at four.

'Don't forget, Olev,' said Damian, as he walked Lev to the kitchen door, 'that a restaurant kitchen operates exactly like an orchestra. Everybody has to focus up and keep time. And there's only one conductor and that's the head chef. So keep alert. Don't rest. Don't take breaks. Keep playing your instrument and play it in time. Then you'll do well. See you tomorrow.'

Lev came out into the sunshine, rolled a cigarette and lit it. On the other side of the street, a few drinkers still occupied a pub table, and their laughter was like the laughter of children, unrestrained and loud. Lev sat down near them and one of the women, a smoker, said flirtatiously: 'Hi, Peaches!' and the men turned round to look at Lev, but only for a moment, because their drinks were what they held to and no stranger could part them from their concentration on those.

Lev ordered a beer. He'd earned this small celebration. He was part of the British economy now. He didn't have to go back to delivering leaflets for Ahmed. He could send another card to Ina, telling her he had a job, paying £5.30 per hour, which was more than he could earn in Baryn in a day.

But then he remembered that money had a new terror here.

The room Lydia had found for him in Tufnell Park was going to cost £90 a week. Added to this would be his Tube and bus fares, and his food and his cigarettes. How much would be left to send to Ina? Would anything be left? Lev looked at the young woman who had called him 'Peaches'. How did she manage to live and grow fat and drink away the hours of a Wednesday afternoon? How did she afford it? The woman repelled him: her bulging belly, the greasy skin of her face flaming in the London sun. He preferred to remain alone, sipping the cold beer. He spread out his Underground map and began to plan his journey to Tufnell Park.

It was a street of choky little houses, called Belisha Road. Rowan trees cast a deep shade down one side of it. The pavement was cracked and lumpy and stained.

Number 12 was on the shaded side and a high privet hedge, overgrown to wide proportions, made the entrance dark. Behind the hedge stood overflowing garbage bins and a bicycle, chained to the window bars.

Lev rang the top bell, beside a card marked *C. Slane.*

He waited. He placed his bag on the step beside him. Down the street, he could hear a dog barking and see a child kicking and shrieking in a pram. The berries on the rowans were beginning to turn gold.

When the door opened, Lev saw a small, elfin kind of man, with pale, nervous eyes and a flare of eczema across his nose. He wore an old white T-shirt and faded jeans too loose for his narrow frame.

'Mr Slane?' said Lev.

'Yes. Christy Slane. Come in, come in. I was expecting you. Your friend, Lydia, telephoned about the room.'

In the dark hallway, several pairs of trainers lay in a sprawling heap, under a line of hooks, where anoraks, scarves, back-packs, fleeces and leather jackets hung.

'None of this junk is mine,' said Christy Slane. 'It belongs to the downstairs people. They don't want the stink of the shoes inside the flat so they leave them outside for me to trip over. They've no consideration and, of course, no imagination whatsoever.'

Lev followed Christy Slane up the stairs. He saw that the door to Christy's flat was painted white and taped to it was a child's drawing of a house. 'My daughter, Frankie, did that,' said Christy. 'She doesn't live here any more. That's why I have the room to let. I should take the picture down, but I can't quite come up to doing it.'

Christy closed the white door and Lev saw that the flat he was in was also painted bright white and it smelled of this fresh paint and of something else, which Lev hoped he'd recognised as cigarette smoke. He looked round at the doors leading off the small entrance hall they were in. He glimpsed a sitting room with a gas fire and two wicker armchairs and a dining-table and a TV. A dented paper lampshade hung from the ceiling. The windows were uncurtained.

'Bare minimum furniture now,' said Christy. 'My wife took her share and then she took *half of my share*. That's English women for you. But she wouldn't take any of the things I'd given her. Nor the things I'd given my daughter. So you're going to share your room with a Wendy house and a little plastic shop I brought all the way over from Orlando, Florida, and a cuddly toy or two. I hope this is all right. If you get peeved with them, you can help me get them up into the loft.'

Now Christy opened the door to the child's room and Lev saw wooden bunk beds and a ladder leading up from one to the other, and bed linen patterned with giraffes. On the window-ledge sat a huddle of soft toys. The floor was carpeted green. On it stood a tiny wooden house with red chimney pots and flowers painted over the door. By the bunks there was a multi-coloured rug, which reminded him of the rag rug in Maya's room.

'Is it all right for you?' asked Christy. 'It's been cleaned and aired. Beds look small, but they're full size. I'll chuck your laundry in the washer once a week, all included in the ninety quid. You can be comfy here, can't you? Not so different from my own little room. When I was a boy in Dublin, I had animals on me pillow. But if they bother you, we can get some other covers, cheap, on the Holloway Road. OK?'

Lev walked into the room and set down his bag. He hadn't understood all of what Christy Slane had been saying, except that he knew this had once been Christy's daughter's room and now that daughter was gone. He looked round at all the child's possessions and then out of the window at a sycamore tree, whose wide branches almost touched the glass. Then he looked at Christy, standing in the doorway, as though not wanting to come into the room, his hands held at his sides in a helpless way, and Lev was transfixed for a moment, recognising something of himself in the other man, some willingness to surrender and not fight, some dangerous longing for everything to be over.

'The room is very good,' said Lev. 'I will take.'

'Right,' said Christy. 'Good. Well, at least Angela left these curtains. And this is the quiet side of the house. Except when they have a barbecue in the garden, if you can call it a garden, the way they keep it, and they've got a puppy there right now that whines in the night sometimes, when they don't bring it in, but otherwise it's quiet. Now I'll show you the facilities.'

The bathroom was also painted white and was brightly lit. The bath, basin and lavatory looked new. Lev saw a wry smile cross Christy's face. 'The *pièce de résistance*. Angela would have nabbed it, if she'd known how to uncouple the piping, but luckily she didn't.'

'Very nice toilet,' said Lev.

'Yes, glad you noticed it. Put it all in meself. That's my trade: plumber. But I'm freelance now – if that's the word for more or less unemployed. Couldn't keep to me job after Angela left. But at least we've got a nice environment to shit in. I'll find you a towel.'

Christy went away and Lev heard him opening a cupboard in another room. Lev looked down at the miniature plastic shop standing by the miniature house. A sign on the shop's door read: *Hi! My Store is Open.*

Christy returned and handed Lev a green towel. 'So,' he said, 'tell me your first name.'

'My name?'

'I'm Christy. I'm Irish, in case you hadn't noticed. Baptised "Christian", but that was too much to bear, too much of a yoke, you know what I mean? But "Christy" is all right. Just call me that.'

'Yes,' said Lev. 'And I am Lev.'

'Right,' said Christy. 'Now, I'll make a pot of tea, Lev, and we can get the money side of things done. Terms are one month's rent in advance, or if you can't manage that right now, I'll settle for two weeks.'

'I prefer two weeks,' said Lev.

'That's OK. I can live with that, fella.'

Lev began counting out notes: almost all the money he now possessed. Once again, he thought about Rudi's assurances that he'd be able to live on twenty pounds a week. 'I'm *informed* about the world,' Rudi had often said. 'I don't just watch the news, I *interpret* it. My judgements are backed up by hours of *further reading*.' Lev also knew that Rudi would argue about the ninety pounds and, in all probability, get Christy to lower the rent by some percentage or other, but that he, Lev, was incapable of such an argument. And he felt lucky to have found Christy Slane, to have been given a child's room. He wasn't too embarrassed or proud to lay his head on a pillowcase printed with giraffes.

'Pity the men, I say,' said Christy as they drank the tea. 'Women have got us by the balls in this century, that's what I feel.'

'Yes?' said Lev.

'I'll admit, my drinking got bad and it's not so fantastic trying to share your life with me when I'm like that. Drink lets loose the shite in me. There's shite in every man – and every woman – it's the nature of being human. But most of the time, it's kept in, you know what I mean? Most of the time, you're not looking at a steamin' pile of manure.'

Lev nodded. Both he and Christy Slane were smoking and the butts in the cheap ashtray were piling up.

'So I have some sympathy with Angela,' Christy continued. 'I can see her side of it all. But then she gets so nasty. You know? She tells me I'm a piece of nothing. And she tells me in front of Frankie, my daughter. Then Frankie won't talk to me, won't let me kiss her goodnight. I go in there – in your room – and she turns her head away. I get one of her toys and I say, "Look, Frankie, Sammy the Clown wants you to say goodnight to your daddy ..." Pathetic this was, because she takes no notice. She pulls the covers over her head, like I'm going to hurt her. And I never hurt her. I swear to God. It was only Angela made her act like that.'

Lev nodded. He saw that Christy didn't really care whether he understood what he'd been saying. Perhaps, he thought, it's easier for him to talk if he knows I don't understand. Because now he was started on the story of his recent life, he didn't seem to want to stop. And Lev didn't mind. He was gradually coming to understand that the Irishman's loneliness was nearly as acute as his own. They were the same kind of age. They both longed to return to a time before the people they loved most were lost.

'What a mess,' sighed Christy. 'Will it ever be cleaned up? I don't think so. I think Angela's got me in a noose. I go to Frankie's school, in their playtime, and I watch her in the playground, I watch her skipping and jumping. But I'm not allowed to go near her. The teachers have instructions: I'm not to try to make contact with her. I'm considered some kind of "unacceptable risk" because I once broke a few plates and glasses. So now I have to go to court to get my rights back, my rights as a father – my rights as a human being. And what if I lose? I'm trying to stay clear of the booze. You can help me, Lev. You're a disciplined man, I can tell this. I'd like you to help me. Don't let me go to the pub. And if I open a bottle of Guinness at home, try to get the fucking thing away from me. Right? Just take it and tip it down the sink.'

'Yes,' said Lev. 'I try. But I have many hours at *GK Ashe* to work.'

'Sure you do. I'd forgotten that for a moment – like I was thinkin' we could just sit here for the foreseeable future drinking tea! I like it when things are nice and quiet like this. Cuppa tea. Smoke. Quietness. I like that.'

'Yes,' said Lev. 'I like also.'

'Tell me about your daughter, then.'

Lev took out his wallet and found the photograph of Maya that he carried there. He passed it to Christy. He could remember with absolute clarity the soft texture of the woollen dress Maya had been wearing that day. He watched Christy look tenderly at the picture.

'Girls,' he said. 'So lovely. Aren't they? So sweet and darlin'. Butter-wouldn't-melt and all that. And then, bang, they turn away from you. They say they hate you. They break your heart.'

He passed the photograph back and Lev put it away. In the

silence that followed, Lev tried to tell Christy about Marina's death, so that this subject would be out in the open and not there to catch him off-guard, at a time when speaking about it would be too hard. When Christy asked him *why* Marina died, Lev tried to explain that cases of leukaemia were common in Auror and Baryn, but nobody knew why. Some people said there was contamination in the water, others that the cancer came from eating too little red meat, or too much rose-petal jam.

His own theory was that Marina's death had something to do with the electricity pylon, whose shadow fell over his house in the late afternoons. He tried to tell Christy that this shadow had a chill to it, a grey chill, which was particular to it, and that seeing it laid out across the garden – across the goat pen and the chicken house and the vegetable patch Marina used to tend with such care – had always filled him with rage and foreboding. He was grateful that electricity had come to Auror, but his hatred and fear of the pylon shadow had never left him.

Christy stared at Lev, with his face resting on his hands, which were bone-thin and scarred here and there with the traces of burns. After a while, he said: 'Why was it the shadow you feared and not the pylon itself?'

Lev thought about this. He tried to say that the shadow *touched* them. It laid a kind of grid over them. The pylon was a little distance away on the hillside behind Auror, but the shadow fell directly onto them and there was nothing they could do about it.

Christy cleared away the teacups. The afternoon was gone now and the sounds of evening in Belisha Road began to accumulate around them. Distinct among these was loud, clanging music coming from the flat below.

'*EastEnders*,' announced Christy. 'You'd better watch it, fella. Tell you a bit more about the mad world you're in.'

Christy heated a steak and kidney pie for them and they ate it with some tinned peas, sitting on the wicker chairs, watching the TV, and when he'd eaten Lev fell asleep to the sound of furious arguments going on and on in a TV place called Albert Square. The sleep he fell into was deep and sound, and when he woke the TV was off and the room was almost dark and there was no sign of Christy Slane.

Lev walked alone through the flat. The kitchen was tidy, the supper plates washed up and put away. He went into Christy's bedroom and saw a double bed, unmade, and a bedside table cluttered with paperback books, letters and pills. Apart from the bed and the table, the room was empty. At the window, a blanket had been hung up for a curtain.

Lev returned to the sitting room. He stared longingly at the telephone. He tried for some time to resist this longing, but it wouldn't go away, so – without any idea what a phone call to his country might cost – he tugged out some coins from his pocket and set these down by the phone. Then he picked up the receiver and dialled Rudi's number. When he heard Rudi's familiar, growling voice, he felt warm in his heart.

'Hey!' yelled Rudi. 'I miss you! Everybody misses you. What's happening over there? Are you ready to come back yet?'

Lev laughed. He told Rudi that he'd found a job in a kitchen, that he was lodging in a child's room, that people in London were fatter than he'd imagined.

'Fat?' said Rudi. 'So what? Don't blame people for being fat, Lev. If we had better food here, I'd be happy to be fat. I'd parade my fat belly. And if Lora grew a big arse, I wouldn't care. I'd hold it to my face and kiss it.'

'Well, OK,' said Lev, 'but I hadn't imagined people looking like this. I'd imagined them looking like Alec Guinness in *Bridge on the River Kwai*.'

'That film was made back in the Cold War, Lev. It was made *before* the fucking Cold War. You're way out of date with everything.'

'So are you,' said Lev. 'You calculated that I could live on twenty pounds a week. The room alone is ninety.'

'Ninety pounds? You're being cheated, my friend.'

'No,' said Lev. 'I looked at about thirty *Rooms to Let* in the newspaper. *ES* newspaper. This was the cheapest one.'

Rudi went silent. Lev let this silence last for a moment, then he asked after Maya and his mother. Rudi replied: 'They're all right, Lev. They're fine. Except one goat went missing. Ina thinks some fucker stole it right out of the goat pen. She thinks he'll take them all, one by one, now that you're not there.'

It was Lev's turn to be lost for the next word. What came to his memory was the delicacy with which the goats trotted around their dusty corral.

'Tell Ina to take them inside the house at night,' he said.

'And put them where?' said Rudi.

'Anywhere. The kitchen.'

'And then they shit all over the floor, and that bastard breaks in the house to nab them. D'you want that?'

'Tell Ina to double-bolt the door.'

'Sure, I'll tell her that. But you know, Lev, she keeps saying to me: "Rudi, why did my son go away? Tell me why Lev went away".'

'She knows why I went away. You all know, so don't torture me with it, Rudi. At the end of next week, my first money will arrive. Then Ina will be happy.'

'OK, OK. I'll tell her that too: happy at the end of next week.'

Lev changed the subject. He asked after the taxi business and Rudi replied: 'Well, nothing's changed since you left. As you know, people don't want to cycle places any more, now they know the Tchevi's available. They want to ride in style on my leather upholstery. But I've just noticed something: they're wearing the fucking upholstery *away*! They let their bums slide around on it. I guess they like the feeling of their bums sliding around, but it's doing my interior no fucking good.'

'If it's just the upholstery wearing away,' said Lev, 'you can live with that.'

'Well, I can live with it, but it makes me mad.'

'Better that than any of the machine parts going wrong.'

'Well said, my friend. You're bright today, I see. But maybe now you'll be able to ship auto parts to me from London?'

'Yes,' said Lev. 'When I get on my feet. When I can find my way . . .'

'You lonely?' said Rudi.

'Yes,' said Lev.

There was another silence now, in which Lev imagined Rudi in his hallway where, on a mahogany dresser, he kept his taxi log and an old cuckoo clock which spat out a broken wooden bird to announce all the hours of the day and the night.

'I saw your Diana card,' said Rudi, after a while. 'Ina showed it to me and I got a hard-on. I thought, Princess, smile me your lovely smile, then come sit on me.'

Lev laughed. He heard his own laughter as a distant and surprising thing. Then, after a moment, Rudi's familiar laughter began to chime with it and Lev remembered the vodka-soaked railway journey to Glic and dancing the tango under the stars and the blue-neon fish of Lake Essel.

'Forget Diana,' said Lev. 'I've got a date tomorrow with two-point-five metres of steel draining top.'

GK Ashe wasn't the way Lev had imagined him; he was a wiry man, not tall, with wild black hair he stuffed inside a cotton hat and eyes of a startling blue. Lev put his age at about thirty-five.

He came into the kitchen just before four and found Lev ready at his sinks with his striped apron on. 'OK,' he said, shaking Lev's hand, 'I'm GK Ashe. Glad you're joining us, Olev.'

'I am glad also, sir,' said Lev.

'Don't call me "sir". Call me "Chef".'

'Chef ...'

'Damian told you I run a tight ship?'

'Tight ship?'

'The difference between a kitchen where some people are lazy and careless and one where everybody's tasking at maximum stretch is the difference between a successful enterprise and a failed one. And the word "failure" pisses me off. I don't want even to contemplate it, right? Everybody in this space has to cut the mustard, OK?'

'Mustard, Chef?'

GK Ashe moved past Lev towards the sinks. 'Now,' he said, 'this station. Treat it like an operating theatre. I want all the stuff – every spoon, every tin, every colander, every bowl, every crusher, chopper, stoner, grater, every last potato-peeler – sterile-clean. When you've scrubbed up a roasting pan, I want to be able to drink a cocktail out of it. OK?'

'Cock tail, Chef?'

'Yes. The hygiene in some kitchens is bloody pitiful. Seventy per cent of cases of food poisoning in this country begin in restaurant kitchens. But not in mine. Not in mine. So see to it, right?' GK put his hand on Lev's shoulder. '"Nurse" is going to be your nickname,' he said. 'That's what I call my KPs: *Nurse*. And you have to live up to your name.'

'Nurse?'

'Yup. Don't take it as an insult. Quite the contrary. It's a *designation*. Just do your work with pride and you'll be OK.'

'I will try,' said Lev.

GK smiled. He pirouetted away from Lev, but turned to say: 'New menu begins this evening, so it may get a bit hot in here, there may be a fair bit of replating going on, but what do nurses do? They stay calm. They clear up the mess. You got it? We're counting on you, Olev.'

More staff began to arrive. They came over and introduced themselves to Lev, and Lev tried to remember their names: Tony and Pierre, sous-chefs; Waldo, pâtisserie and pudding chef; Sophie, vegetable and salad preparation; then the waiters, Stuart, Jeb and Mario. All were younger than Lev and they seemed solemn, as actors seem when they're nervous.

At five, the group sat down at a table at the back of the restaurant and Jeb served poached chicken legs with celery, carrots and *gnocchi*, cooked by Tony. Lev ate very slowly. There was some cleansing herb in the *gnocchi* he wanted to identify. He savoured the delicious potato ball, rolled it round in his mouth. Parsley, that was it. He ate it silently, wondering how it was made, while all around him the dishes for the new menu were being discussed and final notes scribbled by the chefs.

'Plating up the trout terrine,' he heard GK Ashe say, 'I want the leaves in a rosette-shape and clear of the slice. I don't want them touching the fish or lying all over the plate like some stupid paperchase. Barely dress them, OK? Just a glisten of vinaigrette. And the grapefruit mayonnaise should look like an army button on the cuff of the terrine. You see the image?'

'Yes, Chef,' said Pierre.

'And keep it small,' GK went on. 'The trout's moist enough, rich enough. What we're saying with this mayo is, OK, we're going to spoil you now, but not too much. You have to *savour* it.'

Lev understood only words here and there. He ate more *gnocchi*. He imagined serving these, in their beautiful chicken broth, to Maya.

The menu discussion went on, charged with intensity. 'The *pintade*, Chef,' said Tony. 'The *vin de noix* is going to make it lovely and dark. I was thinking ... lay on the breast three batons of ... maybe steamed beetroot, and get a nice vibrant colour contrast.'

'No,' said Ashe. 'No beetroot. *Cèpes*. We discussed this. Just the *cèpes* and the little sandcastle of potato gratin. Now, everybody OK with the halibut?'

'Yes, Chef.'

'Did you get some nice endive, Pierre?'

'Yes, Chef.'

'Don't overcook it, then. I don't want to see my lovely halibut sitting on bogie-slime.'

There was a clatter of laughter. Sophie said: 'You're putting me off my grub, Chef.'

'Good,' said GK. 'You're too fat as it is.'

The group went silent. Lev looked up and saw Sophie blush and lay down her knife and fork on her half-finished meal, and he remembered Lora once saying: 'In a workplace, as a woman in this country, you're fighting a war. Every day.'

He looked away from Sophie as Stuart and Mario cleared away the chicken plates and Waldo brought in a dish of *crème brûlée*, its crust still bubbling from his blow-torch.

'Chef,' said Waldo, 'I want everybody to try this. I'm using blueberries, just cooked for one minute to soften their shape, as a nice astringent base to the *crème*.'

'OK,' said GK. 'Give us a spoon.' Then he turned to Lev. 'You taste this too,' he said. 'We call desserts "puddings" in England; hangover from the days when that's what desserts were: steamed puddings. It's probably why Queen Victoria was the shape she was. But in Britain now a pudding can be a mint sorbet; it can be a poached lychee in a spun-sugar basket. You get it, Olev?'

'Pudding?' said Lev. 'Yes. I know English pudding.'

'Sure,' said GK, lightly investigating the *brûlée* crust with the edge of his spoon, 'but now you can know it properly – know it for what it means. If you're coming to work in a kitchen, Olev, you have to get the words right. You have to get the *glossary* into your head.'

'I will, Chef,' said Lev. And he wanted to add, as politely as he could, that there was one word GK Ashe himself could get into his head and that word was 'Lev', but when he opened his mouth to speak, GK had turned away and everybody was concentrating on Waldo's *brûlée*.

'I like it,' said Damian. 'It's quite refreshing.'

'Bloody nice, Waldo,' said Mario.

'It's OK,' said GK, 'but vary the fruit base over the week. Try rhubarb. Try damsons.'

Lev tasted the pudding. The texture of the cream was delicate and cool and the crust hot and sweet and, once again, he had no idea what had gone into the making of this dish or how these surprising contrasts were achieved. He thought of his father saying: 'Things can only be *what they are*. We Communists always understood this, but the new generation doesn't. They need reminding: a loaf of bread is just a loaf of bread. It's not a bag of gold. It's not a ruddy musical box.' And then Lev remembered Ina standing up to Stefan, for once, and saying: 'If things can only be what they are, why has the Church of St Nicolas at Baryn been turned into an indoor swimming-pool?'

Now Lev's arms were deep in his sinks. Round his head, GK Ashe had tied a clean white cotton bandanna. He'd done this almost tenderly, tucking Lev's springy hair underneath it. 'Nurse's hat,' he said. 'Keep it tight, OK, Olev? I don't want human DNA in the dishwater.'

Lev worked, trying to keep pace with the rising tumult at the chefs' stations. The hot water, the grandeur of the steel surfaces, the fierceness of the rinse-faucet made him forget that this was a lowly job. Steam clouded the tiles. On his right-hand surface, the chefs hurled down mixing bowls, strainers, knives, stock pans, whisks and chopping-boards, and Lev's hands took them up and immersed them. He'd been nicknamed 'Nurse', so now, in his imagination, he became a nurse to these objects. He told himself to examine each pan, each utensil, in a clinical way, to coax the dirt out of it, to keep watch, moment to moment, over its arduous alteration.

After a while, running clean hot water, beginning everything again with, at his back, the chefs hunched over their burners and the smell of poaching fish fumigating the air, Lev's mind began to drift. He imagined himself, dressed in a nurse's white cotton clothes, walking down to the sulphur lake at Jor and immersing helpless people in the grey deeps. Storks on a chimney top regarded the people as the lake water washed over them and their pale skins began to shine through the bluish mist.

One of these helpless people was Marina, and Lev started to scrub at her flesh. He scoured her neck, her armpits, her arse, her feet, her ears; he rinsed her mouth. Then she lay back on the surface of the water and Lev's arms lifted her up and wrapped her in a clean white towel and set her down where the other people waited, on a wooden balcony. She wasn't cured, of course. His task had only just begun. What would cure her was his nurse's endurance, his willingness to repeat the immersion and the harsh but inevitable scraping and scouring of her flesh, to repeat it over and over again, without giving up, without breaking ...

A food-scented presence at Lev's elbow woke him from his reverie. GK Ashe threw a mop into his hands. He pointed at the floor. 'What's that?' he said. 'You're turning my kitchen into a fucking inland sea!'

Lev looked down. His brown shoes stood in a puddle. A scum of water lapped against the back of the vegetable chiller. His apron was soaked and even his trousers were wet and clung to his legs. 'Sorry, Chef,' he said.

Ashe snatched up a red plastic bucket from under one of the sinks. He hurled this at Lev and it struck him on the thigh and bounced away onto the slippery floor.

'*Swab it!*' he said. 'And stop dreaming. I've been watching you. Concentrate!'

Mario, headed for the restaurant door, carrying three servings of venison *ragù* with pasta, called out: 'Table four's away, Chef!'

Ashe turned, almost lunging at Mario. 'I don't call that "away", Mario,' he shouted. 'Where's the *ballotine*?'

'Coming next, Chef ...' said Mario and disappeared, leaving Ashe mumbling: 'Don't say a table's away when it isn't away. Can't anybody here count?'

Ashe moved away from Lev's station and Lev filled the bucket from the rinse-faucet and began to mop the floor. Now that he'd left the lake at Jor and was back in the kitchen, he realised that his eyes were stinging and that an immovable pain had lodged itself between his shoulder-blades. He longed for a cigarette. The water all round him surprised him, but he knew he had to vanquish this, too, keep on mopping and squeezing out the mop until the tiles were dry. But he couldn't get them dry. He couldn't even get them clean because where his own feet trod, grimy footprints remained.

He looked around for a floorcloth or a rag. (At home, when Ina washed the floor, she, like Ahmed, laid newspaper over it and the paper slowly darkened with moisture and Maya sometimes knelt down on it to watch the people in the photographs gradually turning black.) Unobserved, Lev snatched a clean tea towel off its peg and knelt and began to rub the floor with this while, at his back, he could feel the heat from the ovens and the burners reach a new intensity.

Lev squeezed out the tea towel and threw it out of sight under the sink. He dried his hands. He stared at a large pan that had arrived beside his sink. It was smeared with what looked like yellow glue. He remembered an article in the *Baryn Informer* about the new craze, in the West, for a peasant dish from Italy known as *polenta*. 'Polenta,' said the *Informer*, 'is maize flour mixed with seasoned water. It is what the poor blacks of South Africa have called "mealie-meal" for generations. It is starvation food, sold at high prices. To put *polenta* on an expensive menu is a mendacious and decadent act.'

Lev lifted up the *polenta* pan. The smell of it was like the smell of a barley field at harvest-time. Lev ran more hot water.

By eleven, Lev could feel the movement in the kitchen slowing and the objects that arrived by his sinks were different: baking trays, sorbet glasses, ramekins, egg-beaters, pastry-cutters, spoons, coffee cups and cafetières. He allowed himself to turn, once, to see what everybody was doing, and he saw Sophie close the vegetable chiller and begin to take off her kitchen whites. When she removed the little cotton hat she'd been wearing, her hair was damp and lying in heavy curls close to her skull, as though she'd been swimming.

'Night, everybody,' she said.

GK Ashe came over to her, put a hand on her wet head and considered her with his ice-blue eyes. 'Nice calm work, Sophie,' he said. 'Everything well co-ordinated. Pretty good.'

'Thank you, Chef,' said Sophie.

The other chefs raised a hand to her and then she turned to Lev. 'Night, Olev,' she said.

Lev felt himself execute a ridiculous little bow, while holding in his hands a bowl and a whisk. Waldo and Jeb sniggered. Sophie smiled. Lev said quietly: 'Sophie, I am sorry. My name is Lev. Not Olev.'

'Oh, right,' said Sophie. 'I'm sorry, too.'

'Nothing to be sorry about,' said Ashe. 'His name's *Nurse*.'

By one o'clock – when the service was long over and the 'front of house' empty of the last customers and the dining room dark and silent – the staff had gone home, and the only people who stayed behind in the kitchen were Lev and GK Ashe.

Ashe sat on a stool at his work station and drank white wine and made notes on his menu pads. His blue eyes darted everywhere, observing Lev as he cleaned the hobs and the salamanders, the plate-warmers and the steel counter-tops. Lev was then reminded to sweep and mop the floor.

'I sacked the last nurse,' said GK, as Lev poured hot water and floor-cleaner into the red bucket, 'because he refused to do this late-night stuff properly. I said to him: "You know you're an idiot? Idiots sleep while the smart guys work." But he didn't get it. So, tough. He was history. Lucky for you.'

'Yes,' said Lev. 'Lucky for me, Chef.'

But he felt as tired as an old mule. His yearning for a cigarette made him shivery. His hands were sore and burning and the ache in his back was like a wound. He longed to lay down his head on the surprised faces of the wandering giraffes.

6

Elgar's Humble Beginnings

The London heatwave lasted a long time.

Dust accumulated on the gates and railings of Belisha Road, and on the tops of cars. In the garden of number 12, the grass turned brown and the malnourished puppy whined all afternoon in the dry shade of the sycamore tree.

Christy Slane kept the windows of the flat wide open and Lev grew accustomed to the sounds of North London, as to a piece of modern music which he knew others admired, but which he couldn't quite bring himself to love. One of these sounds was the council chain-saw biting into the limbs of the rowan trees.

Some afternoons, Lev just sat in his room, smoking and wondering and concealing ten-pound notes in brown-paper parcels padded with newspaper to send to Ina. On other days, when he felt strong in his limbs, he walked to Parliament Hill and watched the kite-flyers launch peculiar buzzing mattresses into the blue air and listened to snatches of conversation by the dark ponds of the Heath. He stared at lovers and young couples with babies, and envied them. The grey skin of his face and arms turned brown in the late sunshine. His hair grew long over his collar.

Most days, both Lev and Christy stayed in bed until midday, then Christy would make tea and crawl out to a Greek shop for fresh bread. Sometimes he cooked bacon and potato-scones and fried tomatoes. Then he and Lev would sit at the table in the window of the bare sitting room, eating and talking about work and money, or trying to sing the nursery rhymes they'd taught their daughters long ago. Christy reminded Lev that Ireland was a land of song. He said music was in the green of the hedgerows and in the bleating of sheep; it was in the dreaming coves of the western shore and in the malting houses of the Guinness breweries. He said England had no songs, only marches and embarrassing old laments for dead glories. 'When you come to a land without song, things are bound to go tits-up, sooner or later,' he said. 'I should have known that before I married Angela.'

Towards the end of the summer, Lev went with Christy to a small shop at Archway, staffed by young Indian men, and bought a mobile phone. From an assistant whose name was Krishna, he chose the cheapest model available. When he and Christy came out of the shop, Christy slapped Lev's shoulders and announced to him that now he was a 'true citizen of London', that he was a 'modern human being', and Lev felt pleased with his purchase. The mobile had a turquoise green casing. He had, as yet, almost nobody to make calls to, apart from Rudi, but he liked to cradle the phone in his hand and re-run the selection of ring-tones. And, in the early hours as he walked home to Belisha Road from his night bus, he would sometimes call Christy – wherever Christy was, in some friend's smoky room, or in some Irish pub that never closed – and say: 'This is Lev. Just phoning in.'

'Lev,' Christy would invariably say, 'good man! I'll be home in a jiffy.'

But he seldom was. If a plumbing job came up, he'd tell the people he only worked evenings, and when Lev left for *GK Ashe*, Christy would be doing a jigsaw puzzle at the table, or hanging up sheets and T-shirts over the bath. Yet one afternoon, before Lev went to work, Christy showed him a wad of money.

'Cash,' he said, 'see it? Cash is gold and don't forget that, Lev. Get paid in cash, and I'm not funding some eejit to knacker the trees or dig up the fuckin' road. I'm not subsidising foreign wars or helping to redecorate the House of Commons toilets. I'm paying for me own life and that's all. And that's the way I like it to be.'

Christy held out the money – a clutch of twenties – for Lev to admire. When Lev had admired them sufficiently, Christy offered to come and talk to GK Ashe, to persuade him to pay Lev in cash, but Lev said: 'No, Christy. Thank you for thinking. But I have bank account now. Damian helped me. Sometimes I go to look at this bank, Clerkenwell branch, to feel pride in my money so safe.'

'All right,' said Christy. 'I appreciate your sentimental attachment to the premises of capitalist extortionists. But it's robbery to get National Insurance and all that extra stuff off you, when the hourly rate is so pitiful.'

'I get free supper meal.'

'Sure. I guess that's worth something. Got a top chef filling your belly once a day. But I've seen you come home. You're beat. They're workin' you like a slave.'

'No,' said Lev. 'I'm OK. And sending money home.'

'How much're you sendin', though? You've not a lot to spare.'

'Depends. Sometimes twenty pound a week. In my country, this can go far.'

'Can it? Well, Jeezus, why don't we all move there, then?'

Christy sat down opposite Lev at the sitting-room table. His thin arms rested on an ancient tea stain. He sighed and went on: 'I'd *like* to move there. Why not? If twenty quid a week can buy you what it used to buy. They could do with a few plumbers, couldn't they? Put in some nice sanitary-ware. Your daughter could have her own little washbasin with dolphin taps, eh, Lev?'

'You don't want to move there,' said Lev.

'Why not? I like the sound of it. Goats tinklin' along in the street. Tin jewellery. Old-fashioned folk-dancing. I truly like the thought of it.'

'No,' said Lev. 'You wouldn't like, Christy. No future there. No work.'

'I'd make me own work,' said Christy. 'Like Rudi and his taxi firm. And we could go drinking all together – you, me and Rudi. And I'd be away from Angela. Away from the lawyers ...'

'But also away from Frankie.'

'Yes,' said Christy, with a melancholy sigh. 'Well, I know. But it's not as if I *see* her, is it? Only those glimpses I get. Oh, and I didn't tell you: Angela's got a boyfriend now. Some eejit of an estate agent. Planning on moving in with him. Her and Frankie. Moving in with *that*. Kills me, it does. If Frankie starts to call him "Daddy", I'll have to murder somebody. I tell you, fella, I'll have to commit a serious crime.'

Lev looked at Christy, who was twisting a rubber band round his wad of twenties. On his narrow face, the flare of eczema was spreading wider.

'Why you can't see Frankie?' Lev said quietly. 'It's your daughter.'

Christy didn't raise his eyes, just stared at the money-roll. After a while, he said: 'Angela made things out. Said I was violent when I'd been drinking. Said I hit her. Said if I hit my wife, I was capable of hitting the child.'

He laid down the money and lit a cigarette. Not looking at Lev, he said: 'I didn't hit Angela. I'm sure I never did. Or if I did, it's just vanished away out of me, into a void. So I had to tell my lawyer: "I don't *know.*" Angela showed me a swollen lip one time. Perhaps I did that. Perhaps I did. But I wouldn't have said such a thing was in me. I wouldn't have said Christy Slane would ever get anywhere near to doin' that. But how do I know?'

Lev sat very still. He wanted to admit to Christy that, where love was concerned, he knew that he himself had been capable of saying and doing things of which he'd later felt ashamed.

But this subject needed time and the cheap clock on Christy's mantelpiece was ticking towards three thirty. Lev had to leave soon and get on his bus. He reached out and took a cigarette from Christy's pack of Silk Cut. The sharing of cigarettes had become a quiet habit with them. It confirmed them, in Lev's mind, as friends. He inhaled and said: 'I believe you didn't do this, Christy. Somewhere in your mind, you would know.'

'But would I?' said Christy. 'That's what I'm not sure about. And that's why I can't defend meself. It's all just gone dark. And now this eejit of a property-shop employee is fucking Angela and reading Frankie bedtime stories. I'm the out-and-out loser.'

When Lev got home from *GK Ashe*, towards two o'clock, he found Christy on the landing outside the flat door, lying in a pool of sick. Lev went into the flat and dampened a sheaf of kitchen paper and came back to Christy and swabbed away the vomit from his mouth. Then he ran a bath and carried Christy into the bathroom and undressed him and laid him in the warm water. Christy was conscious by now, and aware of where he was. His face was very white, except for the sore band of eczema, and his voice sounded thin and hesitant, like the voice of a person on the end of a waver-ing mobile-phone connection.

'Sorry, fella,' he said to Lev. 'That's fuckin' disgusting. Me ma used to say to me: "Wouldn't mind Dad's drunken rages, wouldn't mind him smashing up Aunt Bridie's tea service, if only he could keep the drink *down*".'

'It's OK,' said Lev. 'It's OK.'

He left Christy soaping his neck with a flannel and returned to mop up the pool of vomit on the landing. Though the smell was foul, Lev could endure it. When Marina had become ill, she had vomited often and he'd just got used to it. It was part of her, was what he used to tell himself. It was everyday human mess. It was proof that Marina was still alive.

Cold autumn arrived without warning.

When Lev left for work one afternoon, the sun was still quite warm on the window-panes of 12 Belisha Road; when he came out into the Clerkenwell night, all the pubs and bars had closed their doors and a freezing wind was howling through deserted streets. Lev set off towards his bus-stop. He tugged up the collar of his leather jacket as rain began to fall. The revolving yellow light of a street-sweeping cart lit up a suddenly unfamiliar city.

Waiting for his night bus, on a tilting bench no wider than a plank, Lev remembered how, when Marina had worked in the Procurator's Office of Public Works in Baryn, he used to imag-ine her as the guardian of his world, used to feel confident that whatever changes might be on their way his wife would be one of the first to know about them. Even changes in the weather. The Office of Public Works had invested in what the Procurator called a 'Reliable Forecasting Facility'. Marina always knew, for instance, when snowfall was expected. Her department would have overseen the oiling of ancient snowploughs and authorised the call-up of the retired drivers of these machines, taken from their homes to be put on a fearful standby in the Baryn transport depot, where the only creature-comfort was an antique samovar bolted to the wall and a stall of rusty urinals that were never cleaned.

'These old men,' Marina used to say, 'have to use the urinals very often. I worry they will get some infection.'

Lev's bus arrived and he climbed on and was glad of the weak warmth to be found inside, and the lemonish light in the darkness. He wished someone could have warned him about the suddenness of change in the English seasons. He knew he'd become so accustomed to the fine weather he'd made no adjustments in his mind for a cold autumn. And now he could see the long tunnel of winter waiting ahead, the dark afternoons, that old middle-of-the-night sadness you could feel when you heard the wind tormenting the trees.

Lev closed his eyes. His back ached from his long shift at the sinks. He stuffed his hands inside the pockets of his jacket and clutched the precious money he found there. Memories of Marina's office in the Public Works building now filled his mind. He could remember its fusty smell and the sound of its heavy door opening and closing and Marina's nameplate on her desk.

It had been in winter that he and Marina had become entrapped in their one furious quarrel. Even at the time, Lev had known that the detestable way he was behaving towards his wife had something to do with the cold season, with lightlessness, with the too-thin blood in his veins. All along that dark time, he'd hated himself – his ranting voice, his hardened heart – but this hatred didn't alter what he felt or what he did. All along that dark time, he had known he was probably mistaken, but he couldn't recant, couldn't cease to believe what had suddenly, in the space of a single day, become his blinding conviction.

He had accused Marina of being unfaithful to him. He believed that her lover was her boss, the Procurator himself, the fifty-year-old Mr Rivas, formerly known as Comrade Rivas.

This belief had been born on a cold Friday afternoon when work finished early at the Baryn sawmill. Lev had walked through the freezing town to Marina's office. He went through the main door of the Public Works building, treading mud and sawdust onto the linoleum floor of the reception area, and the way was barred by the ugly, fire-breathing receptionist, who instructed him rudely to take off his shoes.

He did as he was told. In Baryn you obeyed public servants without questioning their authority. But Lev's socks were damp and had holes in the heels. Climbing the stairs, clutching his muddy shoes, he felt humiliated and poor. He arrived at the corridor outside Marina's office and, without knocking, opened her door.

She was sitting at her desk, reading some paperwork. The Procurator, wearing his smart suit, was standing behind her, also reading – or pretending to read – the document on her desk, with his arm round Marina's shoulders.

Lev stared at this tableau. Comrade Rivas jumped, withdrew his arm and straightened up. Marina let out a tiny strangulated sound, which Lev heard as the sound of guilt. His gaze went from one face to the other. Nobody spoke until Marina said: 'Mr Rivas and I were just going over some new costings from the District Office of Heat and Light.'

Rivas looked at his watch. 'Well, it's true it's getting late for a Friday,' he said. 'Please do accompany your wife home.' Then he walked past Lev, without looking back at Marina, *click-click*, *click-click* in his shiny shoes, and went into his own office and closed the door.

Lev sat down on a leather chair. He laid his filthy work boots on the floor. His eyes didn't leave Marina's face. She began to tidy the documents on her desk and wouldn't look at him. He could see that her face was red, that this blush had crept down her neck, and he imagined it spreading underneath her neat white blouse into the cleft between her breasts. 'What have I just seen?' he asked.

Marina continued tidying the papers. 'You haven't seen anything,' she said. 'Let's go home.' She took her coat off its peg, wound a woollen scarf round her neck, patted her hair.

'Oh, yes,' said Lev, 'I'd do that if I were you: check your hair, where his hands have been. Check your lipstick, too? Or perhaps there's no lipstick left on your mouth.'

'Don't think what you're thinking, Lev,' she said. 'The Procurator behaves in an affectionate manner towards all his staff, because he believes this humane attitude to be more productive than—'

'More productive of what?'

'More productive than old-fashioned hierarchical severity and—'

'I said more productive *of what*?'

'Please don't shout in this office. Of cohesion. Of everybody working together—'

'And doing what else together?'

Marina didn't answer. She took out a headscarf from her coat pocket and tied this round her hair. The sweetness of her face inside the scarf made Lev's heart falter. 'I hate you,' he said. 'You've just ruined my life.'

They cycled home through the falling night. Lev rode ahead of Marina because he couldn't bear to look at her, but all the while he could see the faint flicker of her cycle lamp following on behind.

It was January or February, the deep cavern of winter, and Lev thought that now this winter would be with him for ever, and that even when spring returned it wouldn't return for him.

Now, aboard the night bus, Lev remembered all the ways in which he'd punished Marina for her supposed love affair with Procurator Rivas. He left their bed and lay down on the floor outside the room where Ina and baby Maya slept. He stayed away some nights altogether, getting drunk with Rudi and finding himself unable to go to work the next morning. His job began to be under threat. He ignored his child. He bullied his mother. For Marina's birthday, he wrapped up a lump of coal and put it into her faithless hands.

It was when Marina unwrapped the coal that she broke down.

She swore on the life of her child that she had never been near the bed of Procurator Rivas. She offered to resign her position at the Office of Public Works. She declared that nobody in Baryn, no woman in the world, loved her husband more than she loved Lev, and now that love was being poisoned – for the sake of a terrible misunderstanding. She beat the wall with her fists, then she laid her head against the wall and wept. Baby Maya, aged two, began screaming and Ina had to pick her up and take her outside, to try to divert her by feeding the chickens.

Lev remembered the sudden exhaustion that had overcome him at the moment when Marina began to beat the wall. It was as if, since the afternoon in the Office of Public Works, he'd been tramping across ice and snow, across glaciers and crevasses, on some fruitless expedition over wasteland and emptiness, carrying a terrible weight on his back, and now he was spent and near to dying – all for nothing, all for the sake of trying to wound the one woman in the world who made him happy.

He went over to Marina and took hold of her hands and stilled them by cradling them against his chest. He laid his head on her shoulder. He asked her to forgive him.

*

When the temperature in London had dropped still further and the pub drinkers of Tufnell Park had swept themselves off the pavements into snug lounges and heated snooker rooms, Lev received a letter from Lydia:

> *Dear Lev,*
>
> *I hope you're surviving well in your job and that your room is comfortable.*
>
> *I would like to say how sorry I am for what happened at Tom and Larissa's house. I was a little drunk that night, and behaving like a schoolgirl – which, perhaps, all women do from time to time. I am sure you are a kind enough man to forgive me.*
>
> *To make amends, I would like to invite you to a wonderful concert Maestro Greszler is giving in two weeks' time with the London Philharmonic Orchestra at the Festival Hall on Sunday, 30 October. The programme is Elgar and Rachmaninov. Maestro Greszler has given me two excellent seats and the soloist for the Elgar cello concerto is the Russian genius, Mstislav Rostropovich. I think this will be an extremely marvellous event. Rostropovich is old and makes only a few appearances now, but his genius is undiminished. I very much hope you will be my guest for that evening.*
>
> *Yours ever, Lydia*

Lev's first thought was that Lydia always surprised him. On the coach, he'd imagined her as a woman of unremarkable gifts. But he'd been wrong. His next thought was that now he had someone else to call on his mobile. He first punched Lydia's number into his phone's memory system (where its alphabetical listing placed it between Damian's mobile and Rudi's distant landline by the cuckoo clock), then he dialled it.

'It's Lev,' he said. 'I have a mobile phone now.'

'Oh, yes?' said Lydia. 'That's very technological of you.'

'I'm a "true citizen of London", so I'm told.'

'Yes, you are. And thank you for calling me on this lovely new phone. I hope it's to say you can come to the concert.'

Lev was smoking one of Christy's Silk Cut. He inhaled deeply, then said: 'I've never been to a concert like this, Lydia, only folk-music performances in Baryn.'

'Well,' said Lydia, 'this is quite far from folk, but I think you would like it.'

'The other thing,' said Lev, 'is that I can't come because I have nothing to wear.'

There was a moment's dejected silence before Lydia said: 'Lev, you know that doesn't matter. Just put on a tie. Won't you?'

'I'm not sure ...'

'Please,' said Lydia. 'You will never regret this. To hear Maestro Greszler conducting and Rostropovich playing Elgar ...'

'Who is Elgar?' said Lev.

'Oh, you don't know? One of very few good English composers. This piece was written in the autumn of his life and the slow movement is very famous and sad. It may make you cry, Lev. Please tell me you will come and cry.'

When Lev said at last that he would accept, he heard Lydia utter a little mew of delight. She told him to put the date in his diary and he promised he would. He didn't tell her that he had no diary or that his days and nights all resembled each other in their unvarying routine.

Christy took him down the Holloway Road where, from a Saturday stall run by Irish friends of Christy's, Lev bought a white cotton shirt and a tie the colour of Waldo's *brûlée* crust. He laid these clothes out on his bunk bed. He took his best pair of grey trousers to the Greek dry cleaner's. He shined up his brown shoes.

'I note that you're taking a lot of trouble for Lydia,' remarked Christy.

'No,' said Lev. 'I take trouble to look smart at concert.'

'Well,' said Christy, 'music is something worth taking trouble for. When I was a boy, me dad used to play the fiddle. We had a neighbour, Stan Lafferty, who must have been ninety if he was a day, but Stan and me dad used to make some good music down the pub on Saturday nights, and I and me ma would sit there, in our Saturday clothes, clickin' our stupid fingers and bouncin' our stupid feet. That's the nearest I ever got to seeing me ma happy. She'd be overcome with that dancing music. Her face would get a grin on it and a shine ... I think that concert's going to raise your spirits, Lev.'

'Yes?'

'Yes, I do. Maybe you'll even find Lydia more charming than before.'

'No,' said Lev. 'I know what is Lydia to me.'

'Sure,' said Christy, 'but it can change. Things like this are never what you'd call *stable*.'

Lev was now crossing Hungerford Bridge. An icy wind blew off the river, but he stopped in the middle of the bridge and gazed out at all the electric light flooding the buildings along the stately embankments of the Thames. Because of his fear of being late, Lev was very early for his rendezvous with Lydia, so he lingered on the bridge.

He rolled a cigarette and smoked it in an easy, automatic way, not taking his eyes from the panorama of the dazzling riverfront. That the steady flood of brilliance which illuminated the buildings had no purpose except to beautify impressed him and troubled him in a kind of equal measure. He couldn't stop himself remembering how precious each hour of electricity was in his country and how people like his mother longed for light that would never go out. In the years since the fall of the Communist government, light-stability was something that had been promised many times, but still the power-cuts continued in Auror. Sometimes Ina would stare up at the electricity pylon in the darkness and curse and say: 'Look at it! Taking the power right over our heads. And we're left without. Nobody cares about the villages.'

Lev stubbed out his cigarette. He felt nervous. He wondered how long the concert would last and whether he could sit through it without fidgeting. He hoped he wouldn't fall asleep, or start coughing. He could imagine all kinds of reproach in Lydia's eyes.

Lydia was waiting for him near the bar, sitting alone at a table, with a glass of tomato juice in front of her. Lev noticed that her hair had been stylishly cut. She wore a black suit with a green blouse.

When she saw Lev, she stood up and they shook hands.

'Lev,' she said. 'What a very nice tie.'

It was still early and the great gleaming foyer had few people in it, but still Lev could feel an air of anticipation about the concert, as if the audience was here to be cleansed or rebaptised.

Lydia was clutching a programme and she said: 'Now, Lev, I will tell you something about Elgar.'

Lev sat down. He wished he was wearing a better jacket than his old leather one, with its stained collar. Lydia's eyes were bright as she said: 'This man was Sir Edward Elgar, and very important to English music in the first part of the twentieth century. But he was like us: the beginnings of his life were quite ordinary. His father owned a little music shop in some provincial town.'

'A music shop?'

'You know, a small place selling instruments and music sheets. There is one in Baryn, on the corner of an old alleyway behind Market Square. Maybe you know that one?'

'No,' said Lev.

'Well,' continued Lydia, 'the one in Baryn is very dusty, with second-hand flutes and violins and so on, and some of the music sheets are torn and with missing pages. So perhaps Elgar's father's shop was like this one in Market Square, because later in his life Elgar would say he was ashamed of his origins.'

'I would have thought a music shop would be a good place to start, if you wanted to be a composer,' said Lev. 'Why be ashamed?'

'Well,' said Lydia, 'you are right, Lev. But, of course, that was very English of that time – for a man like Elgar to make his way, then feel ashamed of a humble past because those around him *made him* feel ashamed. Just as now, in our country, there is some shame among the old Communists because they are *made* to feel this shame. Communism was not their fault, just as to be born in a music shop was not Elgar's fault. Do you see my connection?'

'Yes,' said Lev. 'I suppose so.'

'But Elgar overcame his poor start with the dusty violas and so forth. He wrote very, very beautiful melodies and his orchestration is extremely fine. You will hear. It is very complete. When he was a boy, he used to sit by the river – some river near that town where the music shop was – and listen to nature. He called it "fixing sound". And he said that the things he could hear made him long for something great. And then, eventually, this greatness—'

Lydia was interrupted by the arrival of a young man, one of the Festival Hall employees, with a name-badge that said 'Darren'.

He bent down towards her. 'Sorry to intrude, Lydia,' he said, 'but Maestro Greszler would like to see you.'

'Oh,' said Lydia. 'Yes, of course. May I bring my guest, to introduce him?'

The employee, Darren, looked at Lev, then back at Lydia. 'Yes,' he said. 'I expect so. Please follow me.'

Lydia stood up. 'You come with me, Lev,' she said, 'and we will see if I can introduce you.'

'It's all right,' said Lev. 'I can wait here.'

'No, no,' insisted Lydia. 'Come on. Then you can write home and tell your mother you've met Pyotor Greszler face to face.'

They were shown into a large, brightly lit dressing room where Pyotor Greszler sat alone, wearing a woollen dressing-gown.

He was seventy years old. His body sagged in the leather and chrome chair. He was sipping morosely from a medicine glass, containing a white substance. His long hair was also white, and a droopy white moustache gave his lined face an expression of pure melancholy. When he saw Lev, he slammed down the medicine glass and made a bad-tempered, sweeping gesture with his arm. 'No, Lydia. No strangers in here! Who is this?'

'Sorry, Maestro,' said Lydia. 'Only my friend, Lev, from our country, who would like to be introduced—'

'No, he cannot be introduced now. He must go,' said Greszler. 'Go. *Go*!'

'I'll go,' said Lev, backing away.

'Come here, Lydia,' said the Maestro, crossly. 'You must help me. We haven't much time ...'

Lev hurried away and closed the dressing-room door. Darren had disappeared. Along the corridor, Lev could hear snatches of music being practised. He felt hot with embarrassment. He wished Rudi were there to make a joke of what had just happened. He tugged at his tie, to loosen it round his sweating neck.

After only a moment or two Lydia emerged from the room. Her face wore an expression of grave concern. 'Come, Lev,' she said, and set off down the corridor in the direction from which they'd arrived. Then she made for the nearest door and tugged Lev out into the cold night.

'What's happening?' he asked.

'Pharmacy,' said Lydia. 'The nearest will be in Waterloo Station.' She began almost to run. 'I only pray it's open,' she said. 'We must walk very fast. Come on.' The scurrying *clack-clack* of her court shoes was an anxious sound.

'What's wrong with the Maestro?' said Lev as he hurried to keep up with Lydia.

'I'll tell you later,' said Lydia. 'Luckily, I know the quickest way.'

Lev looked at his watch. The concert was due to begin in thirty-five minutes. His image of Pyotor Greszler, slumped in his chair, sipping the white medicine, remained vivid in his mind.

Lydia's pace was such that, soon, both she and Lev were out of breath. Lev could feel his smoke-addicted lungs begin to complain, but Lydia kept hurrying on. 'God!' she exclaimed, as they rushed onto the station concourse. 'The human body. So sublime and yet so weak.'

They raced towards the chemist's shop, with Lydia already tearing money from her purse. She instructed Lev to wait by the door while she went in.

Now, Lev was waiting for Lydia again, back at the same unadorned bar table where they'd started the evening. After the dash to Waterloo station and back again, he was glad to be sitting down. In the foyer, a bell was chiming repetitively. There were now three minutes left before the start of the concert. Lev watched the audience all around him finish their drinks and start moving up towards the auditorium. He wondered whether there would be any music after all, or whether some grave managerial person (of the kind who used to work with Marina at the Office of Public Works) would come onto the platform and announce the cancellation of the whole evening.

With the third or fourth chiming of the bell, Lev found himself alone in the bar seats and the echoing foyer was deserted except for a few people, far off, ambling round some photographic exhibits.

In the silence that had fallen, he thought, not without wonderment, how the next few moments of musical history might depend upon Lydia.

And now he saw her running towards him. Lev noted with tenderness that, after all the dashing through the damp night streets, her former elegance had been compromised. On her brow there was a film of sweat and her nicely styled hair had become wilfully curly. 'Lev,' she panted, 'I'm so sorry. To put you through all this. Let me catch my breath and then we can go in.'

Lydia sat down. She wiped the sweat from her face with a tissue. She combed her hair. She asked Lev to get her some water from the bar. She said the performance was going to begin late, so there would be plenty of time in which to drink it.

Lev brought the water and sat down again.

Lydia gulped it. 'My God,' she said. 'My God. I hope he will be all right. I never thought I would have to go on such an errand.'

'What's the matter with him?' asked Lev.

'Well ...' said Lydia, in a whisper. 'I will tell you now. Maestro Greszler told me he couldn't conduct the Elgar cello concerto with so many poisons in him. He had been trying to evacuate the poisons, but he wasn't able to succeed. He said he absolutely had to be purged before he could go on stage. I had to get suppositories for him, to bring about an evacuation. He was embarrassed to ask any English person. He feels that we, as a people, are a mystery to them: a mystery and a terror. But all I hope, now, is that the suppositories have worked!'

Lev smiled. He took Lydia's hand and held it for a moment. He thought her valiant and suddenly found himself wishing – for her sake as much as his – that she was prettier than she was.

With her hand in his, Lydia let her large eyes come to rest on his face. Then she looked down. 'What I said is true,' she said. 'That is a very nice tie, Lev.'

Inside the auditorium, Lev stared with awe at the big, breathless space and the orchestra tuning up on the brightly lit stage. Lydia hurried them to their seats and he could smell on her the odour of their coach journey, of perfume or deodorant mixed with sweat, and he thought how incredible it was that they were now sitting side by side in this famous concert hall.

Minutes kept passing. The orchestra waited. The audience went silent. Individual bouts of coughing came and went in different parts of the hall. Lydia's breathing was still slightly laboured. On her green blouse was a tiny stain of tomato juice Lev hadn't noticed before. He could feel her deep anxiety.

To try to calm her, to help her pass this bit of agonising time, he said quietly: 'Tell me something more about Elgar.'

'Well,' began Lydia, 'what can I tell you? You will hear, in this concerto, a big nostalgia, a big longing for some time or place that is gone, or perhaps it's a longing to find some perfect place that cannot ever be found. I think I read somewhere that he said he only loved one thing in the world and that was a river somewhere in the west of England. Probably the river where he was when he was a child, where he "fixed sound". I don't know.'

'Do you have "nostalgia" for our country, Lydia?'

'What? Do you mean am I homesick?'

'I mean, do you think you made the right decision to come here?'

'Yes,' she said emphatically. 'There was nothing left for me in Yarbl. Only my parents, set in their old ways. Here, I am starting again. I'm determined to have a life.'

Now, at last, there was movement on the left-hand side of the stage, and here he came, Pyotor Greszler, the most famous person their country had produced in the last fifty years, upright and smart in his tail-coat, making his way through the orchestra, with his hair neatly brushed and, on his formerly melancholy features, the beginnings of a smile. He walked with a firm step, almost bounced onto the podium, and raised his hands to acknowledge the applause that greeted him. Lydia began to clap violently. She turned and smiled at Lev and said: 'His colour's better. I think the suppositories worked. I'm so happy.'

Maestro Greszler now looked over to the door from which he'd entered. He raised his hands again in a gesture of welcome as Rostropovich made his slow and careful way to the soloist's chair.

The applause grew in passionate intensity. One or two people stood up. The elderly Rostropovich inclined his head. The lights gleamed and flickered on his spectacles. Next to him Lev could feel Lydia's rapture. Now, in moments, the beautiful music was going to begin.

Gradually, the audience fell silent. Rostropovich settled himself around his instrument. Greszler waited, baton in his hand. The musicians were still, but poised on their chairs, watching Greszler. No silence that Lev had witnessed had ever been so choked with expectation. And it endured. The great cellist was very old now: he needed to take his time. On the podium, Greszler held his elbows out, waiting, still, for the moment when his baton would take flight.

It was in this rapt silence that Lev suddenly became aware of an unexpected, but somehow familiar sound. It seemed to be very near him. And he was conscious of people turning and staring at him and the man next to him giving his arm a violent nudge. Then he realised: his mobile phone was ringing! The latest ring-tone Lev had selected was called 'Carousel' and he'd chosen it for its touching resemblance to the fairground music at Baryn, and now, in this fatal moment before the Elgar cello concerto began, it was playing merrily along.

Lydia put a hand over her mouth, as though this gesture might stop the phone's insistent ring. 'Turn it off!' she hissed.

Lev fumbled to find it. His jacket had many pockets. The 'Carousel' ring-tone was programmed to increase in intensity after the third ring. Lev's hands searched uselessly. On the platform Greszler had turned angrily towards the audience. He made a gesture of despair. 'Mobile phones off!' he yelled. 'Please, *please*! No barbarians in here!' And the hundred outraged faces of the orchestra looked in Lev's direction. Lev thrust his hands into this pocket and that. He found money, keys, comb, cigarettes, but no mobile. Sweat began to pour down his back. Lydia kept growling his name in despair: 'Lev, Lev, *Lev*!'

The phone wasn't in Lev's jacket. The merry 'Carousel' played blithely on. Lev bent down, his face burning, and fumbled under his seat. Even as he told himself that he wouldn't find the mobile there, that it couldn't have jumped out of his pocket, the ringing stopped. Slowly he straightened up. He was trembling. He saw Greszler still glaring out at the audience. He knew that the profound spell cast over the hall just seconds before was irretrievably broken – and he had broken it. Worse, he still hadn't found his phone. It might ring again. And at any moment it would certainly send the loud beep-beep 'missed-call' signal.

In a daze of mortification, Lev stood up. Without glancing at Lydia, he pushed past fourteen or fifteen furious concert-goers, ran down the steps and out of the auditorium. He kept running. He found the nearest exit and went out into the night.

7

The Lizard Tattoo

Christy Slane was doing the ironing when Lev got home to Belisha Road. He was drinking Coke. He'd had no alcohol for a week, in preparation for his appearance in court, which was coming up soon. The silent flat smelled of scorched fabric, like toast.

'Shame you missed the music,' Christy said, folding a faded giraffe pillowcase.

Lev had made himself a ham sandwich. He ate this slowly and thoughtfully. Guilt at his desertion of Lydia had now turned to anger. 'I don't belong in those places,' he said. 'Muswell Hill. Festival Hall. That is not my world. I work in kitchen! I should have told Lydia, that is wrong, that is *shit*.'

'Ah, well,' said Christy. 'From the sound of it, shit's the default word for the whole *dee-backle*! But I often say that human society is ninety per cent muck that won't disperse to the appropriate location. That's why I chose the profession of plumber. Someone has to be on hand to get it all washed away to the sea.'

Lev had found his mobile, in an inside pocket of his leather jacket he didn't remember encountering before. Now he placed the phone on the table and looked crossly at it. He knew that soon it was going to ring, and it was going to be Lydia.

'I can tell her you're ill,' offered Christy. 'I can say you've got food poisoning.'

'Yes?'

'Sure I can. I can say you ate a lethal prawn baguette on the way to the hall – that's why you had to rush out.'

'OK,' said Lev. 'You tell her that. Then, in some days, I will call her.'

'Fine,' said Christy. 'But more to the question is: Who was calling *you*, Lev?'

'Calling me?'

'At the critical moment – when you heard those lovely little "Carousel" tones?'

'Oh,' said Lev. 'I don't know.'

Christy put down the iron and picked up Lev's phone. He showed Lev the number listed as a missed call. 'Whose is it?'

Lev stared at it. It wasn't Damian's or Rudi's.

'Could be somebody in Bangladesh trying to sell you double-glazing,' said Christy. 'Or could it be old GK himself, inviting you over for a spot of Sunday-night bubble-and-squeak? But I expect I'm being far-fetched. Why don't you call it and see?'

Lev lit a cigarette. He noted that the time was nine forty. He imagined Lydia coming out of the Festival Hall into the cold night and walking away towards Waterloo station.

'Shall I call?' he said to Christy.

'Yes,' said Christy, 'call.'

Lev pressed the 'call' key and waited. The phone rang six times, then a voice cut in and said:

> *Hi. You've reached Sophie's phone. I'm either at work or out getting plastered. Please leave a message and I'll get back to you when I'm next capable of doing so.*

On Monday evening, *GK Ashe* was what Damian called 'clientele lite'. By ten forty-five, the service was done and the customers had paid and left, and GK Ashe announced to his staff that he was making tomato-and-dolcelatte crostini 'for a late-night feast'.

Lev's work was far from finished when Jeb laid the familiar table at the back of the restaurant, so he kept at his scouring and rinsing when the others went to sit down. He watched Ashe hurl his crostini under a salamander and the smell of the bubbling cheese woke in him a beautiful hunger, like the innocent hunger of a child.

GK carried through the dish of crostini and Lev could see Mario opening beers. The combination of hot cheese and cold beer suggested itself to Lev's mind, at this moment, as the most delicious one the human mind was capable of inventing. He saw the others begin to eat. They, too, seemed to have the hunger of children. He heard their teeth crunch into the crisp, oil-soaked bread.

'Nice night,' he heard Ashe say. 'Lite but good. Everything lovely and organised. No cock-ups. Wicked salsa with the sea bream, Pierre.'

'Thank you, Chef.'

'Brown-bread ice-cream with the cinnamon pears is a winner, Waldo.'

'Good. Glad you think so, Chef.'

'This is how it should be every night, though. Even when we're chocka. It should purr like that. Well, cheers, everyone. Where's Nurse?'

They looked over to where Lev stood at his sinks. 'Come on, Nurse!' called Ashe. 'Come and get your crostini before Miss Sophie Greedy-Guts eats it!'

Lev wiped his hands on a clean towel. He unwound the bandanna from his head and dabbed his face with it. As he sat down, a beer was put into his hands. 'Cheers!' said Ashe again.

Lev drank and ate. Though the familiar ache was in his back, he understood, at this moment, that he was fortunate. If he could hold down this job, rewards like these would be his. He would tell Ina in his next letter that he was working for a good establishment. He would compare the beautiful food he was given here to the crude starch-laden stuff he and Stefan used to eat at the Baryn lumber yard.

He looked over to Sophie, whose curly hair had recently been dyed a shade of robin red. She'd taken off her whites and Lev noted that her arms were plump and still brown from the summer heatwave and that near her shoulder there was a tattoo in the shape of a lizard. He wondered whether he was going to ask her why she'd tried to contact him. He tried to imagine telling her about the embarrassment of the ringing phone in the Festival Hall, but felt that he wouldn't find the right words. And perhaps, anyway, her call had been an error. Perhaps she'd wanted Mario's mobile number, or Jeb's, and Damian had given her Lev's by mistake.

'English girls,' Christy had commented. 'There's only one

trouble with them: they're racist. They don't see themselves like that; they'd hate it if you accused them of it, but they are – or a lot of them are. And you and me, we're foreigners, both. All Angela could say to me when things started to go wrong was "I shouldn't have married a fucking foreigner". That's what she called me. I speak the same language. I've lived in London fifteen years, but there you are, I'm still a "foreigner" to her. That's English girls for you, I'm telling you. Or, rather, I'm warning you. Don't get involved with an English girl.'

'I will not involve with anyone,' Lev had said.

'Well, that's OK, then. But if you do, don't choose Miss United Kingdom.'

Lev looked away from Sophie. He felt GK Ashe's hand on his shoulder. 'You're doing all right, Nurse,' he said. 'No mice. No cockroaches. Not even a silverfish. Not yet. Keep up the standard, though. Don't let things drop. Eh?'

Ashe went home at half past twelve and, one by one, everybody left and Lev was alone, mopping the floor. But he didn't mind. His head felt light from the beer. He mopped in time to an old folk song he sang in his mind. Optimism seemed to have caught him unawares.

Then he heard the outside door open and Sophie was there, wearing a ragged sheepskin coat and a yellow football scarf.

'Came back to help you,' she said. 'I suddenly just didn't like it that we all left you.'

Lev straightened up and looked at her. He thought, I like her clothes.

She began unwinding the football scarf. 'What can I do?' she asked. 'Take the bins out?'

Lev smiled at her. Underneath her shaggy coat, she wore a red sweater the approximate colour of her hair and a beige leather skirt.

'It's OK,' he said. 'This is my job.'

'I know it's your job,' said Sophie, 'but I'll bag up the rubbish and get it out for you, right?'

'You don't need—'

'I know I don't. Stop saying that. I'd like to do it. Then you can get home.'

Lev watched her lifting out the black bags and tying them and piling them up by the door. As she worked, she suddenly said: 'I called you the other night. Damian told me you live in Tufnell Park. I go to a pub there sometimes with my friend Samantha: Sam Diaz-Morant. She works in fashion. We thought it would be a laugh to buy you a drink.'

'Yes?' said Lev.

'You wouldn't have come, though, would you?'

'I don't know . . .' said Lev.

'You just keep yourself to yourself. And, actually, I admire that. Most men are such fucking prostitutes.'

Lev didn't understand this. He shrugged. Then he said: 'I know you called. I was at Festival Hall.'

'Yeah? You were? What were you doing there?'

'Well. Elgar. You know him?'

'Yeah. "Land of Hope and Glory". All that stuff.'

'Yes? I didn't know him. You know he began very poor, with his father in small poor shop, selling music?'

'Did he?'

'Yes. Very poor.'

'Yeah? Well, good on him. Now he's on the twenty-pound note!'

'That's Elgar?'

'Yup.'

'It's some businessman. No?'

Sophie rummaged in her coat pocket and brought out a cheap plastic purse. She produced a twenty-pound note, took it over to Lev and pointed out the name, Sir Edward Elgar 1857–1934.

He recognised the face he'd examined on the coach, with the set expression of a banker, and multiple lines of radiance shining down on him. He began to smile. Leaning on his mop, he told Sophie how he'd studied the face of Elgar on his journey to England and then almost heard his great cello concerto but had been prevented at the last minute.

'What prevented you?' asked Sophie.

'You,' said Lev.

'Me?'

'We are waiting for Elgar when my mobile rings. I am only man with ringing phone. And ringing is you.'

Sophie shook her head as she laughed and her robin-red curls gleamed under the bright kitchen lights. 'Fuck,' she said. 'Never imagined you at a posh concert. Imagined you all alone in some room. That's how wrong I often am.'

Lev looked at Sophie's soft arms and the lizard tattoo. And he thought how, just for a moment, he would like to stroke those arms or rest his head against them. He resumed his mopping, while Sophie went in and out with the rubbish sacks and gusts of the night air intruded on the still-warm body of the kitchen.

When the work was finished, Lev offered Sophie a cigarette and – flaunting GK's laws – she took one and they stood by the two-point-five metres of steel draining top, smoking.

'So,' said Sophie, 'would you like to come drinking with me?'

'Yes?' said Lev.

'You don't sound too sure. But I don't blame you. Sam and me, we can get a bit out of order. People drink in your country?'

'Yes,' said Lev. '*Vodichka.*'

'Is that, like, vodka?'

'It *is* vodka. It means "darling little vodka".'

'Right. Well, we drink "darling little gin and tonic" or "darling little Stella" with rum or whisky chasers. We tried absinthe one night, but I tell you, that makes you insane and we were sick as pigs.'

'Why do you drink?'

'Why do we drink? Well, why does anyone drink? Just for the way it makes the world start to look. You know?'

'Yes.'

'I work at a care home for the elderly most Sundays. Ten till six. You need a drink after that lot. No use being squeamish around old people. But they're a laugh, too. I love them, really. You know what their favourite game is?'

'Yes?'

'Slagging.'

'Slagging?'

'Yeah. Slagging people off: criticising them. They say: "I never liked so-and-so." Their son-in-law, say. Then it crescendos: "He's such a slob. He's a bad driver. He sends crap Christmas presents. He dyes his hair …" You know? On and on. "He's useless with a drying-up cloth. He wears white socks with black shoes. He broke the bird-feeder". It gets hilarious. I encourage them. I say, "Right. Today over tea we're going to have a slagging competition. See who can be nastiest". And they hoot with joy. I'm not kidding.'

'Yes?'

'Hate keeps people alive. One old guy, Douglas, says to me, "I refuse to die before my sister. She's looked down on me for seventy-five years. Now I want to look down on her – in her grave." And he's still going strong. He thinks up different ways to kill her. One of these was, he was going to break into her house and take down her curtain rails and fill them with prawns and put them back up again.'

'Prawns?'

'Yes. What GK calls "shrimp" – just because he once vacationed on Long Island. Wait for her to suffer with the stench. Drive her mad because she can't find the source of it. Because she's house-proud as hell, so Douglas says. Has every surface smelling of some crap polish. Dusts the lightbulbs! And the thought of her being driven away from her home by the prawn stink gives Douglas real pleasure. And I can understand that. I had a boyfriend last year I wanted to kill.'

'You wanted to kill?'

'Yeah. Haven't you ever felt that?'

Lev remembered the longing he'd had to put a knife in the heart of Procurator Rivas, remembered lying awake on his sad bed on the floor and imagining this scene, with Marina screaming and Rivas clutching his fatal wound and falling backwards in his chair, with his clomping, institutional feet sticking up in the air. Lev picked up a cloth and began gently polishing the edge of the draining top. 'Maybe ...' he said.

'I did,' continued Sophie. 'I'm not joking. He was a PE instructor, my boyfriend. Fit as shit. Like an Olympic gymnast. But he kept showing his fitness off. What a wanker! He could do a back-flip from a standing start. It was his party piece. And everybody went "Ooh-aah, my God, how brilliant is *that*!" But you get tired of someone doing back-flips. I did. I kept hoping the next time he did a back-flip he'd break his fucking neck. But he never did. I'd like to marry a fire-fighter. Someone who does something non-wanky. Know what I mean?'

Lev stared at Sophie, trying to fathom what she was saying.

Her face was wide and dimpled and her breasts large, and her legs looked chunky and strong. There was nothing about her that resembled Marina in any way. But this otherness, this *newness of form,* fascinated him. It made her exotic, like some far-away, sun-soaked place that smelled of sugar. And he wondered what it would feel like to go to this place and breathe the candied air.

'What're you looking at?' Sophie asked, confronting Lev's gaze.

'Sorry,' he said. 'Only looking at tattoo. Does this hurt you?'

'Nah,' said Sophie. 'He's just my lizard. He's called Lenny. Had him done two years ago. They all know him in the care home. They say, "How's Lenny today, dear?" and I say, "Oh, Lenny's fine, he'll give you a little lick on the nose if you eat up your bread and butter". That's how terrifyingly juvenile and crazy I am.'

Lev smiled. 'Not crazy to me,' he said.

'Well, I am crazy,' said Sophie. 'I love Lenny. When I settle down to sleep, I sometimes put my arm round my face, like this, and Lenny looks at me and we have conversations in the dark.'

Lev switched off the lights and they stood at the door for a moment, listening to the hum of the chillers in the darkness. Then, they went out into the street, where a few snowflakes had begun to fall. Sophie wound her football scarf round her head. Lev pulled up his collar. He wondered where he would be able to find a winter coat he could afford.

Sophie took the padlock off her bicycle and bundled up the chain. 'Night, then,' she said. 'See you tomorrow.'

'Yes,' said Lev. 'See you tomorrow.'

He watched her pedal off along the empty road, with the snow falling all around her. Then he made his way to the night bus stop, where he sat on the plank seat and smoked and rubbed his hands on his knees to try to warm them.

When he got home to Belisha Road, the lights were still on in the sitting room, but Christy was asleep. It was late, but Lev felt wide awake and restless. He made a cup of tea and carried it through to his room and sat down on his bunk, drinking the tea and staring at the Wendy house and the shop and the soft toys on the window-sill. One of these was a clown. Lev took it down and looked at its painted rag face and its tall felt hat. The feel of its body was squashy and soft and Lev could imagine how much Maya would like it.

Lev looked at the time. He suddenly, desperately, wanted to call Rudi – to get news of Maya – and after some minutes of indecision, in which he imagined Rudi snoring peacefully by Lora's side, he took out his phone and selected Rudi's number. The phone was picked up straight away.

'Hi, Lev,' growled Rudi. 'Glad to hear your voice, comrade. No, you didn't wake me up. Couldn't fucking sleep at all. How're things?'

'OK,' said Lev. 'Good. My job's working out pretty well. Has Ina been getting the money I sent?'

'Yes. Sure she has. I took her to Baryn last Monday and we bought her a new Calor-gas heater for her jewellery-making shed. She'll be all right now when the snow comes.'

'That's good. It's snowing here. What about Maya?'

'She's fine. We were going to take her to the fair next Saturday, but I've got problems with the fucking Tchevi. That's why I can't sleep.'

'What problems?'

'Belts on the automatic drive.'

'Yes?'

'So she fucking *creeps*.'

'Creeps?'

'Yes. I'm manoeuvring out of a parking space, say, so I get into "drive" to move her forward a bit, then I select "reverse" and I expect her to obey me and go fucking backwards nice and slowly, but she doesn't: she creeps forwards before starting to acknowledge the gear she's in. Then she lurches back, like a fucking kangaroo.'

'What can you do about it?'

'Fit new belts. Except I can't locate any belts.'

'So?'

'If I had the fucking solution, Lev, I wouldn't have been awake for this telephone call. Keep searching for belts, I guess. Or bribe somebody to make them. All I can do. But it kills me when the Tchevi's sick. I love that car like I love my own liver.'

'I know you do.'

'And it's my livelihood. But, meanwhile, Lora and I have dreamed up a new scheme: horoscopes.'

'Horoscopes?'

'Yeah. Everyone's into astrology suddenly. They didn't know what it was in the old days, but now they're flocking to it like swine to the swill. All you gotta do is keep filling the swill bucket.'

'What are you going to fill the swill bucket *with*?'

'Got a few astrology books from the library. Lora's mugging it all up. She's got a fast-learning kind of mind. Then we're going to advertise star-sign readings. People send their birthdates, accompanied by some hard cash, and we give them a personalised prediction of their immediate future. Four or five euros a shot.'

'Right. What if their immediate future doesn't turn out the way you predict?'

'It *will* turn out the way we predict. The knack with astrology is you word everything in such broad fucking terms, it can all be made to fit. But we just have to get in fast, before some other fucker gets the same idea.'

Lev smiled. 'I'd like to know my future,' he said quietly.

'Yeah?' said Rudi. 'Why? Something happen to you? You sound different.'

Lev was silent. He looked over at the clown, lying on the floor with its soft limbs in an attitude of surrender. 'No,' he said, 'nothing's happened. Tell me more about Maya.'

Lev heard Rudi's broken cuckoo blurt out three o'clock. Rudi coughed, then said: 'She's OK, Lev. Truly. No more goats stolen. Oh, yeah, she lost another tooth. I told her she looked like a vampire. She said, "What's a vampire?" but I couldn't fucking remember. My mind just wouldn't conjure it. I said we might see one at the fair, but now I don't know if we can get to the fair.'

'Tell her to write something to me, or send a drawing.'

'OK. What d'you want the drawing to be of?'

'Dunno. The house, maybe. She likes drawing houses. Or a sunflower.'

'It's not sunflower time, my friend, it's nearly winter, in case you'd forgotten.'

'I hadn't forgotten. She can imagine a sunflower. Tell me more news.'

'What news? You know nothing happens here. You tell *me* more news.'

'Well,' said Lev, 'I almost heard a concert.'

'Almost heard? Is that some kind of new grammatical tense?'

Lev told Rudi and Rudi laughed so loudly that he woke Lora and Lev heard Lora's voice in the background saying: 'What's going on?'

'Nothing,' Rudi told her. 'Just hearing about Lev making his mark in London.'

'It's three in the morning, Rudi,' said Lora.

'I know,' said Rudi. 'So talk to Lev.'

Lora came on the line and said: 'Lev, we miss you. So does Maya. She's afraid she'll never see you again.'

Lev was silent for a moment. Then he said: 'Don't let her think that, Lora. I'm going to be sending some toys.'

He dreamed of a woman. It was the first dream of its kind Lev had had for two years. He lay down in the snow with the beautiful woman and unwound the rags that covered her, and these rags were like a skin she was discarding to reveal a body soft and shining. He told her he'd forgotten how to love, and she said, 'No, I don't believe that for second,' and she put a hand on his neck and pulled him down towards her and kissed his mouth.

He knew he shouldn't name the woman. Naming her would break some unspoken bond, some tacit understanding. Yet he wanted to name her, to make her real to him in this way. He felt as though he'd choke if he didn't say her name, but he kept a rein on himself and stayed silent.

When he woke, his phone was ringing. It was Lydia.

She said: 'Lev, I'm trying hard not to be angry with you, but I think your manners are very bad.'

8

The Need to Shock

From an Irish stall on Holloway Road, Lev bought an anorak with a fleece lining and a trim of nylon fur round the hood. He put it on as soon as he'd paid for it and walked away, feeling warm and glad. Then he turned and went back to the stall and bought another one, in a child's size but identical to his, and posted it to Maya. He knew that imagining Maya in her little identical coat was going to become a habit of mind with him as the winter passed.

Christy admired the anorak. He said: 'I think it looks good on yer – and I'm sayin' this stone-cold sober.'

He was trying to stay sober most of the time now. The court had granted him 'chaperoned visits' to his daughter, who was living with Angela and her estate-agent lover in a loft conversion off the Farringdon Road.

'Trouble is: the chaperone is Angela,' said Christy. 'I think that's unfair. I can't see Frankie without seeing the woman who took her away from me. D'you think that's right?'

'No,' said Lev. 'Maybe I can be "chaperone"?'

'Well, I wish. But they said it has to be the mother or some female social worker. And Angela never wants to go out anywhere. I said I wanted to take Frankie to the zoo, but there was a drop of drizzle in the air so Angela says, "No, we'll get soaked going round the zoo." Then I suggested a film.' Christy pronounced it *fillem*. 'But she says, "No chance. I'm not going up the West End, it's too hideous." So all we do is, we sit there and do bits of colouring or Lego. And I try to talk to Frankie about school or about her friends. She answers me, yes-no, yes-no, but she won't look at me.

She looks down at the Lego, or up at her mother. And the light in that place is so glaring, it makes me eyes sore. One whole side of the living-room wall is glass, and there's glass all above you in bloody enormous panels. God knows how it gets cleaned and God knows how you sleep, with the rain clattering down and the light flooding in. I wouldn't like to live there at all.'

When Lev asked about the owner of the loft, Angela's lover, whose name was Tony Myerson-Hill, Christy said: 'The less I hear about him, the happier I am. His furniture's ugly: big black-leather sofas, tubular-steel tables. And everything has to be in its right place or he has an epileptic fit. How he can put up with a five-year-old, I've no idea. And the shower's weird. Big walk-in thing, tiled in grey granite, but with no door on it. No privacy at all. What kind of interior design is that? I think the man's a fashion victim of the first fucking water.'

Then he told Lev that once when he was visiting Frankie all Frankie wanted to do the whole afternoon was polish stones.

Tony Myerson-Hill had bought a stone-polishing machine and said he would pay Frankie 10p for every stone she polished. Then she laid the newly shined stones in a line along the walls of the granite shower and she said Tony would be 'really, really happy' about this arrangement and might take her to the zoo at the weekend.

'Get that,' Christy went on. 'The zoo! I suggested the bloody zoo the very first time I went to that place. So either Frankie had no memory of it, or else she said it just to hurt me. God knows. I look around that effing glass-house and I see the huge plasma-screen TV and the seven hundred and seventy-nine CDs and DVDs and the three computers and I think I'm done for. I think about this place and that little shop in your room that Frankie never played with, and I see that Myerson-Hill and loft conversions in EC1 are the future and I'm the past. As far as Frankie's concerned, I'm pretty much over.'

Lev barely knew what to say to this. He remembered his father, Stefan, saying that life had moved on and left him behind – and he had been proved right. So he knew this wasn't a thing that he could mention to Christy. Instead – as some kind of appropriate response to the desperation Christy was feeling – he began talking about a trip he'd made with Rudi to the Kalinin mountains, a year after Marina had died.

Christy sat down in one of the wicker chairs. 'Yeah, tell me, fella,' he said eagerly, as though he was glad not to have to talk about Frankie any more.

Lev explained that the trip had been Rudi's idea. Rudi had told him that he, Lev, needed to walk, to lose himself, to stop lying in his hammock, sunk down in sadness. Lev had said that he was all right in the hammock, but Rudi said, no, it was time to get up now, time to set himself some kind of test. And Rudi had this 'test' already planned and funded, so arguing with him against it was going to be fruitless.

They packed rucksacks with supplies and sleeping-bags and strong boots and bought lengths of rope. Neither of them knew how to climb a rockface. Rudi said that their destination was a cave, on the lower slopes of the Kalinin range. If they could reach the cave, they would have achieved their objective. When Lev had asked what that objective was, Rudi had replied: 'To embrace something.'

They took three days of their leave entitlement from the lumber yard. It was early spring in Baryn, and cold, and the new green on the larch trees was a pale dust, barely visible to the eye. But even as they set off, Lev had felt his heart lift. To be travelling somewhere was, after all, better than staring at Ina's yard, and he liked the idea of going into the mountains and becoming lost in a place where there were no people.

To reach the cave, they followed the line of the Baryn river to its stony source. There was no path, only narrow tracks here and there, made by mountain goats. Underfoot was slippery schist and ragged clumps of heather. The steady ascent made Lev's lungs burn and he had to stop frequently to recover his breath. During these moments of rest, he looked about him and saw the snowcaps way above him and, below, the long, beige scars on the hills where pine and fir had been felled for the Baryn mill. The air was damp and clean and fragrant in a way it no longer was in Auror, and Lev became aware of a feeling of poise within himself that he hadn't known for a long time.

After four hours Rudi and Lev stopped again and drank tea from a flask and ate bread and smoked herring, packed by Lora. They sat on a lichen-covered boulder, smoking and staring at a lone bird, turning and dipping, turning and dipping towards some invisible prey. Rudi's plan was to reach the cave before nightfall, make a fire and sleep there on its earth floor. To keep them warm in the night, he'd brought a flask of Ukrainian brandy.

'Ukrainian brandy,' Christy interrupted. 'What the hell's that like?'

'As you would expect, poor quality,' said Lev. 'But very cheap. And in cold air you don't taste difference.'

'OK,' said Christy, 'I get the drift.'

Lev sat down opposite Christy. He lit a cigarette. He told Christy that they had come to the rockface below the cave in early afternoon, with a hour or two of remaining light. Set into the rock was an iron ladder, which went almost vertically upwards for a hundred feet, and near the base of the ladder, they discovered, among the scrub and stones, rusty tins that had once contained liver sausage and sardines and condensed milk. They examined these objects, to which faded labels still clung in spite of their scorching by time and weather. Then they looked at the ladder. It was as rusty as the tins, and the bolts that held it to the rockface were missing in places. Several of the rungs were broken. But neither Lev nor Rudi had commented on the ruinous state of it.

'I will never forget going up there,' said Lev. 'All around me space and air. Nothing to hold. Only the ladder, so broken. But I say to Rudi, "I am going first and you stay on the ground until I reach cave." If one of us is die, I want it to be me.

'So I climb. And my pack feels very heavy. Heavy like a child on my back. And each moment, I think, Now the air takes me and I fall and that is end of me. But you know something, Christy? For all that time I am climbing I don't think about Marina. All I think about is getting to cave. Like cave is made of gold, or something. You know?'

'Well, I never believed in caves of gold meself,' said Christy, 'but I can see how that might take your mind off everything else.'

'On I go,' continued Lev, 'my arms in pain. Pain everywhere. How many steps? I don't know. We never counted. But many, many. I think to myself, This have no end.'

Above the ladder, in front of the cave's mouth, was a broad ledge and it, too, was strewn with old food tins and plastic bottles. Lev hauled himself onto this ledge and lay, face down among the debris, breathing hard. Up here, the wind was strong and dust swirled at the cave-mouth.

Lev didn't want to go into the cave before Rudi arrived. He let his rucksack fall and knelt at the top of the ladder, facing the void, watching Rudi climb. Rudi was heavier than he was. Lev heard the metal sing, could feel it shudder as the weight of Rudi's boots fell on each rung. It was at this moment – with Rudi half-way up the ladder – that he heard himself whispering to his friend, 'Don't look down ... don't look back ...' and he felt that he suddenly understood why Rudi had brought him here and that the thing he had to embrace was the idea of perseverance.

The mist had cleared by the time Rudi and he went into the cave. By the last rays of the sun, they could see something lying on the cave floor. They crept towards it and then they stopped. There lay a huddle of human bones, clothed in what looked like a dusty military uniform, stained a deep brown. Lev and Rudi stared at the place where the skull should have been, but there was no skull. Resting on the ribcage, where the buttons of the uniform had once shone gold, was an old Kalashnikov rifle. On the ground beside the bones lay more empty tins and a metal spoon.

'Jesus Christ!' said Christy. 'Didn't the body stink?'

'No,' said Lev. 'Flesh gone.'

'What about the head? Did you find it?'

'No. But pieces of bone. We think he put rifle, here, under chin, and shot his head away.'

Christy got up and went to the window. He looked out at Belisha Road, where a police car was shimmering by, lit up by its blue, shrieking light. Then he turned back to Lev and asked: 'Who was it? Did you ever find out who it was?'

Lev sighed. He said: 'Well. It was me.'

Christy stared at Lev. The flashing police car could be heard accelerating up Junction Road, towards Archway. Christy opened his mouth to ask another question when Lev said: 'Rudi knew this dead man was there. A colonel or general from Communist time before our country's new era. And this colonel or general, he couldn't make any progress with his life. He was ended. He lay in the cave – like I lay in my hammock – and ate food out of tins. And when tins ran out, he shot his head away.'

Christy's hands were shaking as he lit a new Silk Cut. After a while he said: 'That fella, Rudi: he goes to some lengths to make a point, doesn't he?'

'Yes,' said Lev. 'But he helped me. From this time, I didn't lie in hammock any more.'

'Well,' said Christy with a sigh, 'that's a nice thing. Survival's always nice to hear about.'

Sophie's friend Samantha was bone-thin, with boyish hair, coloured white-blonde. In the noisy pub, she was wearing a short, low-cut black dress and purple snakeskin boots. Everyone called her Sam. Sophie told Lev that Sam Diaz-Morant was becoming a famous name in the world of hat-making. Her youngest clients were the princesses Beatrice and Eugenie.

'Yes?' said Lev.

'Yes,' said Sam. 'Poor mites that they are. They're doing their level best to become beautiful, but nobody's giving them much of a hand, except me.'

Sophie, who was wearing jeans and a tight cream sweater, explained to Lev that most of Sam's hats were miniatures, like the one she was wearing to the pub tonight, a baby black topper, attached to her head by spangled elastic. She said: 'Sam believes that the days of the unironic hat are completely past. Unless you have an exceptional face – which rules out ninety-nine per cent of everybody. So she's doing pastiches of old styles, in titchy form, and they've caught on amazingly. She's getting rich now.'

'Yes?' said Lev.

'Not rich-rich,' smiled Sam. 'Just comfy.'

'She goes to film premières and all that shit. Don't you, Sam?'

'Sometimes. I just treat them like personal catwalks. I go to parade a hat.'

'She had a big show at London Fashion Week.'

'Not big-big.'

'She's an amazing star.'

'Not amazing-amazing. I still live in Kentish Town.'

The Amazing Star was looking Lev over. Her ferret eyes flickered from his newly washed grey hair to his mouth, and then to his left hand, on which he still wore his wedding ring.

'I didn't know you were married, Lev,' she said, sipping the vodka and tonic Lev had bought her.

'I told you, Sam,' said Sophie quickly. 'Lev's wife died.'

'Oh, yes. Wow, sorry. I forgot. I've got a show coming up and my brain's gone into coma mode. Tell me about hats in your country, Lev.'

'Hats in my country?'

'I get inspiration from all round the world. Spain was fantastic. The mantilla is such a flattering idea. Virtually everyone looks good in it, because you can get the lace to cover half the face, if necessary. God, I'm nasty! But, to be fair, most women also look reasonably brilliant in those wide-brimmed hats the picadors wear. I've just adapted them a bit with trailing ribbons. I've never visited your country, but somehow I imagine women in headscarves. Am I right?'

'Sometimes,' said Lev.

'I don't mean the full Muslim scarf thing, the *hijab* or whatever it's called, but headscarves like the Queen wears, right?'

'Yes.'

'But things are changing now, right? Women are smartening themselves up. Are hats coming back?'

Lev conjured up a street in Baryn or Glic. He saw women hurrying through the rain, clutching cheap, flimsy umbrellas or holding magazines over their hair. He couldn't see or imagine a single hat.

'No,' he said.

'Right. Not worth making the trip to Jor or somewhere, then?'

'Well,' said Lev, 'in Jor, you can find some nice clothes, these days. Quite expensive ...'

'No, I don't mean for shopping. I mean to get a look at ethnic headwear. What about at weddings?'

Lev was about to reply that Ina kept in a drawer the embroidered cap she'd worn in 1959 at her wedding to Stefan and which Maya had once found and tried on. This trying-on of her wedding cap had upset Ina for reasons Lev could only guess at and she had snatched it out of Maya's hand. But as Lev opened his mouth to speak, Sam turned away from him to embrace a young man with floppy hair, wearing dark glasses. 'Andy,' she said, '*darling*. How's it going?'

'Good,' he said, removing the glasses to reveal narrow, sleepy eyes, which rested on Samantha's skimpy cleavage. 'How're you, beautiful?'

'Insane,' said Sam. 'Bloody show in two weeks. Look at my fingers. Raw with stitching.'

'Love the dress. Love the boots. And *love* the dinky topper!'

'Yeah? You do? Relieved about that, petal. But tell me about rehearsals.'

'We're not in rehearsal yet. We're still casting – or trying to …'

'Oh, who? Tell me who.'

'Well, long story, babe. We'd been pretty hot for Sheridan Ponsonby, but then we realised the posh arsehole just didn't begin to understand the play.'

'Oh, pants, Andy. I adore Ponsonby!'

'Really? I used to like his work. Now I think he's a vain twat. He's not Brain of Britain, I can tell you, Sam, despite going to bloody Eton. I mean, he kept saying the whole play was "transgressive" and I had to keep reminding him, "That's the whole fucking point, luv, this is a totally transgressive story. We're testing good taste boundaries, we're testing audience-shock. We're way beyond *Jerry Springer – The Opera*."'

'I *know* you are, darling.'

'Why are actors so fucking thick? But, fingers crossed, we've got Oliver Scrope-Fenton. We're talking deals with his agent now.'

'Ollie Scrope-Fenton. Brilliant! I love him! It's going to be such a totally ground-breaking piece of theatre.'

'I hope. Who knows? Anyway, how're you, sweetheart?'

'I'm good.' Sam turned again towards Lev and Sophie. 'Sophie you know, darling. And this is Sophie's friend Lev, who also works with GK. Andy Portman, the extremely famous playwright.'

Lev held out his hand and the famous playwright, Portman, gave it a violent shake. 'Hi, Lev,' he said. 'How's GK treating you?'

'OK,' said Lev. 'He calls me "Nurse".'

'Yeah? Why's that?'

'Well, I keep everything clean …'

'Oh, right. Right.'

'C'est le plongeur,' Sam whispered to Andy, 'mais il est assez beau.'

'Right,' said Andy, again. 'Drink time. Everybody OK?'

Andy Portman disappeared into the crush of people near the bar. Sam Diaz-Morant took a cigarette-holder from her bag, looked at it longingly, caressed it for a moment with her lips, then put it away again. 'I'd better explain,' she said to Lev, 'that Andy's written a brilliant play, *Peccadilloes*, which is being done at the Court. Alias the Royal Court Theatre. Opens in the New Year. It's going to be unlike anything the British stage has seen.'

'Peccadilloes?' said Lev. 'What is that?'

'Oh, you know. Explain it to him, Sophie.'

'No. You explain it.'

'Well. Doing little naughties ... Isn't it, Sophie?'

'I guess.'

'Not the world's most catchy title,' said Sam. 'Confused it with *Piccalilli* when Andy first said it.'

'Piccadilly?' said Lev.

'No. Piccalilli – gherkiny table sauce my mum serves with cold meat.'

'I am confused ...'

'Oh, well, never mind. But what the play's about is the extreme forms desire can take. It's about the total infiniteness of the human imagination.'

'Is "infiniteness" a word, Sam?' said Sophie.

'Well, "infinity". Whatever. I don't fucking know. Anyway, *Peccadilloes* is a ground-breaking play.'

There was a silence. Sam Diaz-Morant adjusted the spangled elastic on her baby hat.

'Sorry,' said Lev. 'Now I am lost ...'

'Right,' said Sam. 'Well, I guess it's complex. Talk to Andy. He's got a whole thesis on the subject. He'll explain it to you.'

Sam turned away and Lev was left looking down at Sophie, who, he noticed, wouldn't meet his eye. His vodka glass was empty and he began, suddenly, to feel the heat and noise of the pub as a desolate vibration in his heart. He set down the empty glass.

Sophie's gaze returned nervously to him. 'Sam and Andy are good fun,' she said brightly. 'You'll see, Lev. They're ambition-crazed lunatics, but they're also good company. We're going to have a fun evening.'

Sophie reached up and stroked Lev's cheek and the unexpected touch of her hand on his face surprised and consoled him just enough to vanquish his longing to be away from there, out in the cold street. He took Sophie's glass and his own and made his way to the bar and put the two glasses down. He took out his wallet. The price of vodka in England shocked him anew each time he heard it uttered.

He found himself standing next to Andy Portman. Portman wore a leather jacket very like Lev's own. Lev stared at him. Then he said: 'Sam told me you would explain your play.'

'Explain my play?'

'She said you had "thesis".'

'A thesis? You mean on theatre?'

'I don't know ...'

Andy sighed, as he ransacked a bulging wallet for drink money. 'I'm kinda tired of explaining all this,' he said, 'but I'll give you the short version, if you want. OK?'

'Sure,' said Lev.

Andy took his change from the barman and took a gulp of his pint of beer. 'Imagine society as a house,' he said.

'A house?'

'Yeah.' Andy wiped foam from his lips with the back of his hand, dried the hand on a small towel set out on the bar top. 'A house. With the usual rooms: sitting room, bedroom, kitchen, et cetera. OK?'

'Yes.'

'Well, British drama, in the 1950s, was stuck in the sitting room – or what people liked to call the *drawing room*. Everything was decorous and unspoken and polite and full of lies. Then, in the 1960s, plays moved into the kitchen. Wesker, John Osborne, David Storey and so on. We had honesty. We had working-class emotion. Then it crept into the bedroom. Did you ever see Pinter's *Betrayal*?'

'No.'

'OK, but you know of it. You're following me, right?'

'Not well ...'

'I'll make it simple, then. I was going to do a riff about Stoppard and Frayn and their intellectual universes, about the clever-clogs vogue for whirling the play *outside* the societal and domestic space, but none of this fits too well with my analogy – and you probably wouldn't get it anyway, right?'

Lev said nothing. He felt helpless and ignorant. Andy Portman's eyes kept flickering round to where Sophie and Samantha stood among the roaring crowd, then returning reluctantly to Lev.

'Do you see where I'm going with the house thing?' he asked. 'Can you tell me what little room has never really been visited on the British stage?'

'I don't know.'

'Well, think. The toilet, of course. What we in Britain term the *loo*. You know this word?'

'Yes.'

'Right. Well, I think it's time we looked in there. It's time we had the courage to look at the filth that's never more than one or two rooms away from us – or, in other words, inside us. Don't you think we should do that?'

The barman arrived in front of Lev at this moment and he ordered the two vodkas. He noticed that his hand holding a ten-pound note was red and raw from its hours immersed in dishwater, like some uncooked root vegetable. And he thought, This is how these people see me – as a turnip with no intelligence and no voice.

'You don't agree?' said Andy. 'I guess you – like almost everybody else – just want to be presented with everything nice and clean and refreshed and made ready for you, and never notice how each one of us adds to the excrement pile?'

'No …'

'You wouldn't be alone. That's exactly what most people in the West feel, even if they don't admit it. But I want to force them to look where they don't want to look: at their dark side, because there is a dark side – sometimes a really seriously dark side – in us all.'

'Dark side?'

'Yup. And one of the things we have to own up to is that the stuff we crave can be absolutely transgressive. We need to look this straight in the eye. And people agree with me, or I'd never have got *Peccadilloes* on. I know it's going to shock, but that's the whole point. I guess maybe you come from a culture that isn't yet aware of the need to shock.'

Lev knew the word 'shock'. Managing a shallow smile, he said: 'There has been "shock" in my country, sir. Very much shock. Many, many years of—'

'Right. Absolutely. I hear you. But I'm not talking about political systems, Lev. And please, for fuck's sake, don't call me "sir". I'm talking about art.'

'OK …'

'In your country, you've got a lot of catching up to do, art-wise. That's fine. I completely understand. I'm sympathetic to that. But here in Britain, we're at the cutting edge of things and the work has to be razor-sharp, otherwise it won't fucking cut.'

Andy picked up his beer. He seemed about to walk away, but then he stopped and looked at Lev's hand, tensed around the ten-pound note. 'You buying for Sophie?' he asked.

'Yes,' said Lev.

'We all love Sophie,' he said. Lev waited for the thing that would follow – some instruction or warning – but it didn't come. Andy just held his gaze for a moment longer, then walked away. Lev looked back at where Sophie was standing, talking to Sam again, and he thought that Sam's miniature hats were ridiculous objects and that they would never make a woman look beautiful, no woman in the world.

Lev paid for the vodkas and put the change into his jacket pocket, but he didn't move from the bar. He tipped the ice out of his drink, and drank the vodka neat, leaning hunched over on the bar counter. He knew that, thanks mainly to Christy Slane, his loneliness had diminished in recent weeks, but now he felt it return as something else, as a feeling of inadequacy and rage. He longed for a cigarette. At his back, rough tides of laughter pushed at him and threatened to knock him down. He could feel the hard floor of the pub through a hole in his shoe. He had a desire to spit and see a gob of his own saliva arrive on the polished surface of the bar. Imagining this gob, this mark of himself, he suddenly heard his name spoken. Without turning, he saw Sophie arrive at his side. She took up her glass of vodka and poured tonic into it, took a sip and put the glass down.

He didn't want to look at her. He wanted to stay folded inside his own fury. Then he felt her soft hand on his neck and the hand pulled his head towards her face, and he saw her mouth open and waiting and let himself be steered towards it. The kiss Sophie gave him was a violently sexual thing and Lev felt her teeth clamping against his, trying to lock him to her, bone on bone.

In his rage and loneliness, he could have held her to him, could have let his arm go round her waist, let himself feel her breasts against his chest. But he didn't do this. He resisted. He broke away from Sophie and walked out of the pub.

Now he was alone in his room in Belisha Road. Below, in the scuffed garden, the dog was whining.

Lev sat on his bed, smoking, staring at the plastic shop and its welcoming sign, *Hi! My Store is Open.* Then he got down on his knees and opened the shop door. Inside, a plastic storekeeper, a figure with a black moustache, was wearing a long hessian overall, tied round his waist. On his face was a cheery smile and he held out his hands, palm upwards, in a gesture of innocence.

Lev examined the miniature wares on the counter: cans of soup, sacks of flour and sugar, boxes of matches, tins of boot-black, and he saw that this was a shop out of some past time, like the shops that existed in Baryn long ago, before the war, when Stefan and Ina were children and wore wooden shoes. Lev held the storekeeper tenderly in his hand for a moment or two, then replaced him behind his counter, where he immediately fell over. He left him lying there and closed the shop door.

Lev lay down on his narrow bunk. He longed to sleep. He wished his mother were there to bring him one of her home-made sleeping draughts and smile her crooked smile. He thought about the poinsettia flowers and Ina's rare expression of joy when she'd caught sight of them on the morning of her sixty-fifth birthday. Then he thought about being a boy in Auror and holding Ina's hand as he walked to school, going all the way there with his head tipped back, marvelling at the speed of clouds as they unravelled across the blue sky. 'Lev!' Ina would scold. 'For pity's sake, look where you're going.'

He got up and began a letter to her. The dog outside in the garden kept whimpering as the night grew colder.

> *Dear Mamma,*
> *I am sending with this letter another £20 for you. I miss you and Maya very much. Tonight I would like to be home with you in Auror, where life is simple. Here, it is so difficult to keep my balance. I am never sure what anybody is thinking about me or what I am really thinking about them.*

I hope the goats are safe and none have been stolen. With this £20 please make sure you have all you need for the winter. Please send me a picture of Maya wearing the coat I sent. Ask Rudi to take it with his Kodak.

I am still working in the restaurant kitchen. Now I ask the chefs how they put together certain dishes and I watch GK Ashe when I can. I am going to try to make some of these Ashe recipes and become a fine cook! I think this could be useful in my life somehow.

One of the good things I can tell you about the GK Ashe kitchen is that there is no waste. All the chicken carcasses and meat bones and the stalks and ends of vegetables and onions are boiled for stock (which the chefs call 'bouillon') and I admire this. Also, the taste of the bouillon is very good. But there is waste left on the plates by the clientele. One of my jobs is to scrape all the uneaten food into the bins and every night at least one bin is almost full to the top and then I take out the plastic sacks and put them onto the street and sometimes I'm troubled by this. Sometimes it is difficult for me to leave the sacks there.

9

Why Shouldn't a Man
Choose Happiness?

The English winter began to bite. The rowan trees of Belisha Road, lopped in their flowering by the council chain-saw, appeared black and dead. Frost quietened the mornings. Christmas lights flickered and swung in the rising winds of the dark afternoons. Waiting for his night bus, Lev sat hunched inside his anorak, with his hands deep in his pockets and the hood pulled over his forehead, and saw that, in this attitude, he was regarded by other people with terror.

At work, Sophie seldom spoke to him now. Her station was just behind Lev's sinks and now and again he would turn and watch her, but her head always stayed lowered. Bright light fell onto the lowered head, onto the soft cap and the red curls escaping from it.

And Lev knew that he wasn't indifferent to this sight. He watched Sophie's hands, paring, peeling, coring, scraping, dicing. He saw how dextrous these hands were and how, in her, there seemed to be nothing that was programmed for illness or death. Often, he found himself thinking about the kiss. He wanted to break the silence between them, but he didn't know how.

He asked Christy Slane's advice. Christy was trying out a new cream for his eczema and his nose and cheeks were slathered green.

'I'm the wrong person to consult,' he said. 'I see now that I've never understood women at all. Never ever. I understand mad March hares better than I understood my own wife. If you ask me, the lot of them belong on the fucking moon.'

Christy was drinking more as Christmas neared. He told Lev

that on Christmas Day he was going to take three sleeping tablets and not wake till it was over. He said: 'The thought of Frankie opening her stocking with Myerson-Hill kills me dead.'

Lev stared at the green cream on Christy's face. Then he said: 'I have good idea. You listening to me, Christy? We make Christmas meal here for Frankie. Pierre will tell me a nice sauce for turkey. And stuffing. I can do this.'

Christy looked at Lev tenderly. His bloodshot eyes glistened, momentarily, with the threat of tears. 'You're a good man, Lev,' he said.

'Why not do this?' said Lev. 'Make everything nice here for Frankie?'

'Well, for starters, because her mother wouldn't let her come. Not in a million years. But it was a fine thought. I'm glad I've got you as my lodger. I was lucky there. If we had any money, we could get on a plane and spend Christmas in your village, eh?'

'We can't do that ...'

'I know we can't, but I still think it'd be grand. Rudi could meet us at the airport. I'd get to ride in the Tchevi. And we could pack up the plastic shop and take it to Maya.'

Christmas. Lev saw how it advertised itself on every street and seemed to preoccupy every mind. He saw its daze and worry everywhere in people's eyes. He understood how Christy, in particular, felt it as a coming ordeal – an armada of sufferings he felt unable to endure. As day followed day, he seemed to subsist on a diet of fret and anxiety, unleavened by the smallest gulp of happiness.

In his free time, Lev walked the streets of the West End, among the litter and the chivvying crowds and the slow-moving buses, staring at the brightness of everything, looking for a present to send to Maya. In his country, toys were quiet things – objects that looked forgotten before they'd been bought. Here, they screeched and flashed from shop windows in vengeful colours, parading huge price tags. Even the boxes in which they were housed appeared expensive.

'Ah, forget bloody Oxford Street and Regent Street,' Christy advised. 'Go to one of the charity shops in Camden. They have home-made kinds of things there. Much better for a little girl than some battery-charged velociraptor.'

But in the charity shop, Lev felt stifled. He crept around, coughing, among old women pushing limp garments along dented rails. The place smelled of worn shoes and chewed-up books. The ugly fluorescent lighting reminded him of run-down stores in Baryn. The few soft toys he found there were hand-stitched in felt and had no life in their faces. He wanted his daughter to be amazed by his Christmas gift.

He came out into Camden Market, bought wrapping paper, decorated with silver penguins, from a stallholder chewing gum to keep his face from freezing in the bitter morning air. When Lev got home to Belisha Road, he unrolled the paper and let the penguins stretch across his floor. He lit a cigarette and looked at them and began to remember Christmases in Auror. He remembered how, during the Communist years, when Christian ceremony was banned, Ina would nevertheless defy authority by getting out a worn gold icon and setting it up on the wooden beam above the fireplace and putting candles round it.

On Christmas morning she would kneel there and say her prayers aloud, and she would show Lev how to put his hands together and stay very still beside her while she asked Jesus and His Mother, Mary, to bring the family better times. Stefan let his wife do this, without comment or protest. In later years, when Lev worked alongside his father at the Baryn mill, Stefan had once observed to his son: 'I've always let your mother pray. I don't believe in all that Jesus superstition, but who knows? Suppose it's true after all? Then Ina's prayers could be like an insurance for me, eh? They could get me through the narrow gate.'

And when Marina died, Ina tried to comfort everybody with the idea that Lev's young wife was in Paradise. Marina's photograph stood on the beam, next to the icon, and Ina's candles cast a golden light on her. 'She's there,' Ina would whisper. 'She's with God, Lev. I know it. Every fibre of my being tells me that Marina is in Heaven.'

These days, religious practice was permitted again. At Christmas time, Ina laid branches of fir in a corner of the room and wrapped small gifts in crêpe paper: wooden toys for Maya, gloves or scarves for Stefan and Lev. The Baryn yard let its workers have the day of the Christian festival off. (The chief supervisor of the mill was a grand adulterer and he liked to cram his atonement for the year's sins into the twenty-four hours of a family Christmas – the better to carry on with his affairs when the new year dawned.)

Ina would kill a goose and cook it with rosemary and chestnuts and Stefan would open a bottle – or two – of his best vodka and the day would slide peacefully towards darkness and sleep. It was a kind of dying, Lev remembered. A surrender. As though, once the senses had been stilled to this deep rest by rich food and heavy drinking, no morning would intrude on them ever again. And when that morning did come, glaring white at the small windows, the three grown-up occupants of the house – the three left alive – staggered out of their beds in astonishment. They felt like Lazarus.

Lev found Maya's present at last. It cost more than the money he sent home each week. It was a doll that resembled a living baby. This baby gurgled and opened and closed its eyes and could be made to wet its nappy. It was dressed in a romper suit and lived in a soft basket under a pink woollen blanket, with its head on a white embroidered pillow. Already Lev could imagine Maya cradling it. She would lay it down to sleep beside her and comfort it with gentle orders and instructions.

For his mother, Lev found a pair of American steel wire-cutters for her jewellery-making and a box of scented soap. And when these presents were wrapped up in the silver penguins and posted, he felt a sudden lightness of heart. He was proud that he'd been able to afford such well-made things.

At the beginning of Christmas week, Lydia telephoned. She sounded very unhappy. She told Lev that Pyotor Greszler's concert programme in England had come to an end and that he'd gone home. She'd looked for other translation jobs, she said, but hadn't found anything. But she'd become embarrassed about staying on so long with Tom and Larissa in Muswell Hill, so she was working *au pair* now for a rich family in Highgate. She said: 'This job is not at all the same as the other. Maestro Greszler respected me. Here, in this household, I am nothing.'

She said she had a Christmas present for Lev. She asked him to meet her on Sunday morning in Waterlow Park, not far from where she worked. She said: 'I will show you this place, where I often walk. I like it very much. It is quite green and quiet and sometimes they hang sculptures in the trees. Then we could go for a cup of coffee in Café Rouge.'

Lev said: 'I have no present for you, Lydia. I spent my last money on a doll for Maya.'

'Oh,' said Lydia, 'I didn't expect you would have anything. But we're still friends, aren't we? We're the kind of friends who could go for a walk in the park. Or am I wrong?'

Lev could hear the agitation in Lydia's voice. He thought of her face with its mud-splash of moles, smiling and flushed in the bar of the Festival Hall, then grave with vexation as he stumbled out, along the row of furious concert-goers. He felt that he was destined always to disappoint her.

'Of course we're friends ...' he said.

'Well, then,' said Lydia. 'Waterlow Park is quite small. Come at eleven o'clock and I'll find you there.'

He did as she instructed. This was the other odd thing about Lydia, he reflected, as he trudged up Swains Lane, with his dented London A–Z in the pocket of his anorak: he always obeyed her – until something happened which made it necessary for him to flee. He thought that he obeyed her because the journey on the coach had bound him to her. It was a peculiar bond, a bond fabricated from hard-boiled eggs and English words rehearsed aloud and the fields of Europe fleeing past the window. It was a bond that should have been broken by now, but wasn't.

She stood on a swathe of muddy grass, a lone figure in a red coat against a lightless December sky. When she saw him coming towards her, she waved wildly, as though summoning rescue. This made Lev smile: the girlishness of it, the unconscious desperation. He kissed her cheeks, pink with cold. She touched his face. 'Your hair is quite long now,' she said.

She put her arm inside his and they set off across the grass towards a gnarled tree. Hanging from its branches were large coloured shapes, made of papier mâché and painted brown and red and yellow. They were light enough to be moved by the wind. They moved silently, sometimes turning on their strings.

'See?' said Lydia. 'Do you like this? I think it is quite original.'

'What are they meant to be?' asked Lev.

'Oh,' said Lydia, 'you can't ask that question any more, Lev. Those kinds of questions belong to the old era. Art is just itself, these days. These shapes are themselves, as you are you and I am me.'

Lev looked at the tree. It irritated him. It reminded him of the trees behind Auror where Stefan used to hang up his spirit rags. He noticed that the objects had been painted the colour of autumn leaves. He thought the wintry tree would look far more beautiful without the hanging man-made things, but he said nothing. They stood and watched the moving shapes and a brown mongrel ran up to them and sniffed them. Lydia knelt down and patted it. She said: 'I would like a dog. Some little creature to love me.'

She then steered Lev towards a shrubbery where the holly trees, bright with berries, had been draped with bolts of scarlet cloth. She said: 'I am happy in this park. I don't know why. I think it is because there is a mind at work here. A mind that is full of surprises. Don't you like what they have done with this holly?'

Lev looked at the cloth. He was indifferent to it. He felt indifferent to all that was untrue. Behind him, somewhere, he could hear a tennis game start up and he envied the players. He thought how, in his life in England, he never *ran* anywhere any more, but only stood at his sinks or crept into bus shelters or wandered the streets with slow steps, like the steps of an old man. And this realisation wounded him the more because he knew suddenly – as he stood and stared at the shining holly so ridiculously festooned – where he wanted to run to. He stood very still, gazing at the ground. Then he pulled free of Lydia's arm and fumbled for a cigarette. He'd shocked himself with his thoughts. He felt his hands shaking.

'Lev,' said Lydia, 'are you all right?'

He lit the cigarette. He inhaled the smoke deeply and waited for it to calm him.

'Lev ...' Lydia said again.

'I'm OK,' he said, 'but it's cold here. It feels like snow. Shall we go to the café?'

'Oh,' said Lydia, 'I had been planning a nice walk before the light goes. See, there is a little sun now. That will warm you. Let's make a tour of the park.'

He let himself be led, smoking all the while. The sunlight came and went and the clouds above London darkened. The sounds of the tennis game grew faint. They skirted a pond, where a few ducks swam in pairs. Lev threw his cigarette into the water and began to walk faster, so that Lydia had to skip to keep up with him. He wondered whether his heartbeat was audible to her as he pounded along. But he didn't care whether it was or whether it wasn't. It was his heart. Its blood beat in his ears. He was a man and he knew that he had decided, on this Sunday in December, to come alive again. He wanted to run now – this moment, without hesitating – to where she lived. He'd known her address by heart for weeks, memorised it off Damian's staff contact list, knowing that one day he'd need it. He needed it now. He was a man and she'd kissed him and now it was time …

'Lev …' Lydia bleated, as she scurried to his side, 'don't go so fast.'

So he had to slow down. He had to tell himself to wait, to pay attention to Lydia. He couldn't desert her yet again with no explanation and no warning. He let her put her arm through his once more. He felt her small hand clutching at his sleeve. She began talking to him about a piece of sculpture, resembling a twisted human torso, set out on a concrete plinth. She said she admired its 'discomforting strangeness'. She longed, she said, to *create* something, to see part of herself expressed in some separate entity that would endure beyond her life. Because she could see, now, the way life gathered speed. Particularly in London. 'At home,' she said, 'every day was always the same and we had no hope of alteration, so time went very slowly. But here, my God, I feel it rushing on. Don't you, Lev?'

Lev nodded. Yes, it was rushing. Today it was. It was going to take him far, far from where he'd been. But what could he say about this to Lydia? Her hand was snug in the crook of his arm. She'd bought him a Christmas present. Together, like a fond couple, they were moving round Waterlow Park. The bolts of red cloth on the holly moved in the wind. The paired ducks called.

'Well,' said Lydia, as they drank the foaming coffee, 'I'll describe to you my situation. I think many young women from our country live *au pair* in London, but now I can tell you that, for me, it's not so good.'

'No?'

'No. Not at all. Perhaps I am not young enough. To me, English children are too little disciplined, too spoiled. They have everything in the world, but they treat everything the same: pick it up and throw it away. Pick people up, throw them away. Hugo and Jemima are their names. They call me "Muesli".'

'Muesli?'

'It amuses them. Because of my face, my moles. Muesli.'

Lev looked up from his coffee. He said nothing because nothing appropriate would come to his distracted mind.

'Well,' said Lydia, 'I see that at least you're shocked. It *is* shocking. I think so, too. I am thirty-nine and these creatures, Jemima and Hugo, are aged seven and nine, and they call me Muesli.'

'You should tell them not to call you that.'

'I have told them.'

'Inform the parents, Lydia. Say you won't put up with it.'

'Yes? And lose this job, when any job was so hard to find?'

'Well …'

'You know I was very happy with Pyotor. My dear Maestro. I miss him so much. As you saw, I did everything for him. We had such a good understanding. I kidded myself that that job would last for ever. But, of course, nothing lasts for ever. I had some beautiful luck and now everything has gone to darkness. That is how it feels to me.'

'Leave this family, Lydia. Find something else.'

'Yes. I could. Except where can I go, when it's winter now? You remember what I warned you about English winters. How long they last. At least I have a warm room in the house, which is a very nice large house. I have a bathroom that is mine. I shouldn't complain, really. It's only that my old job was so lovely and now I'm with monsters. You see? And there is no culture in that house. Only TV and PlayStation games. All violent. I offer to read bedtime stories, but no, they laugh at me. They even tell me to F off. Can you imagine?'

'That's bad …'

'But I see you are bored. Of course you are, because here I am, complaining once more. Let's drop this subject. It's not nice at all. Talk to me about your life, Lev.'

Lev blinked. His pulse was still racing. He found saying words an ordeal. He was dizzy with excitement and terror.

'It's OK,' he said flatly. 'I was lucky with the room you found for me. I'm very grateful to you. Christy Slane is a good man.'

'Yes? Tell me about him.'

'Well. He has his troubles. But it's too long a story to tell you now. I must go soon.'

'Oh, no. Don't go, Lev,' said Lydia. 'It's Sunday, remember? Why don't we order some lunch?'

'I'm not really hungry.'

'We can just get a nice baguette with chicken. Or a salad.'

'I'm not hungry, Lydia.'

'Ah,' said Lydia with a smile, 'but I remember this in the bus. At first you said you weren't hungry and then, after a while – after not so long a time – I'm sharing my eggs and my rye bread and my chocolate, and soon it was all gone. You remember this?'

'Yes.'

'I think I shall call the waiter for the menu. It's not expensive if we just have the baguettes.'

'No. I don't want to eat.'

'I shall pay for you, Lev. It will be my treat.'

'No! I have to leave.'

She heard the firmness in his voice and looked at him four-square. He thought that this was how she would look at the children who called her Muesli, with her brave stare, with her eyes very wide and blue. And then she would give up on them and turn away, as she did now. She bent down to where her bag sat at her feet and pulled out an oblong package, carefully wrapped in shiny paper, and handed it to him.

'Well,' she said. 'I am quite hungry, but never mind. Here is your present. Merry Christmas, Lev.' Her voice was fragile and quiet.

Lev reached over and took it. He wished he'd bought something for her: a scented candle, a phial of bath oil ... *something*. A cheap gift for her would have rescued the moment, made him seem less selfish and uncaring.

'Thank you,' he said.

'You can open it now, if you want.'

So then he thought, If I unwrap it, I can thank her again and then I can leave. Opening the gift will bring the meeting to an end and allow me to escape. He looked at it in his hands. On a gift tag were the simple words: *To Lev from Lydia.*

'Wouldn't you like me to save it for Christmas Day?' he asked.

'No. Open it. Why not? Then I will see whether you like it.'

He began to tear off the paper. Lydia brought out a small handkerchief and blew her nose. She said: 'You may think it a strange present – not what you were expecting.'

'I wasn't expecting anything.'

'But you will see why I thought it appropriate. I think you will see …'

It was a paperback copy of *Hamlet*. Lev opened it and read in English: *The Tragedy of Hamlet, Prince of Denmark*. Act One.

'Oh,' he said. 'Thank you, Lydia. I once saw some Russian film of this, but I have never read it.'

'No. I didn't expect you had, Lev. Who has read *Hamlet* in Auror? But this edition has very thorough notes to help you understand. If you turn to the back, you will see there are notes.'

'I expect I will definitely need them …'

'And I think for us, who are exiles, or whatever you like to call it, this play has very much meaning. You may see this as you read. Because Prince Hamlet, you know, he is cast out. Or, rather, he casts himself out, so that he can make things right in the place that he's left behind.'

'Yes?'

'Yes. And all the time he is haunted by the past. You will see.'

He thanked her again. He put the book into his anorak pocket. He didn't know what more to say. He pulled out some money to pay for the coffee and set it down on the wooden table.

He was away now. Away from Highgate. Coming up into the frosty air from Kentish Town Tube station. Running along Rossvale Road. Door numbers flying past. Her street. For why shouldn't a man choose happiness? Didn't he, didn't everybody, have the right – no matter if his wife had died, no matter if he'd told himself that this was the thing he'd never do again – to make a bid for a new beginning?

It had begun snowing. The whirling snow was soft and cool on Lev's face. He hoped it would fall all night, coat the city with silence, wall him up in the room he was running to, bring him a soft, purple-white dawn, like the dawn that broke that morning long ago when he and Rudi drove the Tchevi home …

Now here he was. 5 Rossvale Road. A bell to ring. Then a wait to endure. Then her voice on the intercom. Her voice that had a little choke in it, which, now he thought about it, had always affected him: the voice that was going to set him free.

'It's Lev,' he said.

He'd run so hard, he could barely breathe. He was giddy with running, with wanting, with hoping.

The intercom was silent. But then he heard the buzz of the door release. He pushed the heavy door open and stood in a small hallway, carpeted blue, strewn with unopened junk mail. He caught sight of himself in a mirror: his colour high, his hair wild, his eyes shining like jet. He wiped sweat from his forehead and tried to smooth his hair.

He looked up the narrow stairs. Sophie had come out of her flat on the first floor and stood, in her doorway, looking down at him.

She was wearing a tracksuit and her feet were bare. In her hand was a newspaper or a magazine. Lev began to climb the stairs. Sophie didn't move, but when he looked up at her, he saw a slow smile dimple her cheeks, as though she'd been waiting for him, waiting calmly and without fuss, in the knowledge that sooner or later he would arrive, that in the end he would need no persuasion, that waiting was all that was required of her.

When he reached her, she pulled him gently inside the flat and closed the door. He leaned her against the wall. He bunched her bright curls in his hand. Now he wanted to tell her everything that he was feeling, but he felt the words float away. He put his mouth on hers. Her breath was sweet as caramel.

10

'Pure Anarchy in Here ...'

On Christmas morning, Lev woke up in Sophie's bed and saw that the sun was shining outside the white-curtained window. He placed a kiss on Lenny, the lizard tattoo. She woke and mumbled: 'Lenny thinks you're really tasty.'

Lev stroked her face, oily with sleep. He said: 'I would like to be Lenny. In your skin always.' She smiled and took his hand and kissed the dark hair on his wrist, then stroked her top lip with it, as though it were fur. And he thought, Yes, this is true, this is what I want now: to be *indelible* in her, never erased. Because he was astonished by her. And this astonishment hardly left him.

When, during their work hours, he looked at her, he felt his heart lurch. He wanted to take her in his arms right there, in front of all the chefs. Through his long shifts at the sinks, he listened for the sound of her voice. His longing for the night was profound. When he looked at his own reflection, he saw a young man, his eyes wild with dreams.

He had to tell Rudi about her. He called early on a Sunday morning, while Sophie slept, and said: 'I think I'm in love now.'

He heard Rudi's cuckoo clock strike seven. Then Rudi said wearily: 'I knew there was something.'

Lev told Rudi that it was all unexpected and had taken him by storm and that he barely knew how to think about it or how to behave.

'Well,' offered Rudi, 'isn't it like riding a bicycle? Doesn't it come back to you?'

'Does it?' said Lev. 'I don't know. It's not like it's *come back* exactly. It's like it's something new.'

'Yeah?'

'With Marina it was beautiful,' said Lev, 'but it went so ... deep. There was always ... there was always something *angry* about it, something dark or difficult. This time it's innocent.'

'Am I following you, my friend? I'm not sure I am.'

'It doesn't matter. How can you describe love, anyway? But it feels ... I don't know ... uncomplicated. You know?'

Rudi yawned and said: '*Uncomplicated* is good. Uncomplicated I like. Try to keep it that way. You're probably not ready for anything else. What's her name?'

'Sophie.'

'Sophie? She's not Russian, I hope.'

'No, she's English. She works in the restaurant. She wants to be a chef.'

'OK,' said Rudi. 'Well, we all have our dreams.'

A silence fell. It was like Rudi didn't want to talk any more about Sophie, so Lev asked, 'How's the Tchevi?'

'Don't ask. I'm in transmission hell, Lev. I still haven't got the fucking belts. I've had to send off to some place in Germany for them. Postage alone is going to cost me a ton. And meanwhile the car keeps bumping into things. I told you, I keep denting the fenders, because the Tchevi doesn't understand which fucking drive she's in.'

'I'm sorry, Rudi.'

'I mean, if she falls apart, what am I going to do? I'm going to have to get back into *grey* stuff. And that gives me such bad dreams, I'm afraid to fucking sleep.'

'What about the horoscopes?'

'The horoscopes? Yeah, well, actually they're OK. We've got a little clientele now – or Lora has. It's a sheer precipice of bullshit, Lev. I feel dizzy when I think what lies we tell. But, hey, we have to stay alive, don't we?'

'Yes. We have to stay alive.'

There was another silence, in which Lev could hear the clock ticking above Rudi's telephone table. After a moment, Rudi said: 'Listen, I'm happy for you, Lev. Really, I am. Very happy. Send me a photograph of Sophie and her birthdate and Lora can work out your horoscopes, see if you have a future.'

A future.

Lev didn't want to consider this. He'd come alive in the present. That was enough.

And, now, on Christmas Day, Ina had her American wire-cutters; Maya had her doll; and he had Sophie.

It was more than enough.

He made love to Sophie very slowly, with the soft morning light falling on them, and they slept again for a while. Then they got up and made breakfast side by side: a Spanish omelette, bread and coffee. While they ate, Lev stared at all the colours of red and gold in Sophie's hair and at her mouth on the rim of the heavy green coffee cup. He thought how much he would like to take her dancing.

She'd warned him it wouldn't be a 'normal' Christmas Day because she was committed to spending most of it at Ferndale Heights care home, with the old people. She explained that few of the full-time staff wanted to work Christmas Day, so she'd volunteered for a six-hour shift. She'd said to Lev: 'For some of the residents, they know it could be their last Christmas.'

Lev had asked her what she'd do there and she told him that she'd help prepare a Christmas meal and then they'd play games and have a sing-song. She said: 'They'll all get squiffy on Asti Spumante and float backwards in time, but I don't care. When you're old, nobody touches you, nobody listens to you – not in this bloody country. So that's what I do: I touch and I listen. I comb their hair. I play clapping games with them. That's a laugh and a half! I hear about life in a post-war prefab or in some crumbling stately pile. I play my guitar and sometimes that makes them cry. My favourite person there is a woman called Ruby. She was brought up by nuns in India. She can still remember the convent school and her favourite nun, Sister Benedicta – every detail, every feeling.'

Lev had said he would come with her to Ferndale Heights, help with the meal and wash it up. When he said this, Sophie put her arms round his neck and said: 'I knew you were good. Hardly anybody is good. But you are. I saw it in your face.'

They washed up the breakfast. They showered and got dressed and Sophie put on make-up. She said the residents of Ferndale Heights were cheered up by the sight of shiny hair and nice lipstick and the smell of perfume. Lev wore his old leather jacket, because

Sophie liked him in this garment and told him he looked sexy wearing it.

They walked hand in hand along Rossvale Road, going towards the Tube station, staring in windows at Christmas trees and paper streamers and fake snow. Sophie carried her guitar in a canvas case. The sun put a shine on the black-painted railings and on the last plane leaves clustered in the gutter and on people wearing new knitwear and on dogs in new collars and leads.

A flower-seller stood in the cold outside the driveway to Ferndale Heights. He wore fingerless gloves and a woolly hat pulled low over his brow. On trestles behind him, among buckets of tall roses and carnations, there was a clutch of poinsettia plants and Lev had to stop and stare at them.

'OK, mate?' said the flower-seller, clapping his hands together to warm them.

'Yes,' said Lev.

'Take a nice Yuletide offering to your relative?'

'Sorry,' said Lev.

He walked on, hurrying to catch Sophie up.

Ferndale Heights stood at the end of a quiet road in East Finchley, looking out over a vale of roofs. It was a three-storey red-brick building with metal window-frames. The brick was stained black in places where overflow pipes had dribbled down the walls onto a concrete path. Green lawns had been laid out around the path. Heavy-shouldered yews dripped the last of their poisonous berries onto the grass, where a few pigeons wandered.

'On fine days,' said Sophie, 'it doesn't look bad. There are worse places to die.'

Inside, the smell reminded Lev of the hospital where Marina had lain for so long: urine and disinfectant mingled, stale coffee, the faint suggestion of some recent, unidentifiable burning. Sophie took his hand. The place felt quiet, as if the residents were all slumbering, and Lev thought about Christy lying alone in Belisha Road, dosed up with his sleeping pills, keeping his room dark all day until darkness fell again.

Sophie led him down a corridor where each door had a name plate beside it: Mrs Araminta Hollander, Capt. Berkeley Brotherton, Mrs Pansy Adeane, Miss Joan Scott ... From some of the rooms came the sounds of small afflictions: the clearing of throats, coughing, a voice crying softly into a telephone.

Lev and Sophie stopped in front of the last door, this one propped open, as if in anticipation of their arrival. Sophie knocked. The name beside the door was 'Mrs Ruby Constad'. They heard slow feet shuffling forward, then Lev saw a large woman, with curly grey hair and eyes that were still almost beautiful in the colourless dough of her face, standing before them. Round her neck was an ancient string of pearls. 'Sophie dear,' she said. 'Merry Christmas! Come in and sit down. Someone sent me some crystallised plums.'

They entered Ruby Constad's small room, which was inhabited to its four corners by antique furniture and framed oil paintings, china ornaments and tarnished silverware. The bed was tidy, topped with an old-fashioned eiderdown covered with green brocade. A commode chair was pulled up close to it.

Sophie laid her guitar against an ornate firescreen that had no fire to screen. 'Ruby,' said Sophie, 'this is my friend, Lev.'

Ruby Constad had taken up the box of plums and, with a fleshy hand that trembled slightly, offered it to Lev. She said: 'I don't know who sent these. Do take one. People send things wrongly addressed. Or the staff muddle everything up. They were probably really destined for Minty Hollander. Most things are.'

Lev obediently took a sugary plum. He didn't particularly want to eat it, but there seemed no other thing to do with it, so he bit into it.

Ruby turned to Sophie and asked: '*What* did you call him?'

'Lev,' said Sophie.

'Lev? Is that foreign, or short for something?'

'Lev's come to England to work. We work together at the restaurant I told you about. *GK Ashe*. D'you remember?'

'*GK Ashe* is the most peculiar name for a restaurant I've ever heard! Why didn't he call it something sensible, like Wheeler's?'

Sophie giggled. 'Things have moved on, Ruby,' she said. 'Restaurants have different kind of names, different kind of food.'

'What kind?'

'Modern food.'

'I used to like Wheeler's. Oysters. Dover sole. We used to think those were quite modern. Do you like the plum, Lev?'

'The plum is good,' said Lev. 'Thank you.'

Ruby Constad examined Lev's features. He felt hot in the over-furnished room and tugged off his scarf. He saw Ruby's attentive eyes gazing up at him.

'Well,' she whispered to Sophie, 'he's quite a dish.'

Sophie giggled again. She put a hand on Lev's arm. 'Ruby thinks you're handsome,' she said, 'and so do I.'

'Yes?' said Lev.

He heard the two women laughing. The sound filled the room. He smiled at the childish joy he heard in it. Ruby put down the box of plums and began to forage under the pillows on the bed. She pulled out an envelope and handed it to Sophie.

'Now,' she said. 'This is for you. For being such a dear darling to a fat old woman. For brightening all our Sundays.'

Lev saw that Ruby's eyes were suddenly brimming with tears. But she snatched a handkerchief from her cardigan sleeve and wiped them away.

Sophie looked down at the envelope. 'Ruby ...' she began.

'Now don't make a fuss and twaddle. Buy a new coat. That sheep's rag of yours looks well past its sell-date, or whatever they call it. Go on, open up the card.'

Ruby turned to Lev as Sophie began opening the envelope. He saw a cheque drop out of a Christmas card and Sophie bend to pick it up.

'In here,' said Ruby to Lev, 'we're all past our sell-dates. Berkeley Brotherton is ninety-three.'

Sophie was staring at the cheque. She crossed to Ruby and put her arms round the wide bulk of her. 'It's far too much,' she said.

Ruby laid a kiss on Sophie's scarlet hair. She said to Lev: 'Sophie is the dearest girl.'

'I agree,' said Lev.

'She's much nicer than my daughter. Alexandra never sings to me. Never helps me with the crossword. Never makes me laugh.'

Ruby invited them to sit down in her cluttered room. She installed herself on the commode chair. Lev perched on a low stool. 'That's a Kashmiri stool,' said Ruby. 'I brought it back with me from India. Most of the silver is Indian, too.'

'Yes?'

'I expect Sophie told you I spent my youth in India – before

Independence, when we had the Viceroy and everything. I was in a welcome pageant for the Viceroy at my school. We made a tableau. We made the word WELCOME in girls across the stage. I was one half of the O. I've never forgotten being half of an O. I sometimes think, That's all your life has amounted to, Ruby Constad, being *half* of something. So silly, the things that remain with you, eh, Lev? Tell me what you remember.'

'Well, I can remember ... my father used to tell me there were wood-sprites in the forest behind our house, and—'

'Wood-sprites? My goodness! I don't think we have *them* in Britain. What did they look like?'

'I don't know. The ghosts of dead people who have suffered. My father used to say: "They can become birds, become women."'

'Oh dear. I wouldn't like a sprite suddenly to become a woman. It could put you in a confusing situation.'

Lev smiled. 'Yes. But I think they only became women in my father's mind.'

'I see. In your father's mind ...'

'I never saw any wood-sprite. I used to look and search. Like for a four-leaf clover. But I never found.'

Lev looked up to see the two women smiling approvingly at him.

Ruby reached out and took Sophie's hand. 'Darling,' she said, 'how nice that you brought Lev to see me.' Then she turned back to Lev. 'Sophie once brought another man, a gymnast. He offered to perform a back flip-flop-over or something, but I had to say, "No, I really don't think we've got the space for it in here."'

Lev and Sophie helped in the kitchen, preparing sprouts, chopping and roasting parsnips, rolling sausages in bacon, while the turkey was cooking. Sophie made a bread sauce scented with cloves. Lev manufactured a bouillon from onions, potatoes and sprout stalks. He then put the jar of gravy granules back into the cupboard and made a dark and fragrant *jus* – as he'd watched GK Ashe make it, using the bouillon, a splash of wine and the caramelised residue in the roasting pan. The two South African girls filling in on Christmas Day gaped at this *jus*. 'Wow,' they said. 'That smells gorgeous. You guys saved us. We're skeleton staff.'

When everything was ready, Lev made his way to the dining

room where the residents were now gathered, supervised by Mrs McNaughton, the director of Ferndale Heights.

Of the seventeen inmates, five were in wheelchairs. Many of them struggled to control Parkinsonian jerking and trembling. Beside each place setting, a single Christmas cracker had been laid. The elegant woman known as Minty picked up her cracker, waved it around in her thin, jewelled claw of a hand and announced, in a voice not unlike the Queen's: 'I just want to say ... listen everyone ... I just want to remind you that last year, the cracker-pulling was completely uncoordinated. We have to pull the crackers *after* the turkey. That way, the gifts don't fall into the food. All right? Did everybody hear?'

'Minty,' said an ancient man, wearing a new Fair Isle sweater over a frayed checked shirt, 'if we pull the crackers after the food, we could, in some cases, be waiting until nightfall.'

'I mean,' said Minty, 'after the *bulk* of us have finished.'

'You mean "the bulk of us *has* finished". "Bulk" is a singular noun.'

'Shut up, Berkeley,' said Minty. 'You're a bloody singular noun and an irritating one at that.'

There were pockets of laughter round the table. Lev heard a hearing-aid whine. 'Hush,' said Mrs McNaughton, sweetly.

'I'm pulling my effin' cracker now,' announced one of the wheelchair occupants. 'I'm not bein' dictated to by Mrs High-and-Mighty. We're all equal in here.' She offered one end of it to her neighbour, a man whose features reminded Lev of his father's, in their gravitational pull towards melancholy.

'Naff off, Joan,' he hissed.

'OK,' she said. 'I'll pull it me blinkin' self.'

'Joan!' shouted Minty. 'Tut-tut!'

'It's your fault for drawing attention to the ruddy crackers, Minty,' said Berkeley.

'All I want is a little bit of *order* on Christmas Day,' bleated Minty. 'Otherwise it's pure anarchy in here.'

The woman, Joan, took her cracker in both hands and began to pull. The cracker crumpled and stretched but didn't burst.

Sophie arrived at Joan's side. 'Joan,' she said gently, 'we're serving up the meal in a minute or two. Do you want me to pull the cracker with you now, or do you want to wait?'

'I just want to pull it when I want to pull it, not when someone else says I can.'

'There's always trouble at mealtimes,' said the wheelchair man, Douglas.

'She's not making trouble,' said Sophie.

'Just because Miss Araminta once worked with Leslie Caron ...'

'I liked Leslie Caron,' commented another woman.

> *'"On to your Waterloo" whispers my heart,*
> *Pray I'll be Wellington, not Bonaparte ...'*

'Singing's for later!' snapped Minty.

'Here she goes again,' said Joan, beginning to wrestle once more with her cracker.

'Let's for God's sake get the food,' said Douglas.

'Douglas is right,' said Mrs McNaughton, briskly. 'Douglas is right. I shall say a grace and then we're going to serve up.'

Joan reluctantly put her cracker down. One of the wheelchair residents gave in to a violent nodding. Mrs McNaughton began to intone: 'Thank you, Oh Lord, on this day of your Nativity ...'

'It's not the *Lord*'s nativity,' interrupted Berkeley. 'It's his Son's.'

'Oh, put a sock in it!' said Pansy.

'Strictly speaking, Berkeley's right,' said Ruby, suddenly. 'Having been brought up a Roman Catholic—'

'I'm going to begin grace again,' said Mrs McNaughton. 'Can we have quiet?'

'But religion's got itself into a frightful muddle in this country ...'

'Ruby? Can we have quiet for the grace?'

'Because nobody knows what they believe any more. They believe bits of this and bits of that, and meanwhile the Millers of Islam—'

'*Mullahs*, you stupid cow.'

Mrs McNaughton stood up and clapped her hands. 'My word!' she said. 'Just because it's Christmas, there's no need to start behaving like children. Now. "Thank you, Oh Lord, on this blessed Christmas Day, for giving us food and wine, for bringing us warmth in the midst of cold, company in the midst of solitude, and for blessing us with your perfect love. Amen."'

For a moment nobody spoke. Mrs McNaughton and Sophie began to go round, straightening wheelchairs, tucking napkins into collars, pouring water into plastic tumblers, cheap red wine into glasses. Joan picked up her cracker again and began to bite it.

Lev returned to the kitchen, carved the turkey and started to plate it up. Once again, he tried to imitate the chefs at *GK Ashe*, laying out six plates, arranging the meat and stuffing very carefully in the centre of each. He showed the South African helpers how to place the roast potatoes, sprouts and parsnips attractively round the meat, keeping the bread sauce and the *jus* simmering while they did this, then spooning it on, keeping the spoon low, so that nothing dripped on the plate rim. The South Africans now stood waiting to take the plates through to the dining room, noting the care with which Lev worked.

'You a chef?' one of them asked.

'No,' said Lev.

He began on the next six plates. The food smelled good. Lev put a piece of turkey skin into his mouth. It was crispy and succulent. He watched his hands arranging and spooning. He thought of his mother's hands, threading delicate shards of tin onto copper filament, picking up the beautiful new wire-cutters, made in America, admiring them as she worked ...

Now the residents were eating mince-pies and drinking the Asti Spumante. The crackers had been pulled and paper hats put on. Douglas announced that he felt sick and had to be wheeled away by Mrs McNaughton, a plastic bowl on his knee. Two of the company had fallen asleep in their chairs. From one end of the table came the unmistakable stench of urine, mingled with the aroma of the flaming brandy poured over the mince-pies. While Lev and Sophie washed up plates and pans in the kitchen, they heard the barter begin for the cracker gifts.

'Berkeley,' said Minty, imperiously. 'You've got no use whatsoever for that sewing kit. I'll swap it for my dolphin key-ring and the joke about polar bears.'

'You'll have to do better than that.'

'I can't do better than that. We only had one cracker each.'

'You've got to *trade*, Araminta. You've got to talk up your wares, like in a *souk*. Have you forgotten the bloody rules?'

'I know the thing you all want is the miniature Woods of Windsor talcum powder,' declared Pansy Adeane, 'but that happens to be mine and I am not ruddy well swappin' it!'

'I don't want the talcum powder,' said Berkeley.

'What will you swap for the sewing kit, then?'

'Nothing. I like the sewing kit.'

'You're a man,' said Minty. 'Men can't sew. But a lovely dolphin-shaped key-ring—'

'If you've been in the Navy, you can sew,' said Berkeley. 'I could sew before you were born.'

'I'm willing to trade this exceptionally useful Bambi stapler for the Woods of Windsor talc,' Lev heard Ruby offer.

'Nobody's getting the effin' talc,' said Pansy.

'Think of what a stapler can do,' said Ruby.

'It can shut Minty's mouth for starters!' said Berkeley.

There was a ripple of laughter as Ruby asked: 'Would you prefer the Bambi stapler to the sewing kit, Berkeley?'

'No, I bloody wouldn't. I can mend all my pockets with this.'

'You mean, make yourself tighter than ever with money?'

'Shut the fuck up.'

'Language, language ...' said Mrs McNaughton.

'I'm putting the talc in my pocket.'

'I'm not giving away the ruddy sewing kit.'

'I've got no use for a stapler.'

'What use is a key-ring if you've no longer got a car?'

'That polar-bear joke was crap anyway.'

'Somewhere over the rainbow ...'

They paused in the argument. Sophie had come back into the room, taken up her guitar and begun to sing.

'... Way up high ...'

The residents of Ferndale Heights put down the cracker gifts and seemed instantly to forget them. They tried to still their tremors and their coughs, stop their stomachs gurgling.

'... There's a land that I heard of ...'

Mrs McNaughton folded her hands on her chest.

'Once in a lullaby ...'

Lev came back into the dining room and, standing quietly with the Asti bottle, watched all eyes turn to the singer. Sophie's voice was melodic, effortless. And he thought how, when you looked at Sophie, what you saw first was her softness and her dimpled, little-girl smile, and then when you got to know her, you began to feel her confidence.

When the song was over, Berkeley Brotherton was drying his eyes on a table napkin, as was Ruby Constad. Clapping broke out and three cheers for Sophie. Then Minty stood up. Her cheeks flushed with the wine, her blue-veined hands ablaze with the diamonds her beauty had bought her long ago, she began to sing, in a quavery soprano:

> *'Some enchanted evening,*
> *You may see a stranger,*
> *You may see a stranger*
> *Across a crowded room …'*

Almost everybody seemed to know this song, and they began to join in, swaying to the melody, waving their arms, trying to follow and keep in time together.

It was dark when Lev and Sophie left Ferndale Heights. As they walked away, Sophie said: 'I hate to think of them lying all alone in the night.'

'Well,' said Lev. 'I know. But it went good. Meal good.'

'Meal *very* good. Everybody enjoyed it.'

'Douglas felt sick.'

'Oh, he ate too much, that's all. He had a huge second helping. Said it was the best bread sauce he'd tasted since 1957.'

Lev smiled as they walked on towards the Tube. 'Nice singing,' he said. 'And Ruby, she loves you so much.'

'She's had a difficult life,' said Sophie. 'Her husband left her for someone else. Then he died. She was about fifty. On her own since then. She hardly sees either of her children.'

'They don't come to visit?'

'Now and then. Selfish pigs. About once a year. You know she gave me a hundred pounds?'

Lev put his arm round Sophie and held her close to him. 'We can go shopping,' he said. 'Buy beautiful dress for you.'

'Nah,' she said. 'I'm going to save it. Definitely. I'm saving it up, like a little squirrel.'

*

When they got back to Sophie's flat, they lay down and slept. Sophie's back was turned to Lev and his arm lay along her thigh.

The evening came on silently.

It was near to eight o'clock when Lev woke. He looked over at Sophie. It occurred to him how strange and lovable it was that young women seemed to sleep without making a single sound.

He dressed and lit a cigarette and went to the living room and sat down by the dark window. On his mobile, he dialled Belisha Road, but the phone wasn't picked up. He wondered whether Christy was still in bed or in the pub. He remembered with a smile that Christy's gift to Frankie – bought with his groceries at the Camden Town Sainsburys – had been a purple ballet dress with a spangled bodice and a spangled tiara for her hair.

Lev smoked for a while, staring out at the night. Few cars went up or down the road. Blue tree lights blinked on and off in the window opposite. The faint sound of laughter came from the pub on the corner. Lev picked up his mobile again. His phone bills were large, but he was keeping pace with them – just. He dialled Rudi's number.

'Comrade,' said Rudi, 'greetings from the home front. I'm the worse for fucking wear! But pay no heed. Ina and Maya are here. Lora cooked your mother's bad-tempered cockerel, but it was stringy. All those months of shagging the hens had worn it out!'

'Yeah?'

'Yeah. But never mind. We washed it down. We've had a nice time. Lora was sent some wine from one of her horoscope clients. And it was fucking good. Talk to Maya ...'

There was a long pause, then Lev heard his daughter's voice.

It sounded very quiet and far away.

'Pappa?'

'Yes, it's Pappa. How are you, my flower? Do you like your new doll?'

'Yes,' said Maya.

'Did you think up a name for her?'

'Lili.'

'Yes? She's called Lili?'

'She can go to sleep.'

'Do you love her?'

'She does pi-pi in her nappy.'

'Right. So you'll have to wash the nappy and put a clean one on?'

'Yes. When are you coming here, Pappa?'

'Soon. You'll have to dry the nappy in front of the fire. But be sure not to let it burn. Grandma will help you ...'

'She's gone,' said Ina's voice. 'All she asks about is when are you coming back.'

'You know the answer to that,' said Lev. 'Tell her I'll come back when I have some money – or you can come here ...'

'Lev,' said Ina, 'it's Christmas Day.'

'I know it's Christmas Day. I was just about to wish you—'

'So don't spoil it by asking me to come to England. I'm much too old to leave my country. If you want Maya with you, then send money and I'll put her on a bus. I'll just get used to being here all alone ...'

'Mamma ...'

Lev looked up. Sophie was standing in the doorway, wearing a tartan dressing-gown. Her hair was wild from sleep.

Ina went on: 'I've lived in Auror for nearly seventy years. I prefer to die here.'

'Don't worry, Mamma,' said Lev, picking up his packet of cigarettes and holding them out to Sophie. 'No one will take you away from Auror. Now, did you get my presents?'

'Yes. Cutters. But they're too heavy.'

'They're too heavy for your hand?'

'Much too heavy. I'd need a man's strength to use those.'

'Oh,' said Lev.

Sophie came and sat beside him and lit her cigarette.

'Lev?' said Ina. 'Did you hear what I said? The wire-cutters are too heavy. It's a waste of precious money.'

'Never mind,' said Lev.

'Never mind? Why "never mind"? You mean you've got money to burn now?'

'No ...'

'From working in a kitchen?'

'No.'

'What did you mean, then?'

'I'll try to find some different cutters – lighter and smaller.'

'It's not worth it. I can manage with the tools I've got.'

'But you got the soap, too. Did you like that?'

'It looks expensive.'

'Not too expensive. But you liked the smell of it?'

'Yes.'

'All right, Mamma. Well ... merry Christmas. Is Maya wearing her anorak?'

'Yes. But you know, in the nights she cries. She says to me, "Has Pappa gone to that place where Mamma is sleeping?"'

'No!' shouted Lev. 'I hate that! Don't let her believe that.'

'Children believe what they want to believe. What can I do?'

'Explain it to her! Tell her I'll come back ... for sure ...'

'When? How can I tell her that if I don't know when?'

'As soon as I have enough money. For heaven's sake, I'm only doing this for her and for you – for us all. You have to help me a bit.'

There was silence. Then Lev could hear his mother crying. He swore under his breath. He almost wished he'd never made the call. He covered the mobile and said to Sophie: 'She's crying.'

Then Ina said, through tears, 'It was a bad idea. England. I read an article in the *Baryn Informer* about the crime there. It's becoming a terrible place. Violence. Drunkenness. Drugs. Everybody too fat. You were better off here.'

'I wasn't better off,' Lev said, as gently as he could. 'I had *no job*. Have you forgotten? Please stop crying, Mamma. Please ...'

Sophie got up and began to wander about the room. Lev watched her, loving the sexy grace with which she moved. Meanwhile, he scoured his brain for something to say that would comfort Ina, but he felt instead only the dark distance that separated him from her, the great continent of Europe that lay between them.

'Listen' he said, with a sigh, 'I have to go now because calls from this mobile are very expensive. But please try to see things differently. I'm sending money ...'

'You should have done like Rudi: found a livelihood in Auror.'

'What livelihood?'

'Taxi driver. Car mechanic. I don't know.'

'You don't know because there was *nothing*. No work. So just stop saying all this. Now, I'm going to say goodbye, Mamma. Right? I'm going to go now.'

'Yes. You go.'

'I'll send another twenty pounds next week. Did you hear me? I'll send twenty pounds next week.'

'Yes, I heard. Goodbye, Lev. Today I asked the Holy Mother to pray to God to bring you home.'

Ina hung up.

Lev sat motionless with the phone in his lap. He felt as if a stone had lodged itself inside his ribcage. He put his head into his hands.

'Tell me ...' said Sophie.

'My mother. She doesn't understand that I'm trying so hard for her and Maya. All she says to me, "Lev, come home, come home." But home, why? Nothing there, Sophie. No work. No life. Only family.'

Sophie handed her half-smoked cigarette to Lev and he took a long pull on it. 'Today,' he said, 'at Ferndale, with you and Ruby and everybody, I was happy. You know? So happy. When I serve up their nice meal, very happy. When you sing, so happy. This was my best Christmas. And now ...'

'I know,' said Sophie. 'Families kill you. It's why I hardly ever see mine. But, hey, listen, the day's not over yet. Let's go to the pub. Get a nice steak pie. Have some drinks. Shall we? It's not as though we haven't earned them.'

Lev reached out for Sophie. He pulled her to him and sat very still, with his arms round her, resting his head against her scarlet curls. He loved the smell of her. Knew the scent alone could drive him wild. Wondered how crazy, in time, he would allow himself to get.

Flooding Backwards

On the morning before the restaurant reopened, Sophie said: 'Lev, you have to go home today. I've got stuff to do.'

Stuff? What stuff? But he didn't argue, even though the day yawned in front of him, long and lonely without her. He told himself he had things to occupy him: his room to clean, money to send to Ina. And he remembered Christy, alone in the flat. Perhaps he and Christy would walk to Hampstead Heath and watch the kite-flyers and the hardy swimmers breaking the ice on the frozen ponds.

Before he left, Sophie offered to cut his hair. She shampooed it and rubbed it roughly with a towel. Then she positioned Lev at her wooden dressing-table and he could see himself, brightly lit, in an old, three-sided mirror, with the towel draped over his shoulders, and he stared at his two profiles and at Sophie's soft hands, caressing his damp head.

Clustered round the mirror were a collection of cosmetic products and a jewellery stand, in the shape of a tree, hung with necklaces and beads. In whichever direction Lev looked, he saw his own image framed by these objects. He sat obediently still, staring at the lotions and creams. And he remembered how, when Marina had been alive, he'd loved this scented, intimate paraphernalia, the modest vanities of her life as a woman: the smell of lipstick and foundation, the one precious bottle of perfume, eked out over time, the stubby pencil with which she drew out the elegant line of her eyebrows ...

He felt tempted to talk about Marina now, to remind Sophie

that he'd been loved before – as if this fact would make him more beautiful to her, more visible and strong. But she was absorbed in the hair-cutting. She arranged his head this way and that. She kept telling him not to move. She was tender towards him, but part of her, he felt, had left him already. The flat had gone still and silent.

Marina became Lev's companion in this silence. It seemed a long time since she'd been there with him, but now she was ...

She and Lev were travelling in a bus going from Auror to Baryn in the heart of winter and, on the way, their baby began to arrive. Little Maya. She beat with her fists and with her feet inside Marina, to throw out the fluid in which she'd been floating, and suddenly the floor of the bus was drenched, and when the driver saw this, he began swearing and swerving all over the icy road.

The bus skidded to a stop. A fellow passenger covered Marina with her woollen shawl. Other women clustered round. The men stared from a horrified distance. Lev asked the driver to go straight to the hospital in Baryn. So the driver let the bus hurtle on, ignoring its scheduled stops, leaving people waiting in the sleet, waving their arms in vain. Marina's contractions were coming every three or four minutes. Lev knelt by her and held her hand. When the pain came back, she didn't cry out, but tightened her grip on Lev's hand and her nails dug into his palm.

The road seemed long and grey and unforgiving. One of the women, a *babushka* with a lined and suffering face, whispered to Lev: 'Comrade, you may have to be a hero and deliver your own child. Do you have vodka for sterilisation?'

Vodka for sterilisation.

The phrase later passed into hilarious usage between Lev and Rudi. When the small frustrations of life got them down, Rudi would say: 'Shit, Lev. We need vodka for sterilisation.'

Lev smiled at the memory of this and Sophie said: 'What are you smiling at?'

'Nothing,' said Lev. 'Only thinking about Rudi.'

She went on snipping and shaping. Lev looked at the grey drifts of hair on the floor beside his chair. He returned to the bus and the shadowless landscape going by the window and the *babushka* rolling up his sleeves for him and pouring vodka over his hands and forearms. And he remembered that, instead of feeling alarmed or afraid, he had begun to feel excited at the idea of bringing his child into the world on the road to Baryn. He began, even, to hope that the bus wouldn't reach the hospital in time. He recast himself as a hero, steadied himself for what might prove to be his finest hour ...

'OK?' said Sophie. 'I think that's finished. Now you don't look so 1970s, man.'

Lev stared at his face, shorn of his long hair, and he thought that it had never appeared to him quite like it appeared now. He reached up a hand and touched his neck: it was unexpectedly smooth and cold. He tugged the towel off his shoulders and held it in an awkward bundle in his lap.

'OK?' said Sophie, again.

'Yes,' he said. 'It's good. Thank you.'

Sophie took the towel from his hands. 'It's a bit short, but in a week it'll look brilliant.'

She lightly kissed his mouth. He got up, brushed the hair from his knees and went into the bedroom where he began to pack his things. He looked out of the bedroom window into Rossvale Road, and it, like the landscape on the route to Baryn, seemed to be without shadows. He watched a young woman walking along, pushing a baby in a buggy. A small dog followed at her heels. Lev sighed as he folded his checked shirt.

For all the dramatic preparations, he'd never had to become the hero in the story of Maya's birth. The bus drew into the Baryn hospital compound in time, and the passengers cheered, the *babushka* smacked a kiss on Marina's cheek and the driver wiped his forehead, which was oily with sweat. Orderlies came running out of the hospital doors with a trolley and Marina was wheeled away. All Lev could do then was follow, aware of the vodka fumes that still emanated from his body.

The hospital corridor was painted green. Lev jogged behind the trolley, trying to keep one hand on it. But then a set of swing-doors loomed up at him, blocking his way. The doors swallowed the trolley with Marina on it, and a white-coated doctor, who appeared from nowhere, instructed Lev to wait on a wooden chair of the kind that furnished the Office of Public Works.

Lev sat down. He could hear his laboured breathing. He was alone in the waiting area and he stayed sitting on the wooden chair for a long time. A tin ashtray piled up with his cigarette butts. The vodka evaporated on his skin.

Then, at last, a nurse came through the doors and held up a tightly wrapped bundle. 'Daughter,' she said curtly. 'Yours now.'

Lev sat with Christy, drinking tea. They smoked and coughed in a kind of unison. He looked up at Christy and noticed now that his eczema had retreated, that there was some colour in his thin face.

'Must be the sleep,' Christy commented. 'Slept for thirty-nine hours – just to be on the safe side, so as not to experience a *chink* of Christmas Day. You know? Heard the phone ringing coupla times. Got up to piss. Drank a glass of milk. Those pills gave me excellent dreams, too. Chipper as a spaniel, I was.'

'Yes?'

'Yes. You know your hair's feckin' short, fella. Was that deliberate?'

'Sophie said I looked like 1970s person.'

'I think it suited you long, but never mind. To go on with me dream: I was at Silverstrand, in Suffolk, where Angela and I once or twice took Frankie. Lovely sea there. Beach nice and clean. I floated along the shore, light as the wind, with all me worries gone. The breakers came tumbling in, and the sun put a glint on the foam and I saw all the beauty in that, every speck.'

'That's a nice dream, Christy ...'

'Well, it is. It was. And when I wake up finally, when the pills have worn off, I feel all optimistic suddenly, and think to meself, maybe, with Sophie as, like, the female chaperone, we could make a day out with Frankie – without Angela peering down me neck. What d'you say, fella? One Sunday. We could all go to the zoo.'

Lev stubbed out his cigarette. 'Or go to that place in your dream,' he said. 'Silverstrand. Why not there?'

Christy stared at Lev. His eyes began their familiar, nervous blinking.

'I don't know ...' he said. 'In the dream it was lovely, but it's a while since I visited ...'

'Walk by the waves,' said Lev, 'or run.'

'Run?'

'Yes. Along the sand.'

'Easy on, fella. Not sure I'm up to running! Might end up face down in a rockpool. Then the gulls would start circling the territory.'

As Christy began to laugh and the laughter turned to a cough, Lev's phone rang and he walked with it into his bedroom because he thought it might be Sophie, summoning him back to her, but it was GK Ashe.

'Nurse,' said GK, 'how was Christmas?'

'Good,' said Lev. 'Thank you, Chef.'

'OK. I'm glad. Well, now listen up. We've got a crisis. Tony's left.'

'Yes?'

'Fuck him. Gave me no decent warning and he's dumped us in the *merde*, because we're full New Year's Eve, absolutely sodding chocka. So here's what I'm doing. I'm going to put Sophie in as the second sous-chef. She's overdue a chance because she's dedicated, and she watches and learns, so I think she can hack it. Right?'

'Good, Chef.'

'And I want you to take on the veg prep. It's not difficult. It's not rocket science, it just needs care. Are you up for it?'

Lev sat down on his bunk bed and looked at the shop and the old-fashioned storekeeper still lying prone behind his counter.

'I will do it, Chef,' he said.

'Good. Good man. If it goes a bit pear-shaped tomorrow evening, it's not so catastrophic, because we're clientele lite, but for the New Year we've got to be up to par. Go and buy some proper knives. Get down to those catering suppliers in Swiss Cottage. I'll reimburse you. And then pick up some stuff – salad, endive, potatoes, carrots, whatever you can find – and start practising, OK? Try to get your chopping speed up. Remember, it's the body of the knife you move, not the tip. And endeavour not to sever your fingers or your hand. I don't want to see blood in the gratin.'

'Yes, Chef.'

'And don't worry about the KP work. I'll find a new nurse. Nurses aren't hard to get. I'll give you and Sophie a week's trial. If the week goes all right, I'll put your money up. Seven pounds an hour. If it's crap, you're back at the sinks. You understand me, Lev?'

'Yes, Chef.'

'Good. So it's up to you. Everything now is up to you.'

The call ended and Lev sat still for a moment, staring at his mobile. Then he walked through to Christy, who was clearing away the tea things. 'Christy,' he said, 'I'm going shopping now. Cook a nice vegetable stew for supper.'

'Yes?' said Christy. 'Well, don't let me stop you, fella. Make a lovely change from milk and pies.'

> *Little Gem lettuce: pare away stalk, separate and rinse leaves, spin-dry, leave ready for the chefs in colander, covered with clean wet towel.*
> *Baby carrots: slice tops, leaving half-inch of clean green, scrape and rinse, leave ready.*
> *Spinach: rinse, wilt over low heat, if requested, leave for chefs to drain and season.*
> *Rocket: rinse and spin, leave in colander.*
> *Haricots: pinch out tops, discard oversize beans (stockpot), wash, leave for chefs.*
> *Courgettes: top, wash and drain, slice or baton-up as requested.*
> *Tomatoes: Blanch and skin. De-seed before chopping ...*

Sophie had written out and pinned up for Lev what she called her 'Veg Blueprint', and now he was hunched over his new station, cutting, rinsing, scraping, separating, slicing. 'Keep your ears pricked,' GK had told him. 'If I need spinach, I'm going to shout out, so will Pierre and Sophie. If we need carrots batoned-up or fennel sliced, again, we're just going to shout it. And then we'll need them fast. You got it?'

'Got it, Chef.'

'Keep your chopping-boards clean. I don't want to experience a courgette seed on my endive. And if you cut your finger, rinse it, dry it, dress it quickly and carry on. Elastoplast and stuff is up there, above your head. Always put on a fingerstall to prevent blood leaking through.'

Lev's bandanna had been replaced by a cotton cap, identical to the ones the chefs wore. It fitted snugly over his shorn head.

Now and again, Lev glanced up at the thin, seventeen-year-old boy who had replaced him as nurse in his old kingdom of the dishwash. This boy wore the bandanna now. He looked, to Lev, like an apprentice pirate, nervous of the vast, steel-coloured sea that surrounded him. Tendrils of his brown hair escaped from the scarf and clung to his neck, damp with steam. His name was Vitas and he was from Lev's country. Lev felt protective towards him, but had no time to give him. The chefs' demands came fast and didn't slacken. Labouring his way through the skinning and seeding of tomatoes for a *coulis*, he was aware that Pierre needed spinach, and GK, who was moulding courgette cakes, shouted to him that he'd run out of mint leaves. Lev left the tomatoes sliding in a bloody mass to the far edges of his chopping area, tore a bundle of mint from the chiller, rinsed it and began picking off the leaves and hurling them into a colander.

'Lev!' shouted Pierre. 'Spinach! You're holding up table six.'

'Coming, Pierre ...'

The mint leaves stuck to Lev's hands. He realised he should have picked the leaves off first and rinsed them afterwards. He saw juice from the tomatoes begin to drip down the front of the work station. He wiped his hands, ran water into his sink, threw in the spinach, then returned to his mint, shutting off the cold rinse-faucet with his elbow. He glanced up to see GK pausing in his own work to stare at him and he knew the import of this electric stare by now. No words were needed.

He thought about the promised seven pounds an hour. With that, he might be able to increase his payments to Ina by about ten pounds a week. And then, instead of bleating on and on about his return, she might at last begin to be proud of what he was trying to do ...

'So rescue it,' he instructed himself, imitating one of GK's per-emptory commands. 'Stay calm, like you stayed calm at Ferndale Heights, and rescue it.'

He set up the spinach colander. With his thumb and first finger he kept jabbing and pulling at the mint. He waltzed the mint round to GK, waltzed back, piled up the clean spinach, pressing it down, piling on more. Pierre was standing and watching him, furious at his own enforced idleness, flicking a tea-towel against his shoulder.

'OK, Lev? Come on! I need the spinach ...'

He saw Vitas turn round and stare at him. The boy's look was one of terror. Sophie kept her back turned. She was plating up lamb medallions, each with a careful spoonful of onion marmalade.

Lev's hands felt raw in the cold rinse-water. GK was again bent over his courgette cakes. Lev prayed he could get the spinach to Pierre before GK looked up again.

It was done now. Pierre snatched the colander from him, threw a fistful of leaves into a waiting pan.

'Lev,' called Sophie, 'I'll need the tomatoes in about two-point-five minutes.'

'Yes,' he said calmly. 'Tomatoes coming.'

He snatched at some kitchen paper and wiped up the tomato leakage, then returned to the dicing. The tomato seeds were stubborn, jelly-like, and clung to the tomato flesh. He had to gouge them away with his fingers. The task was almost complete when he saw a spinach leaf arrive in the tomato bowl. 'Cooking,' GK had once said to him, 'is at least eighty per cent about separation and amalgamation. The chef is almost always addressing one or other of these processes. A restaurateur I knew in France used the terms *divorce* and *amour ...*'

So now Lev had this amorous green spinach leaf lying on the inviting tomato flesh. He smiled as he plucked it out and denied it a second life in the stockpot. He finished dicing the tomatoes and took the bowl to Sophie. He saw the skin of her face pink and moist under the soft cap and the tip of her tongue innocently caressing her top lip as she carefully laid a spear of asparagus across each medallion. Sudden desire for her made his head swoon. She looked critically into the tomato bowl. Then she smiled at him and said: 'OK. Nice.'

The smile made him mad to touch her – just stroke her cheek or, better still, slide his hand over the sweet contours of her arse – but she'd made him agree, made him promise, that the affair had to be kept from the staff at *GK Ashe*. She said it would 'muddy' the feeling of everybody working as a team. She said it would make GK nervous.

So he left her and returned to his station. He felt order beginning to return there. Beside him, the vegetable chiller hummed in the rich and humid air. He carried the empty tomato bowl over to Vitas, who was scouring a roasting pan. He saw Vitas's feet awash, his trousers soaked. He took down the mop and bucket and gave them quickly to the boy. 'Mop it now,' he said quietly, 'before the Chef sees it.'

*

It was a crostini night.

When they were settled with their beers and the hot, oil-scented food, GK said: 'Not bad, considering. Well done, everybody.'

'Chef,' said Lev, 'tomorrow I will get faster.'

'You did OK. The thing was you didn't panic. I registered you *not panicking*, and I liked that. But come in earlier tomorrow, Lev, get more of your prep done before the service starts.'

'I will, Chef.'

'Sophie did very good,' said Pierre.

GK turned to Sophie and ruffled her curls. Lev saw her blush. 'I agree,' said GK.

'Table seven commented really favourably on the medallions, doll,' said Damian, swigging lager from the bottle.

'I think I overcooked them by about half a minute,' said Sophie.

'Well,' said GK, 'learn from it. We'll put them on tomorrow. Get them perfect tomorrow for New Year's Eve.'

'She did good, though,' insisted Pierre. 'First night as sous-chef. Didn't she, Chef?'

'Yes,' said GK. 'I said so.' He turned away from Sophie and glared at Vitas, after glancing through into the kitchen, where unwashed pans, utensils and plates were still piled up. Lev watched Vitas, who was gulping his beer and seemed unaware of GK's glare. Lev noted that the boy's eyes were bruised with exhaustion and that his hair hung limply round his pale and serious face.

'What about you, Nurse?' said GK. 'Got away from you a bit, did it?'

Vitas looked blank.

'Because it's a mess in there. Isn't it? And that was a lite evening. What went wrong?'

'I am tired,' said Vitas.

Damian grimaced. 'Lad,' he said, 'didn't I tell you? "Tired" is not a word we use in this kitchen. We live with it, but we don't talk about it. We just carry on.'

GK nodded his agreement. He said to Vitas: 'The kitchen has to be clean before you leave it, right? You understand, Nurse?'

'I come here in morning ...'

'No,' said GK, 'you do not come here in the fucking morning.

In the morning, we're stocking the fridges and the chillers. Waldo's in, making puddings. I may be prepping. And none of us is setting *foot* in a dirty kitchen, right?'

Vitas blinked. He said to Lev in his language: 'The Chef does not understand that I have to sleep now.'

'What's he say?' said Damian to Lev.

'He says he is very tired, but he will do it. I will help him.'

'OK, but you shouldn't have to help him. You're on veg prep now.'

'I know,' said Lev. 'But tonight, I will.'

Lev saw Sophie looking at him. The look was amused, sexy and tender. He returned her the ghost of a smile. Then he finished his beer and stood up. 'Come on, Vitas,' he said. 'In one hour, you'll be able to go home.'

Now the place was empty except for Lev and Vitas. Lev had watched Sophie riding off into the darkness on her bicycle, with her football scarf wound round her head. Then he'd resumed his old place at the sinks, giving Vitas the tasks of scouring the burners and salamanders and mopping the floor. In the corner of his eye, he could see Vitas moving very slowly, almost dreamily, seeming not to see what his work entailed, staring blankly at areas of grease, then dragging a cloth uselessly over them, the scourer forgotten in his other hand.

Lev finished the pans, put the washer on its final cycle, polished the sinks, threw the damp tea towels into the laundry basket and hung up new ones on the steel pegs. He gazed almost fondly at the station where he'd reigned for what seemed like a whole lifetime, then looked at his watch. It was 12.55. He knew where he was going to go ...

Vitas was leaning on his mop. And now Lev saw that tears were dribbling down his face. Though Lev longed to leave, he knew he couldn't abandon Vitas. He crossed to him and took the mop from his hands. 'Just need some sleep, do you?' he said.

'I can't do this job ...' sobbed Vitas.

'No?'

'I miss my dog.'

'You miss your dog?'

'My dog, Edik. I think of Edik, waiting for me, by my mother's door. I wanted to bring Edik to England, but I wasn't allowed. They said he might have rabies. But he doesn't have. He's the best dog ...'

A storm of weeping overtook Vitas. Lev handed him a damp dishcloth, then sat down on the stool where GK often sat, late at night, to plan his menus.

'Edik is a one-person dog and that person is me.'

Lev stayed silent while Vitas went on sobbing, then he got up and went through to Damian's bar area. He took down a shot glass and poured out a double tot of vodka. He brought this back to Vitas. 'Drink,' he said.

Vitas gulped the vodka. His weeping subsided at last. He wiped his eyes with the dishcloth.

'How do you survive here?' he said. 'This fucking place ...'

'I work,' said Lev.

Vitas looked forlornly round at the kitchen, still not clean. 'I hate this,' he said. 'And I hate the Chef!'

Lev shrugged. 'Try not to,' he said.

'Why? That man is horrible. He's rude. I *hate* him. He's an arrogant bastard. The way he calls me *Nurse*. I'm not a fucking nurse.'

'I know. Just ignore that, Vitas. Stay with GK and you may have a future in England.'

'I don't want a future in England. I hate England. It's like that shit-hole Jor, except with more Muslims and more blacks. I want to be back in my village with Edik.'

Lev looked at the boy, remembering how extreme youth is almost always touched by extreme melancholy.

'Where are you staying?' Lev asked.

'Some tip of a room. Hackney Wick. And the Wick's full of immigrant scum.'

Lev ignored this. He said: 'Do you know your way home?'

'Yeah. Night bus.'

'Right. Go home, then, Vitas. I'll finish off in here.'

Vitas was silent. He now appeared slightly sheepish. He pushed a strand of damp hair out of his eyes. He blew his nose on some kitchen paper. 'Where are you from, then?' he asked, after a while.

'Auror,' said Lev. 'Small village, like you. Above Baryn.'

'That place where they're going to build the dam?'

'What?'

'I heard they were planning to make some dam – on the Baryn river.'

'Where did you hear that?'

'Dunno. Somewhere. Perhaps it was someplace else.'

Lev stayed very still. He thought about the Baryn river and how it came down from the once-forested hills above Auror and ran through the pastures beyond Ina's garden. He thought about the fact that this was the only river that flowed into Baryn.

'I think if they were going to build a dam near Auror I would have known about it,' he said.

'Maybe,' said Vitas.

'In the old days,' Lev said slowly, 'I certainly would have known, because my wife worked in the Procurator's Office at the Public Works building in Baryn. But my wife died.'

'Your wife died?'

'Yes. So you see, Vitas, you're not the only one to feel sad.'

After Vitas had left, Lev sat on in the kitchen and again broke one of GK's cardinal rules by smoking a cigarette. Images of Auror filled his mind. He saw the rags shivering in the trees above his father's grave. He saw Ina's goats, huddled together in their pen. And he heard the silence of his village, that sweet silence of the night, never broken by the spirits to whom Stefan used to utter his peculiar prayers, but only by the calling of owls.

He got out his phone and punched Rudi's number. Lora answered in a sleepy voice. 'Lev, Rudi's out,' she said. 'Driving some people home from Baryn.'

'How's the Tchevi?' Lev asked.

'Still jumpy. But he's got the belts, finally. From somewhere in the Ruhr. He's going to fit them on Monday.'

'Good,' said Lev.

There was a moment's pause and Lev could hear Lora yawning.

'I'm sorry to call late,' he said, 'but I heard a rumour tonight, about a dam they're planning to build above Baryn. "Above Baryn" must mean on our bit of the river.'

'A dam?' said Lora. 'We never heard anything about a dam.'

'There's a boy who works in this kitchen, from some village near

Jor. He told me.'

'Perhaps they're going to make a dam above Jor?'

'No. He said Baryn. So we have to find out, Lora. Can you go and talk to Procurator Rivas?'

'You know I don't like that man, Lev.'

'I know. But people in Rivas's office would know.'

'They may know, but that doesn't mean they'd tell us.'

'This is meant to be the new era of openness.'

'Sure. But old attitudes are hard to shake. How do we know whether to believe what they say?'

'Well, a dam above Baryn would wipe out Auror. About this, they would have to tell you.'

'Wipe out Auror? Wipe out our homes?'

'Yes. If you dam a river, it floods backwards. Auror would be under water.'

'They can't do that, Lev ...'

Lev lit another cigarette. He stared out at the mess left untouched by Vitas. He said wearily: 'Probably not. Perhaps the boy said it to frighten me. I don't know, Lora. But find out, OK? If you don't want to see Rivas, get Rudi to go.'

'Oh God, now I'm frightened, Lev. Suppose it were true? Suppose we lost our village?'

'I guess there would have to be compensation.'

'Compensation? What would *that* do? Where would we go?'

'I don't know, Lora. We'd have to figure it out. Tell Rudi I'll call again in a few days. Try to get an appointment with Rivas.'

'What would Ina do, Lev?'

'I don't know.'

'She just wouldn't survive that.'

'She'd have to survive it.'

'All the old people. Imagine it. To leave Auror would be the end of their world.'

This was what he thought about as he completed the work left unfinished by Vitas: his mother dismantling her jewellery shed, packing up her belongings, taking up the rag rug from the floor of her room ... visiting Stefan's grave for the last time, gathering a scant bunch of wild marguerites and putting them there, on the rough stone under which he lay ... sweeping the corners of the empty house ... slaughtering her goats ...

Pray it doesn't happen.

Lev could imagine his mother's face, close to the candlelit icon, close to the photograph of Marina, whispering to the God-Who-Had-Been-Asleep in her country for all her lifetime, but whose picture her parents had kept safe in a dark cupboard, obstinately believing that, one day, He would be allowed to return, obstinately telling their child that, in secret, she should pray, that this God-Who-Had-Fallen-Asleep nevertheless saw everything on earth.

How can a God who is asleep in a dark cupboard see everything on earth?

His mother used to wonder about it. She had told Lev that, as a child, sometimes, she used to unwrap the icon and bring it forward on the shelf, so that a corner of light fell onto its golden surface and she would stare at the chubby legs of the Christ-child and think: In time, those fat legs may grow, and what will be asleep in the cupboard will be a man. And the idea of a sleeping man in the cupboard thrilled her. She used to listen to see whether she could hear Him breathing. But He never made one single sound.

'And yet,' she once said, 'in a way I was right. God slept, but then He woke at the beginning of the 1990s. He took back His power. And He was grown up by then. He knew how to bring the people back to Him.'

The news about Auror had taken away desire.

His body aching, Lev rode forlornly home to Tufnell Park. But as the night bus was lurching up Kentish Town Road, his phone rang and it was Sophie.

'Lev ...' she said, and across the single syllable of this word, Lev heard the little, irresistible break in her voice.

'Sophie ...'

'Shall I tell you where I am?' she said. 'I'm in bed, and I put on some new sheets, and they're satin, and they're driving me completely wild. So I was hoping you were on your way ...'

Lev smiled. He cradled the phone to his ear. 'Sophie,' he said, 'I want to hear you say something to me. Then I will come.'

'Then you'll *come*? Right. Say what?'

'I want you to say you love me.'

He heard her laugh. Then she said: 'You're so sweet. Men are boys, really. But, yes, I'll say it. "We're both chefs now, and I love you." Have you *come* yet?'

12

A Visit to the Lifeboat Museum

With the new year, mild weather arrived, unexpected and consoling, as though spring were already returning. Lev remarked that he could hear birds singing in the bare plane trees outside Sophie's flat.

'They're deluded,' said Sophie, brightly. 'They'll start building nests and then the snow will come.'

She was happy. 'Happy-crazy', she called it. She took photographs of Lev making breakfast, sitting in the bath, lying naked on her bed. And in their scented nights she was as shameless as the whores of Baryn whom Lev and Rudi used to visit long ago. She made the pronouncement that love-making like theirs was a war – with two winning sides.

Lev knew that her success at *GK Ashe* played a part in her mood. The trial week had gone smoothly. Sophie was a sous-chef now, on seventeen pounds an hour. Already, she told Lev, she could imagine opening her own restaurant one day, 'and this,' she said, 'would be the most brilliant life I can think of. Be my own boss. Design my own menus. Somewhere less high-end than *GK Ashe*. More buzzy, less expensive: food for people who want to eat well and have a good time and not take out a fucking bank loan to pay for it.'

'Where will it be?' Lev asked.

'Dunno. North London somewhere, I guess. Except every second shop is turning into a food outlet these days. Banks are morphing into pizza emporia. I saw a funeral parlour that had become a tapas bar. What premises are left?'

They lay in the dark, swapping their private dreams. Lev said that his ambition, now, was to learn to be a chef, too. He said that he'd spent forty-two years not thinking about food. Now he thought about it for hours at a time. All through his vegetable prep, he kept watch on what GK and Sophie and Pierre were making. He made notes on a pad he kept in a pocket of his whites.

With the fine weather, Christy Slane began thinking about the day out with Frankie. He said he was coming round to the idea of going to Silverstrand. 'The only thing we have to do,' he told Lev, 'is get you vetted by Angela. She'll never let Frankie go anywhere with people she's never seen.'

So Lev and Sophie were sitting, now, in the front room of the flat in Belisha Road, waiting for Angela to show up. It was mid-morning and Christy had set out the coffee-making equipment in a meticulous line on the kitchen worktop. He said: 'I was going to buy some pastries, but I thought better of it. When you offer Angela something, she never bloody well wants it. She only wants it when you're way past offering it any more.'

'I wouldn't have minded a pastry,' said Sophie.

'Oh, right you are. Shall I go and get some after all, then?'

'Nah. I'm fine. But you know this vetting's a farce, Christy. It's like parents' day at school.'

'I know. I know it is, but what can I do?'

Angela came in, wearing a smart red coat. She was tall and big, with wide hips and a tall woman's lofty smile. Beside Christy, she looked huge. Her eyes were brown and slightly protruding.

Lev stood up and kissed her hand. He could tell by her embarrassed smile that she thought this ridiculous, yet found herself girlishly flattered by it.

Sophie said: 'Hi, Angela. I'm Sophie. I work with Lev at *GK Ashe*. I live in Kentish Town. I'm twenty-nine and I have no children.'

'It's not an interrogation,' said Angela.

'Oh, right,' said Sophie. 'I thought it was.'

Lev caught Christy's stricken look. 'Angela,' Lev said quickly, 'Sophie is just saying … we tell you anything you want to know. Who we are. Everything. Then you will be happy.'

Angela looked round at the three of them. It was a look that asked, Is everybody in this room mocking me? and Lev saw her turn, as though starting for the door. But Christy jumped to her side. 'Take your coat, love? Come and sit down. Put the gas fire on, if you're cold.'

Silently, slowly, Angela surrendered her coat, which Christy went to hang up in the entrance hall. He called out that he was now making the coffee.

Angela stared at Lev and Sophie. Lev noticed that, in contrast to Christy's suffering face, Angela's skin was flawless, like the skin of Diana, Princess of Wales. Yet he also saw a woman whose youth was disappearing and who knew that this was so.

'Well ...' she said.

She looked around, not knowing where to sit, as though she'd forgotten that she'd taken away most of the furniture from this flat.

Lev offered her his chair and he went to stand by the window, where the winter sunlight put a grey sheen on the dusty net curtains.

Sophie said: 'So, do you know Silverstrand, Angela?'

'Yes,' said Angela. 'Of course I do. I was born there.'

'Oh, right. Christy didn't tell us that.'

'Well, Silverstrand's not much to write home about. The sea's nearly always grey and full of muck. I was glad when my parents moved.'

'Kids love the water, though,' said Sophie. 'I did. We used to go to Hove. Put up our stripy windbreak ...'

'How would you get to Silverstrand? I'm not letting Frankie go in a car with Christy driving.'

'Train,' said Sophie. 'Change at Ipswich. Only about an hour and a half. And we've been saving up for candyfloss, haven't we, Lev?'

'Yes. Because I never tried that. I am like a child ...'

Angela shifted position, so that she was facing Lev. Under the red coat she was wearing a woollen dress, and she kept pulling the hem of the dress down, to try to cover her fleshy knees.

'Coffee almost ready!' called Christy, and Lev could hear the panic in his voice.

Lev found his wallet, took out his picture of Maya, walked over to Angela and offered it to her. 'My daughter,' he said. 'In my country. Maya. Age five.'

Angela took the photograph and gazed at it blankly for a moment, then handed it back. 'I hope you're sending money home,' she said with a sniff.

'Yes,' said Lev.

'Lev's had lots of practice with children,' offered Sophie.

'Practice?' said Angela. 'That's a funny word to use.'

'Why?'

'As if caring for a child was like riding a bicycle. It's knowing how to behave in your own life that matters.'

Christy appeared, carrying the coffee tray. His hands shook and Lev could hear the mugs rattling. 'Everybody OK?' he said.

Lev went to his side. 'Christy,' he said. 'I pour the coffee. Chef's technique.'

'Thanks, fella,' said Christy. Then he babbled: 'I was going to get pastries, Angie ... but I thought you might not ...'

'Thought I was big enough? Quite right. Tony keeps telling me I'm too big. But then he goes on taking me out for meals: expensive meals, too. I keep saying, "Tony, I thought you wanted me thinner and now look, more champagne, more lovely sauces. How am I to lose weight with all this?"'

'Who's Tony?' asked Sophie bluntly.

Angela turned to face her. 'Tony?' she said. 'Well, not that it's any of your business, but Tony is my partner.'

'Right.'

'He's in real estate.'

'Is he? Oh, how lovely.'

Lev could hear a laugh beginning to surface in Sophie's voice. And he felt the moment sliding towards catastrophe. He took the coffee quickly to Angela and knelt down by her chair.

'Angela,' he said. 'I am lodger with Christy for many months now. Hardly ever does he drink any more. I swear this. But he is, like me, so sad for his daughter, so sad for Frankie ...'

'He doesn't need to be sad for Frankie. He needs to be sad for himself.'

'This I mean. I'm sorry my English is not good. I mean that Frankie is missing ... he is missing her so much.'

'He may say that now, but what does he do when we all lived here? Just fucks off out all the time – not to work, hardly ever to work. Fucks off to the pub. She kept asking me, "Where's my dad?"'

And what was I supposed to say? Then he comes home and throws up in the hall. It was an absolute bloody fucking nightmare!'

'But now ... almost never the pub ... almost never.'

'So you say.'

'It's true, love,' said Christy. 'I know I was bad for a long time. But I've got a real grip on it.'

'He has,' said Lev. 'A very good grip. So all we're asking is, please let us make a nice day for Frankie. All together. By night-time she is back with you. Everything nice and safe: walk on beach, play kiddie golf, eat fish and chips. Everything lovely, like that.'

Angela put sugar into her coffee and stirred it vigorously. 'I'm not deciding now,' she said, 'so don't pressure me.'

The room went silent. Lev got up from his knees. He took out a packet of Silk Cut. 'Will it trouble you if I have cigarette?' he asked Angela.

'Suit yourself,' said Angela. 'It's not my flat.'

Lev offered the packet of cigarettes to Christy and he took one with a trembling hand.

'What Lev says is true, Angie ...' he began.

'Oh, leave it out, Christy!' she shouted, slamming down her coffee mug. 'This whole charade pisses me off, well and fucking truly! You make my life a misery for five years and now you want to pretend it's all going to be OK, all fucking fine and dandy. Well, it's not! You've got to do more than bleat on about not going to the pub. You've got to do more than live off the rent of innocent people from a foreign country. You've got to start working again. You've got to prove – not just to me, but to the courts – that you're a rational, responsible human being again and a fit father. Then I might consider what you're asking. Meanwhile – and I want to tell you this now, so your new friends can restrain you when you throw some Irish epileptic fit – Tony has asked me to marry him, and as soon as the divorce is through, that is what I'm going to do. I've told Frankie and she's fine with it. She adores Tony. He's becoming the father she never had.'

Christy sat down on a hard chair. His blue eyes blinked and blinked. This blinking reminded Lev of the terrified beating of an insect's wing.

Sophie said quietly: 'I'm not from a foreign country. My parents live in Sussex. They breed lurchers.'

Angela got up. She hadn't touched her coffee. She turned to Sophie and said: 'I don't care who you are or where you live, dear. You're not part of this. This is between me and Christy. But if you want to be his friend, tell him to stop pestering me about seeing his daughter. He should have thought about all that long ago.'

'Angela . . .' Christy began.

'I'm not listening!' she said. 'I don't know why I even agreed to come here. I only agreed because Frankie wants her shop, so I'm going to get that now and then I'm leaving.'

Angela stomped out of the room. Lev turned to Christy, who didn't move. The cigarette had fallen out of his thin, burned hands, which he clasped and unclasped under his chin. Lev went over to him and picked up the cigarette and lit it and gave it to him. Sophie looked at Lev for guidance, and Lev made a decision.

He turned and left the room, and walked along the corridor to his own door. The sight of Angela, large and angry in his bedroom, offended him. He saw her bend down and pick up the miniature shop, with its old-fashioned commodities and its little optimistic sign, *Hi! My Store Is Open*. He watched the moustachioed storekeeper fall out and bounce onto the floor.

'Oh, bugger!' said Angela.

Lev picked up the storekeeper. Angela said: 'I need a carrier-bag, or something, to put this lot in. Can you find me one?'

'It's a shame . . .' said Lev.

'Eh?'

'I'm thinking . . . I am quite fond of this store assistant. I will miss this shop.'

'What?'

'True. I will miss. But it's OK. This is nothing. But if you take away Frankie from Christy, this is bad. He is the father, as I am father of Maya. He will suffer . . .'

'Listen,' said Angela, with a heavy sigh. 'You seem like a perfectly nice man. I hope England treats you fairly. But just don't meddle with things you don't know anything about, right? Christy Slane is not going to be allowed to ruin my life, or my daughter's, and that's all I have to say. That's it. *Finito*. So could you just get me a carrier-bag and I'll be on my way?'

Lev handed her the storekeeper and she threw him into the door of the shop.

'I have no carrier-bag,' he said.

'Oh, never mind!' said Angela. She walked to the hallway, grabbed her red coat from the peg and, carrying the shop awkwardly under her arm, let herself out of the flat. Her heavy footsteps clumped down the stairs.

Lev told Sophie he'd have to stay at Belisha Road for a while, to keep Christy company, to try to stop him going to the pub.

'You're at work half the night,' she said, 'so what difference can that make?'

'Maybe some. If he knows I will be back. If we make breakfast in the mornings ...'

'You're naïve, Lev. If someone wants to drink his life away ...'

'I know,' said Lev. 'But I can try this. Christy has been my good friend.'

They were at *GK Ashe*, at the end of a long, busy night. Sophie turned away from Lev and said: 'OK. Fine. You stay at Belisha Road. I've got stuff to do, anyway.'

'What "stuff"?'

'Same stuff as you: taking care of my friends.'

'But some nights you could come there. To my room ...'

'What? Screw in a kid's bunk? I can't, Lev. It's too totally bizarre.'

On the other side of the kitchen, Vitas was toiling over his sinks and drainers. That same night, GK had said to him: 'You're hanging by a thread, Vitas. Today I found gobs of goat's cheese still stuck to my salamander; I found a smear of blood on the floor.'

'Not blood, Chef.'

'And don't argue with me. Just never do it. You've got till the end of the week to get your ducks in a line or you'll be out. You'll be picking sprouts in fucking Lincolnshire.'

Later, when GK and Sophie had gone, Vitas said to Lev: 'What is Lincolnshire?'

'Oh,' said Lev, 'it's the countryside, somewhere.'

'I'd rather be there than here, then,' said Vitas. 'I miss trees.'

The idea of the dam had washed against Lev's heart, like silt. In his dreams, he'd seen the school-house in Auror floating on the water like a wooden boat, then slowly sinking, and, for a moment, he'd thought this vision of the slowly sinking school-house oddly beautiful – until he realised that all the children, including Maya, were still inside it. Far off, on the water, he could hear them screaming.

He told Christy about the dam. Christy said he had to light a fag and make a cup of tea before he could bear to think about it. Then, with the cigarette and the strong tea in his hand, he said: 'Public Works, Lev. You know, the very term terrifies me to the gills. Because you can never imagine anything good coming out of there. It's meant to sound philanthropic, but what it signifies to me is some consortium of strangers replacing a thing you love with a thing you don't need.'

Christy's hand shook as he drank the tea, but he was holding himself together. The thing that seemed to be holding him together was a 1000-piece jigsaw puzzle of Van Gogh's *Sunflowers*. He'd spread it over the table and he worked on it for hours and hours at a time, drinking tea and smoking. At the end of the conversation about the dam at Auror, he said: 'The thing we've got to try not to lose is our reason. We mustn't end up like this fella Vincent.'

Lev put off calling Rudi, in case the news from Auror was bad. Then, one Sunday morning, he felt he couldn't put it off any longer and dialled the familiar number.

'Tchevi's fixed!' Rudi announced triumphantly. 'Now I suddenly love Germans. I kiss their arses. They make belts that fit.'

'She doesn't creep any more?'

'No. It's like she's been to dog-training school, come back a different animal! All I gotta do now is punch out the dents in the fenders and polish up the chrome. Then she's good as new.'

Relief about the Tchevi seemed to have made Rudi impervious to any other misfortune. When the subject of the dam came up, he still sounded blithe. 'OK.' he said. 'Lora got to see someone in Public Works. Not that bastard, Rivas. Some thin creep with a squint. Dunno his rank. It's possible it was low.'

'Tell me what he said.'

'Usual department crap. But I think it's OK. He said a dam above Baryn had been a "provisional project" for something like two years.'

'But nobody's known about it?'

'I guess some people know. But Squinty told Lora there were no plans to *actuate* it. "Actuate", eh? That's a typical Rivas word, isn't it?'

'No immediate plans, or no plans ever?'

'You know Public Works, comrade. They don't deal in concepts like "ever" or "never". Everything's *provisional*. I think there's probably this team of celestial engineers, going round designing dams and hydro-electric plants and reservoirs on every fucking river in the country, and they all coo over their drawings and imagine the prosperity these projects are going to bring and the rewards they're going to get – and then nothing happens because there's no money from Central Government. So there you are. I guess Auror's pretty safe.'

Lev wanted to feel reassured by what Rudi had told him, but he sensed that the information was inadequate and this maddened him. He felt sure that if Marina had been alive, she would have ferreted out the truth. But now they were like everybody else – isolated by distance, at the mercy of a bureaucracy in which lying was still the chosen mode of communication.

'You've got to keep watch, Rudi,' said Lev, after a moment. 'Watch for surveyors. If a survey team arrives, that'll be the first sign.'

'Not necessarily. You know what those dozy government departments are like. They despatch a few men with clipboards. They trudge up and down. They look important, so everybody starts panicking, but all they're doing is measuring the length of their own dicks!'

Rudi laughed his habitual explosive and infectious laugh, but on this occasion Lev didn't join in.

'OK,' he said, 'but if rumours about a dam at Baryn have got as far as the villages around Jor, then someone knows it's going to happen. They *know*.'

Rudi's laughter died and Lev heard him coughing.

'Well,' he said, 'what more can we do? You tell me. "No plans to actuate" means what it says, no? Unless Squinty was bullshitting.'

'There were "no plans to actuate" the closure of the lumber yard.'

'That's different. They ran out of fucking trees!'

'Just as they keep "running out" of electricity. But build a hydro-electric plant above Baryn and you've got uninterrupted, renewable power for the whole region way into the future.'

'Except half the region will be drowned.'

'Exactly.'

Lev heard Rudi sigh. 'I'll keep my ear to the ground, Lev. I promise. Hope Rivas's official car breaks down, so then he'll have to hitch a ride in the Tchevi – and he'll be at my mercy. But enough of all that. It tires me out, thinking what the world could do to us. Tell me about *l'amour*, Lev. Are you acting like a teenager? Are you spending all your hard-won cash on red roses?'

When Lev got home to Belisha Road late one Friday night, he found Christy sitting in front of two unopened cans of Guinness.

'Celebration,' he said, as soon as Lev came in. 'Angela changed her mind. We can take Frankie to Silverstrand on Sunday.'

Lev took off his anorak and sat down. Kissing Sophie in the street, then watching her ride away from him, had left him feeling frustrated and cross. He'd felt almost violent towards her, capable of pushing her against a wall and fucking her right there in the street, like the desperate adolescent Rudi imagined him to be. In his mind, he accused her of playing games with him.

'After all that bloody palaver,' Christy continued, pouring the stout, 'after making me suffer like that, she just phones up and says OK she'll bring Frankie round Sunday morning and we can go to the sea if we want.'

Lev and Christy drank the Guinness. Christy laid his head on the heel of his hand. 'I think she's only agreeing,' he said quietly, 'because Myerson-Hill's taking her out somewhere and she doesn't want Frankie to ruin their lovely romantic day. Expect they're going to Hampton bloody Court in a barge, or something. But I don't care. As long as we can have a beautiful day, I don't mind.'

Lev smiled. He felt himself begin to transcend his frustrated mood. He imagined gulls bickering above a quayside and the scent of seaweed and a salt wind. 'Don't worry,' he said. 'We will have a beautiful day.'

On the train to Silverstrand, Sophie suggested a game of 'I Spy'.

'Are you sure you want to play that, darlin'?' Christy asked his daughter tenderly. 'Because I'm not sure your spelling's that good, yet.'

Frankie didn't reply, just pushed at Christy's thin arm, trying to move him further away from her.

'I bet her spelling's brilliant,' said Sophie. 'So: I spy with my little eye something beginning with … F.'

'What's F?' said Frankie.

'You have to do phonetic stuff, Sophie,' said Christy. 'That's the alphabet she knows. F is *fuh.*'

'Oh, right,' said Sophie. 'You can tell I'm a totally sad person upon whom nobody has fathered a child, can't you? OK, Frankie. Something beginning with *fuh.*'

As Sophie said this, she looked at Lev and giggled. He thought: She's like some exotic dish that I don't yet know how to make, but yearn for in my dreams. He turned away from her, moving his gaze to Frankie, who was staring worriedly out at the fields of Essex. She had a small, angular nose that she began to press up against the glass.

'Give up,' she said.

'No. Bollocks. Don't give up,' said Sophie. 'Something beginning with *fuh.*'

Frankie was wearing pink jeans with a pink top and a little furry body-warmer. On her knee, she carried a matching pink rucksack, which she'd refused to surrender as they'd boarded the train and now clutched tightly to her.

'Come on, Frankie,' said Sophie. 'Something beginning with *fuh.*'

'Tree?' said Frankie.

'No. That begins with a T.'

'*Tuh,*' corrected Christy.

'OK, *tuh.* You see? I'm rubbish at this game. Whose *name* here begins with *fuh*?'

'Give up,' said Frankie.

'No, no,' said Christy. 'Just think.'

Frankie pushed again at Christy's arm. Outside the window, Lev could see the winter plough, dusted with new green shoots, and squalls of dark birds wheeling above the hedgerows. Strong sunlight brightened the pale edges of woods and glimmered on flooded beds of bulrushes and reeds.

'You're not looking in the right direction,' said Sophie to Frankie.

So Frankie turned away from the window and looked round at the people with her. Her gaze swept past Christy to two young women, drinking Stella and talking on their mobile phones. Lev saw her staring at their teeth, crunching Walkers crisps, then at their shiny mobiles, on which the sun glinted, as their heads moved restlessly about.

'Phone,' Frankie announced, triumphantly.

Sophie smiled. 'Good try,' she said. 'Pretty good guess, girl. But the word "phone" has a weird kind of beginning ...'

'And it's not a name, Frankie,' said Christy. 'Sophie told you, this word is someone's *name*.'

Frankie still refused to look at him.

'Give up,' she said again.

'No,' said Christy, crossly. 'You're not bloody well giving up.'

'Mum says you shouldn't swear,' said Frankie.

'Well, yer mum's right. I shouldn't. I'm sorry. But goodness me, is this what your mother lets you do these days, give up on everything before you've hardly begun?'

'No ...'

'OK. Now, *think*, then. There are four of us here and only one person's name begins with *fuh*. Whose is it?'

'I don't know his name,' said Frankie, looking at Lev.

'Yes, you do. I told you, darlin'. His name is Lev. That doesn't begin with a *fuh*, does it? Nor does mine, nor does Sophie's, so ... ?'

She squirmed and slipped about in her seat. She hugged the pink rucksack to her, like a shield. After a while she said: 'Frankie.'

'There you are, then!' said Christy. '*Fuh* for Frankie. Easy, you see? Wasn't it? Easy as pie. Now, sit up, darlin'. You just need to concentrate.'

Frankie let herself be pulled up, then she turned away and put her face close against the window once more. She said she didn't want to play 'I-Spy' any more. She said she was going to count the number of horses she saw in the fields.

Christy rubbed his eyes. Since Angela's visit, his eczema had returned and crept to their rims and flamed them with a red crust. Under his breath, he said to Lev: 'They're neglecting her education. I can feel that already.'

Lev didn't feel like talking. Like Frankie, he wanted to watch the countryside beyond the train window. He wanted to remember, as the lines of hedges unrolled and isolated farms came and went, how this part of England had appeared to him from the bus that had brought him to London from Harwich on the early morning of his arrival, with Lydia beside him. He smiled as he recalled the commentary Lydia had begun, as soon as the sun rose, drawing his attention not to the shimmering wheat nor to the dark shade made here and there by English oaks in full leaf, nor to the stone churches, which so frequently appeared, but to the signs that came and went from view: '*Little Chef*,' she would say, 'and look, Lev. *Little Chef* again! So many of these.' She murmured new words under her breath, like an actor saying lines. '*Royal Mail Depot ... Kendon Packaging ... Multiyork ... Atlas Aggregates ... Notcutts Garden Centre ... Pick Your Own ...*'

'What is *Pick Your Own*?' Lev remembered asking.

'Oh,' said Lydia. 'I don't know. I think it's quite a puzzling sign because it appears grammatically incomplete.' She thought for some time, then sighed and said: 'I'm sorry, Lev, I can't translate "*Pick Your Own*" yet. Perhaps I am deluded in my expectation of a translator's job.'

It seemed long ago.

It was as if *that* Lev had been a different man. And he began to think how strange it was that the person Rudi still knew, the person Maya would remember, was this other Lev, this old, sorrowful, anxious man. He wanted to apologise to them. He wanted to reassure them that he'd be better company now.

'Right,' said Christy, to break the silence. 'Time for sandwiches.'

They arrived at Silverstrand near to midday, with the sun at its height, and hardly any wind, and they ran straight down towards the sea. The tide crept sedately in over a wide, beige-coloured beach, chivvying the sand-ripples, breaking in shallow wavelets, silvery-white under the arc of blue sky.

'Hey!' said Christy, grinning at the beautiful sight. 'I think this is all right, everybody. Look at this, Frankie. Isn't this a morsel of OK?'

She'd put down her rucksack. For the first time that day, her flinty eyes were bright. She made little hopping and skipping movements on the sand.

'Smell the ozone!' said Christy. 'Or is it the bladderwrack, or the shells or what? I've never known. On the west coast of Ireland they always used to say, "Smell the ozone".'

'It's definitely ozone,' said Sophie. 'And we're in it. Breathe, Lev. Every breath cancels out forty fags.'

Suddenly, without warning, she snatched Lev's hand and began to run with him towards the water, then turned and pushed him playfully forwards, so that the waves almost surged over his feet. He resisted and tugged her to him. He wanted to pick her up and walk into the sea with her. He felt strong and wild, as though he could hold her in his arms above him, like a dancer.

'No!' she giggled. 'No!'

'You started this,' he said. 'Now you punish!'

'No, Lev! The water's freezing! Christy, help me!'

He loved the feeling of her struggling with him. Though he could have lifted her up immediately, he let her whirl and fight. He could smell the salt sea and the perfume of her body and was a youth again, a blithe idiot, full of joy. His hand went under her skirt and he bunched the flesh of her arse in his hand and lifted her high.

'Put me down, Lev! Put me down! If you drop me in the water, I'll kill you! I'll die of fucking frostbite!'

She was yelling, but laughing all the while. Lev walked with her into the sea and the cold waves began eddying round his ankles and soaking into his shoes and socks. He could feel the iciness of them, biting on his skin, like sherbet.

'Lev! You're crazy!'

'Yes,' he said. 'I'm crazy. Crazy for you.'

'Put me down!'

'You know I'm crazy for you?'

'I know, I know. Go back.'

'I don't think you know how crazy ...'

She had to cling to him to keep from falling. He wanted to kiss her, but he was afraid to become more aroused than he already was, so he turned and ran with Sophie, testing his own strength, feeling the power in his limbs. He could see Frankie jumping up and down, waving her thin arms, and Christy holding the pink rucksack and, further along the beach, a line of smart little painted huts, from which children, dressed in startling colours, ran to and fro, and he thought how wonderful a thing it was for the world to seem so bright in winter.

He set Sophie down and she cuffed his head. 'Nutter,' she said. 'Aren't you?'

'Look at that, Frankie,' said Christy. 'Now his trousers are waterlogged. What a fine example to set!'

'I want to go in the sea!' said Frankie. 'I want to go in the sea!'

'Jesus,' said Christy. 'Now look what you've done, Lev. The sea's cold, Frankie. Cold as snow.'

'I don't mind. I want to go in it!'

'No, no, look at the state of Lev's shoes. You don't want to get yours like that.'

'Yes, I do. Yes, I do!'

'OK. OK,' said Christy, throwing down the pink bag. 'We'll go in the sea, but take your shoes and socks off first, and I'll do the same. Did anybody bring a towel? Sophie?'

'No. Only this madman had the idea of getting soaked.'

'Never mind. Sun'll dry us. Shoes off.'

Christy and Frankie sat down on the sand and took off their shoes and socks. Already, the colour in Frankie's cheeks was high and strands of her wispy hair had broken from their band. She waited obediently as Christy rolled up the bottoms of her pink trousers, then stood up. For the first time that day, she reached for her father's hand.

'OK,' he said. 'Here we go. Guess this is the way we do things at Silverstrand. Hold tight!'

Lev watched them run towards the water, both of them thin and nimble and moving fast. When they reached the sea, they let out high-pitched yells of shock and delight. Christy began to jump over the wavelets as they broke and Frankie did the same and water sprayed all around them, catching the sunlight, and after a moment or two, Lev saw that they jumped in unison, like children playing a skipping game.

Lev dug his feet into the soft sand to dry them. Sophie stood laughing as she watched Christy and Frankie. 'It's bloody February!' she said. 'We're all mad as hatters.'

Behind the beach huts, installed on a piece of vacant ground, there was a winter fair and it was here that Christy led them next. The place was small and almost deserted. Stall-holders sat about on plastic chairs, blinking in the sunlight, surrounded by their own litter of dented Styrofoam cups and sweet wrappers and old cigarette packets. A sign advertising *Freddo the Fire Eating Fiend* lay forgotten and half hidden in the dead weeds of summer. The candyfloss machine was taped up with the message *Out of Order*. But tinkly music was playing and in the middle of the ground stood a children's carousel, set up with miniature cars, aeroplanes, space-ships and tanks. Frankie ran immediately to this and Christy paid for her ride. She was the only child on the carousel, but the young attendant stood watchfully at the centre of the machine, turning like a figure on a music box while, above it, seagulls shrieked in the blue air.

Christy, Lev and Sophie stood in a line, smoking, while Frankie went round and round, sitting proudly in a miniature fire engine with, on her head, a plastic fireman's helmet. She waved to them like royalty, her hand stiff and flat. But there was a smile on her narrow face and Christy said at last: 'She's happy now, or am I wrong? She's having a good time, isn't she?'

'Brilliant time,' said Sophie.

Christy touched Lev's sleeve. 'Shame Maya couldn't be here with us,' he said. 'D'you have these merry-go-round kind of things at home?'

'Yes,' said Lev. 'But I must say more beautiful than these military cars: nice painted horses and other animals, made of wood. Very old-fashioned. The Communists never got so far as these to break them.'

'That's interesting,' said Christy.

'Perhaps a fair is very proletarian already, no? Not worth bother to destroy that.'

'Could be, could be.'

'In Baryn, the fair was a nice place. We used to go there. Even grown-ups like this place very much. You eat roasted sunflower seeds and you can hear a folk band and shoot at tin birds. Long ago there were prizes, but now there are no prizes.'

'Why's that?'

'Because what has anyone to offer for a prize? A piece of coal?

Some wild flowers? But I used to shoot the tin birds just the same.'

'Did you hit them?' asked Sophie.

'Yes,' said Lev, putting his arm round her shoulders, 'my father taught me. We used to practise on real birds, in the woods, before the woods were cut down.'

'Practise on real birds?' said Sophie, pulling away from Lev. 'That's barbaric.'

'No,' said Lev. 'I was joking. We killed them to survive.'

The ride slowed to its end and Christy lifted Frankie out of the fire engine and returned her little helmet.

'Good kid, innit?' said the attendant.

'Aye,' said Christy. 'She is.'

She was looking all around her for the next treat, the next excitement. She spied a hot-dog stall and led them towards it, and Christy bought dogs with onions and mustard and they sat on an iron bench eating them. A seagull landed at their feet and snapped at their crumbs. Frankie began pulling off hunks of her bun and throwing them to the bird.

'Don't do that, sweetheart,' said Christy. 'You said you were hungry. So you eat it.'

Lev said to Frankie: 'The first food I ever had in Britain was a hot dog.'

'Why?' said Frankie.

'Why?'

'She means "where",' said Christy. 'Don't you mean where was it, Frankie?'

'Yes,' said Frankie.

'Well, Frankie, it was by the river. In London. I watch the big tourist boats. I think, I am alone for ever ...'

'Why?' said Frankie.

'Oh, diddums,' said Sophie. 'Isn't that heartbreaking, Christy?'

'Yes, it is.'

'And then you met us: a Celtic plumber and a Size 14 Wannabe-Chef, born in Godalming! Bet you never saw *them* coming!'

Christy chuckled. Lev blinked. He knew that Sophie had said something he should probably be laughing at, but he didn't know what it was. Sometimes his understanding of English failed him, failed him suddenly without warning, like a spasm of deafness. He stared at the seagull, cramming its sharp beak with the dropped food. He was aware of Frankie staring at him, as the remains of her hot dog went cold in her hand. He sensed that something fundamental about the day had changed, but couldn't quite recognise what it was.

'Sun's gone in,' said Christy, looking up at a grey-white sky. 'What about a visit to the lifeboat museum?'

13

The Pitch of It

A text from Lydia came to Lev's mobile: *Important news. Meet me in Café Rouge Highgate for lunch Sunday?*

Lev called her to say he'd promised to go to Ferndale Heights on Sunday, and Lydia said disconsolately: 'Well, you've been avoiding me for a long time. So carry on. I'm used to it by now, Lev. Perhaps you've got a girlfriend. But don't worry. Soon I'll be gone.'

'Gone?'

'Yes. Don't you want to know where I'm going?'

'Where are you going, Lydia?'

'It's a long story. I can't tell it on the phone. If you don't want to meet me, you may never know it.'

Lev began to say that he was working long hours, had no time ... but the silence he heard now, at the other end of the phone, was so reproachful, it made him feel mean. He told Lydia he'd meet her at noon in Highgate the following day.

'OK,' she said. 'That will be nice, to see you at last. How are you getting along with *Hamlet*?'

Lev didn't want to tell her that he'd hardly opened the book, that it was lying under his bunk at Belisha Road, alongside empty Silk Cut packets. Instead, he said: '*Hamlet* is difficult for me. My progress is very slow.'

'Well, I think you should persevere, Lev. You may recognise something of yourself in the character. See you tomorrow.'

He bought her some flowers – freesias, yellow and purple. Although it was almost spring, now, these freesias had no perfume.

But Lev thought, That doesn't matter, because Lydia will pretend they do. She will say: 'Oh, Lev, what a lovely scent!'

And sure enough, when he gave the flowers to her, she pressed them to her face. 'Beautiful!' she said. 'I didn't expect these. Now I remember that my first judgement of you was correct: you're a thoughtful man.'

In the dimly lit barracks of the Highgate Café Rouge, they ordered the chicken baguettes Lydia had wanted the last time. She also insisted on ordering two shots of vodka, and when these were brought to the table, she said: 'Some of the waiters here are from our country. That thin one is from Yarbl.'

'How do you know?

'Because I come here alone sometimes, on my day off. I drink hot chocolate. I talk to the waiters – just to hear our language, to escape from being "Muesli". Like us, these people send money home. But this life in North London is soon going to be over for me. So I shall tell you my news. Are you prepared for a shock?'

'Yes,' said Lev.

'Very well. I'm going away with Maestro Greszler.'

'Going away? Yes? Going where?'

'Wherever he goes. First will be Vienna, next month, in April. Then Australia. After that New York. Then Paris. Sometimes we shall be back in London and then I shall call you and say hello.'

'Well, that's great, Lydia. I know you loved that job with Greszler.'

'It's more than great.'

'But why does he need you in Vienna? You don't speak German.'

'Well, I do, a little. But you see …' and here Lev saw her pale face bloom with a sudden flush of pink '… he wants me not only for the translating.'

Lev drank his vodka. Lydia was fanning herself with her paper table napkin. 'I told you it was a long story. But I'll make it short. I should have mentioned to you before, when I was working in London with Maestro Greszler, how he very often tried to kiss me, but I would never let him. He has a wife at his home in Jor. A wife and three children and now grandchildren. I thought I shouldn't allow myself to be touched by such a man, who could never be mine. But since his leaving, I've been getting letters from him – two or three a week – telling me he's fallen in love with me and wants me to be his mistress and go with him all over the world.'

'His mistress?'

'I expect you're going to remind me that he's old—'

'No, I wasn't.'

'And that he suffers from constipation.'

'No.'

'But I don't care, Lev. I've put away my scruples about everything. Even about his wife. I'm someone in need of love and I can love Pyotor Greszler, despite all these things. He tells me he's still virile. He says he makes love to me in his dreams.'

She was flustered and smiling like a girl. She looked around for the waiter from Yarbl, to order a second shot of vodka. She laughed a hectic little laugh.

'Oh Lev,' she said, 'I hope you don't look down on me – to become the mistress of a famous man, to be a kept woman. But, you know, my life here since Pyotor went away has been so bad, I feel I've lost all my pride. I am just "Muesli" now: a slave to spoilt English children. And I can't go on like this. I would die.'

'You don't have to justify it, Lydia. I'm sure hundreds of women would like to have a life with Maestro Greszler. He's a genius. And if he loves you ...'

'Well, what is love when you are seventy-two? I don't know. But I'm going to take my chance. I'm almost forty. I've always longed to see the world. I think, when I get to New York City, I may die of wonder! And with Pyotor, we'll be in the best hotels, the best rooms. My God, I sound worldly. I must have caught the English consumer disease! But never mind the hotels and so forth. When I think of my dear Maestro, it's with great tenderness. I never pulled away from his kisses out of revulsion. It never bothered me to help him with his bowels ...'

The vodka was warm inside Lev. His old admiration for Lydia returned to touch his heart. He said gently: 'When you're not travelling with Greszler, where will you live?'

Lydia put down her vodka glass and patted her hair. 'He's already thought about that. He is so very considerate. I'll live in Yarbl, with my parents. He is going to help us with money, for a new refrigerator for Mamma, and for me a small car so that I may sometimes drive to Jor to see him.'

'Do you know how to drive, Lydia?'

'No. But I'll get lessons. You don't think I can master this?'

'I'm sure you can. I'm sure you will be a very good driver. Have you told your parents yet?'

'Yes. Except not the mistress side of it. They need never know about that. Only that I'm going to be Maestro Greszler's assistant on his concert tours. They're very proud. They're already telling their friends about it.'

Lev reached for Lydia's hand and brought it to his lips. Her face was close to his, radiant and warm.

'It was you, of course,' she said, 'who reminded me of what I could feel for a man, Lev. I know you never had any feelings for me, but that doesn't matter. No, don't say anything. I'll never forget our journey. Will you? It was the most important journey of my life and I made it with you.'

At work, that evening, Lev's concentration was bad. His head was full of his own language. His mind kept conjuring images of Lydia in her new life: Lydia wearing a fur coat and high-heeled shoes, walking into some smartly decorated hotel lobby on Greszler's arm; Lydia in Greszler's dressing room, administering stomach powders, fixing his white tie, allowing him to whisper to her some secret, pre-concert endearment; Lydia in a king-size bed with her elderly lover, his flowing hair soft and copious on the crisp white pillowcase …

The chefs, including Sophie, screamed at him: 'Asparagus, Lev! Leeks, Lev! Salad leaves! Mushrooms! Fennel! Where's my okra, Lev?' At one moment, he found GK's face suddenly close up and shouting: 'What's the matter with you tonight? Don't you know who's in? Didn't word get to you who's in?'

'No, Chef.'

'Howie Preece. OK? Table three, with the noisy party of nine. Howie fucking Preece, right? Get it? So move your arse. Start focusing up.'

'Sorry, Chef. Who is Howie Preece?'

'Oh, that's great!' exploded GK. 'I've got one of the most famous young artists on the planet in my restaurant and I'm employing staff who don't even know who he is!'

GK hurled a ladle away from him and it bounced and clattered on the tile floor near Vitas's feet. Vitas let out a shriek. GK snapped his fingers. 'Pick that up, Nurse. *Now*!'

Vitas wiped his hands on his sodden apron and hurried to rescue the ladle. He made to offer it back to GK, who snarled: 'Don't be stupid, Vitas. Fucking *wash* it!'

GK pirouetted back to his station, his shoulders taut with anger. Lev returned to his preparation of button mushrooms, which tormented him by bouncing and jumping out of his fingers. At his back, he could feel Sophie's eyes glued to him. Suddenly she replaced GK at his side and whispered: 'Don't screw up, Lev. Not tonight.'

Lev tried harder to concentrate then. Usually he prided himself on keeping pace with the chefs, even pre-empting their demands by listening to the orders as Jeb and Mario called them out, stacking them up in his mind in the correct sequence and selecting the right vegetables before the chefs even asked for them. He was slow tonight, he knew, not only because he was day-dreaming but because of the vodka he'd drunk at lunchtime. He hoped GK couldn't smell alcohol on his breath. He longed for the service to end. He felt tired and sexy and sad. Images of Marina laid themselves in strange configurations over images of Lydia in his weary mind. He knew that only making love to Sophie would be able to console him and bring him back to himself.

The hours felt long. Though most of the clientele had gone by eleven thirty, the party at table three kept right on ordering more wine, puddings and coffees. GK peered through at them, his eyes lingering greedily on the artist, Howie Preece. On a whim, he ordered Damian to offer them free champagne. 'Call it a loss-leader,' he whispered to Damian, 'I want Preece and his friends back in here on a regular basis. Serve two of the '05 Mumm with the chef-proprietor's compliments, and then I'll come through and say some charming how's-yer-father, right?'

'Will do, Chef. And you know they've had four bottles of the '96 Château Margaux.'

'Bingo!' said GK, punching the air. 'That I totally like.'

Lev had finished his work, but he didn't want to leave without Sophie, so he went to his old station to help Vitas. As they worked, Vitas whispered to him: 'Don't tell the boss, but I'm quitting soon. Friend of mine, Jacek – the one who got me my mobile phone – has heard about a job coming up in the countryside, picking vegetables. Good money. So I'm taking that. And we live for free.'

'Live for free how, Vitas?'

'Caravan. Luxury motor-home. Me and Jacek sharing. Jacek is fixing it and I'm definitely going to go.'

'I think it's a shame,' said Lev. 'You've got on top of the job now. You should stick it out here.'

'No. I hate it. I told you. I hate that man. I'd like to cut his balls off and salamander them and throw them to the dogs.'

They washed up in silence for a while. Then Lev said: 'How is your dog, Vitas? Have you heard?'

'Heard from my dog? No. Didn't you know? Dogs in our country are very backward: they haven't learned how to write letters. But what I am going to do, with Jacek: we're going to steal a dog and keep it in our motor-home. It will be ours. That way I'll forget Edik – until I go home.'

'What will happen to the dog you steal when you go home?'

'Who can tell, comrade? What will happen to any of us when we go home?'

The pans were almost done. Lev set another cycle for the glasswasher and began to wipe down the draining tops. When he turned, he saw Sophie. She'd put on clean whites and her mouth was newly scarlet with glossy lipstick.

'Lev,' she said quietly, 'I'm going through into the restaurant with GK. I know Howie Preece, through Sam and Andy. GK's asked me to help with the chat-up thing.'

Lev stared at her, at her shiny mouth. He felt his heart suddenly beat faster. 'No ...' he said.

'Told you, got to do it, Lev,' Sophie hissed. 'Don't make a fuss. Just accept it. See you tomorrow.'

Waiting for Lev at Belisha Road was an envelope in Ina's writing. She'd spelled London 'Lodnon' but the letter had arrived just the same. Inside there was a drawing of children skating, done by Maya. The children all wore fur-trimmed anoraks, like the one Lev had bought for Maya on the Holloway Road. Their feet were huge in their brown skating boots.

Lev lay down on his bunk bed and smoked and held the drawing close to his face. He tried to recognise which child was Maya and he thought how quickly children's faces altered and how, when he saw her again, Maya would no longer be the daughter he held in his memory. On the other side of the drawing was a message:

Dear Pappa,
I hurt my nose. I fell down on the ice. My nose has gone blue.
Lili is crying. I wash her nappy. Love from Maya XX

Lev closed his eyes. The cigarette burned low in his hand.

In his mind, it was the night of Marina's thirtieth birthday. He and Marina were eating goose and roast potatoes and drinking red wine under a big apricot moon, with Rudi and Lora. On the table on Rudi's porch, red candles flickered in the night-time summer breeze, and on Marina's feet were the red shoes Lev had given her, which had brought tears of joy to her eyes.

Folk music was playing – from an old battery-operated cassette machine Rudi had picked up at the flea-market in Glic – and when the food was gone, all four of them got up to dance. The moon went down and they danced on. The candles went out and they kept dancing under the stars. Rudi poured more wine. They danced with their glasses in their hands. They drank toasts to Marina's long life and Lev kissed her mouth and tasted the wine on her tongue and told her he would love her until he died. They began their famous tango and he heard the click and stamp of Marina's new red shoes on the wooden floor of the porch and saw her slim, brown legs kick out. And she called out to the dark night that she wanted a child. She told the whole village of Auror.

Dogs barked and night birds shrieked from the hills.

She was as drunk as a tsarina, but she didn't care. Rudi and Lora began stumbling about, trying to clear the dirty plates and dishes from the table. 'Give her a child!' shouted Rudi, as a waterfall of cutlery tumbled onto his shoes. 'Tonight we're not mortal, comrade. We're beyond mortal. Give her an immortal child!'

So then he was lying with Marina in Rudi and Lora's back room. An oil lamp flickered on the whitewashed wall. A patchwork coverlet, smelling of mothballs, covered them, but they were naked except for the red shoes, which Marina had kept on. Lev could feel the high heels digging into the flesh of his arse and the touch of the shoes reminded him, as he made drunken love to his wife, how easily wounded was his human form, how agile and marvellous and alone.

Lev stubbed out his cigarette and returned to staring at Maya's picture. She had been born eight and a half months later. Was she conceived on that famous night – his tango-girl, his apricot moon-girl, his girl of the summer stars? He and Marina often amused themselves by trying to work this out, but they knew they would never really know the answer.

Lev dozed in the silent flat. His mobile was by his bed, but it didn't ring. He woke and imagined Sophie still drinking and talking with animation to Howie Preece and his party. It was after 3 a.m. He fell into a dream of skating. On the shimmering ice, his skates made no sound.

When he got up, Christy was there, making breakfast. Christy said: 'I thought you wouldn't be here. I thought you'd be with Miss Sophie. Then I heard you snoring.'

When Lev mentioned Howie Preece, Christy said: 'Ah, that fella. I was taken to see a piece of his work once. It was a model of the double helix constructed out of old tennis balls. The frayed condition of the balls was meant to indicate the fragility, ha-ha, of human DNA. I just kept wondering how he came by all those balls.'

'Well,' said Lev, 'to GK, and to Sophie I think, he's very important.'

'OK, but I doubt he truly, objectively, is. He has "concepts". You can see his mind doing it. He could be sitting on the toilet when it happens. He's understood all right that the word begins with *con*. So he thinks up any old supposedly serious thing. Like, say, double helix/tennis balls/mortality. *Eureka*! Gets some badly paid studio assistant to make the feckin' object. Doesn't even get glue on his hands. Just twiddles his thing and waits for the cheque. To me, he's the embodiment of everything that's half-baked about this country. Nobody's using their feckin' eyes any more. You've got a clutch of emperors walking around without a stitch and nobody's noticing. And in times of stress or extreme penury, this can royally piss me off.'

They sat drinking tea and eating bacon sandwiches. The sun came and went from the window. Christy stared at it and said: 'The thing I loved most about our day at Silverstrand was that jumping about in the freezin' water. That was the best moment.'

Lev reminded Christy that there had been other good moments: playing clock golf and letting Frankie and Sophie win; going back to the beach as the sky cleared again and the sun went down and shimmying stones across the low breakers; watching some riders on white ponies come galloping along the sands ...

'Sure, you're right,' said Christy. 'It was all-in-all a beautiful day. Why does the brain keep on selecting things out, keep on and on with all that measuring and comparing? I've never known why I'm so prone to it either. Haven't the first clue.'

Lev was silent for a while. They both lit a Silk Cut. When Christy had fetched the tin ashtray, Lev said: 'You think Sophie really likes me, Christy?'

'Right,' said Christy, crossing his thin legs in their faded jeans, 'here comes one of the Big Questions once again. So, let's consider. But listen to me, fella. How would I know whether she does or doesn't? If anyone here's going to know, it's you. So what do *you* think?'

'I don't know,' said Lev. 'This is why I ask. Sometimes, I think yes, sometimes, no ... .'

'Well,' said Christy, 'I've been trying to use me eyes. Sophie's a bonny girl. She has a heart, unlike Angela, who has an old rotting watermelon where her heart should be. And she obviously likes whatever you do in bed, or she wouldn't stick with that. But as to love, how am I meant to fathom it?'

'I don't know.'

'All I'd say is, don't assume there's a bright and starry future.'

'Assume?'

'Don't *count* on anything. English girls, like I once said, they're fickle as the tide, Lev. Perhaps, even now, she's in the sack with that bag of frayed DNA, Preece.'

She told him, no, she knew she was a flirt, but she was his girl now, Lev's girl, so why didn't he just forget all about it? It was late on Friday night and she lay stretched out on a rug in front of her gas fire, wearing a turquoise bra and G-string. She uncoupled the

G-string and knelt on all fours and said: 'Fuck me like this. Like the bitch I am.'

He barely moved in her. His wanting of her had become so intense, he knew he'd come in seconds. She yelled at him to go faster, to *hurt* her. He tried to tell her, no, he'd be gone, it'd be over, but she kept screaming at him, like the screaming was part of it, part of what she needed. So he let everything happen as she wanted it, and the pitch of it was so deep, the room went dark and he fell forwards on her, like an animal, spent and dying.

In bed, she turned away from him and curled to sleep on her own. He lay awake and listened to the street sounds and to the quiet of her breathing and to his own heart, which was still beating hard enough for him to hear it. Then he got up and walked silently about her flat, examining her life in the near darkness, aware that this was all he knew of her, this place he could barely see.

He lay down eventually on her sofa, covered himself with his anorak and tried to sleep. But his mind wouldn't rest. To try to soothe it, he made soup recipes in his head: a fish soup with John Dory, whiting, squid, onions, tomatoes and wine; a borlotti bean soup with parsley and lemon oil; a pea and potato soup made with ham stock and cloves; a minestrone with pancetta; a mushroom soup with sour cream ... Putting together a smart court-bouillon, priding himself on the ends and pieces of things he was able to use, he drifted to unconsciousness at last, just as the March dawn broke over London and the traffic on Kentish Town Road began its slow, maddening roar.

Two hours later, when the morning arrived, Sophie was quiet, even sad-seeming. The crazy girl of the turquoise G-string had vanished. She stroked Lev's face. Then she said: 'Lev, I can't go to Ferndale Heights on Sunday. My mum's poorly, so I've got to go home to Godalming. Can you go without me?'

'I don't want to go without you.'

'Please. See Ruby. She's been ill, too. I was going to take her some fruit. Ruby would like to see you.'

'No. Ruby likes to see *you*.'

'I can't, Lev. Haven't been down to visit my mum for ages. Please go to Ferndale. Help them make a nice lunch. Get as many of the residents as you can out into the sunshine to see the daffodils. But especially talk to Ruby. She's so lonely.'

So he said, reluctantly, that he'd go on his own. When this was agreed, she thanked him and stroked his face again and said: 'OK, listen. Sunday week, there's the press night of Andy Portman's play, *Peccadilloes*, at the Royal Court. It's a must-go event. Do you want to come to it with me?'

Lev looked at her. He didn't want to have to think about her friends. He wanted to take her gently to bed, make love to her again in a tender way.

'Lev. Tell me whether you want to come or not. If not, I'll invite someone else.'

'Yes? You invite, for instance, Howie Preece?'

'No. All those people will be there anyway. But I can't go alone. We could go shopping, hey, buy you some nice stuff so you can look handsome for me at the press thing. Because you're actually bloody tasty. You just need better clothes.'

Lev lit a cigarette. His head hurt from his sleepless night. He looked down to see that his hand was shaking. He said: 'Sophie, I have been asking myself ... do you truly like me ... ?'

'Lev,' said Sophie, sharply. 'Don't start on that. How much reassurance d'you need? I beg for it, don't I? Look at me on the rug last night. God almighty, I was Miss Shameless. Wasn't that a sign?'

'I don't know.'

'Course it was. Just because I won't sleep in that kid's bunk bed, with Christy Slane listening through the wall ...'

'Not that.'

'What, then?'

'Nothing. Only, I wish I knew.'

'Knew what?'

'What to hope for.'

'Just don't be so anxious about it, Lev. Like, take it easy, OK? Everything will become clear. So tell me whether you want to come and see the play or not.'

'Yes,' said Lev. 'All right. I will. Now, will you come back to bed with me?'

He saw her hesitate, but then she let him take her hand. They went into her bedroom and drew the curtains on the spring day. He held her chastely at first, like a girl, with her head lying on his shoulder.

*

It rained on Sunday morning and the residents of Ferndale Heights seemed subdued. 'It's Berkeley,' said Minty Hollander to Lev. 'He's in the Royal Free. He can be very argumentative, but we're so short of men here we're all praying he pulls through.'

'What's wrong with Berkeley, Mrs Hollander?'

'Pneumonia, darling. The Old Person's Friend. And, actually, Berkeley is – unlike some of us – what you could genuinely call an *old* person. But I do miss him.'

Lev went to the kitchen and offered to help the kitchen staff, Mrs Viggers and her daughter Jane, make Sunday lunch. The two women, both wearing yellow overalls, stared at him, hands on their haunches, which were huge with flesh.

'Who're you, then?' asked Mrs Viggers.

'I am Lev. I helped here Christmas Day – with Sophie.'

'Oh, yeah, we heard about that: posh gravy, innit? You a chef, then?'

'Training to be a chef.'

'Well, we're not "chefs", are we, Jane? We're just nice plain cooks, but nobody's ever complained.'

Jane came close up to Lev and stared at him. She reached out a hand, as though she wanted to touch him, then withdrew it.

'Jane!' snapped her mother. 'Give the man a task. Give 'im the Paxo to mix.'

Jane jumped. Her pouchy little eyes were moist and startled. Slowly, she reached up and took a packet out of a cupboard and handed it to Lev.

'What's this?' he asked.

'Stuffin', dear,' said Mrs Viggers. 'For the roast pork. Just mix it with water. Give 'im a bowl, Jane.'

Lev looked at the packet, then laid it aside. He began walking round the kitchen, opening cupboards. He found a bag of dried apricots and a jar of dried rosemary and set them down on the worktop. He picked up some onions and parsley from the vegetable rack. 'I make a stuffing with these,' he said. 'You got bread for crumbs?'

'Apricots? With pork?' said Mrs Viggers. 'They won't eat that.'

'They will,' said Lev, and began chopping.

Mrs Viggers shook her head as she reluctantly handed Lev a

sliced white loaf, then moved away, but kept glancing at him from her task of peeling potatoes.

'You got a visa then, Olev?' she said, after a while.

Lev went on with his work. He threw butter into a pan and began to sweat off the onions and apricots with the herbs.

'Bet 'e don't 'ave no visa,' said Jane. ''E's illegal.'

'That it?' said Mrs Viggers. 'Asylum-seeker, innit?'

The apricots began to release their perfume. Lev made breadcrumbs in the snarling old blender. He snatched the apricot pan off the heat, grabbed salt and pepper and began to mix his stuffing. Then he said: 'Can you show me the pork, please?'

'Show 'im the joint, Jane. He doesn't want to talk, and I know why ...'

Jane set the meat down on a dish, a vacuum-packed leg of pork boned and rolled and with a thick rind. At *GK Ashe*, Lev had watched GK scoring and preparing pork rind, and he took up a knife and sharpened it. The two women stared at him.

'Aren't you afraid, like, Immigration could come here and whack you down the nick?'

'Whack me down the nick? What is that?'

'He knows nothin', bless 'im. You don't know nothin', luv. That Immigration, they've got officers everywhere, in disguise. I could be from them, for all you know. Then you're done for. You're back on the first plane.'

'Yes? Back to what place?'

'To wherever you came from: Bela-whatsit, Kazak-wherever.'

Lev unpacked and dried the meat, loosened it from its strings, and laid in his stuffing. Then he scored the pork rind to strips narrow as matchsticks and began to rub in salt and mustard powder. He retied the joint.

'Mum,' said Jane. ''E's makin' lines.'

Mrs Viggers shuffled over to where Lev was working and rested her elbows on the chipped Formica top. Her breasts hung over her forearms. 'If you're trying to get it to crackle, don't bother, dear. That meat never crackles. They put 'ormones in the swill so it stays rubbery.'

'This will crackle,' said Lev.

'And, anyway, they can't eat bloody crackling. They hain't got no bloody teeth!'

'OK,' said Lev. 'But when is crisp, is light, you know. Then maybe they can crunch.'

Jane Viggers had a satanic laugh. It came echoing out now in the dingy kitchen and made Lev shiver.

'Crunch-crunch!' said Jane. 'Crunch like a Crunchie bar!'

'Don't start, Jane Vig,' said Mrs Viggers. Then to Lev she said: 'Jane sometimes gives the wrong impression. But she's as normal as steak and kidney pie.'

Later, in Ruby Constad's room, he said: 'I think the cooks here are crazy.'

'Are they?' said Ruby. 'How fascinating.'

'Jane is definitely crazy.'

'I have heard a funny sound coming from the kitchens now and then. But perhaps it doesn't matter with cooking.'

'I think, to cook very well, you must be quite clever.'

'Do you? That's probably why I was never a proper cook. Not clever enough. I used to boil things – chicken and silverside of beef – and make dumplings. That was about all. Otherwise, after I was on my own, I ate Marks & Spencer ready-meals.'

Ruby looked pale and tired. She'd had a bout of gastric flu, she said, which was why she hadn't been able to manage the roast pork. 'I just ate a little of the stuffing, Lev,' she said. 'With a couple of sprouts. That made a perfect small meal.'

'I'm glad you like ...'

'Anyway, I'm on the mend now, but my sleep is very bad.'

Lev said: 'My friend Rudi, he always sleeps so well. Like a baby. He is lucky that way. But me, not.'

'No. Well, it's bad luck. It's how you're born, they say. And now I have such dreams, so full of guilt at how useless my life has been. Night after night. But what can I do about it?'

'I don't know.'

'The only thing left I can do is alter my will. I have stacks of money – all inherited, nothing from any proper work. I could leave more to Africa. Or to some institution in my beloved India. I could endow something. Couldn't I? What do you think, Lev? What's the best thing I could do? I asked Berkeley – Captain Brotherton – but all he said was: "Don't let the taxman get it." But I said: "Berkeley, who cares if the taxman gets it? Tax is roads, isn't it, and hospitals and places for the homeless?" But he couldn't seem to see the value of those things. I expect it's his upbringing, or his sheltered life in the Navy.'

'What about money for your children?' Lev asked.

Ruby shifted in her chair. She closed her eyes. 'I hardly ever see my children,' she said. 'This happens in some families. You think your children will always be there for you, but then you find you're wrong. And you suddenly see it: you're not even in their minds.'

Lev waited for Ruby to say more. But she folded her heavily ringed hands across her bosom, like someone preparing for sleep. Lev sat silently near her feet, on the stool from Kashmir.

'Enough about me,' she said, after a while. 'Tell me about your life.'

Lev looked away. Outside, the rain had stopped and a weak sun fell onto the green spaces around them. 'May I light a cigarette?' he asked.

'Yes,' said Ruby. 'Put the ash in the pot-pourri dish. It needs chucking out anyway.'

Lev lit a Silk Cut. These days, when he had to spend so many hours without smoking, cigarettes had taken on the sweetness of mountain air. He inhaled deeply. Then he turned towards Ruby and said: 'My life is a puzzle. Is that my word?'

'I expect it may be, yes.'

'I feel … I don't know anything. I am waiting – you know? You understand me? Like I think, One day, Lev, you will *know* the future. You will see everything clear. I work and wait. But I know nothing.'

'Tell me about the past.'

Lev sighed. Then he began talking about Marina. Ruby listened attentively, now and then eating some of the grapes Lev had brought.

'I see,' she said softly. 'Your wife died. That changed every-thing.'

'Yes.'

Lev smoked quietly for a moment, then he said: 'Before, I was a happy man. You know what I'm saying? I was OK, despite what happens in my country. Happy and strong, like Rudi. But now. Sad inside. Sometimes, with Sophie, OK for a while. Laughing, kissing, everything. Then it comes back.'

'I know. It comes back.'

'Maybe for always. Who knows? This I would like to know, Ruby. Will I be free of this?'

'Lev,' said Ruby, 'when I was younger, I always told people the things I thought they wanted to hear. But I don't do that any more. It's a cruel thing to do. So I can't say to you now you will be free of it and move on, because I just don't know the answer.'

There was silence in the room. Lev finished his cigarette and stubbed it out among the dusty petals of the pot-pourri dish. Ruby's old-fashioned bedside clock ticked on past three. The traffic on Finchley High Road made a distant, surging sound, like an angry river.

After a while, Ruby reached out and took Lev's hand in hers. She held it lightly, as though weighing it in her palm. 'Thank you for coming to see me today,' she said. 'Did I tell you I was brought up a Roman Catholic, by nuns in India?'

'Yes.'

'Oh, yes, of course I did. Well, sometimes I say prayers to the Virgin Mary. Just out of habit. I say them somewhere unlikely, like the bathroom. I remember when my husband was very ill I used to pray in the bathroom of our Knightsbridge flat. The wallpaper had a pattern of kingfishers on it, which I can see to this day. I have no real belief that my prayers go anywhere – they certainly weren't answered when I prayed with the kingfishers – but the Virgin was always a dear sweet thing, with a lovely smile. Tonight, when I'm cleaning my teeth, I'll have a word with her about you.'

14

Jig, Jig ...

In the noise and deep darkness of the Royal Court Theatre bar, Lev was striving to become invisible.

He was leaning against a wall. The air he was forced to breathe had about it the overwhelming, gamey perfume of success. And Lev sensed that this was not mere innocent chatter that thrummed and trilled round him, carelessly thrown out: it was a studiously composed *symphony* of talk, a *performance* of conversation, which presupposed some silent, admiring audience, mute in the shadows, as Lev was, unregarded in his new suede jacket and stupidly expensive shirt.

Although he'd arrived with Sophie and queued at the bar to get her a drink, she'd snatched up her vodka and tonic and turned away from him, pushing through the scrum to find her friends.

It was as though she'd closed a door on him. So he decided to go in search of shadow. He turned his back on *her*, inching his way from the bar to this space by a wall. He let some minutes pass before he looked up to see where she had gone.

He saw her close to her friend, Sam Diaz-Morant, who was wearing one of her miniature hats, a spangled gold bowler, and whose laughter now and then floated clear of the conversation-symphony's bass notes, like the rattle of a tambourine.

In the group talking to Sophie and Sam, Lev's eye lit on a razored head, big and blue-toned under a pencil spotlight. He knew who this head belonged to: it belonged to Howie Preece.

Sophie was wearing a new dress that looked as though it was made of shimmering spirit rags. With a dipping, uneven hemline, it was cut across her right shoulder into a tight bodice that lifted her full breasts and left bare her plump and irresistible left arm, where Lenny the lizard, who had been given a dusting of sequins for this one night, flashed fire from his tail. Lev had never seen Sophie look quite like this. From the start of his love affair with her, he'd been in slavery to her clothes (sometimes even feeling an embarrassed sadness about the plain blouses and skirts Marina used to wear and which he'd thought so beguiling at the time) but this outfit was the wildest he'd seen. He knew Sophie knew how sexy she appeared. He knew she knew she looked whorish and that she didn't care. Her mouth was a crimson pout, her thick curls new brash colours of auburn and plum. As Lev watched her, envy of Lenny, irrational as he knew this to be, invaded him. He wanted to be lying on Sophie's arm, one with her scented skin, parading his sequined tail ...

Success. Celebrity. Christy had once remarked to Lev that 'Life's a feckin' football match to the Brits now. They didn't used to be like this, but now they are. If you can't get your ball in the back of the net, you're no one.' And Lev saw how right Christy had been. He wished there was other air than this rarefied, celebrated air to breathe, but as the minutes ticked down towards the start of the play, more and more luminous, scented people crammed into the bar, thickening the atmosphere still more with their perfumed exhalations. And they began to bring to Lev's mind not only modern-day movie stars or sports stars, with perfectly toned bodies, but also the once-beautiful, absurdly dressed aristocrats of another era – the people his father used to revile as he ate his heel of salami in the Baryn lumber yard, the people who had brought about the suicidal stampede towards Communism – those long-dead members of the ancient nobility, sweeping forwards, always forwards, in their jewels and furs and pheasant-tail feathers, going towards lighted rooms, towards concerts and *soirées*, towards ten-course banquets, past the unseen poor ...

Lev took a sip of his vodka and the tonic in it tasted like bitter marmalade. He wondered whether he was allowed to smoke here. He turned and looked towards the exit. He imagined himself walking out into Sloane Square and going down into the Tube and riding the underground trains in silence till he reached Tufnell Park and the solace of his child's room ...

He saw Sophie look round now – to see where he was, or only to try to spot which other famous faces were arriving? Howie Preece, too, swivelled his dome of a head, and Lev realised that it was the playwright himself they were greeting, the author of *Peccadilloes*, Andy Portman. They embraced him and clung to him and he to them, and Lev could imagine how Sophie would be reassuring him, wishing him luck, telling him the play was going to be brilliant, a winner, a ground-breaking moment in the history of British theatre ...

Lev was weary. For days now – he didn't know why – this tiredness had been killing him, giving him bad dreams, black thoughts, thoughts about Marina, a feeling of being adrift once again. 'It comes back,' Ruby Constad had said, and she'd been right: his old feeling of misery was creeping in round the edges of things. He'd clung to his work, to Sophie, to the rhythm of his days, to the onset of the reluctant English spring, but now, in this bar, he just wanted to lie down and be carried away on some dark tide of sleep, to become invisible even to himself. Lev closed his eyes, but even as he laid his exhausted head against the hard wall, a voice announced that the performance of *Peccadilloes* would begin in five minutes.

In the stalls, five or six rows back from the stage, Lev sat between Sophie and a bulky middle-aged man, stinking of some sickly aftershave, with jewelled rings on his fat fingers and a caramel-coloured cashmere overcoat pushed down between his legs. The man's right leg set up a non-stop bouncing and trembling so close to Lev's seat that it made it shake. This trembling repulsed Lev. He longed to put out a hand to still it.

He looked away from the man, towards Sophie's profile in the near-darkness. He wanted the profile to turn towards him, but it didn't move. The play had hardly begun, but already Sophie was rapt by her expectations, surrendering to her belief in the genius of Andy Portman.

Lev turned back to face the stage. A purple light came up on a double bed. It seemed, at first, the only object there, but then, revealed in a dim corner, there was a white wardrobe, with, in ornate writing, the word 'Hers' painted on it. Wardrobe and bed. Bed and wardrobe. Already there was something in these waiting objects that made the audience snigger.

A man and a woman came on. They were about Lev's age, with a cool air of prosperity, dressed in evening clothes. They sat down on either side of the bed and undressed and put on identical silky dressing-gowns, the colour of veal. The woman began to brush her hair. The man thumbed a magazine called *AutoMagnate*. While brushing and thumbing, they talked about their evening and how boring it had been and how everybody at the party had been 'arseholes'. They made jokes about these arseholes, at which the audience laughed loudly. They left their smart clothes in two piles on the shiny wooden floor. (They were rich, but they didn't seem to possess any coat-hangers, just left their expensive things lying, as though evacuated from their bodies.) The wardrobe door remained shut.

The woman, whose name was Deluda, began to kiss the man, whose name was Dicer. They lay on the bed in their silk night-robes, touching each other. Then Dicer suddenly sat up and told Deluda he'd 'forgotten to say goodnight to Bunny'. Deluda told him this didn't matter, but he insisted that it did, that without his goodnight, Bunny would have bad dreams. He broke off from what had seemed to be a preamble to sex, and went off-stage. Deluda lay still for a moment, clearly frustrated and angry, then reached under the bed for a hidden gin bottle and took a long swig. Again, the audience tittered.

After a few moments, Dicer came back. But not alone. With him was his daughter, Bunny, a child of nine or ten. He sat Bunny down between him and Deluda on the bed. Deluda hid her gin bottle. Bunny had a sleepy, dreamy look in her eye. Dicer told Deluda that Bunny was having nightmares.

Deluda sighed. But she was Bunny's mother. The parents, Dicer and Deluda, had to comfort Bunny. They began to tell her fairy tales from memory; 'Once upon a time, in a lonely forest, there lived a cruel beast …' Dicer stroked her hair. Not long after the beginning of *Beauty and the Beast* she put a thumb into her mouth and seemed to be drifting off to sleep.

Deluda, still yearning for sex with Dicer, ordered him to put Bunny back into her bed. He looked at Bunny asleep and stroked her face. Then, almost reluctantly, he took her up in his arms and carried her away. Deluda waited for Dicer, snuggling into her pillows as though they were a body beside her.

Dicer returned from Bunny's room at a run. He kissed Deluda and then mimed making love to her with desperate haste. She urged him to slow down. But he seemed to convey that he couldn't hear her: he was inside his own head. His eyes were closed. He called Deluda his 'little darling', his 'naughty rabbit'. The scene ended with Dicer shouting and screaming as he reached his climax and falling inert across the unsatisfied body of Deluda, who slowly extracted her arm from beneath Dicer's weight and groped for the gin.

The audience tried another snigger, then seemed to find this inappropriate and went quiet. The purple light began to fade.

At Lev's side, the bouncing leg was at last at rest, the jewelled right hand spread calmly across the meaty thigh. Lev looked up and round at the packed theatre, heard in the near-darkness a rumbling far beneath him, as of an underground train accelerating out of a station. He reached out and stroked Sophie's arm. For a second, he found himself sweetly reassured that it was still warm to his touch. But then Sophie jerked away from him, as though the stroking hurt or offended her. 'What's the problem?' she hissed. 'Don't you understand the scene?'

Lev withdrew his hand. 'I understand,' he said, and turned back to staring at the dark space above him and listening to the train moving away and to the near-silence it left behind.

The next scene took place in an office boardroom of a company called PithCo. Dicer's boss, a smart, suit-clad woman called Loyala, was urging some promotion for Dicer on the board of slick young men. She referred to Dicer as 'a business brain *par excellence*, but also just the most regular guy you could ever wish to meet'. The board of young men looked bored. They sent Loyala out and began to discuss Dicer. But they were all preoccupied with other things. Their phones and their BlackBerrys kept ringing and bleeping. Two of them couldn't seem to remember Dicer's name. They referred to him as 'Dick'. But they were in a hurry, so they all pronounced themselves in favour of his promotion, except one, a man, a little older than the rest, named Clariton.

Everybody on the PithCo board turned to stare at Clariton. Clariton expressed what he called 'a personal doubt' about Dicer, but when pressed to say what this was, all he could come up with was that he had a 'feeling' about him. The mobiles chimed and

flashed and beeped. Clariton was told that feelings were 'unverifi-
able moments of consciousness and nothing more'. He had to give
in and let his doubts about Dicer be overruled. A vote was taken.
Dicer's promotion was agreed.

Dicer was then called in. When told of his promotion, he looked
relieved. Then he began a speech about how twenty-first-century
Britain was 'a mucky place, a place adrift on a tide of moral uncer-
tainty, a place that some us don't recognise any longer …' Then
he said that he, Dicer, and the company, PithCo, had to resist this
tide, make ethical decisions, behave with responsibility in a global
world …

At these words, while the heads of the board nodded their agreement, the bouncing and trembling of the leg next to Lev began
again. The jewelled hand bounced with it. *Jig, jig, jig, jig, jigger, jig,
jig, jig … Jig, jig, jig, jig, jigger, jig, jig, jig …*

Lev thought, I won't be able to bear this, I'll have to strap his leg
to the floor … And then what was going on in the scene slipped
away from him and he began to consider how this might be done,
how a leg might be immobilised in the darkness of a London
theatre, without anybody crying out, without causing undue pain,
just to end the torment to its neighbour …

When he focused again on the play, Deluda and Bunny were
dressed for a journey and had come to say goodbye to Dicer. Lev
had missed why they were leaving. Everybody appeared anguished.
He watched the gestures of the girl playing Bunny. She was playing the scene, once more, as though she were in some distant,
dreamlike sleep, all of her own.

She disappeared and Deluda disappeared. Now, Dicer was alone.
He sat at a computer. A big screen was lit behind him, on which
what Dicer was seeing on his computer monitor was replicated.
Dicer tapped and clicked. Images of naked children came and
went, seen for a flickering second, then gone. Dicer kept searching for something, clicking on boxes marked 'View Merchandise'.
And now, on the giant screen, appeared an inflatable doll, made
of rubber or latex, or some flesh-like substance: a young girl with
no breasts and an open, rosebud mouth and a little slit between
her legs. Dicer stared longingly at this girl doll. Lev could sense
the audience staring at it, too. And the leg stopped. *Jig, jig, jig, jig,
jigger, jigger. Rest.*

On the screen, a box marked 'Customise' appeared. Dicer clicked on this. Another box came up: 'Scan Photo'. At his desk, Dicer was now becoming excited, his breathing laboured. A photo of Bunny's face appeared in close-up. She looked younger than she'd seemed on stage. Her mouth was open. Dicer raised both his arms, as if to embrace his daughter's face. On the screen a box saying 'Confirm Customisation' came up and Dicer clicked an arrow on the box and began to shout, 'Customise!' He said it several times, with mounting passion: 'Customise! Customise! *Customise!*'

The audience had gone quiet. Lev looked at Sophie. Her face was calm and still. Lenny glittered on her arm. She seemed spellbound by all this 'customise' business.

Lev felt unbearably hot, suddenly, as if in the grip of some colossal embarrassment. He began to tug at the sleeve of his new suede jacket, to take it off. He was aware of being the only person in the auditorium not sitting obediently still, and the task of removing his jacket now seemed peculiarly difficult, as though he were trying to get himself out of a straitjacket. He tugged on the sleeve, pulled at the neck, tried to push away the lapels, felt his shoulder collide with the man with the bouncing leg, who flashed him a furious stare. But he had to get the jacket off or he was going to suffocate. He was going to faint. He longed for water on his brow, in his mouth, over his sweating body. He longed for a cold river, like the river that flowed down into Auror ...

'Lev!' he heard Sophie hiss. 'For fuck's sake ...'

The jacket was off now. At last. He felt cooler. Visions of the cold river faded in his mind. He looked up. What had he missed? Once again, he'd forgotten he was at a play. It had moved on and left him behind. But what did it matter? It was a disgusting play. It wasn't even a proper *play* when a giant screen had to be used. It was a kind of half-film, wasn't it? He looked away again, folded his jacket on his knee, glanced sideways at the leg. A tiny tremble, a shivery *jig-jig-jig*. Then stillness.

On the stage, Dicer was sitting at a candlelit dinner with Loyala. Loyala was talking fast and in a masterful kind of way, spouting words Lev couldn't recognise. He supposed this was meant to be business language or jargon or whatever people called it. It felt a bit like listening to Rudi talking about his 'belts' and his 'automatic drive', without bothering to explain what these things were, as though the whole world was meant to know without ever being told. Except Rudi knew in his heart that no one else was interested, that his love affair with the Tchevi was a lonely thing, but here it became clear that Loyala thought her corporate-speak was seductive. She thought Dicer was fascinated. She was making a pitch for Dicer and she was using these things as her weapon – her superior knowledge of certain facts and percentages, her understanding and manipulation of terms.

Lev looked at Dicer. From the actor's expression, it seemed as though he was trying to follow Loyala, trying to let her seduction of him work, and at the end of the meal – when silent waiters came and went, bringing and removing empty plates – he was holding her hand across the table.

Lev glanced down at his watch. Its tiny luminous hands told him that almost an hour had passed since the beginning of the play. But how long did plays last? Were they as long as ballets or concerts? Because this was all he knew of theatre: old American soaps on the TV; one performance of *Giselle* by the Glic Ballet Company; a few visits to Jor, where Marina's favourite folk singers, the Resurrectionists, often used to play.

Wearily, Lev looked up. The bed appeared once more. Bed and wardrobe and the purple light. As though the play were beginning all over again ...

Dicer came in alone. He sat down on the bed, exactly as he'd done in Scene One. He took off his clothes and left them in a pile and put on the veal-coloured silken robe.

The play *was* beginning again. Only without Deluda.

Lev closed his eyes. He tried to remember the words of Marina's favourite song by the Resurrectionists. Something about drinking vodka in the morning, sleeping in the sun, feeling lonesome for the moon: '*Oh, I'm so lonesome for the moon ...*'

Lev opened his eyes. Dicer was walking towards the wardrobe now, the wardrobe marked 'Hers'. He opened it, and there were coat-hangers and there were dresses and skirts. Dicer moved these along the clothes rail, then from underneath them he dragged out an inflatable doll-child, with the face of his daughter, Bunny. He held the inflatable Bunny in his arms. He arranged her legs wide apart, curving round his legs. He pulled her to him and stuck his tongue into her open mouth. Then, baring his arse in the face of the audience, he began to mime fucking.

The curtain fell. The lights in the auditorium came up.

Lev sat very still. The clapping all around him was loud and enthusiastic. It felt as though the play might be over. But, of course, it wasn't over. This was just the interval. Lev considered the word 'interval' and thought, Did someone once understand that, in some circumstances, the 'interval' had to become permanent, that what it temporarily ended couldn't be returned to?

Beside him, Sophie stood up. She touched Lev's arm. 'Bar,' she said. 'Howie ordered champagne. Come on.'

Obediently, Lev got to his feet. His body ached. He put on his jacket, whose newness was so pungent to him it was as though the suede was still part of the heifer, still grazing on pristine grass. Sophie pushed him on and they inched back towards the bar, where Lev could hear the sound of champagne corks popping.

Now, suddenly, he heard a burst of laughter behind him. 'Lev!' said Sophie. 'You've still got the price tag on your jacket!'

He felt her reach up and wrench away the label. That the people in the row behind him might have been staring at it all the way through the first bit of the play should have embarrassed him, he knew, but all he felt was the sweet absurdity of it and he began to laugh.

'It's not funny,' said Sophie. 'This is a press night. It just makes you – and me – look like panty-hose.'

'I think it's funny,' said Lev, loudly. 'I think it's more funny than a purple bed.'

'Ssh, Lev. Just keep moving. Keep moving forwards.'

'I think it's more funny than a man wanting to fuck his daughter.'

'OK,' said Sophie, pushing past Lev. 'There's Howie. Follow me if you want some champagne.'

'No,' said Lev. 'I don't want champagne. Why drink champagne? To celebrate why? To make a toast to this horrible play?'

'Shut up, Lev. Please ...'

'You know, even the names are ridiculous. I know English enough to know this. "Dicer". "Deluda". Why couldn't Portman think of better names?'

The people round Lev were turning to stare at him. Sophie

gripped his arm and tugged him towards the tall figure of Howie Preece, who was waving a champagne bottle above his head.

Preece, whose single diamond earring glittered in the pencil spotlights, said: 'Good girl. What a bun-fight. Have a dose of Bolly.'

Sophie took the glass of champagne and Howie Preece turned to pour another one. 'This is Lev,' said Sophie quietly.

Howie Preece kept pouring and didn't look up. When the second glass was full he offered it to Lev.

'No, thank you,' said Lev.

'Right. All the more for us. I'm Howie Preece.'

Lev nodded. He saw Howie Preece waiting for the *thing* to appear in his eyes – the *awe* or whatever he might have called it – the thing that people couldn't help but reveal in his presence. And when he didn't discover this awe in Lev's face, Preece, for a moment, appeared disconcerted. He shifted his expectant gaze to Sophie. 'That creature,' he said, 'on your arm. What's it meant to be?'

'Oh,' said Sophie, 'that's Lenny the lizard. He kisses me good-night.'

'Yeah? How does he kiss you?'

Sophie brought her arm to her face and let the sequined Lenny brush against her lips.

Howie's slug-white jowls dug themselves into a leer. 'Sexy girl, Sophie, in't she?' he said, as if to Lev, but still gazing at Sophie with large, sleepy eyes.

Lev saw her blush. He wanted to … oh, he couldn't say what he wanted to do, but the sight of her showing Lenny to Preece was bitter.

'So,' said Sophie, brightly, to Preece, 'what d'you think of the first half?'

'Well,' said Howie Preece, 'it's Portman. Portman's a genius. He's always right on the fuckin' button. Bet half the fuckers in Chelsea are screwing their kids senseless.'

'I think it's brilliant,' said Sophie.

Preece was about to speak again, but Lev snapped: 'Why?'

'What d'you mean, "why"?'

'Why you say this is brilliant, Sophie?'

'Because I think it is.'

'Why?'

'Because it *is*. Because it's radical and brave and—'

'It's shit,' said Lev.

'Well, there's a downer for Andy!' said Howie. 'The man from a distant country thinks *Peccadilloes* is a piece of—'

'I could kill this man!' said Lev.

'Excuse me?' said Preece.

'To see this: a father, a doll, his daughter … How can he show this?' Anger and misery swept through Lev like a rising tide of sickness. He jabbed a finger at Sophie – an authoritarian gesture he detested in other people – saw her try to recoil but be prevented by the crush in the bar. He knew he was becoming out of control, knew he should have tried to master his feelings, but why master feelings that, in this unreal world he'd just entered, felt real and true?

He jabbed at Sophie again. 'You!' he said. 'I understand you now. You don't see *anything*! You see what is "fashion", what is "smart". That's all that matters to you. Because you don't know the world. Only this small England. You know nothing, *nothing*.'

'Hey,' said Preece. 'That's a bit out of order, isn't it? What's the matter with you?'

Lev was trembling. His arms felt like wires, sparking with electric current. He felt their lethal power. 'The matter is I'm mad,' he said. 'Crazy, maybe. But I'm not sick, like this play. At home I have a daughter, Maya. I love this daughter—'

'Who cares?' said Preece. 'That's *so* not relevant. Who cares if you've got a daughter? This is *art*. This is cutting edge—'

'OK. Then I cut!' yelled Lev, passing a finger across his throat. 'I cut!'

'Listen, why don't you shut up?' said Preece. 'You're just being an arsehole.'

'Oh, yeh?' shouted Lev. '"Arsehole", like in the play. So funny, uhn? Well, this arsehole can cut! I cut the neck of Portman! I cut everybody! You want to see?'

Lev grabbed Sophie and locked her body to his with his arm round her neck. Her glass fell and broke. She began to choke and gasp. Preece reached down from his superior height and took hold of Lev by the chin. His huge hand squeezed and squeezed until Lev felt as though his jaw would be crushed to shards. 'Let her go,' said Preece. 'Let her fuckin' go or I'll break your fuckin' face!'

Lev stared at Preece, his white, glistening cheeks, his high forehead, his stubbled chin, his fleshy lips, the whole terrifying amalgam of him, and thought: He's my enemy now. He hated him almost as much as he'd once hated Procurator Rivas. He was aware of people round him, gaping, gasping, almost comic in their terror, but he cared nothing for them. In that moment, he knew that his love affair with Sophie was doomed.

'Let her go!' shouted Preece, again. But already Lev's arm had freed her. He waited for Preece's grip on his jaw to slacken, and when it did he hurled himself away from him and began to walk towards the steps and the foyer and the cold April night.

Not to think about it, not to *feel* inside him the finality of what had just happened, that was all he craved now. Nothing else. Nothing beyond or after or yet to come. None of that. Only the feeling of *not feeling*.

He was a stranger to this smart bit of London. But he didn't feel capable of walking far. He turned right out of the theatre and went into the adjacent pub-restaurant.

It was choked with people, waiting to be seated at tables, but Lev pushed past them. When he reached the bar, he lit a cigarette and ordered Guinness, then vodka ... ah ... his darling *vodichka* ... then more Guinness (he had the taste for it, now, just like Christy Slane) and more *vodichka*. Then he went to the cloakroom and pissed it all away and returned and began again with the Guinness. He sat in a shiny wooden chair and listened to his bones polishing its surface. He watched the moon faces of his fellow drinkers circling him in a slow, ponderous way, heard the diners chattering and braying behind him. He was a stopped river. He was mute, a puppet or doll. He was a forgotten song: *Oh, I'm so lonesome for the moon ...*

If people spoke to him, he didn't recognise the words. If there was music playing, who knew the melody? Not him. He knew nothing. His brain was as small as a pellet of bran. And as black, as dark as darkness could be anywhere.

He knew he was losing touch with where he was. This wasn't his fault. It was the fault of the world. Because nothing in the world stabilised for long. Nothing was the right way up for long. There was always something, some silently approaching event, such as the opening of a play, which, you knew ... you *knew* was going to turn everything on its head. Nothing could, or would, ever be the right way up. Or if it was, it wouldn't last. One moment you could be flying like a swallow. You could have the world spread out below you. Then it was gone. It was way above you, crushing you again, with all its effluent running into your ... yes, into your heart, until your heart was black and choked like a sluice.

Oh I'm so lonesome for the moon ...

He wanted more Guinness, more *vodichka*. He tried to tell the man behind the bar to keep the drinks coming, but now there was a problem: he was being asked for money. He searched his new jacket for his wallet. This pocket. That pocket. The bar-tender looked at him, square and ugly. This pocket. Another pocket. No wallet. Nothing there in the beautiful suede: only a cotton handkerchief, a comb for his thick hair, his mobile phone. There were two barmen staring at him now. He could hear their breathing. He thought: Everything multiplies. Sorrows. Accusers. Woe. And he held up his arms to the barmen, the gesture of an innocent man, a gesture that said: 'I have nothing. Everything's been taken from me. Do what you have to do.'

They were leaning right into his face and shouting at him. He could smell their brandied breath. And he wanted to be away from this, now, go out into the night air, breathe in the darkness. So he renewed his search for his wallet. Trouser pockets. Shirt pocket. Hip pocket.

There it was.

Its leather worn and curved and stained. Inside, his picture of Maya. His beloved daughter. Innocent, *innocent* child. He tugged out the photograph, tugged with trembling hands, and set it down on the bar top. And he looked at it and saw that it had faded. All the once-bright colours were vanishing, leaving only a trace of themselves, tinged with green, with the bluish green of the sky ... when evening was coming ... the sky behind Auror ...

Now the cold wind was blowing him along the pavements. Blowing everything north. Dust. Leaves. Garbage. Which? Who cared? Everything blew north in time. Everything came to its icy destination.

He knew he was lost.

His bladder ached. He clung to a tree and pissed onto the ground and his hand, holding his cock, was frozen. And he told himself, when parts of his body began to freeze like this, it was time to creep away somewhere, find shelter, somewhere unseen, and lie there till the earth turned and brought whatever it brought in the form of light ... whatever it was that would have to pass for morning.

Down. It was better to creep downwards, inwards, towards the centre of things, like a fox. So silent, so like an animal, that nobody would see or hear. Down and down. And here, in this city, this London, there was always, sooner or later, such a place, and then ... well ... there you could lie, with the traffic above, with the road bearing the weight of all that it had to bear, with steps ascending and descending ... And this was all that was asked of you ... that you lie there and be still.

Here they were, the steps, not the same ones as before, yet similar, found once again, ascending, descending, with iron railings above, as though the old spirits might have need of a hand-hold, to pass from one world into another ... the spirits no one cared about any more, the ones who used to flit round in the brains of the ageing men who sat on hard chairs in the lumber yard, blithering about this, yammering about that, full of hurt, used up by work ... the spirits of Stefan.

But these steps were not properly aligned to Lev's sight. He knew he was about to fall, but he couldn't let himself fall there, into that slippery void.

He lay down where he was, on the street.

15

Nine, Night-time

Somebody shouting at him. A smell so foul it might have been the stench of a cancer ward. But no memory of any ward, no memory of where he was or why these things were as they were ...

Lev opened his eyes. Far above was a man's face. Lev's gaze flickered downwards and he understood that the face was attached to a heavy, uniformed torso, and this torso to a black leather boot. Then the boot seemed to shuffle away and the face came nearer and was staring at him.

Next, a memory. Rudi's stricken look, once, remembering a violent arrest in the night: 'If you wake up with a man's face in yours, Lev, it's not a faggot dream, it's the fucking Militia.'

Now, an arm on his, helping him up. Bright light, hurting his skin. A voice very close to him, but not unkind: 'Right, sir. You OK now? You've been sick. Do you want me to call an ambulance?'

Lev looked down. He'd puked all over his suede jacket. But why was he here, in this harsh daylight, in this street he'd never seen before?

A woman's voice now, high and anxious. 'Can you get him away now? Please take him away.'

'He's going, love. He's on his way.'

Lev saw the woman now. She was standing on her front steps, regarding him with a look of terror. He was led towards a police car. Two police officers with him.

'Do you have a home to go to?' asked one of them.

Lev nodded. Slowly, agonisingly, it was creeping back into his memory: the hurtful play, his fury in the theatre bar ...

He began hitting his head. 'Sir,' said the second policeman, 'I wouldn't do that to yourself, if I were you. Suggest you go home now, right? Go along quietly, or we'll have to charge you with causing alarm and distress.'

Alarm and distress.

He understood the words.

He walked away. The street seemed to tilt under him, like a boat on a queasy sea. He had no idea where he was walking to. Which way was north? He knew he had to walk north, but how far? In this labyrinth of London, where was the haven of Belisha Road?

He had no idea. He was lost once more. He'd brought this dereliction on himself. He'd sworn, in England, to keep his temper under control, but he'd failed. Now, he was cast out.

He came level with a garbage bin, overflowing with the obscene bags of someone's leavings, and he thought: I've made my life obscene. He kicked out at the bin, wanted to see it fall, wanting to see everything spill out onto the pavement, but it didn't fall. He began swearing. He snatched the lid off the bin and hurled it into the road. Heard footsteps thundering towards him.

The policemen seized his arms. He felt the icy pain of handcuffs going on. Then hands searching his pockets and one of the voices again, loud in his ear: 'Right. You are now under arrest. We warned you. We suggested you went home without causing any more trouble, but you didn't listen, did you? So you are under arrest for an offence under Section 5 of the Public Order Act.'

In the police car now. Unfamiliar streets going by in the still-early morning. An ache in his skull. Shivering with cold and fear, yet finding it difficult to bear his suede jacket on him because he'd fouled it. Unable to take it off because of the handcuffs.

The voice of the law saying what the law required it to say. '... detained to enable the investigation of this offence. You do not have to say anything ... anything you say may be given in evidence. Do you understand?'

Lev shook his head. He had no idea what law he'd broken. He'd thought he was free and walking away and suddenly he wasn't free but handcuffed and pressed into the back of this car.

The two policemen were talking to each other now. Lev strained to hear, couldn't understand them, but knew that his fate was in the hands of the law and things might go better for him if he were contrite.

'I am sorry,' he said.

One of the heads turned. Lev saw the face close up, death pale after winter, scarred with old acne burns.

'You speak English, then?'

'Yes.'

'How much English?'

Lev stared out at the traffic and at the grey sky.

How much English?

Enough to understand a play. Enough to know that his girl with her strawberry curls was no longer his girl ...

'I speak good English,' he said carefully. And he heard something peculiar in his voice: a kind of inappropriate pride.

He was led into a police station, still clutching his fouled jacket. He saw flecks of vomit on his shoes. He tried to cradle his aching head.

He was told to wait on a plastic chair in a drab corridor. The door to the toilet was pointed out to him. Near him, three youths, two white and one black, also waited, glancing up at him from the depths of the hoods of their fleece jackets, giving him a stare of pure indifference, a stare that said: 'We're on our own chairs, motherfucker, with our own reasons for being here, locked away in our skulls, and we don't give a fucking toss about you or anyone else.' They were half Lev's age.

Lev got up and went to the toilet and pissed, then ran hot water and washed his hands. He turned on a cold tap, stuck his face underneath it and drank, prayed this was drinkable water and not tainted.

His suede jacket hung over the edge of a washbasin. Lev looked at it, all £170 of it. He emptied the pockets of everything they contained, which turned out to be nothing at all except a comb. Then he rolled up the stinking jacket and put it into the plastic waste-bin, knowing that, even if it could be cleaned, he'd never wear it again. Never.

Lev returned to the corridor, where the youths still lounged, airing their groins. He turned away from them and counted four fire extinguishers, bolted to the grey wall. A digital wall clock told him that the time was 9.47 a.m. Six hours before he had to go to work at *GK Ashe*. Six hours before he had to see Sophie again …

A door opened and a fair-haired constable beckoned Lev forward. He got up and was shown into a room with no window, furnished only with a table, two chairs and a radiator that gave out heat of a disproportionate intensity, as though it were filled with burning sulphur.

The constable set up a laptop computer on the table and, without glancing at Lev, without acknowledging by a single gesture that there was another person in the room, began to punch in codes or numbers. Lev waited. He noticed that the only object on the table, aside from the constable's laptop, was a box of Kleenex tissues.

'OK,' said the constable, looking up from the laptop at last. 'You speak English, I gather?'

'Yes.'

Lev was asked to give his name, age, country of origin and address in the UK. While the constable typed these in, a robust-looking black woman in a green overall came into the room and put down a cup of tea in front of Lev. He thanked her. On the saucer were four sugar lumps and Lev put all of these into the tea, stirred it and began to drink. As he drank, the woman, pausing at the open door, winked a seductive brown eye in his direction. Then the door closed.

'Date of entry into the UK?' asked the constable.

Lev thought that this should have been engraved on his memory, but the date felt so long ago, it had gone from his mind.

'July last year,' he said. 'I can't remember which day.'

The constable's hands caressed the small black keyboard. 'What means of support do you have in the UK?'

Lev began to feel the blessed, sugary tea enter his bloodstream.

'I work at *GK Ashe*,' he said.

'*Cheeky Ash?* What's that?'

'The restaurant,' said Lev. '*GK Ashe*. You don't know this?'

The constable didn't reply or move a muscle of his face. He disregarded the question and just went on typing, with diligent care, as though the computer were the vulnerable living thing and Lev the inanimate piece of technology.

'What's your wage at Cheeky Ash?'

'Not Cheeky. Letters: GK.'

'I didn't ask for comments, sir. Please tell me your weekly wage or your hourly wage.'

'£7 an hour. £280 a week after tax. I send money home to my family.'

More typing. More communing with the clean, obedient little machine. Then the constable looked up at Lev, face to face. His pale eyes held Lev in a steady, unfrightened gaze. 'Right. So, you understand that you are being issued with a PND: a penalty notice for disorder.'

'I told the policemen in the car I was sorry.'

'Yes? Well, I'm sure they were glad to hear that. Now, a PND carries with it a fixed fine of £80, which must be paid now. Are you with me, sir?'

Lev was silent. He wished there was a window to look out of, a view of the sky, or birds coming down to settle on a tall roof. His mind made a terrifying addition: £170 for the suede jacket; £42 for his unnecessary shirt; now an £80 fine. A total of £292 *wasted*.

'Are you listening? Did you hear my question?'

'Yes,' said Lev.

'Then answer it, please. Do you understand the charge and the fine accruing?'

'Yes.'

'So how are you going to pay?'

Now a terrible image swam into Lev's mind: his wallet on the bar counter, and near it, among the beer slops, his precious picture of Maya ... He began to search the pockets of his trousers. Side pockets. Right. Left. Hip pocket. Side pockets again. Right. Left ...

'I'm waiting, Olev. Just tell me how you wish to pay. Cash or credit card?'

Nothing in any pocket. Only a few coins, some crumbs of tobacco and an old packet of Rizla papers.

Lev put his head in his hands. No money. No picture of Maya. No credit card. No phone. He felt a sob welling up in his chest, pressed his palms into his eyes.

No Sophie.

He let the sob break. It reminded him of a wolf-cry.

'I don't know how to pay,' he stammered.

'Cash or credit card.'

'I have nothing. My wallet is gone.'

The constable waited, staring at Lev's distress, as though it might have been a TV programme that bored him. He pushed the box of Kleenex towards Lev and sighed and said: 'If the accused is unable to settle the fine, we suggest recourse to a third party.'

'Sorry?' said Lev.

'We call it "phoning a friend".'

'Sorry?'

'*Who Wants to be a Millionaire?*, on TV. Don't you watch it?'

'No. I work in the evenings.'

'Never mind. Want to phone a friend, d'you?'

Lev blew his nose. The bitter dregs of his sickness seemed to be lodged there. He wanted to throw the tissue away, but there was nowhere to throw it. He saw the constable pick up a clear plastic envelope and take a mobile phone out of it. He set the phone down in front of Lev. By its turquoise casing, Lev recognised it as his.

'Or don't you have any friends in England?' said the constable.

Lev stared at the phone. Then he picked it up and held it tenderly in his hand. 'I have friends,' he said.

'Right. Suggest you call right away.'

Lev drank the last of the tea. He punched in Christy's number at Belisha Road. He heard the voicemail click in:

> *Hello there. You're through to Christy Slane. Try not to hang up before you've left a message or, if it's urgent plumbing work you're after, call me on me mobile, 07851 6022258. Be back to you shortly.*

'Christy,' said Lev. 'It's Lev. Got a bad problem. I try your mobile.'

But Christy wasn't picking up his mobile, either. Lev figured that he was probably still asleep, or else already gone out on one of his infrequent jobs. He left another message.

'No luck?' said the constable.

'He will call back.'

'What? In five hours' time? OK. Up to you, if you want to spend them here. I don't know what time you have to be at work, but if it were me, I'd try another number.'

Lev was sweating now in the tropical heat of the room. He wiped his forehead. For a moment or two, the temptation to call Sophie visited him with a sudden stifling of his breath. But the knowledge that she'd probably refuse to help him made him lay this temptation aside. Sophie was with Howie Preece, anyway. Lev was sure she was. The whole *Peccadilloes* evening had been leading her there. She'd be lying next to his big, ugly head. His huge hand would be kneading her breast in his sleep …

'Come on,' said the constable, 'stop day-dreaming. I'm beginning to be tired of you, Olev. Make another call.'

Lev was back on the plastic chair in the corridor when he saw her arrive: his habitual saviour, the plain woman whom two pampered English kids mocked with the cruel nickname 'Muesli'. Here she came again, wearing a new beige coat, with her hair stylishly short, but on her face the familiar, persecuted look, the look that said: All right. I forgive you one more time, Lev. But soon, very soon, you will have tested me too far …

She sat down beside him.

Aware of his ghostly appearance, of the smell of puke still on him, he hung his head, said: 'I'm so sorry, Lydia. I'm sorry to have asked you to do this. I'll pay you back, I promise.'

'Well,' said Lydia, with a sniff, 'I don't know when you're going to pay me back. I leave for Vienna tomorrow. You were very lucky to find me still here.'

He looked at her profile, held aloof from him, then at her feet, neatly arranged side by side in their black court shoes. Tenderness towards her suddenly choked him. Only the thought that she'd soon be embarked on her new life with Pyotor Greszler and gone from his altogether prevented him breaking down into tears of shame at his own repeated and unsavoury betrayals of her loyalty.

'I'm sorry,' he said again. 'All I do is cause you grief. I know. If only I hadn't lost my wallet …'

'It's all right, Lev. Now, where do I pay the £80? I have a lot to do today, all my packing, then I'm going over to see Tom and Larissa to say goodbye. So …'

'Did you bring cash, Lydia?'

'Yes. I'm not an idiot, you know. Now, where do I pay?'

*

They walked out into the rain.

The Chelsea streets were unfamiliar to them both. Lev, shivering again, clung to Lydia's arm, holding a flimsy umbrella. He walked without seeing, hoping vaguely that she knew where they were going, but she soon stopped and declared herself lost. She looked all around her, at the street of smart, white-painted houses, at wrought-iron balconies ornamented with topiary.

'Pelham Crescent,' she said. 'I don't recall it.'

To be warm again. To be clean. To eat something bland and sweet. To sleep for a while. These longings preoccupied Lev's mind to the exclusion of all other thought. He saw Lydia staring at him and perhaps she understood this, because she let go of the umbrella and ran towards a woman emerging from a Range Rover outside one of the fine front doors with its sentinel bay trees, and Lev heard her say: 'Excuse me. Can you help me? Where is the Tube, please? My friend is ill.'

Lydia came back to Lev and led him forwards like a child, found an Italian café near South Kensington Underground station and sat him down on a wooden chair. She took off her beige coat and put it round his shoulders and he felt the warmth of her body, still, in the silky coat lining. He heard her order coffee and pastries.

'Lev,' she said, after a while, when he'd gobbled the first pastry and was warming his hands on the foaming coffee mug, 'Lev, there's only one thing that worries me.'

He looked up at her: about-to-be-mistress of the famous Maestro Greszler, her days of knitting jumpers, subsisting on eggs, behind her. Without her, he'd still be sitting on a plastic chair in the police station. Without her, he might still be delivering kebab leaflets for Ahmed, sleeping in Kowalski's yard ...

'Are you listening to me?' she said.

'Yes.'

'Whatever has happened – and I'm not going to make you explain it to me because I can feel that you don't want to – whatever has happened, you have to stick with your job at *GK Ashe*. That is what most concerns me. That you'll give up this job. And then I think you would be lost. So promise me you won't?'

Lev nodded. Then he said quietly: 'I've been watching the chefs. Making notes. I'm going to collect all the recipes in a notebook.'

'That's very good. Very good. But you must stay in *this* restaurant, where GK helps you learn. In other places they might treat you like shit and you'd learn nothing. You must keep going on this track.'

Lev was silent now. He wanted to tell Lydia how hard this was going to be, working with Sophie, seeing her day after day, catching the scent of her in the humid kitchen air, obeying her chef's orders, watching her put on her football scarf to go home to Howie Preece's bed ...

'Lev? You hear what I'm saying?'

'Yes.'

'When I'm in Vienna or Salzburg, I'm going to call you up and ask you what the chefs made today at *GK Ashe* and I hope you're going to be able to answer.'

'I will.'

'Promise me?'

'Yes. I promise.'

'All right. Well, I'm going to go now. You're near the Tube. You remember? Just turn left out of here. Here's change for the train.'

Lydia stood up. She put three £1 coins down on the table. Gently, she took her coat from round Lev's shoulders. Lev reached up, drew her face down towards his and kissed her cheek, putting his lips softly among the moles.

'Lydia,' he said, 'you've been my good friend. I hope you're going to be happy now. I hope you're going to have the best life ...'

'Well,' she said, 'at least I won't be "Muesli" any more. I shall have a little dignity. Not too much, so that it goes to my head. Just enough, so that I can hold my head up.'

'I know Pyotor Greszler will be good to you.'

'Of course he will. Well, goodbye, Lev. I'll send postcards. Send you pictures of Paris and New York.'

'Goodbye, Lydia.'

Lev watched as she walked away from the table, heard her footsteps, neat and regular as ever, *click-clack, click-clack, click-clack*, till she was out of the door and gone.

It was after one o'clock when Lev climbed the stairs to the flat in Belisha Road. He called out to Christy, but there was no sign of him. Lev ran a bath and lay in it till it almost went cold. He fell in and out of an exhausted sleep. Then he dragged himself to his room, drew the curtains, got into bed and closed his eyes.

He dreamed about Marina. He was back in the bad time of Marina's supposed affair with Procurator Rivas. He was fly-fishing, with Rudi, on the river above Auror, on a summer evening, and they could see clusters of gnats, lit by the sinking sun, hovering above the water, and Rudi said: 'They only live one day. I read that in a nature magazine. Imagine. They get to late afternoon, like now, and they start panicking and saying: "Where did the day fucking *go*?"'

They fell into their old, familiar laughter. They were pulling grayling out of the river, happy as herons, and then they saw a figure on the opposite bank, poaching on their fishing beat. It was Procurator Rivas.

'Fuck him,' said Rudi. 'Why doesn't he stay behind his desk? I don't want to see his legs. I thought all those Public Works people ended at the waist.'

'He's on our stretch,' said Lev. 'Tell him to move downriver.'

He stared at Rivas. He wore a cumbersome coat, a kind of padded oilskin, and this made his movements awkward.

'Look at him,' said Rudi. 'Look at his pathetic casting. Where's he ever fished before? In the public drinking fountain?'

Their laughter pealed out across the water and Rivas raised his head and Lev saw on his face an expression of pure spite. So they stopped laughing and Lev said: 'Let's go further upriver.'

They wound in their lines, began to load up their fishing gear and their bag of grayling, and then they saw that Procurator Rivas had hooked a fish and was trying to land it. His rod was bent in a frightening arc, as though it would snap at any minute, and he was breathing hard, struggling to wind in the fish, which pulled him further and further towards the water. He waded in up to his groin. His face was sweating. Then he let go of the rod and reached down into the river and lifted out the head and shoulders of Marina.

Marina was naked and her body was grey and slippery, like the bodies of the grayling. Her hair trailed on the shimmering surface of the water. Procurator Rivas tried to gather the slippery, grey-blue body to him, so that Marina's head rested on his shoulder and her breasts sank against his barrel chest in the oilskin coat. He kissed her forehead, called her name: 'Marina. Marina.' But she was a dead weight in his arms.

'That's ridiculous,' said Rudi. 'Why can't he see she's been dead a long time? What an idiot. Why can't he fucking *see* it?'

Lev woke and it was dark in the room. A voice was saying his name. With the nightmare still filling his mind, he turned his head and saw Christy bending over him.

'Lev,' he said. 'I just got in, fella. Didn't you oughta be at work?'

Lev hurled himself up in the bed, slamming his head against the bottom of the upper bunk. 'What time is it? What time is it?'

'Well,' said Christy, 'it's after nine.'

Nine? How could it be nine? How in the world could it be nine o'clock?

'Nine, night-time?'

'Yes. Or perhaps you got the night off, did yer?'

Lev switched on his light, rubbed his head. 'Oh, God …' he said. 'Did GK call?'

'Haven't checked the voicemail yet. Shall I do that now?'

Christy went to the living room. Lev grabbed his mobile and stared at the screen. No indication of a missed call. He dialled 901 and was told he had one saved message. Before he could switch this off, he heard Sophie's voice – from weeks ago – saying: '*Hi, sexy. Hope you can still move. Are all the guys in your country as wicked as you?*'

Lev deleted the message, slammed down his phone, began to tug on clean clothes.

Nine o'clock.

He was *five hours* late! The service would be coming up to full pitch. But everything would be slow, fatally slow, because the chefs would have had to do their own veg prep and GK would be going crazy …

'No messages,' said Christy, at the door. 'Only one from you, saying you had a problem, like. What was the—'

'No time, Christy. Tell you later. Lost my wallet. Can you lend me some bus money?'

'Sure,' said Christy, rummaging in his trouser pocket. 'Full of cash, I am. Went out to Palmers bloody Green to fix a boiler.

Took me all day, but it was worth it. Indian woman. Wearing a sari with all the trimmings. Disconcertingly beautiful, I found it. And she smelled delicious – sort of like bread sauce, you know? Her boiler should have been junked in about 1991, but I got it going. Jasmina, her name was. *Jas-meena.* She was so grateful she hung money on me, like on a bride.'

'Good, Christy. Good.'

'*Jas-meena.* Now I can get that Spiderwoman outfit Frankie wants.'

Lev arrived at *GK Ashe* at ten minutes to ten.

He entered the kitchen, tugging on his whites. GK whirled round and stared at him. Held high in his hand was an egg-whisk, which began to drop cloudlets of beaten egg-white onto the floor.

'Chef ...' stammered Lev, '... I'm so sorry. I fell asleep. Please forgive me. Will never happen again ...'

Lev saw GK look towards Sophie, who was engaged in some elaborate flambé. She didn't glance at Lev, or at GK.

'So what's fucking going on?' said GK.

'My fault, Chef,' said Lev. 'I promise you, will never happen ...'

GK looked at his watch. More blobs of egg-white dripped from the whisk. Then he said: 'It's nearly ten o'clock. Do you imagine we've sat around waiting for *six hours* for you to de-pith a marrow? You can take those whites off. And go home, as far as I'm concerned. We've done your work for you.'

Lev looked helplessly around. Sophie now had her back to him, ostentatiously turned, the familiar sweet curve of her, with her arms moist in the kitchen heat.

'You didn't call me, Chef. Why you or Damian didn't call?'

'I'm not a fucking alarm-service! I expect my staff to get to work without needing to be *woken up.* Now go home.'

'No, Chef ... I help Vitas with the wash—'

'Vitas? He's history. Gone to pick cabbages in East Anglia. Got a new nurse from Bongoland or somewhere. Hey, Nurse, where did you say you were from?'

'Niger, Chef.'

'That's it. Pronounced *Nee-shair.* Unused to so much water. Rains unreliable there. But he's doing OK. So leave him be, Lev. Just get in here tomorrow at three thirty and see me, right?'

'Please, Chef. Let me do some work.'

'No. I told you. We *did* your work. You're superfluous. Go home.'

GK turned back to his egg-whisking. Lev stared at Sophie, paralysed. She was now plating up her flambéed duck breasts, head bent low over her task. By each duck breast lay a julienne of carrots and courgettes. He watched her spoon juniper berries from the flambé pan and arrange them on the golden skin of the duck. She lifted the plates onto the hot counter. 'Table four!' she called, and turned away.

Lev took off his whites and hung them up. He saw the boy from Niger turn and stare at him. He walked out of the kitchen and stood by Damian's bar, from where he could see into the restaurant. It was the usual Monday 'clientele lite', but at the far end, among a group of six or seven, with Damian fussing over them, he saw what he had expected to find: the big, gloating face of Howie Preece.

16

Exeunt All but Hamlet

'If people do lovely work and get paid a royal ransom for it, I'm fine with that,' said Christy Slane, 'but look at this. Reminds me of the stuff they used to make with milk-bottle tops on Blue Peter.'

Christy pushed a copy of a weekend colour magazine across the table where they sat, drinking tea. It was late.

Up Belisha Road came the sound of a posse of drunk youths kicking their way homewards round the rowan trees and through the litter. Lev read the headline: *Preece Wraps It Up*. Underneath there was a photograph of a curved white panel into which had been inserted hundreds of lightbulbs. Lev stared at it. Then his eye moved down to the caption:

> Bubblewrap *by Howie Preece, one of six new works on show at the Van de Merwe gallery. Preece employed two studio assistants to assemble this complex, symmetrical construction out of epoxy resin and 60-watt bulbs.*
>
> *'Its fluid shape,' comments Nicholas van de Merwe, 'suggests a cunning absence of rigidity. Preece's explorations of the way one object, by mimetic appropriation, gives new meaning to another confirm him as one of the most interesting artists working in Britain today.'*

'See what I mean?' said Christy. 'Frankie could've made that. Feckin' lightbulbs!'

'Preece didn't even make it,' said Lev. 'Studio assistants made it.'

'Well. And that gets on a man's tits, doesn't it? Won't get his fingernails dirty. Won't put in the hours.'

Lev turned the page of the magazine, saw a photograph of another work by Howie Preece, entitled *Wimbledon*. At first glance, it looked like a square of bright green turf, striped by the heavy roller of the lawnmower. He read the caption.

> *Arduous hours went into the making of* Wimbledon, *assembled with more than eleven thousand one-inch nails. Preece comments: Nails present as a powerful signifier for the lawn tennis championships. What you have here is lethal grass.*

Lethal grass. Lev ran his fingers over the photograph. Had to admit there was an illusion of softness in it, even a kind of silky shine, such as a lawn wears after a night of dew. He turned the magazine round and showed it to Christy. 'This one is better,' he said, 'maybe quite clever ...'

Christy glanced at *Wimbledon* as he sipped his tea, and a drip from his cup fell onto the picture. He blotted it with his thin, scabbed hand. 'What's with Preece and Wimbledon?' he said. 'He used tennis balls to make that DNA piece of shite. My guess is the man can't master his top-spin.'

With the tea, Lev and Christy were eating chocolate digestive biscuits. They took one biscuit after another till the plate was empty. Then they stared at the plate. 'I think that's it,' said Christy. 'I think we finished the packet. Got it from me ma, love of those. She used to be munching chocolate digestives in the dead of night. Said to me, "Life's taken away me appetite, Christy, so it has. But somehow, I can still swallow those."'

'Yes? They're nice and soft, that's why.'

'Comforting, they are, I suppose. Crumble to mush in yer mouth. But there was always mice in that house, scuttling round after the cookie crumbs. And she wouldn't set traps. Said there was too much cruelty in the world without her adding to it. Alley cats used to creep in the back door, sniffin' the vermin, but me ma would shoo them away. It was how she was.'

'When did she die, Christy?'

'Long ago. She wasn't even fifty. Just ate her biscuits and closed her eyes ...'

Though Lev was tired, he didn't want to move from the table. To lie in his bunk and be haunted by all that had happened in the last twenty-four hours: the mere thought of this made him feel empty, lost. 'Tell me more about your ma,' he said.

Christy rubbed his eyes. 'Well,' he said, 'what can I tell you? She was the daughter of a pig-man in County Limerick. Know where that is?'

'No.'

'In the south-west of Ireland. Beautiful as anywhere on earth, but poor as ninepence. A drunk, he was, me granddad. Champion pisser. "Pig-man" in more ways than one. Used the strap on all his children. Makes me sick to think of it. And she was a beauty, my mother. Ella Slane. Wouldn't believe it, to look at me, would you? But she was. Eyes the colour of scabious flowers. Know what those are?'

'No.'

'Wild things, like blue daisies, growin' about the meadows. Elizabeth Taylor had eyes that colour. Swear I can remember sitting on her knee – me ma's, I mean, not Elizabeth Taylor's – staring up at those scabious eyes. But what's life going to be like if you can't get away from all those poor places?'

Lev nodded, his thoughts wandering to Auror, to its low houses, its yards full of scratching animals, its pot-holed roads.

'She did get away, though,' Christy went on. 'She married Jimmy Slane, me pa, who worked for the postal service. Step up from the pigs, that was indeed. He had a uniform and the promise of a pension.'

'They went to Dublin?'

'Yes. They got out of Limerick. Used to ask me ma if she missed it, that green countryside, but she always said, no, it wasn't green in her mind, it was black.'

'It was black?'

'I think it was the darkness of night she must have been thinkin' about. Or the peat bogs in winter. Or God knows what other ugly business. The thing with your parents is, they keep coming out with stuff you can't make head nor tail of, and then they die and you're left with a lifetime of wondering.'

'Yes,' said Lev, 'or, like my father, they say stupid words. And you think, How could he believe that? I have arguments with him in my mind. Still I have them.'

'Do you? Well, I don't argue with Ella Slane, bless her. I just remember her scabious-blue eyes and think, What a waste ...'

'What happened in Dublin?'

'Well, they scrimped a house from offa the council list, where I grew up. Small place with no heating. That's where the mice always frolicked about. Ella worked in a laundry. Told me her hair had once been straight, but, gradually, it went curly, in all that laundry steam. And, gradually, another thing started happening: me pa started drinking. He lost his job as a postie and then everything began going down the long slide, includin' trying to rearrange his son's face every now and then. I know it's not an oil painting. It's a face that could do with some readjustment, you might say. But that killed Ella. I swear it was that. To see that start happening all over again ...'

'Yes?'

'But it's in the family, see? The drink is in the family on both sides, and that means it's in me blood. It's why I'm so prone. But in all honest-to-God truth, I never once laid a hand on Frankie.'

Christy got up and went to the window and looked out on the sodium darkness of Belisha Road. He lit a cigarette. After a few moments, he turned round and said: 'You know something, Lev?'

'Yes?'

'Well. This was a bad day for you. Shite twenty-four hours. And I'm sorry for it all. But for me it was pretty good. I mean, I have to say it was exceptional, really. When I got that boiler going for Jasmina – and it was a wreck a of heatin' system – I had this sudden feeling of ... *euphoria*. Know what I mean? Complete fuckin' eejit joy! And I thought, Jesus, Christy Slane, maybe after all you can quit the booze and get back to work. I thought that for the first time in months. Because, you know, I *like* that plumbing work. I've never not liked it. I can get a hard-on looking at a nice run of compression fittings. I'm not jokin'.'

'That's good, Christy. Very good.'

'Yes, it's good. Suddenly I want to get back on me feet. I do. I think you've taught me a thing or two about starting over. I know I've got it in me – somewhere – to do it.'

'You have ...'

'You know what she said to me, Jasmina, she said: "You've saved my life, Mr Slane!" That's when I got that euphoria thingummy.'

*

GK Ashe was waiting in the kitchen for Lev when he arrived at the restaurant at 3.30. Waldo was there, making puddings, and the air was scented with lemon and chocolate, but Waldo didn't look up when Lev came in and there was a dead quietness in the place.

GK, who had been leaning against the vegetable chiller, was wearing a black T-shirt, cream chinos and cream-and-red suede sneakers. His arms were folded across his chest. His hair, untamed by the chef's hat, looked wild and boyish, but his face was solemn.

'OK, Lev,' he said. 'Let's go through into the restaurant and sit down.'

It was almost dark in there, with the window blinds pulled down on a grey afternoon. They sat where the chefs always sat, at the big table at the back, near the bar. Lev began to reach for a cigarette and GK said: 'Sure. Smoke if you want to.'

'No. It's OK, Chef.'

'No, go on. Here's an ashtray. But it's killing you, I expect you know that?'

Lev fumbled with his Rizla paper. His hands shook. He said: '*This* kill me, that I was late yesterday, Chef. Well, more than late. But I can explain—'

'Listen,' said GK, cutting him off, 'I have some respect for you. In fact, I have a lot of respect for the way you've worked here. You've worked well and I think you could go on in this industry, because you're not afraid to get in the hours and you're as nosy as a ferret; you *watch* how things get done. And there's no substitute for that; it's how people get on in this circus. But I've got to get straight to the bottom line, Lev. I'm letting you go.'

Lev looked up. Had he heard correctly? Had he understood? Did 'letting go' mean what he dreaded it meant?

'I'm sorry about it,' GK went on. 'No bullshit. I really am. As I say, I have no complaint about your work.'

'For yesterday, Chef ... I can explain ... please ...'

'Don't make it hard for me. I'm not changing my mind.'

'I had a bad experience, I lost my wallet, I was ill—'

'It's not only about yesterday, Lev. It's about *mess*.'

'Please, Chef?'

'I can't run this kitchen if there's *mess* around me. I can't have *muckiness* of any kind. This is a small space – like a ship. And I have to keep it ship-shape, or it'll fall apart. And you and Sophie – that messes it up big-time. You see? I have to put the business first.'

Lev was silent. The cigarette he'd managed to roll was droopy and thin, almost not worth lighting. Yet he lit it now, with his shaking hand, pulled hard on it for the comfort of the nicotine.

'I'd already got a sniff of what was happening,' GK went on. 'I felt the vibes. But now I've got it story-boarded, right? Frame by frame. I made Sophie tell me the whole thing, including what's happened with Preece. And to keep the two of you in this kitchen with all this *mess* going on is professional catastrophe. It's the most damaging stuff I could envisage. So I'm sorry, Lev. I know it's tough on you. I've got no choice.'

Lev looked up at GK. Emboldened by something in the man's face, an expression almost sorrowful, Lev said quietly: 'Chef, this was my *best* job in my life. Truly, I am happy in this kitchen. More happy than I can tell you. Especially now I am doing veg prep. Always, I try to keep ahead of the orders, have everything ready for the chefs …'

'I know,' said GK. 'It actually cuts me up to get rid of a good man, if that's any comfort to you. But what can I do? I can't have emotional stuff going on in my kitchen. I'm not running an agony column. You've got to understand this, Lev, and just accept it and move on.'

Move on.

Lev looked past the bar into the kitchen, where Waldo was rolling out pastry. Beyond Waldo, he could see his old station, the two-point-five metres of steel draining top. A feeling of protective love, as fierce as any he'd ever felt for a particular place, choked him. If the cabinets and the hotplates, the burners and the salamanders, the ovens and the fridges, the plate racks and the sinks, the dishwashers and the steel hooks and the tea towels had all belonged to him, he couldn't have felt more sorrowful to part from them. To his embarrassment, tears welled in his eyes.

'Listen,' said GK, 'I'm going to be generous. I'm not known for my generosity, but I feel you've earned it. I've put together a package for you.'

'Oh, please, Chef, give me one more chance.'

'It's *over*, Lev. I'm sorry, but that's it. The decision's made. Now listen, right? I'm giving you a week's wages and a bonus of £100. Total of £380. I think that's pretty magnanimous. And I've done you a written reference. Here.'

GK took a piece of paper out of his pocket and handed it to Lev. Lev stared at it, tears blinding him to what it said. He saw the signature, GK Ashe, at the bottom of the page and knew, at the edge of his understanding, that he was being given something of value. But at this moment all was desolation.

As calmly as he could, trying to choke back the sorrow, Lev said: 'Chef, *please*, if you could only change your mind and give me one chance, I promise ... I swear on my life, I will not be any different from how I was. I will do my work as best as I can do. If you want, I shall not talk to Sophie. We can be like strangers. If you will only let me work ...'

GK shook his head. Ran a hand through his wild hair. 'Can't be done, Lev,' he said. 'It's you or Sophie. And I'm not being pushed into letting Sophie go. She's too well-connected.'

Lev stared helplessly. His thin cigarette dropped a sliver of grey ash onto the white tablecloth. He felt icy cold, as though he were being thrown into the sea.

GK waited. Lev wiped his eyes. From the pocket of his cream chinos, GK took out a bulky envelope and handed it to Lev. 'Here's the money,' he said. 'You know what the margins are like in this business, so I think you'll agree it's more than fair.'

Then he stood up. He held out his hand to Lev and Lev forced himself to take it.

'Good luck,' said GK. 'Use your ferret eyes. Stay tuned.'

Lev sat on the rough grass of Parliament Hill and stared up at the kites, like mattresses, buzzing, swooping in the luminous green evening sky. Now and again his eyes flicked downwards to the kite-flyers, so intent on the task of keeping these wild things aloft. Mostly they were men, with small children running and bouncing near them, and Lev thought, This is what men love to do, snatch the toys from the kids, to become children themselves, to *experience* it again, that time when the world moves slowly, when love can be given to a dancing object in the sky ...

He smoked and did arithmetic in his head. Felt the air cool

and darken round him. It was still only April. The kite-flyers went home. The tall trees in the far stand looked black against the declining sun. He could hear birds still singing in the last light.

Of the £380 GK had given him, he owed £90 to Christy for rent, or £180, if he included next week. He was already a week behind with money to Ina, which meant he had to send at least £40 to her.

If he paid Christy the full amount and sent only £30 to Ina, this would leave him with £170, to last him for the whole, uncertain stretch of the future. £160, if he sent Ina £40. Then there was the question of his debt to Lydia. He knew he'd despise himself if he didn't make some effort to start paying this off. But how much could he spare? Could he risk sending Lydia £50 and leave himself with just £110?

These sums were simple, but Lev's mind kept redoing them, altering them here and there each time, to get more favourable answers. He knew, for instance, that Christy would accept £90, leaving him with £270, if he sent Ina £40 and 'forgot' about paying anything to Lydia until he'd found another job. If he sent Ina nothing, this £270 rose to £310, which sounded much more reassuring. But no ... there was a mistake somewhere. The very least he could pay Christy was £90 and £90 from £380 was £290.

He was £20 out ...

A familiar sound woke him out of the ache of his money reverie: his mobile ringing. He took it out of his pocket and stared at the tiny lit screen, now the only light in the near-darkness of his part of the Heath. He half hoped to see Sophie's name there, but knew this hope was vain. The caller was Vitas.

'Vitas,' said Lev. 'How are you doing?'

'I'm good,' said Vitas's distant-sounding, reedy voice. 'I'm in Suffolk. We're picking salad. Then, in a couple of weeks, we move on to asparagus. It's nice here, Lev. Got a caravan, rent-free, sharing with Jacek, my friend from Glic.'

'OK. I'm glad. I'm glad it's working out ...'

'We're a small team, mostly from our country. But there are a couple of Chinese boys, too. Illegals, but no one cares. Sonny and Jimmy Ming.'

'Sonny and Jimmy Ming?'

'That's what we call them. They probably have proper Chinese names, but no one bothers saying them. Their English is hilarious. Keeps us all entertained. And our boss, Midge, isn't a bad guy. Fat as a hog, but far nicer to us than that GK shit-head. So, how is the bastard?'

Lev was silent. He was getting cold now. He could hear the trees sighing. He stood up and began to walk across the grass towards Highgate Hill.

'Lev? You there?'

'Yes. Lost reception for a moment. What did you say?'

'I asked how GK was.'

'Well, Vitas ... I'm not there any more. GK had to let me go.'

'Let you go? *Sacked* you?'

'Yes.'

'Why? You worked like a fucking slave in that place. You did five people's jobs.'

'I know. GK had his reasons. Too long to explain to you. I guess I'll start looking for another job tomorrow.'

'Shit. You don't deserve that. You were ... you were ... *kind* to me. What a sadist. I hate him. What're you going to do?'

'Dunno. Stay in the catering trade, if I can.'

'Why do that? It's just a hierarchical nightmare. It's like the time of landlords and serfs at home. Why don't you get on a train and come down here? I'll talk to Midge. There's space in the Mings' caravan. And we're in the open air. It's green countryside. And there's a farm dog called Whisky. He's a mutt, but he's nice. He comes out with us sometimes and just follows along behind the rig.'

'How much are you paid, Vitas?'

'Minimum wage. But, like I said, no rent. And we buy our food cheap at the Co-op. And Midge gives us free potatoes.'

'Free potatoes? That's good.'

'Yeah. Better than stinking London, I'm telling you. You should come.'

'OK, I'll think about it.'

Lev walked slowly home, past the deserted tennis courts and the beds of roses, all weeded and tidy for the day when their petals opened. Found he was making a picture in his mind of Vitas's life, living in the middle of a field, frying potatoes on a single-burner stove, staring down lines of lettuces translucent in the dawn.

Back in Belisha Road, Lev heated a tin of beans and ate these ravenously, with a spoon, then he lay down in his room, propped his head up with the faded giraffe pillows, and began to read *Hamlet*.

It wasn't that he really wanted to struggle with it, endure the difficulty of it. He began to read as a kind of atonement for his treatment of Lydia.

He opened the paperback. Didn't glance at Lydia's inscription, or at any of the learned introductions. Hurried on to Act One, Scene One.

Who's there?

Right. Well, he understood the first line. It struck him as a thrilling way to begin a play. *Who's there?* The notes in the back of the book explained to Lev that these characters, Barnardo and so on, were soldiers, keeping watch on a *platform*, a place where guns stood. So, OK, it was a guard's nervy utterance. But wasn't it – also – the question he kept asking himself: *Who's there in my life? For me or against me. Who's left? Who's yet to come?*

He returned to the soldiers. Couldn't imagine them yet, so long ago, in Denmark. Only remembered how, in Baryn and in other cities, he used to stare at the faces of army personnel. Always, they looked right past your stare, kept their far-away gaze, apparently seeing some orderly vista of which you formed no part. He'd both feared and pitied them. Their hats were stiff and round, like boxes of chocolates. They clutched their old Kalashnikovs to their chests.

'Tis bitter cold,
And I am sick at heart.

Lev liked this, too. For this was how the soldiers struck you when you'd passed by, when you were out of the orbit of their expressionless faces: this was the afterthought, that they were freezing in their lonely sentry posts, in their desolate walking up and down. And didn't Rudi once say, as they passed two boy conscripts guarding some ministerial blockhouse in Glic, 'They look heartsick. Like they were weaned from the tit too soon.'

Enter the Ghost.

Lev saw this instruction waiting on the right-hand side of the page, skipped some stuff he didn't understand to get there.

So, it was going to be a story about the dead. Probably this was why Lydia had selected it as her Christmas present to him: knowing him better than he'd ever admitted, seeing him still haunted by his father, by his old life at the mill, by Marina.

And now haunted by yet other things: by the kitchen at *GK Ashe*, by the black trees outside the windows of Sophie's flat, by the flare of happiness that had lit up a pathway and then gone out ...

Better to read on, though, to try to become immersed in *Hamlet*, than to think about all that. Lev waded through speeches where meaning went out suddenly, just like the happiness-flare.

It was about to speak when the cock crew.

Lev closed his eyes and let the book fall. It was so absurdly difficult. This difficulty was of a different order from most day-to-day things. But Lev felt Lydia's critical eye on him, a look that said: Don't let me down, don't do what you always do and set me aside. So he tried to obey her. Picked the book up again, struggled on ...

A king and queen came whirling in with their retinue, but what was their connection to the ghost? What was an 'imperial jointress'? Who were Young Fortinbras and Old Norway? What were 'suits of woe'? Back and forth to the notes. Then he skipped on, not lingering on Old Norway, to get to Hamlet himself, as if thinking, Once he's alone and talking directly to us, all might be clear. Stared at the words *Exeunt all but Hamlet*.

Lev lit a cigarette. He took the smoke deep into him, imagining Hamlet alone on the stage now, ready to speak what was in his heart. He'd be young. Probably about thirty. Young and thin, like the boys who used to come down to the Baryn lumber yard, in winter, looking for work. Not princes of Denmark: boys who'd never known work. They used to stand around, silent in the low light, watching the shrieking saw coughing out sparks and orange dust as it ate into the pines. Imagining how it would be to join this world where men laboured through every season – in snowfall, under arc-lights on black afternoons, in driving rain and raw cold, in the first songstruck days of spring – and took home money, week by week. Lev hated to see them there, didn't like to look at their faces. Afraid to see his own face in theirs.

> *... O God! God!*
> *How weary, stale, flat and unprofitable*
> *Seem to me all the uses of this world!*

This was better. He could understand more words.

> *Heaven and earth! Must I remember?*

Remember what? Back and forth, back and forth to the notes, his mind a saw, trying to shriek through a tough bark of words.

> *A little month ... .*
> *... Within a month ... she married.*

So that was it. A woman's treachery! As it would be, thought Lev. Because it's what the *women* do that kills us. On our own, even out in the cold dark of the lumber yard, we men survive. We stamp our feet in the snow. We drink tea out of old flasks. Someone tells a joke. Our shoulders ache like the shoulders of an ox under the eternal yoke. But we shake each other's hands, plan fishing trips, get drunk together, carry on ...

Lev heard the doorbell ringing, but didn't move. It was past midnight.

> *... married with my uncle,*
> *My father's brother: but no more like my father*
> *Than I to Hercules.*

The bell rang and rang. Wearily, Lev climbed out of his bunk and shuffled to the door. He picked up the intercom.

'It's Sophie. Let me in, Lev.'

He said nothing, did nothing, just held the intercom receiver to his ear, as though waiting for some further instruction.

'Lev. Please let me come up.'

Already he was feeling it, that thing he felt when he heard the choke in her voice. He wanted to send her away, shut himself out from everything that belonged to her, everything that surrounded her – her celebrity friends with their crass achievements, the disdain they showed him – but he just wasn't able to send her away, not when she talked to him in that sexy voice of hers.

He pressed the door release. Heard her footsteps on the stairs. Opened the flat door and retreated to his room, as if here, where she'd never deigned to sleep, he'd be safe from her. Fumbled for a cigarette.

She stood at the door and looked at him. Her cheeks were pink from the night air, her hair flattened by her cycling helmet. But he could smell the kitchen on her, the beautiful steel kitchen from which he was now cast out. He lit the cigarette, picked up the copy of *Hamlet*, which had fallen onto the floor, folded down the corner of the page he'd reached.

It is not, nor it cannot come to good.

'Wow,' said Sophie. 'You reading *Hamlet*?'

'Yes.'

'Isn't it difficult for you?'

'Sure. Everything is difficult.'

She looked hot and awkward, standing in the door, wearing her cycle gear. She began unwinding her scarf. That same yellow scarf: the one he'd always loved. Lev looked away from her. She came and sat down on the floor, where Frankie's shop had once stood. She was wearing red-and-black striped stockings and black boots. She took off her black velvet jacket.

'Lev,' she said gently. 'I came to say I'm sorry about it all.'

'Yes?'

'I didn't mean it to go like this. But – I don't know … it's like Howie's just *overwhelmed* me. I've never felt so ridiculously in love before.'

She lowered her head. She seemed contrite, like a child. Lev thought that it wasn't difficult to imagine Preece's body crushing hers. She looked up and said: 'I want us to be friends, Lev. You mean a lot to me and I really want us to stay friends.'

Friends.

A little month . . . .
. . . Within a month . . .

Not anything like a month. A matter of days . . . *hours*. She had a new lover, a man so rich and famous he could buy her anything she asked for. He had nothing. No love. No job. Nothing. He smoked and stared at her. Knew this silent stare discomforted her.

'Lev?'

He stared at her knees. Wanted to put his hand there, let it move slowly upwards, find the stocking top, pause there, wait to see what she did, hear her breath, once more, close to his . . .

'I know it's really tough on you, what GK decided,' she said. 'It's very tough, and I'm sorry. I didn't ask him to do that, but I guess it wouldn't have worked any other way . . .'

Lev smoked. He just didn't want to talk to her.

'Lev, please. Try to understand?'

He looked not at her face, with its dimples and its high colour, only at her clothes and her body beneath: the red skirt tight across her rounded stomach, a jumper of the same red colour, soft over her breasts; remembered the turquoise bra and G-string, her arse lifted towards him in front of her fire . . .

'I mean, I tried to tell you, quite a few times, that it would never've worked, *long term*. All my friends knew that. *I* knew it. Because we're too different. But we had some nice times, didn't we? That day at Silverstrand?'

Was she wearing a G-string now? Did she lift herself like that, crouched on all fours, like a raunchy, smooth-skinned bitch, for Howie Preece? Did she beg *him* to hurt her?

'Remember Christy and Frankie jumping in the surf? The way the sun shone?'

Yes, but the sun had gone in. Had she forgotten that? Or hadn't she noticed? Just as now she sat there chatting to him – almost brightly – as though he had no feelings, no longing, no lingering susceptibility . . .

'Lev, please, please talk to me . . .'

He stubbed out the cigarette. Got down on his knees. Still didn't look at her face. Slammed out one arm, surprising her with the sudden movement, pressing her collar-bone, pinning her against the wall. With the other hand, pushed up between her thighs, finding the stocking top, the hard bud of the provocative suspender belt, the solid flesh ...

She tried to push him away.

He was over her now, his head nudging the wall beside hers, his hand finding ... no G-string ... no knickers ... nothing ... just her briny cunt, open to the world. So he told himself she was a whore, told himself what he already knew, that she was no better than a prostitute, no more decent than the brothel-scum he and Rudi used to visit in Baryn, long ago. She was English: that was the only difference. But Christy had been right: English girls were racist, promiscuous, shameless. They – she, all of them – deserved what he was going to do. They deserved shame.

'Lev, we can't do this any more ...'

She was Howie Preece's girl. His faceful of jowls lay beside hers on the pillow. His tongue explored her mouth. When he woke, he heard her irresistible voice, guided her hand to his preening cock ...

'Lev ...'

He was unmoved, hard as knuckle bone. Hadn't she always been violent *with him* in their fucking?

He pressed her down now, onto the green carpet, her curls touching the door of the Wendy house. Closed his eyes. Closed his eyes and kissed her, like she'd once kissed him in the crowded pub, months ago, his teeth grinding against hers. And as he searched her mouth, he felt her tongue ... despite everything ... despite his present cruelty ... begin to tangle with his, a remembered passion seeming to flood back into her, her resistance to him weakening, altering ...

He hauled her legs up, up till her calves were resting on his back. Never left her mouth, not for a second. She was half crying, moaning, but not in fear – he could tell, couldn't he? Couldn't he tell that her fear was gone and she had it all back, her appetite, her insatiable, irresistible greed for the male ...

Sophie.

Howie Preece's whore, moaning like a fox. Beneath him and ready ...

When he slammed into her, she was silky as oil. Straight away, she began to move with him. She clung to him. He fastened his sinewy arms round her, pitched and rocked like a boat plunging through a humped sea, heard her head knocking against the child's wooden house, felt her boots kick and bruise his arse, and liked it, liked the pain, pressed down on his thigh bones, to get even deeper in.

He still wouldn't open his eyes to see her. Didn't want to feel love for her. Told himself she was his *animal,* nothing more. She bit his lip, the vixen, drew blood, bit again. Harsh pain, but he felt this begin to trigger him. Oh, God ... Blood all over their chins. Wanted to curse and swear and say her name, heard words choked out of his blood-filled mouth. Then the trigger tightened, eased, tightened again, trembled, tightened hard and slammed home.

He surfaced from darkness to feel her sliding out from under him, pushing him firmly aside.

He turned and saw her refastening one of her striped stockings, her sweet head bent over the task. Felt remorse, pure and deep.

'Sophie,' he said, 'I'm sorry. I was rough. I didn't mean ...'

She didn't reply, just went on with the tasks of fixing her stockings, smoothing down her skirt.

'Sophie,' he began again, 'did I hurt you?'

'Yes,' she said. 'You did.' Turned away from him, picked up the velvet jacket and tugged it on.

He got to his feet, went to her and tried to hold her. She pulled away, snatched up the scarf from the floor, started to wind it round her neck and chin.

Remorse and shame. His body still trembling from the delirium of fucking her, but the shame flooding in ...

She moved to the door. The blood on her face covered by the scarf.

He reached for her hand. A single caress. A gesture of forgiveness, of recognition that their old passion was still there; that was all he asked.

But she pulled her hand away. 'Goodbye, Lev,' she said. 'And please don't come round to the flat, or anything. It's better if we never see each other again.'

17

Lady Muck of the Vegetable World

'Midge' Midgham brought the old Land Rover round to the three caravans at seven thirty in the morning. He picked up his foreign workers and drove them out to his thirty-acre asparagus spread, where the tractor and the rig waited.

The tractor had to haul the rig in a straight line down the furrows. No use letting it buck or slide out of alignment. And it had to go nice and slow, letting the asparagus cutters – the human hardware – keep pace. Housed in the wide steel arms of the rig were plastic crates: five, six in a line, depending on how many cutters were following. The system was simple but effective. The cutters bent down and cut with a knife, making sure there was no wastage, that they sliced each stem just *under* the earth – not a prodigal inch above it – massed a bunch of stems in their left hands, as if they were gathering flowers, then laid the bunch carefully in the crates, spears all facing the same way. In the old days, hundreds of man-hours had been wasted decanting the full trugs carried by the pickers into boxes at the field's edge. With the rig, the asparagus was cut and crated in one smooth operation. Twice a day, the crates were loaded into the Land Rover and driven down to the chiller in Midge's barn.

The owner of the spread had to be vigilant, that was all. Midge drove the tractor with his big belly squashed up against the wheel and his neck half bent round most of the time, keeping watch on how the cutters were working. If he saw anybody *throwing* the spears into the crates, he'd yell at them.

'Now, yew listen up,' he'd told them on their first day. 'Asparagus en't sugar beet! It en't blusted Brussels sprouts. It's got a good pedigree. It's Lady Muck of the vegetable world: grows overnight, needs harvesting fast, or it go to seed. And it damage easily. So yew treat it with respect. Yew tug your forelocks to it, or you'll be off this blusted farm.'

Midge told his farmer friends at the Longmire Arms: 'These bors from Eastern Europe, they're used to field work. At home, as kids, I reckon they'd be up at dawn to feed the family chickens, same thing after school, milk the cows, water the cabbages, all that carry-on ... So they're decent pickers, see, because they understand the land.'

Of the two young Chinese men, Sonny and Jimmy Ming, Midge said: 'Denno 'bout them. Can't seem to get their tongues around the language. And Sonny Ming, he cuts too high up the stem because he's dreaming half the blusted time. But they're good-natured. I give 'em that. Laugh a lot, they do. Den't know what at, but who cares? And they never seem to mind the rain.'

But this year Midge had only seven cutters when he could have done with nine or ten, because the asparagus was showing up nice, after a spring that had been just wet enough and after his seaweed mulch, spread on in late autumn, had been broken down by hard winter frosts. The crop had just the right amount of body to it – stems not too fat, not too spindly – and this April was warm; you could practically *see* the stuff growing. So when Vitas came to him and asked him to take on his friend, Lev, a man in his forties, he'd said, 'Awright by me, Vitas, if he don't mind sharing a van with the Mings. And if he'll put his back into it.'

Lev didn't mind sharing the leaky old caravan. He didn't mind any of it, chose to regard the discomfort as a punishment for the way he'd wrecked the life he'd had in London. Because it had been a beautiful life – he saw this now. His friendship with Christy Slane, their tea-and-toast conviviality, had been consoling. He'd begun to love his work. He'd been favoured by a beautiful, sexy girl; a girl who spent half her Sundays working for no money in a care home for the elderly. And now he'd lost them all.

'I screwed up, comrade,' he told Rudi. 'That old anger of mine made me act like an imbecile. It's like I put lumps of coal into everybody's hands.'

'Well,' said Rudi, 'love makes people mad. Don't be too harsh with yourself.'

'Why not?' said Lev. 'I deserve it. I half strangled Sophie in that theatre, and then ...'

'And then what?'

'When she came round to see me, I was rough. You know what I'm saying? I told myself she wanted it because she'd always been quite hot for me. But I guess it wasn't really far from rape.'

Rudi was silent. Lev could imagine him worrying what to say. After a while, he heard a heavy sigh and Rudi mumbled: 'Men are having a tough time in this century. We just don't seem to know where we fucking are.'

'Well, I'll tell you where I am,' said Lev. 'I'm back with the dispossessed.'

There were no curtains at the caravan windows, so most mornings Lev woke at six, when it got light. He made tea on the two-ring burner and usually took the mug outside, to escape the fug of the caravan, to watch the sun come up behind a stand of poplars and feel the fresh air on his face.

It rained often. The field where the vans stood was always muddy, from the trudging back and forth of the gang of workers. This half-acre of mud reached to where a washing-line sagged between two posts, usually draped with towels, cheap bed linen, frayed T-shirts, grey underwear, took in a rubbish heap of pallets, boxes, timber offcuts, lengths of grey piping, steel brackets and plastic shelving, and a Portaloo, narrow as a phone box, jacked up on some concrete blocks. Once a week, the toilet was emptied and refilled with olive-green detergent, sharp in your nose as a dry martini.

Drinking tea and smoking, Lev walked out to where the grass shone with dew, towards hawthorn hedges and a field of raspberry canes, still almost bare of leaf. Beyond the canes, a lush meadow on rising ground, where Midge's geese sometimes wandered, bickered and lay down, like snow-white meringues. Beyond this, the poplars and the big sky. Standing in this place, Longmire Farm, in the quiet of morning, Lev now and again felt something of what Vitas had described to him – that it was all right, better than a thousand other places, despite the mud, like a corner of England from long ago.

But his back ached. Not just from bending all day in the asparagus fields but from the bed he'd been allocated. Everything in his caravan was old, worn, used, stained. Lev slept on a block of petrified foam-rubber, which, in the daytime, was kicked upwards into a rigid fold, to form bulky bench seating for a pull-down Formica table. The foam was upholstered in a prickly brown weave. Lev's thin nylon undersheet slithered around on this weave. All night, his body itched and rolled about. He thought longingly of his bunk at Belisha Road and remembered how, when he'd said goodbye to Christy, he'd felt like weeping.

One morning, after a night of almost no sleep, Lev attempted to ask Midge Midgham for something – a soft blanket or quilt – to put between the sheet and the foam, but he knew that Midge was selectively deaf, so he wasn't surprised when the man simply turned away from him and strode towards the waiting tractor.

Midge Midgham. The Chinese boys had nicknamed him 'Big Berri'. Often, when the pickers assembled for the day and Midge shouted his orders as the rig began its slow forward creep, the Mings' faces broke into smiles and these smiles sometimes widened into unstoppable laughter. *'Hor-hor-hor-hor! Hor-hor-hor-hor-hor-hor!'* It amused Lev to watch them: Sonny and Jimmy Ming, bent over the furrows, weeping with mirth at the sight of Big Berri on his tractor with his stomach punched into an agonising fold by the steering-wheel and his thick neck twisting round to let his puffy eyes keep their vigil on the pickers' pace.

'Wha's the matter with them?' Midge sometimes innocently asked. The mongrel dog, Whisky, might be snapping and yapping at their heels, but they didn't heed him. Their laughter seemed a sweet intoxication from which nothing could part them.

'In China,' Vitas might offer, 'people laugh quite more.'

Or his friend, Jacek, a rosy-faced boy with blond hair, might add: 'Don' worry, Midge. No laugh at you. Maybe plan something. Plan Whisky kidnap. In China, everybody eat dog!'

'Well,' said Midge, 'tell them I'll put their blusted eyes out if they lay a finger on my dog.'

And so the morning would roll on, Lev's world shrinking to the grey-brown furrows, the green stems, snapping cleanly under the knife, wild weeds in the ditches, sun or rain on his back, diesel fumes from the tractor sullying the freshness of the air.

There was a kind of camaraderie in the line. Lev liked to hear his own language pass from voice to voice. It reminded him of beating the woods behind Auror for rabbits and pigeons when he was a boy. Sometimes, breathing in the diesel smoke, he caught a memory-whiff of the Baryn mill, half expected to look up and see his old friends standing at the edge of the wood: ghostly faces under hard hats.

Mainly, Lev himself was silent, listening to what Vitas and the others talked about: the girls they fancied at the Co-op checkouts or in the Longmire Arms, the motorbikes they itched to buy and flaunt, the flavours of crisps they preferred, their discovery of Pot Noodle, the money they were saving, the rules of bar billiards …

One afternoon, as they ate their lunch in the corner of a field – floury baps filled with corned beef, pickles, processed cheese, washed down with Pepsi – he told them the old story of buying the Tchevi and pouring vodka on the windscreen as they drove it home through the ice. And he saw that they were held by this, just as Lydia's friends in Muswell Hill had been held. Everybody stared at him: Vitas and Jacek and the other young men from his country, Oskar, Pavel and Karl. Only the Mings looked blank. When he spoke his language, Sonny and Jimmy Ming didn't understand a single word.

'I'd like to drive an American car,' said Vitas.

'I'd like to meet Rudi,' said Jacek.

The others nodded, concurred. They'd like to meet Rudi *and* drive the car. And Lev thought, yes, Rudi was everything this story had made him out to be – and more. He was a force of nature. He was a lightning bolt. He was a fire that never went out.

Lev called him often. It felt to him as though Rudi was once again his only friend in the world. He knew that his money – money that he should have sent to Ina, money that should have repaid his debt to Lydia – was leaking away on mobile-phone debt, but his loneliness was so acute that he had to keep Rudi near him somehow, or go insane.

One evening, Rudi said to him: 'Well, I've got troubles too, Lev. The Tchevi's playing me up again, fuck it.'

'Yeah?'

'Yeah. Get this. I'm going along Route 719, way out towards Piratyn, in the middle of nowhere, with this lard-faced granny, carrying two live hens in a coop, in the back. Thinking to myself, I hope she's got money and isn't going to try to pay me in fucking *eggs*. And then I see steam coming out of the hood. *Steam!* It's billowing out in massive clouds. I feel like I'm in some old Communist horror movie, starring a tank-engine.'

Lev couldn't suppress a smile. 'What did you do?' he said.

'Well, what could I do? I pulled over. Switched off. Granny leans back on the upholstery, like this is completely normal. Just closes her eyes. Hens fast asleep, too – or dead. So I get out, get the hood up. Everything's *boiling* in there. I'm not kidding, Lev. I can hear bubbling going on, like Lora was cooking face flannels.

'Everything way too hot to touch. So I know we're stuck. No option but to stay there and wait till it cools, then refresh the system. But we're middle of Route 719, nothing in sight but rocks and scrub and one seared old oak tree. Freak temperature: 85° Fahrenheit. And suddenly I'm thinking, It's still eight or nine miles to Piratyn and I've got no water to top up the fucking cooling system!'

'Right. Well, you're alive to tell the tale.'

'Yeah. But it got surreal. I'm waiting there, apologising. I feel like such a loser. I feel worse than you're feeling, comrade. Granny hauls her arse out of the car, twitches her patched-up old skirts, tells me she has to answer a call of nature. So, Bingo, I think to myself: Liquid! And I'm about to ask her, "Would you mind saving your body fluid for my poor sick car?" but then I remember, no, fuck it, I've got no receptacle. Nothing to collect it in.'

Lev heard Rudi's voice begin to break up into laughter as he went on: 'So figure what I do, Lev. While Granny's off into the scrub, I wrap a snot-rag round my hand, get the cap off the cooler tank, and I lean over, nearly scalding my balls off, and I piss into the fucking tank. Jesus Christ!'

Lev joined the laughter. Felt it bubble up in him from wherever it had hidden itself. Rudi began coughing, then collected himself and said: 'Well, we got there. Chicken shit all over my upholstery, and God knows what uric acid does to an engine, but we survived. Never been so glad to see that dump, Piratyn, in my whole life. Got some coolant into the system, courtesy of a bribe. I swear every last citizen of Piratyn's a born-and-bred *grey*. Fucking garage people looked at the Tchevi like she was primed with a terrorist bomb. Cost me almost my whole fare. So bang goes another afternoon's work and the engine still smells of piss and the cooling system's leaking like hell and still not fixed and not going to *get* fixed unless I can cannibalise another motor for a new pump. I tell you, Lev, sometimes this country—'

He broke off. Lev heard the maimed cuckoo come shrieking out of its home in the wooden clock. 'Oh well, I needn't tell you,' sighed Rudi, 'you know only too well. That's why you're picking asparagus in the mudflats of England.'

The afternoons felt long. On fine days they worked nine, ten hours. Worked till the light began to go, till the rooks began to shuffle in the high trees, till Lady Muck became almost invisible in her green sheath. Then they fell into the Land Rover, mute, aching, hungry, and were driven back to the caravans. Took turns at the hot shower, a big empty walk-in space, fixed up by Midge next to the chiller. Heated up the cheapest tinned stuff they could buy – ravioli, baked beans, mulligatawny soup – and spooned it in like starving children, bulked out with thick-cut bread. Slaked their sugar-thirst with canned peaches, mandarin oranges, Mars bars. Wandered outside to smoke, if the night was fine, and stared at the stars, clear and bright, over the quiet land.

Around nine o'clock, Vitas and his friends would invariably set out on the quarter-mile walk to the pub, the Mings following in their wake, and Lev was alone.

He walked in the beautiful silence to where the white geese lay down in their field. Lev leaned on the gate, smoking, trying to empty his mind of everything but this: the May darkness, the moon's borrowed light, the feeling of being alive. But often, like a movie suddenly beginning in his brain, scenes at *GK Ashe* would come pelting in: GK shouting at the waiters, the nurse from Niger banging down heavy skillets on the steel draining top, every sound bouncing and echoing off the hard surfaces. Then the noise lessened and there was Sophie .... selecting a knife, pinboning a sea-bass with deft cuts, making this look as easy as slitting open an envelope, as easy as sliding a scalpel across a vein ...

He'd leave the gate, leave the geese, alert for foxes and night creatures. He'd start walking again, as if trying to escape, fleeing

Sophie's knife, but there was nowhere to go, except further into the darkness, to where the poplars sighed like the sea. Sometimes, as he turned round and went slowly back to the caravan, Lev looked over at the lights in Midge's farmhouse. To push Sophie from his mind, he began to wonder about Midge, 'Big Berri', lonely lord of his fruit and vegetable kingdom, too fat for his clothes, tender towards his dog, spending his life hiring strangers. Had he had a wife once? Had he ever danced a tango? Did anyone alive care about the answers to these questions?

Then Lev would sit at the table, on his bed in its folded state, reading *Hamlet* under the single bulb hanging from a black wire draped across the ceiling of the caravan. External electric sockets on the wall of the chiller fed the three vans, wires bunched up with brown tape and pushed in through tilting windows. When the wind blew, the light above the table swung back and forth, throwing shadows everywhere, like spirit rags.

> *Angels and ministers of grace defend us!*
> *Be thou a spirit of health or goblin damn'ed ... ?*

Lev's eyes were bent low over the page. It was so difficult, he heard himself cursing Lydia for expecting too much of him. But he had nothing else to read here so he laboured on, and, for some reason, whenever the ghost appeared he felt his understanding make a forward surge.

> *I am thy father's spirit ...*

He read till his eyes were closing, then put the sheets on his scratchy bed, and lay down. He was usually asleep by the time the Mings returned from the pub, but he'd wake to hear them laughing, see their light come on through the curtain that separated their sleeping area from the rest of the van. Sometimes Jimmy (or Sonny) would stumble out again, still convulsed with giggles ... *hor-hor-hor-hor-hor-hor* ... and see Lev sitting up, watching him.

'Sorry, Rev. Forgot piss.'

More unstoppable laughter from the one left behind. *Hor-hor-hor-hor-hor-hor!* Then a moment's silent repentance, a dark head appearing through the curtain. 'Sorry, Rev. We waken you?'

'It's OK.'

'We drinking rotsa beer!'

'You have fun?'

'What you say, Rev?'

'You enjoy the pub?'

'Yah, yah. Good-shit. Sonny win bar birriads. Night, Rev.'

He'd drift back to sleep, but wake again, hear them talking, then sighing, moaning and whimpering in their sleep. It seemed to him that their rest was fitful and short, yet in the mornings they always greeted him brightly: 'Morning, Rev. How you today?'

If it was raining, they'd appear with their yellow oilskins zipped up to their chins and their sou'westers already pulled on over their thick black hair. In the Land Rover, they sat tight up against each other. They reminded Lev of two obedient brothers at his school, near in age, who went everywhere together and couldn't bear to be separated. Rudi had nicknamed them 'the KGB'. He told Lev they had a family secret too terrible to let out, had to spy on each other night and day, in case one of them talked. To Vitas and the others, the Mings seldom spoke. Only, sometimes, to laugh about Big Berri. Or when it was their turn to work in the chiller, to rub their gloved hands and say: 'Big cold, this chirrer! Cold like China winter.'

It was an old stable block with a sagging roof, refrigerated to 8° Celsius. The pickers took turns to do a two-hour evening shift in there, washing, weighing and bagging up the asparagus, reboxing it for delivery to local shops and supermarkets. They wore oilskins, and rubber gloves and boots, like the trawler crews. They worked in pairs, under dim rods of industrial lighting, using conversation to try to keep them warm.

Working in the chiller with Vitas, who was trying to grow a fussy little triangle of beard under his lower lip, Lev asked: 'You going to stay with Midge all summer?'

'Yeh,' said Vitas. 'Do the tomato poly-tunnels next. Then the beans and the soft fruit. Go home in August with a suitcase full of cash. Start my engineering course in Jor in September.'

'You want to be an engineer, Vitas?'

Vitas had chosen to work with a woollen scarf wrapped round and round his head, like a bandage. 'I want to be *something*,' he said.

Lev was silent. He stared at the writing on the asparagus bags: *Produce of Longmire Farm, Suffolk. 'Only the Best!'* Thought, Yes, this was what, in the end, drew you on over the years, in spite of tragedy and loss, the idea that you could make some kind of mark, that through the slowly accumulating weeks and months you would somehow become the kind of person you might stop to admire. *Only the Best.*

'What are *you* going to do?' asked Vitas.

Lev went on with his work. He thought about all the recipes he'd painstakingly learned at *GK Ashe* and written out on pieces of paper and stashed in his bag when he left Belisha Road. 'I don't know,' he said to Vitas. 'I still haven't figured it out.'

Midge Midgham invited Lev to his house one May evening, said he'd found a bottle of vodka at the back of his drinks cupboard, assumed Lev liked vodka.

They sat in Midge's living room, drinking out of shot glasses, munching stale Ritz biscuits, with the dog, Whisky, asleep on a frayed hearth-rug and one window open on a warm but windy night.

Big Berri. His room was full of dust. You could smell it in the upholstery, see its grey bloom on the mantelpiece, on the pewter plates tilting there, on the tops of the huge old loudspeakers, positioned like sentries either side of the fireplace.

'You like music, Midge?' asked Lev.

Midge shifted in his armchair, stared at the speakers, appeared at a momentary loss. 'My wife, Donna, she liked pop music,' he said. 'R.E.M. The Strokes. Keane. Beyoncé Knowles. She used to jive around in here. Swish her hair about, like Tina Turner. Had a body on her, even at the age of forty-seven. Me, I hated that blusted music. I like quiet. Or else Barbra Streisand. But watching Donna used to get me worked up. Crikey. I'd put up with her music just to see her move.'

'Yes?'

'Yep. She'd been married before. Now she's married again – to her hairdresser. Me, I was just a whatsername, an interlude. But she tried to get the farm off me. And tha' riled me, I can tell yew. I've put my life into this farm and what did she ever put in? Used to pick fruit, that was all. Feed the geese sometimes ...'

Lev shook his head in sympathy. The vodka was as stale as the biscuits, but still comforting.

'Know what lawyers cost in this country? Tha' nearly broke me, but I fought Donna all the way on the farm – and I won. But if I hadn't, I den't know what I'd've done. I'm telling yew I den't. I might have killed the girl. Because is tha' right that she could walk into my life for three or four years and try to take half of everything I had, everything I'd built up? I'm asking yew if tha's right.'

Midge downed his vodka, got up to break out more ice and to refill the two glasses.

An image of Procurator Rivas, smug behind his huge desk, suddenly appeared in Lev's mind. 'No,' he said. 'Not right, Midge.'

'Tha's what I'm saying. Wouldn't happen in your country, would it?'

'Well,' said Lev, 'in Communist era, people owned nothing in my country. Now, maybe small flat or house – if they're lucky – or, like my mother, a few goats and chickens, one small shed, so …'

'Yep. Commies were little devils, eh? Got everybody in a blusted straitjacket. Glad we din't have 'em here. But what happened to yew, bor? I ben asking myself … Why's a man of your age picking vegetables with young kids? Your wife steal your farm?'

'No,' said Lev. 'My wife died.'

He saw Midge's huge hand falter as he broke out the ice from the rubber tray. He looked up at Lev, smoothing back from his shiny forehead some wisps of grey hair. 'Tha's rotten,' he said. 'Couldn't have been that old, could she?'

'Thirty-six.'

'Oh, crikey, tha's tough. Wish I hadn't asked now. Here …' He handed Lev his refilled glass. Went to his dusty stack of CDs and selected one. 'Like to hear some Barbra Streisand?'

'Sure.'

Midge put the CD on and the swoony orchestral sound floated out across Longmire Farm, joined with the sighing of the trees. Whisky stirred on the rug and shook himself, and when Midge sat down again, climbed onto his lap. Midge stroked the dog's head. 'He's my only companion now,' he said. 'Can't even get people to help me on the land any more – only immigrant labour. The English used to love the land. Specially Suffolk people. Den't know where that love went. Had three men working for me on this place, once. Now, it's just me and the pickers and the dog.'

'People ...
People who need people
Are the luckiest people in the world ...'

Barbra sang on. Lev relaxed into his chair.

'I know the vans aren't up to scratch,' said Midge, after a while. 'It's why I den't charge rent for them. I'd've got them fixed up this year, but my cash flow's poor. Had to whack down a lump sum in '04 to get Donna off my back. And, crikey, tha' left me rocky.'

'The van's OK,' said Lev. 'Only ...'

'Windows den't close properly. I know tha'. Get water in when it rains?'

'No,' said Lev. 'Only my bed, Midge. I tried to tell you before. Scratches my skin. Maybe you can find something soft to put under my sheet.'

Midge stared at Lev in alarm, as though he'd asked him for a loan or a percentage of his takings on Lady Muck.

'Right,' he said. 'But I den't know what. I'll look in the airing-cupboard. Donna would've known, but tha's all women are good for, if yew ask me – feathering their blusted nests.'

When Lev got back to the van, swaying from the vodka, his head dying for sleep, he found the Mings putting away their mah-jong pieces at the Formica table. They looked at him worriedly.

'Rev, your phone cawring, cawring ...'

'Yah, cawring five, six time.'

Lev stared round the van. He knew it was late – later still in Auror. Dread tugged at his heart. He found his phone and stared at the screen. Four missed calls: Rudi's number each time. '*Call me*,' said the voicemail. Rudi's voice thin and choked.

Lev took the phone and walked out again into the night. A bright moon came and went among fast-scudding clouds. The washing left on the line billowed in the wind. Lev took big gulps of air to try to clear away the vodka fug. Dialled the number.

Lora answered. 'Oh, Lev,' she said. 'Such sadness for our village. I can't tell you. I'll get Rudi ...'

Rudi came on. 'Where you been?' he said frostily. 'I've been trying your number all fucking night.'

'Nowhere, Rudi. Having a few drinks ...'

'OK, well, you're going to need a drink in your hand now. We got bad news, Lev, unbelievable news.'

'Say it.'

'I can't hardly bear to.'

'Say it, Rudi.'

A silence. A breath. Then Rudi's voice, very quiet: 'It's not good, my friend. They're going ahead with the Baryn dam.'

Just for a moment, relief. Relief that the call wasn't about Maya or Ina. But then he had to *make sure* they were all right – before he could concentrate on the news about the dam. 'Just tell me first, Rudi, are Maya and Ina OK?'

'As of now, they're fine. But when they know about this ... when everybody in Auror wakes up tomorrow and learns about this ... they're not going to be OK.'

His daughter was safe. His mother was safe. Rudi and Lora were safe. But now something terrible was arriving. Lev cursed Midge for plying him with vodka, kept inhaling the sweet night air to try to get some clarity into his brain ... 'Tell me, then, Rudi. About the dam.'

'Oh, shit ...' Rudi exhaled a long, shuddering sigh, then said: 'Well, like you predicted, surveyors came. Pretended to Lora they were testing the drinking water. But we kept our eyes on them. Back and forth, back and forth, upriver, with their stupid theodolites – or whatever you call those fucking things. I said to Lora, "When did anyone need coloured sticks and expensive lenses to test drinking water?"

'Then, tonight, after dark, I'm coming home from Baryn in the Tchevi, and I see shadows. I see these *ghosts* creeping round the village, sticking up flyers on walls. Jesus! What a way to do it! Stick up notices. No village meeting. No advance warning. Just these bastards, these *cowards*, slapping up pieces of paper!

'They thought everyone'd be in bed, that they wouldn't be seen, but I wasn't in bed. My headlights got them in their glare, like fucking rabbits. I stopped the car. Ripped down one of their flyers and read it in the lights.'

'Tell me what it says.'

'Got it in front of me now. You won't believe the language they're using, Lev. Bastards! I nearly exploded. Got this one ghost by the scruff of his municipal collar, said, "What is this? What is fucking *this*? What the fucking shit is this FUCKING NOTICE?"'

Lev waited. He could hear Rudi's breathing, distressed, wheezy, like the breathing of an asthmatic. Imagined him leaning on the hall table, his hair wild, his body wrapped in his old tartan dressing-gown.

'Sorry, Lev,' he panted. 'But this thing's got my heart into such a state I can't hardly get my breath …'

'OK. Take your time. Is Lora there?'

'She's in the kitchen, making tea. Guess we're just going to sit up all night, because how can anyone here ever sleep again? If Marina had been alive, we'd have known, wouldn't we? We'd've been able to prepare ourselves – somehow. Or maybe it wouldn't have made any difference. God knows. The thing's not signed by Rivas. It's from the Central Office of Planning in Jor. But Lora and I keep saying, "If only Marina had been alive … "'

'Sure.'

'I know I shouldn't say that to you. Doesn't help one fucking bit. But it's what I keep thinking – that she *protected* us from a lot of bad things, because she understood how bureaucracy works and how to fight it. And now there's no one to fight it.'

'I know, Rudi. I know …'

'OK, I'm sorry, Lev. I don't know why I keep bleating on about Marina. I'm going to read the shitting thing to you now.'

Lev waited. He sat down on the cold grass. The wind flapped foolishly in the legs of his trousers.

'Here goes,' said Rudi. '"*The people of Auror District … are hereby informed … that the Central Office of Planning (COOP) … has given the Baryn Dam Project Code One Status as a Project of Outstanding Public Utility (POPU). The COOP accordingly … serves upon the people of Auror District Compulsory Purchase Orders (CPOs) of all Property, whether domestic or commercial, before the end of the calendar year, so that we may proudly begin*" – proudly begin! – "*construction work on this POPU. All residents currently housed in Auror District … will be relocated at the State's expense to apartments now under construction in Baryn Perimeter Zone 93 …*"'

Silence in Rudi's hall for a moment. Then another sound: a

sob rising in Rudi's wheezing chest, a long whine, then a breaking down into a storm of weeping.

Lev felt dizzy, sick. Only once in his life had he ever heard Rudi cry before: when they scattered Marina's ashes. Now, Lev wanted to hold onto something, saw only the swaying posts of the washing-line, too far to reach. Put his head between his knees, still clutching the phone to his ear. Heard Lora trying to comfort Rudi, felt relieved she was there, because what could he say, far away as he was, what could anybody say when their village, Auror, would soon vanish under the water. And now he saw it: the dam itself – ten million tonnes of concrete – rising like a tidal wave between the southerly hills.

Rudi kept crying. Lev fought down his sickness. He heard Lora repeat Rudi's name, helplessly: 'Rudi, Rudi … please, come on, Rudi …'

The wind kept blowing over Suffolk.

18

It Almost Had a Scent

The feeling that he was responsible, that his abandonment of his village had brought about its fate, began to cling to Lev, like a chill. He knew this wasn't rational, but it gripped him now, a clammy fever of guilt. As though he'd been the one to decide to build the dam. As though it were he who'd reduced Rudi to tears.

The fever deepened after he'd talked to his mother. On the phone, Ina said to him: 'I'm not leaving Auror. Not for anyone on earth. No one's going to put me in a hutch in Baryn. You'll just have to drown me.'

So then Lev sweated through nightmares, not only about Auror disappearing under the water but about his mother's death. Sometimes she simply lay down in the middle of the road and waited for the river to rise. Groups of villagers gathered round her. 'Come away, Ina. Come away, dear, before it's too late,' they begged. But Ina refused to move. In other dreams, she weighted herself down with her jewellery – her head tugged forwards by the tonnage of rusty tin that hung round her neck, her skinny feet hobbled by ankle chains, hammered out to resemble garlands of leaves – and walked into the reservoir. Lev stood on the shore, helpless, unable to call out, watched Ina float for a moment or two on the pearly surface of the water, the shards of tin glinting in the sunlight, then disappear without a sound. Ripples fanned out from where her body had once been.

He kept working. Something about each bright May morning drove him on. In fleeting optimistic moments, he told himself it would come to him soon, the thing he had to work out, the plan he had to make, to find a future for himself and his family. Meanwhile, he tried to save his money. Kept his phone switched off most of the time. Bought fewer cigarettes, gave up Pepsi, looked for the cheapest bargains in the Co-op – beans and ravioli, ravioli and beans – lived on these and water and stale loaves and Midge's free potatoes.

He wondered, through this pathetic scrimping, whether he should abandon everything – abandon the whole arduous enterprise – and go back to Auror. Sometimes he went there in his mind, organised protests against the Central Office of Planning in Jor, imagined himself scribbling on billboards and banners, marching up and down in the rain. But part of him knew this was useless. He knew the ways of the Central Office of Planning. The people of Auror were too few in number to matter.

Maya had whispered into the phone: 'I'm frightened, Pappa. When are you coming back? *When?*'

Lev had to tell her, 'Not yet, angel. Hang on. Keep practising your skating. Because I heard you're getting really good at it. I want to see some beautiful spins ...'

But, whispering still, she said: 'I can't go skating any more, Pappa.'

'Why not?'

'Because the bus comes at the wrong time.'

'Doesn't Rudi take you in the car?'

'The car's sick.'

He could barely hear her, this quiet little mumble of hers. 'What, Maya? What did you say?'

'The Tchevi. It can't take me to Baryn. It can't move.'

So this began to torment him, too, the knowledge that Maya was deprived of the thing she loved, and that all his consoling images of her small, graceful body leaping and gliding over the ice were now inappropriate and had to be put aside. When he next spoke to Rudi, he heard himself say crossly: 'Is it true you can't get as far as Baryn in the car?'

'Yes, it's true,' said Rudi, his voice slow and weary. 'The Tchevi's *kaput.*'

'What? The cooling system?'

'And other things now. Tyres worn out. Fan-belt broken. It's a heap of junk.'

Lev knew what this meant: no taxi business, no money. 'Can't you get it fixed?'

'No. I can't get the parts and I can't afford the tyres. It's over, my friend. Everything's over.'

So it came down to this. This was what he had to fight: not only the chill of guilt but the idea of final catastrophe. Because no one back in Auror was fighting any more – not even Rudi. The flame of the fight had to be kept alive by him and him alone.

But it was tough. He didn't yet understand how to do it. His thoughts turned in circles. As he followed the rig along the grey furrows, he kept asking himself whether he was wrong to stay on with Midge, where he lived for little but earned little. Should he bolt back to London, take whatever job he could find? Should he try to get a loan, so that he could bring Ina and Maya to England? If he got them here, where would they live? How would he support them? Should he try to unravel the complexities of the Benefits office? Who would help him? And even if he found the means to support them, how would Ina survive in London with not one word of the language? So the circles wound on, always beginning again where they ended ...

'Rev,' said Sonny Ming, sadly, 'this bad-shit for you. We know. China-side, many dams. Many, many virrige gone. Fuckin' bad-shit.'

'Yah. We know gubman bodies. Lirrel people wipe-out.'

'Yes. That's what they're doing, wiping us out.'

'What you do now, Rev?'

'I don't know.'

'But what you do, Rev?'

'I really don't know. I'm trying to work it out.'

They were tender towards him, as though he'd become the third brother. They tried to teach him mah-jong. During the mah-jong games, they sometimes stroked his hands. Out on the asparagus fields, they slowed the line if he was failing to keep up, but keeping up – or trying to – was what got him through the days. He prayed for fine weather so that these days would be long and the pay at maximum; he offered to work overtime in the chiller for extra cash.

Midge Midgham knew his plight. Came down to the van one evening carrying a brand new mattress cover he'd bought in Asda.

Said to Lev: 'Reckon it's hard to sleep, eh, when you're worrying about this blusted dam business? Whack this on the bed, bor, and yew may get better nights.'

He was touched by the kindness of these people whom he hardly knew, people who'd never seen Auror or anywhere like it. Only Vitas was fierce. 'I told you,' he said moodily, 'I told you about the dam at Auror way back in the winter and you didn't believe me. Like you *still* don't believe me that GK Ashe is an arsehole.'

To be, or not to be ...

Lev reached these famous lines on a night of sudden rain, with the new mattress cover soft under his body and the Mings sighing and whimpering in their complicated sleep. He remembered with a smile how, on the bus, Lydia had confused the words with the term B & B. He read on:

> *To be, or not to be: that is the question:*
> *Whether 'tis nobler in the mind to suffer*
> *The slings and arrows of outrageous fortune*
> *Or to take arms against a sea of troubles*
> *And by opposing end them ...*

Lev lay back and let the book rest beside him. Even he, with his still-flawed understanding of English, could admire the economy with which this question was expressed. And he wrestled with the thought that if only language could always be as simple, as sweet and unambiguous as this, then life itself would somehow be less complicated.

To be, or not to be.

He said it over and over. Tried to translate it into his language. Fell asleep saying it, remembered in his dreams how, when Marina had died, he'd wanted *not to be*. But woke the following morning with the early sun, and no will to die. Though he was in a 'sea of troubles', he'd find the means to 'take arms' against them. Somehow, he would.

*

His phone rang and it was Lydia, calling, very late, from Paris. She thanked him for the fifty-pound cheque he'd managed to send her, then said: 'I just learned about the Auror dam, Lev. Pyotor and I are so shocked. I told him I had to call you.'

'That's kind of you ...'

Her voice was soft and affectionate; no trace of exasperation or anger. 'I'm calling on the phone in our private sitting room in the Hôtel Crillon,' she announced gaily. 'Pyotor is asleep next door. He's very tired after the concert tonight. Sibelius: exceptionally demanding. Such a complex score, you know.'

'Yes? More complex than Elgar?'

'I think so. But we'd better not talk about Elgar, Lev. We're going to talk about Baryn. However, before we discuss that, shall I describe our bathroom to you?'

'Yes, describe your bathroom to me, Lydia.'

She told Lev the bathroom had two washbasins and a floor of marble. The shower cubicle and the side of the enormous bathtub were also tiled in marble. The space was lit with thirteen halogen spotlights and the taps were gold. What she loved most were the bathrobes, thick and white as bales of cotton, put out for her personal use.

Lev stared at the crumbling furniture of the caravan, the filthy two-ring burner, the tilting cupboards, the sink crammed with unwashed crockery and stinking of baked beans. But kept his voice bright when he said: 'That's thoughtful of you, Lydia. Now, I can imagine you in the Hôtel Crillon. Are you wearing one of the bathrobes?'

'Yes, I am, as a matter of fact, Lev. But you were never interested in what I was wearing, or what was underneath it, were you? So all I can report to you is that the robe is very comfortable. Now, tell me what you are feeling.'

'About what you've just said?'

'No. About the Baryn dam.'

He wanted a cigarette, fumbled in the half-light to find and light one. Behind their curtain, the Mings snored.

Lev inhaled deeply and said: 'What am I supposed to feel, Lydia? My mother says she's going to let herself be drowned with the village ...'

'Oh,' said Lydia, with a sniff, 'ignore that. This kind of emotional pessimism, or pessimistic emotionality, is typical of our older generation! Just for heaven's sake ignore that completely.'

'Well, I guess—'

'She won't do it, Lev. You know that. She may keep threatening it, because it's so lovely and dramatic, but she won't go through with it. You'll see. Your mother will rebuild her life in Baryn and you will help her.'

Lev was silent. Stared at his hand, burned by the English sun, holding the half-smoked cigarette. Then he said: 'I don't know how to help her, Lydia. Not really. I don't know how to help any of them.'

'Hold on a minute,' said Lydia. 'I'm just going to walk through into the lovely bathroom. I don't want Pyotor to be disturbed.'

Lev heard a heavy door closing, imagined the hotel taps, mirrors and washbasins shimmering with light.

When Lydia came back on the phone, she said: 'Are you there, Lev? Right. Well, now, listen to me. The first and most important thing is to fight for the best choice of the new accommodation in Baryn.'

'Yes. And then what?'

Lydia sighed, said: 'Just do one thing at a time, Lev. Get the accommodation sorted out first. Are you still sending money home?'

'Yes. When I can. But I earn so little now.'

'Well, never mind. Tell your mother to go to the offices in charge of rehousing. Tell her to go with your friend, Rudolf.'

'Rudi.'

'Rudi. OK. He's a fixer, from what you've told me. Get a wad of money to him. Send him fifty pounds and tell him to use it. The housing people will have a *grey* side, for certain, but fifty English pounds should go quite far with them. Some of the new apartments will be on the river. Get him to acquire two of those, one for him and his wife, one for your family.'

'On the river? There won't be much river, Lydia. Not downstream of the city.'

'Of course there will! I thought you used to work with engineers. The dam will create a reservoir and a falls. The falls will drive the electric turbines. Where d'you imagine electric power will come from, if not from the falls?'

'I know. Sure, but ...'

'So where will the water from the falls run to? Into Baryn city and out again the other side, precisely through the new designated "Perimeter Zones". And water's still a nice thing to see. Or do you want your apartment to look out on a factory wall or the back entrance to a brothel?'

He had a first glimpse of it then, the place where his life would eventually have to be lived. He saw it as a small but clean place, painted white, with electric heaters attached to the white walls. He imagined the river swirling along – still agitated from its fall – outside the window.

'Lev? Are you listening? Sometimes I think you're very obtuse. Sometimes I don't know why I bother to help you.'

'I agree. I don't know why you bother to help me. But I'm grateful. And don't worry, I haven't forgotten the rest of your loan to me ...'

'Don't send me more money. I don't want it. This Crillon bathrobe I'm wearing costs almost two hundred pounds and Pyotor would buy it for me if I asked him. Send money to Rudi.'

'I'm going to honour my debt, Lydia.'

'Sure, but not now, don't be stupid. Pyotor gives me so much, you can't imagine. Today, he bought me oysters, followed by sole, for lunch. Then from Hermès, the most beautiful silk blouse, almost three hundred Euros ...'

She couldn't disguise it, the pride in her voice: pride that love – love for the woman once mocked as 'Muesli' – could be measured in the finest luxury commodities.

Lev smiled and said: 'Tell me more about your new life, Lydia. Are you happy with your Maestro?'

'Well, you know, Lev, my life is really incredible.'

'That wasn't precisely my question.'

'No.'

Lydia was silent for a moment. Then she said, in a whisper: 'At the moment, Pyotor has very bad bowel trouble. Concert stress makes life quite difficult for him. I could kill Sibelius – were he not already dead. But I do my best to comfort my dear Maestro. Now, I want to tell you what he said about Baryn ...'

'Tell me that you're happy. I'd really like to know this.'

'Yes. I am happy, Lev. Now Pyotor is a wise man and he has

seen how the future could be for a city like Baryn.'

'Do you make love?'

'Well, my dear, that's really none of your business.'

'True. It isn't.'

'But we do, yes. When he's free of his intestinal pain, he can be very intense. Are you satisfied now?'

Lev lay on his elbow, smoking. He could hear a night bird chirruping alone in the darkness outside. 'OK,' he said. 'Tell me what Pyotor says about Baryn.'

'Well, this is very good news, Lev. Are you going to listen to me when I tell you some good news?'

'Yes.'

'Good. Well, Pyotor believes, once the dam is built, Baryn will become quite a prosperous place. Bring power to a city like that, reliable power, and a lot of other things follow. New businesses will come. New housing will be built. Parks. Facilities. Smart cafés and shops.'

'It's hard to imagine a lot of smart cafés and shops in Baryn,' he said.

'I know. It's remained backward. But that's going to change. Why make the dam if they didn't think it could change? Pyotor points out that its situation is good: fine countryside around it – at least to the south, where they didn't use up all the trees – winters cold, but summers quite long. Perhaps they'll make a *lido* on the new reservoir. I don't know. Anything one can imagine might arrive there in time. A football stadium, maybe. A new ice rink, with spectator seating.'

'A new ice rink?'

'Yes. Sure. Why not?'

Lev was quiet for a moment. Then he said: 'I hope they'll do that. Maya loves to skate. She's on her way to achieving toe-loops.'

Early the following morning, Lev was riding the tractor with Midge along a narrow lane, hauling a wooden trailer to pick up straw bales for the summer fruit. The dog Whisky was between them, with his dog stink, but his nose cold and his tail wagging. Poplars bordered the lane, their leaves flashing grey in the sunshine. At the feet of the poplars, swathes of damsel's lace. And Midge nearly let the tractor swerve, his pouched eyes were so fixed on this sight.

'Worth the winter,' he said. 'Eh, Lev? Worth all the dark days, to see that.'

Lev looked at it: white embroidery on a flounce of May green. He let his gaze wander there, in its fragility and in its permanence, and it was at this moment that his Great Idea arrived in his mind.

The Idea was beautiful.

For a moment, it deprived him of breath. He felt it as something irresistible, calling him on. It seemed as obvious, as elegant, as a theorem, proved beyond doubt.

He almost blurted it out to Midge, then recognised, no, it had to grow in secret, like the hedgerow lace. He had to hold it inside and he vowed to do this. Long ago, in his boyhood, Lev had understood that secrets gave him a feeling of power. This power was at its most intense when the secret was one he was capable of keeping from Rudi.

The Idea needed three things: information, money and will.

It made his heart beat wildly to consider how he could set about acquiring these. His mind boiled with audacious tasks and hopes. Already, on this early May morning, as Lev helped Midge load up the bales of straw, he began to make lists in his head. The dog danced round him, yelping wildly, as though he could smell a world that was suddenly new.

'What's wrong with Whisky?' said Midge. 'Yew got choc-drops hidden in your pocket?'

Lev bought a ruled notebook and started to scribble in it. Instructions to himself tumbled out so fast that later he found them almost illegible. At night, he lay on his bed, dreaming everything into existence. He could see it all and he wanted it, *wanted it*. He felt like a youth, in the grip of an obsession. The seductive power of his Idea was so strong, it almost had a scent. And, as with all obsessions, it wore him out and wouldn't let him rest. After five or six sleepless days and nights, he began to long for respite.

On the evening of his forty-third birthday, he walked through the dusk to the Longmire Arms with Vitas, Jacek and the Mings. He decided to be reckless with his carefully saved money, bought beer and vodka chasers for everybody, and waited for the drink to still his raging mind.

The Mings, always sensitive to his moods, stood close to him, watching him, examining his expressions, as if wondering at his new euphoria.

'Rev. You OK?'

'Rev. You lirrel crazy?'

'Yeah. I guess. It's my birthday. I'm a little crazy.' But he wanted to say to them, No, not crazy exactly: *lost*. Lost in the Secret, lost in the Idea.

He draped his arms round their shoulders. Wanted to ask them: Help me go somewhere else, you and the *vodichka,* help me find a few moments of peace ...

They drank and drank. Played billiards. Snagged up the baize with some outlandish shots. Had the landlord bawling at them: 'Fucking immigrant idiots!' Caught the Mings' contagious laughter. *Hor-hor-hor-hor! Hor-hor-hor-hor-hor-hor!* Stood in a huddle, with their bodies gyrating to some wild tune. Vitas and Jacek took off, but Lev and the Mings stayed on, swaying to beer, swaying to vodka, munching crisps and peanuts, laughing till their sides contorted. Laughed at Big Berri, at the shitty caravan, at yellow oilskins, at Lady Muck, at what beans did to the gas in your gut, at the catastrophe and joy of being alive. Money dripped away ... dripped and leaked away and was gone ...

'Money gone, Rev?'

'Yeah.'

'Bad-shit. Wha' we do now?'

Hor-hor-hor-hor! Hor-hor-hor-hor-hor-hor!

They staggered the quarter-mile home under a bright moon, heard a fox howling. Lev was half carried by the Mings, one on either side, his brothers, his sweet protectors.

They put him into their bed. It was scented with their bodies.

'Rev,' they said. 'We care of you? You wan'?'

'What?'

'We think you wan'. You a lonely man. Care of you now.'

Soft hands unclothed him. Felt the cool of the air on his naked form. Saw two faces looking down on him, with tender smiles. Then, on his cock, careful, gentle fingers, slippery with some perfumed oil, soft and unhurried as a girl's. A ripple of quieter, less violent laughter, like a stone skimming on water ...

Thought, So this is what I hear in the nights, this is the meaning of the sighing and crying, the fretful sleep. But always gentle, like this ... as if it were hardly happening at all ... as silent as a kiss ...

Tears on his face. His or theirs? Gratitude? Or sorrow that he would refuse what they were offering?

He reached down, to move the hand away, but his yearning to still his mind to rest prevented him.

'Rev. We care of you. You don' wan'?'

'Rev. You don' wan' lirrel Tong Zhi now?'

The voices so sorrowful, so tender ...

'Jimmy, Sonny ... I don't know. I'm very drunk ...'

'Ssh, Rev. No hurt you. We care of you, that awl.'

'On your bir'day. Then sleep.'

He woke in his own bed, the sheet and blanket covering him, the morning a lemon haze at the tilting window.

His head ached, but his mind felt stilled and calm. He looked over to the Mings' curtain and saw it drawn across their part of the van, exactly as it always was. He could hear their soft snores, regular, untroubled.

He dressed quietly, picked up his mobile phone and went outside. Looked over at the raspberry field and saw that the canes were suddenly coming into leaf. Thought, Things happen unseen; they overtake prediction. Regret isn't always appropriate.

He went into the shower room and stood under the warm water for a long time, then dried himself and dressed again and sat in the sunshine not far from the washing-line. He noticed diminutive violets pushing up among the new grass.

He knew it was too early to call Christy, but he had to find out about the room at Belisha Road. He punched the number there and got the message machine, then tried Christy's mobile and heard the familiar voice, husky with sleep.

'Christy Slane.'

'Christy, it's Lev. Sorry to call early.'

'It's OK, fella. Hold on a tick ...'

He heard Christy talking to someone, then a door closing.

'Christy,' said Lev, 'got a question for you. Did you let my room?'

'No. Agents couldn't find me anybody yet. Told me I should replace the bunk beds. Said people don't like sleeping piled up like that, like in a prison cell. But that was Frankie's bed. I can't get around to throwing it out.'

'Sure, it's Frankie's bed.'

'You understand why I'm reluctant. Keep thinking she may be allowed to stay over one night.'

'I understand. But listen, Christy, I have to come back to London. May I have the room? OK?'

'Sure. Excellent. Be glad to see you. How are you, then?'

'OK. I'll explain to you when I get home.'

'"Home". It's nice you used that word about Belisha Road. I'd have missed you more, except I'm not there that much.'

'You working?'

'Yeh. Got some smart new cards done. *Christy Slane: All Your Plumbing Problems Solved. Count on Me for Fair Hourly Rates.* What you think?'

'Good. I like.'

'Got me energy back for it, that's the thing. Probably because I'm not drinking. Jasmina doesn't like me to drink alcohol.'

'Jasmina? You at Palmers Green, Christy?'

'Right first time. Lucky fella, aren't I? Me eczema's cleared right up. I'm going to introduce you to her when you get back. So, when do you plan to get here?'

'Maybe tonight?'

'Tonight? Well, the flat'll be a bit dusty. Haven't visited it for a while. Couldn't be certain there aren't oranges going grey in that old Pyrex bowl. But you won't mind, eh?'

'No.'

'Only one other thing to tell yer: Angela came and carried off the Wendy house. I said: "Oh, you're going to live in that now, Angie, are you? Tony Myerson-Hill's shown you the door, has he?" But she wasn't amused.'

Lev began to walk in the direction of Midge's house. He knew that lonely people woke early. The dog came running to him and he stroked its neck. The back door was ajar. Lev could see Midge Midgham in his kitchen, lumbering between table and stove.

'Want some porridge?' he said.

They sat down and ate. Whisky waited in his cracked old wicker basket, impatient for the day.

'So,' said Midge. 'Come to tell me you're moving on?'

'You guess?'

'Reckon I can see it in your face.'

Lev looked up at Midge. Big Berri. Lev thought, He looks as stupid as a cake of mud, but deep down in the cake is some unexpected ingredient.

'If you want me to stay one week, I will,' said Lev.

'Yew leave when you like. I know the damn dam business has got you jumpy. Crikey. You got things to take care of, I see that.'

The porridge was comforting and good. He remembered GK once saying, 'It's what I always have for breakfast. Lasts you the day, if it has to.'

Midge poured tea, so strong it was almost black, from a stained blue teapot. Whisky turned circles in his basket and lay down. Outside, the sun was already warm.

'Forecast good,' said Midge, staring at the window. 'I think we're getting lucky with the weather. Should be able to pick for nine hours or more today and t'morrow. Hard on yew, those long days, but the bors don't seem to mind. Vitas and his bunch can get a bit crusty, but I have to hand it to the Mings: never seen them anything but happy, have yew?'

'No,' said Lev.

'There's a knack, eh? Never been like that. Wish I were. Always laughing, joking. Always grinning away like Punch and Judy. Wish I knew their secret.'

'Well ...' said Lev.

'Yep?'

'I think, in England, they feel more ... free than in China. And this freedom gives them happiness.'

'Yew reckon?' Midge seemed to ponder this for a long while. Then he said: 'Never think of our lives as "free", do we? Think of them as one long work shift. If yew asked me what freedom meant to me, I wouldn't rightly know what to answer. But perhaps, in this country, we take a lot for granted. I den't know. 'Spect that's why Donna got sick of me: never knew much 'bout anything. Used to say to her: "Den't you ask me, girl. Den't you go botherin' asking me, for I den't know nothin' at all. Only about Lady Muck. She, I know, awright. All her moods, all her likes and dislikes. Tha's why I can make a living. But she's about the sum of it."'

Midge finished his breakfast and took down the pay ledger he kept on a sideboard, which, during Donna's brief day, might have been set out with glass or china, but was now piled up with machine catalogues, magazines and newspapers, old Jiffy-bags, maps, broken pens, secateurs and balls of garden twine. He put on a pair of narrow spectacles and squinted through them at his own untidy handwriting.

'Looks like I owe you £133. Four extra hours in the chiller this week. Right?'

'Yes.'

'Shame you can't stay for the soft fruit, later on. We do Pick Your Own at weekends.'

Pick Your Own.

Lev had a sudden memory of Lydia seeing these words through the coach window and admitting that she didn't understand them.

'What is *Pick Your Own*, Midge?' he asked now.

'Fruit,' said Midge. '*Pick Your Own Fruit*. It's when I let the public loose in a strawberry field. Come swarmin' in on fine days, they do. Never know who you're going to meet there.'

Pick Your Own.

Lev smiled. He imagined the silence of Longmire Farm broken by the laughter of women in pale summer clothes. 'That's good, Midge,' he said. 'Maybe you meet someone new this year.'

'Who knows? But is it worth it? Crikey. All that aggravation. Perhaps I'm better off with just me and the dog.'

Midge went out and returned with Lev's money in an envelope.

'I've called it one three five,' he said. 'Haven't got the coins.'

'I give you change?'

'No. Yew keep it. You earned tha', fair and square. Sorry to lose yew, I am.'

There was a part of Lev that wished he could just slip away from the Mings without saying goodbye: tenderness and embarrassment mingled.

But when they saw him packing his things, they came and stood at his elbow, staring sorrowfully at him.

'Rev. Why you reaving?'

'Rev. You hate us now?'

'We no' hurt you, Rev ...'

'You in crazy mood, Rev. So we take care you. Is awl.'

He reached out for their hands. They came to him and he held them close to him, like children. He said he was grateful that they'd taken care of him, that he would always remember them.

They clung together, the three of them like that, for a moment. Then they heard the toot of Midge's Range Rover, summoning the Mings to the asparagus fields. They grabbed their old canvas satchel, which contained their lunch, tugged on their boots, and scuttled out into the sunshine. Before they reached the car, they turned and waved.

'You good man, Rev!' called Sonny.

And the echo from Jimmy: 'Yah, you good man, Rev!'

19

The Room of Coloured Glass

A Greek friend of Christy Slane's, Babis Panayiottis – usually known as 'Panno' – ran a popular taverna in Highgate Village. Christy had recently replumbed Panno's kitchen, installed a new hot-water boiler, a glass-washer and some deep-bowl sinks and smart drainers, overseen the setting up of a gas-fed charcoal grill. And Panno had said to him: 'Lovely work, Christy. Just how I like it. From now on, you be my guest sometimes.'

Staff came and went from Panno's taverna. He preferred to employ Greeks, or Greek Cypriots, claimed the customers liked to be reassured, in a city of mixed-up cultures, that people were who they pretended to be. But he admitted to Christy that hiring Greek staff was difficult. 'A lot of Greeks get miserable in London,' he said. 'Not their fault. They just can't take the climate.'

When Christy told Panno about Lev, his willingness to work hard, his spell at *GK Ashe*, Panno said: 'Does he look Greek?'

Lev took a waiter's job at Panno's. Six pounds an hour, plus tips, evenings only, six to midnight, six nights a week. The taverna was a twenty-minute walk from Belisha Road, so he'd save on fares, save on time. And he liked Panno. A stooped man in his fifties, with a melancholy face. Brows singed by his charcoal fire. A wrestler's handshake. In his eyes, a fierce patriotic Greek pride.

Compared to the menu at *GK Ashe*, Panno's was simple: fish, chicken, lamb kebabs, steak, spiced Greek sausages, seared on the grill; beef stifado, lamb kleftiko simmered in a low oven; sage-scented moussaka mulched with a thick head of béchamel;

prawns and octopus fried with green chilli salsas; courgette rissoles; stuffed mushrooms and tomatoes and vine leaves; oily hummus and tarama; butter-bean stew; aubergine pâté; fried halloumi cheese; bowls of fleshy green olives; charred pitta bread and Greek salads …

'Never changes,' explained Panno to Lev. 'My regular customers know the menu by heart. It's what brings them back: good food, but simple. Adriatic food. Sometimes, depending on what looks nice at the market, I put on different fish or I make a fish soup. But if I changed the menu, there would be a Highgate mutiny!'

Lev was told to wear his own clothes. 'Black or grey trousers. White shirt. Keep everything fresh and clean.' Tied round his waist was the taverna's hallmark, a blue-and-white apron, striped like the Greek flag. Lev liked its heavy cotton texture, didn't mind that it was a kind of uniform.

The place was full most nights, crazy on Fridays and Saturdays. Lev and the other waiters, Yorgos and Ari, walked a full ten kilometres in their six-hour shift, back and forth to the kitchen. But Lev's sinews were toughened by his time on the asparagus fields. He was nimble and fast. Soon got the art of balancing three plates up his arm, acquired that left-of-vision knack of seeing the raised hand, the wine bottle held aloft. And he didn't mind being front-of-house. After working behind the scenes in the high-velocity kitchen at *GK Ashe*, it was interesting to be in this other arena, the dining space, taking the food to the tables.

The customers got drunk on Greek beer, wine, retsina, raki, but Lev noticed that they usually seemed to have a good time. The food brought out in them a kind of abandonment, an emotional outpouring, as though they were on a Greek-island holiday for a few hours. There was a lot of laughter, a few arguments, some weeping. Mostly, the tips were generous.

'The British need Greece,' Panno was fond of saying, shaking his grizzled head, as the last inebriated customer staggered out into the summer night. 'Always did. Even before Lord Byron. It's where their hearts feel most free.'

Lev had little time in the kitchen to note how Panno's dishes were prepared, but he kept a notebook anyway, understood how cheap lamb shanks could become succulent kleftiko – the dish named after the *kleftes*, the robber bands who fought against

Turkish rule of their homeland in the 1800s – when braised slowly with garlic, wine, onions and tomatoes, how vinegar tenderised the stifado beef, how the split prawns had to flare like firecrackers on the charcoal to get their 'butterfly' shape, how olive oil flowed over everything like a benediction ...

'You got eyes, Lev,' Panno said to him one night, as they were finishing up the service. 'I've seen it. But it surprises me. Not many people from your country are interested in good cuisine.'

'No,' said Lev. 'That's because we've eaten Communist food for sixty years. But now it's changing.'

Lev walked home from Panno's taverna through the dark, often choosing the route down Swains Lane, past Highgate cemetery, locked and barred against intruders and desecrators of Jewish graves. Christy had told him that Karl Marx had been buried there after his 'long, sleepless night of exile'. Lev wondered if he'd go and stand at the headstone one day and tell the bones underneath that, in a grave above Auror, lay the body of a man who'd held on, held fast to the old Marxist ideas till his last breath. Then Lev would add: 'But in another year, Karl, the graves will be under fathoms of water. And who knows where the occupants of them are going to be rehoused?'

Sometimes, at one in the morning, Lev heard noises in the weed-choked hinterland of bushes and dusty trees that bordered the cemetery, noticed litter lying there, tyres, a child's broken bicycle. Once, a cat streaked out in front of him, shivering through the railings, like a phantom. Another night, he stopped, listened, heard a wailing, which might have been feral or human, it was difficult to say.

On the opposite side of the road, where the roots of the plane trees pushed upwards and cracked open the pavements, were parked two ancient camper vans, curtains drawn across who knew what scenes of ecstasy or woe. The vans never moved. The curtains were never drawn back. Sometimes rubbish sacks were left out beside them in the gutters. Quite often, Lev saw vomit staining the wheels, runnels of piss flooding in and out of the sidewalk cracks. One night, a police car was parked there, its blue light slowly turning, but the car was empty and the vans were as closed and as silent as they ever were.

Lev enjoyed the solitary walk home. The nights were warm now. They reminded him of the nights he'd known when he first arrived in England, almost a year ago. With his body tired from his shift at Panno's, he let his mind rampage around his Great Idea, which was becoming more real to him now that he was back in London. He congratulated himself on how far he'd come, and wondered how far it might be possible to go …

Back in Belisha Road, he'd make tea, sit dreaming at the window, postponing, till he felt his head fall, the moment when he'd lie down in his room and sleep. Or, if Christy was there, stay talking till they both started snoring in their chairs.

One night Christy said to Lev: 'There's something on your mind, Lev. I can see it in your look. D'you want to tell me what it is?'

'Yes,' said Lev. 'Soon, I will tell you, Christy. When everything is more clear to me.'

'Fair enough,' said Christy. 'But the Irish are good at keeping secrets, you know. Maybe because our heads are so chock full of them. Me ma used to say, "If walls could see into our minds, the house'd fall to pieces".'

Mostly, these nights, Christy talked about Jasmina: the immaculate colour of Jasmina's skin, her glossy hair, scented with almond oil, the way the blood-red lacquer of her toenails startled you, the sexy Indian poshness of her voice. Lev hadn't met her yet, but began to feel he knew her. 'Like you,' said Christy, 'she's got a love-in going with food. I eat her cucumber and mint *raita* for breakfast, spoon it over me Weetabix. Sometimes we lie in bed and she brings tiny little samosas and baby meatballs and we feed them to each other. I'm puttin' on a ton of flesh, but who cares? Flesh is all we are – Mary, Mother of God, forgive me. Why not have a bit more of ourselves?'

Jasmina had been married once – an arranged Hindu marriage – but divorced by her husband, Anand, because she couldn't give him any children. Anand had married again and fathered five living daughters and one dead son. Jasmina was forty now. Alone for a long time. Never thought she'd fall for a Westerner. But then Christy Slane had fixed her boiler and that was it. 'Gave her back a bit of heat, I guess,' he said, with a grin he couldn't suppress. 'Realised how cold she'd been.'

Christy's behaviour towards Jasmina reminded Lev of how his

had been with Sophie. When Jasmina couldn't see Christy for a couple of days, he fretted. He'd phone or text her in the middle of the night, at dawn, at ten-minute intervals … He brought her name into every conversation, caressed it with his voice: *Jas-meena. Jas-meena.* Said he'd even come round to liking Palmers Green. Pink magnolias grew in front gardens there. Indian music floated out of doorways and onto patios. Children wore clean white socks.

'Of course,' he said, 'there's a lot of drug shite goin' on, and Jasmina's had two break-ins, but that's standard issue anywhere in London. And wait till you see Jasmina's front room. Now there's a thing. The colours of that place get right into me dreams.'

As instructed by Lydia, Lev had sent £50 to Rudi, and told him to use it as a bribe at the Office of Rehousing in Baryn. But Lora, weeping, called to say that Rudi was in bed, that he'd been there for thirteen days, reading old car magazines and staring at the wall.

'If he doesn't get up, he's going to die, Lev,' sobbed Lora. 'What am I meant to do, if he won't leave his bed?'

Lev was silent. Thought how much he'd relied on Rudi and how Rudi had never let him down. Knew that he'd somehow believed this pattern would continue for ever …

Lev took a breath and said: 'I'm working on a plan, Lora. But I've a way to go yet. It involves money. Other things, too. You just have to trust me.'

'What "plan"?'

'It's a plan for getting your lives going again – afterwards, in Baryn. But someone has to secure two apartments: one for you and Rudi and one for Ina and Maya. Can *you* go to the housing office?'

'I'll try. But I'm busy, Lev. A lot of people are coming now for horoscopes. They want to know if they've got any future. I'm doing palm readings, too.'

'Good, Lora.'

'Rudi says it's dishonest, taking people's money to tell them things that can't be known.'

'Not if it consoles them, helps them to carry on.'

He heard a voice in the background. Rudi's. Shouting at Lora not to use the phone any more: it was a waste of money.

'I'd better go,' she said.

'No,' said Lev. 'Put Rudi on.'

An argument between them then. Rudi didn't want to speak to anybody. Lora pleading with him: 'Talk to Lev.' Eventually, a curse as the phone was dropped, then picked up, then Rudi's weary voice: 'Lev, I got nothing to say, buddy. I'm sorry.'

'Did you get the money, Rudi?'

'Yeah. I can't go to Baryn. The Tchevi's sicker than me.'

'OK. How did we get to Baryn before you had the Tchevi?'

'What?'

'How did we used to get to Baryn?'

'You know how. Fucking bicycle. In the shit cold of winter. Froze our faces off. I'm not doing that any more.'

'It's not winter, Rudi.'

'Yes, it is. It's winter HERE! In my fucking heart, it's winter. Guess you haven't understood, Lev, because you're arseing about in London, with some ballbreaking bit of English totty who treats you like the cat's dinner, but we're finished here. All of us. No work. No house. No transport. No money. We're dead. You got it? We're stone fucking DEAD!'

The phone was slammed down. Lev stood in his room and stared out at the patched and tilting roofs of Tufnell Park and the sky above, streaked with vapour trails. Even the *idea* that Rudi might die made him feel panicky.

He let a few minutes go by, then called back. Lora told him she had a client arriving.

'Won't keep you long,' he said. 'Just get to Baryn, Lora, and sort out the apartments.'

'I'll try, Lev. But the only income we've got now is from the horoscopes and the palm readings. I need to be here.'

'It'll only take a morning. Get the early bus. Please do this. Leave the rest to me.'

Leave the rest to me.

How pompous that sounded! A braggart's boast, absurdly confident. It was also tainted with a lie: the lie of implied certainty. And there *was* no certainty, only this wild dream of his, this thing he called his Great Idea, built on hope and nothing else. Lev cursed himself for even mentioning it to Lora. Could already imagine Rudi saying: 'So what does he think he's going to do? Stick his fucking finger in the dyke and hold back the water, or what?'

*

On a Monday afternoon, Lev kept the appointment he'd had to beg for with GK Ashe.

'I'm not taking you back, Lev,' GK had snarled on the phone. 'I've replaced you. Got it?'

'I'm not asking for my job, GK. I swear. Got a job in a restaurant in Highgate now. Swear on my daughter's life.'

'All right. So, what d'you want?'

'One hour of your time. I need advice, information about an Idea I have. One hour of your time. Please, Chef.'

There had been a long silence. Then GK said: 'OK. An hour and that's it. Out of the kindness of my heart. Come at three.'

They sat at the familiar table, near Damian's bar, the smell of the place bringing back feelings of agony, feelings of joy. Waldo, bringing them coffee, gave Lev a weak, commiserating smile.

Lev put his notebook in front of him and opened it. GK's blue eyes watched him. Lev felt like a fish in a bowl. His shaking hands clutched the two open covers of the notebook. He took a breath. Now, he had to begin to make real the Thing that, until this moment, had substance only in his mind. As he spoke, he worked hard to keep his voice steady.

'This is it,' he said. 'This is my Idea. I am going to open my own restaurant.'

Lev stopped. He swallowed. Waited for GK's look of disdain or disbelief, but it didn't come. So he summoned up a stronger voice and went on: 'My restaurant will be in the city of Baryn, where new hydro-electric power is coming. I believe that, following from this, many businesses will come to this city, so for my restaurant, I think the time will be right.'

He waited again, looked up at GK. Sure the put-down was going to arrive now. But all GK said was: 'Your English has improved.'

Lev thumbed his notebook, tried to imbibe, from all the optimistic words he'd written there, a heartful of courage. 'My plan is, I start with a small premises. Maybe forty covers. Maybe fifty maximum. I will be chef-proprietor. I will give my people food like they've never had. I don't mean like here at *GK Ashe*. I know I could never—'

'Why not like here?'

'You have years of training and work, Chef. A big talent. I could never—'

'Why not aim high? You said "food like they've never had". If this is an expanding arena of new capitalism, it'll be chocka with restaurants before you can say *beurre noisette*. So, how're you going to make yours the best?'

Lev gaped. But what he liked already – what was making his heart race with joy – was that GK was taking him seriously.

'Chef,' he said, 'of course I want this. I want mine to be the best. But in my country most people are still poor. They can't afford high-end cuisine.'

'OK. So what are you going to cook?'

'Chef ...'

'Simple question. What are you going to cook?'

Lev turned to his clutch of recipes, most of which had been filched from GK's menu. 'I haven't decided quite—'

'Right. OK. Give me some paper. Let's get some sense into this.'

Lev tore out a sheet from his notebook and GK snatched it from his hand, unsnapped a pen from his pocket. The coffee stood forgotten at his elbow. He began to scribble fast in his large, unruly writing. After a while he turned the page round towards Lev. He jabbed a finger along the lines of writing as he spoke.

'Number 1,' he said. '*Style of cuisine.* Decide on it. Stick to it. Pin your name to it. Keep it authentic. Right?'

'Yes.'

'If you want my advice, don't fart around with fucking fusion. I could name you ten restaurants in London that've gone under by flirting with cardamom pods. One foot in Paris, one in Bom-fucking-bay. And that's a recipe for disaster, because the clients don't know what the hell they're meant to be savouring. Right? So, let me ask you again: what do you want to cook?'

Lev rubbed his eyes. 'I suppose ... what I imagine is ... like here,' he said. 'This kind of food. Very fresh ingredients. Meat never overcooked. Nice sauces and *jus*. Nice vegetables ...'

'OK, but you have to *formulate* it. A lot of my cooking was learned in France. But it's modern. It's even quite minimalist. This is right for London at this moment, but you have to decide what's right for your town.'

'My town, Chef, has never known good food.'

'No, I hear you. OK. You've got everything to play for. But you're also going to have to educate people. You're going to have to persuade them it's worth spending real money on something that's going to end up in the toilet in twenty-four hours. Which brings me to *Costings*.'

GK began to scribble again. Then he looked up and said: 'Margins aren't big in catering, except on booze. Price your food too low and you'll be paddling backwards into Debt Creek. Price it too high and you won't get any customers. You have to judge what your catchment area can take. And you have to judge it right.'

'I know ... and this is difficult.'

'My advice would be: keep the menu small. Don't offer fifteen choices, offer four or five. Or three, plus one or two specials, based on what looks nice in the market that day.'

'Yes. I was thinking that, Chef. At least, to start.'

'OK. Good. Small menu, but that brings us to Number 3, the Big Number 3: *Supply*. And remember, this will dictate your style of cooking. If you can't get a game supplier, you can't cook game. If nobody grows tomatoes, you can't make pasta. From what I've heard about your country, all anybody's eaten in the last century is goat meat and pickles, so you've got a free hand, but it won't be free if you can't get the ingredients. Have you thought about that?'

'Yes,' said Lev. He skipped hurriedly to another page of his notebook. 'Supply is what I've worked on, Chef. Before I start, I will buy a car, or a pickup, go round very many small farms. These were once part of our national farmsteads, but now they are individual and people work very hard on them. So I talk to these people, place my weekly requirements: chickens, geese, ducks, pigs and so forth. Also to local allotment zones, give my requirements for vegetables. Buy direct. And I know the limits of my country's allotments. No point thinking about kiwi fruit or avocados.'

'Right. What about red meat?'

'Same idea, Chef. Buy locally. Visit the hunters, like my father once was, who kill rabbits and wild boar. And fish. May be difficult at first. But above Baryn will be a new reservoir. Very, very big. In time, maybe trout and pike, salmon, freshwater eel.'

'OK. Excellent. Local ingredients are the best. But you can't always be prepping and cooking *and* collecting poultry and listening to game hunters' reminiscences all in the same fucking day. You'll have to delegate.'

'I know.'

'So you have to factor this in to your costings: what you pay other people for deliveries and all the stuff you can't physically do yourself. Nobody will work for you for nothing.'

'I know, Chef.'

'What about staples? Aren't these in short supply still? Flour, rice, butter, oil, sugar?'

'No. You can get these. Baryn market.'

'Regular? No hitches? Remember, a restaurant has to keep going round the year, day on day, or the clientele falls away.'

'Yes.'

'Right, moving on to Number 4: *Look*. Is this a modern brasserie? Or a fuggy bistro? Is it a nostalgic old Russian tearoom? Who's it aimed at? What bit of the city is it going to be in? Whose corner restaurant is this going to become? You've got to get your *Look* aligned with your *Style*. And you've got to know all this before you start. Which brings us to Number 5, which really should be number one: *Setting-Up Cost*. How in hell's name are you going to finance this?'

'Chef, this is really why I came—'

GK's features froze. He threw down the pen. 'You came to ask me for capital?'

'No. Of course not,' said Lev. 'Only to ask you, could you list for me *everything*? Everything I must put in before I can be running. I mean all the equipment. Then I can begin my sums.'

GK ran a hand through his turbulent hair. He stared at Lev in an almost frightened way, then looked down again at the piece of paper, picked up the pen and stuck it into his mouth. 'Yeah. OK,' he said, after a moment. 'I can do this for you. Fifty covers, you said?'

'Yes.'

'So, two in the kitchen? You and a commis. Share all the prep?'

'Yes.'

'Two on tables. One nurse. That it?'

'That's it. And the car or truck. Second-hand.'

'I'll need to think about it. Get it right for you. Half the *matériel* I've got through there you won't need. Got a name for this place?'

'Yes,' said Lev. 'I will call it *Marina*, after my wife.'

GK smiled. He laid down the pen once more. 'Right,' he said. 'At least you got that settled.'

He stood up and went to the bar. He took down a bottle of Cognac, poured two shots and returned to the table. He proposed a toast to *Marina*, and they drank. Lev's heart was beating so fast that he gulped the brandy to try to still the roar of it.

And then he and GK Ashe sat on. Lev smoked and they talked about the future, about the importance, in any life, of having at least one Big Idea, something you could believe in. After a while, the talk drifted to GK's father, who'd wanted him to be a lawyer, had all chefs pinned down as weird, gay or poor, couldn't see how his son might make a profession out of that and hadn't been interested when he had.

'Doesn't he ever come to eat here, Chef?'

'No. Never. He came to the opening, that was all. Stayed about half an hour. If I was head chef at the Dorchester, or somewhere like that, he might come, but even then, I doubt it. So I live with that. I have to. Sometimes you just have to say, "Fuck the parents", and not mind.'

'I know this, Chef,' said Lev. 'I know this very well.'

Time passed, and next door in the kitchen Lev heard people coming in and the staff meal being prepared. He knew he had to leave soon, before Sophie arrived, but now GK seemed to want to keep talking. He described his mother, 'a truly lovely woman', who'd died in a car accident on the M4, and the step-mother who had replaced her, and the knowledge that this had brought him that life was 'a miserable travesty of our dreams'. GK refilled the shot glasses. The Cognac modulated his voice, brought a softer look to his blue eyes. It felt, to Lev, as though GK had suddenly passed from being an employer to being a friend. This friendship had a kind of radiance about it, in which it was tempting to bask.

Then a familiar voice intruded. 'What's going on, Chef?'

Sophie was standing by the bar, staring at them. They both turned and looked at her. Lev saw that her hair was shorter and spikier and her face thinner than he remembered it. Even at this distance, he believed he could catch the scent of her, the scent that still had the power to overwhelm him. He looked away and began to gather up his notes.

'Nothing's going on,' said GK. 'Lev was just picking my brains. He's starting his own place.'

Sophie gaped. Lev could hear her thinking, He's nothing, he's no one. How can a nobody open his own place?

'His own restaurant?'

'Yes. In his own country.'

Lev didn't look at her, but he could feel her tension diminish. In his own country. That's all right, then. In a country far away . . .

Lev thought he should stand up, shake GK's hand, leave there and then, but some stubborn defiance in him insisted on his right to stay where he was.

'So,' said Sophie to Lev, 'you've decided to go back?'

He inclined his head. This tiny movement could have been taken for a nod. But he saw that they were waiting, Sophie and GK, for him to speak to her. He didn't want to speak to her. He thought, All conversation with her now is like trying to scrape the dregs, the *dross*, out of an empty barrel – and then you scar the barrel itself.

They both stared at him, but he didn't open his mouth or let his glance even flicker in her direction. And it seemed she understood that he'd given her all the answer she was going to get. While he clutched his notebook, while he saw his hands tense to yellow bone, she disappeared back into the kitchen.

GK waited a moment, then said quietly: 'Preece leads her a dance. But he gets a lot of important people swilling at my trough, so who am I to complain? That's the way of the bad world, I guess.'

'Yes,' agreed Lev. 'That's the way of the bad world, Chef.'

He found himself shivering. He took a sip of the cold coffee. He was in a kind of shock, but didn't know what had agitated him more, GK's unexpected, thrilling support for his Idea, or the unexpected, teasing sight of Sophie. He still wanted her, and that was the bitter truth of it. Just catching sight of her made him ache to fuck her. And he felt that, far into the future, he would remember her – her voice, her smell, her clothes, her laughter, her dimpled cheeks, her full breasts, her tattoo, her arse, her salty cunt

– and want her still. When he imagined her making love with Howie Preece, he felt himself fall into a trance of desolation.

It was a while before Lev was allowed to meet Jasmina.

'She's a very modest person,' Christy explained. 'It would embarrass her to sleep with me at Belisha Road, with you in Frankie's room.'

'Yes? You want me to stay away, Christy?'

'No, not at all, fella. It isn't only that. I think she's also frightened of Angela, of finding, like, the *residue* of Angela in the flat. You know? Or that Angela could turn up and whip the bed out from underneath us!'

Then on a Sunday evening in June, warm and dry, Jasmina invited Lev to her house in Palmers Green. He and Christy drove there in Christy's van, with the plumber's gear clanking and jumping about behind them, like some toddlers' orchestra trying to assemble itself. 'Ah, shut up!' Christy yelled at this orchestra a couple of times. 'Can't hear meself drive.' And when, out along the North Circular Road, a spanner came flying forwards between the seats and whacked the gear lever, Christy said: 'Christ almighty, will you look at that? I've never been able to control me tools. Never at all.'

They arrived at last in a quiet road of low, semi-detached houses with bay windows and tended front gardens. Christy slowed the van, said, without moving his head: 'See the net curtains twitch. Everybody knows everybody's business here. Worse than Limerick. Looked on me as a scallywag when I first started coming to visit Jasmina. But now they're all after me to refit their kitchens. I've got more popularity on this street than anywhere else on earth.'

As soon as they got out of the van, Jasmina's front door opened and she came out into the evening sunshine with her arms held wide. Lev saw that she was a plump woman, whose sari seemed too tight for her body. Her eyes were magnified by the complicated lenses of her spectacles, but beneath these, a smile of some beauty was occurring. At the sight of her, Christy's face blushed an all-over red. She embraced him and Lev saw him almost disappear beneath or behind her when a gust of wind blew the loose folds of her sari round his narrow shoulders.

He emerged from her to introduce Lev.

'Welcome,' she said to Lev. 'Come into the house. My God, it's such beautiful weather, I can't believe it. Come on, come on ...'

Her path was made of some granite-like material with shards of mica that glittered in the soft light. Under the curving window, fat hydrangeas were poised on the brink of a blue flowering. Her front door was bright white PVC with a brass door-knocker in the shape of a lion's head.

From a carpeted hallway Jasmina led them into her front room, and here Christy turned to Lev and said: 'Did you ever see something like this, Lev?'

The small room had been fitted out with glass shelving, running right round it to a height of six or seven feet. The shelves were lit from above with halogen spotlights and on the shelves stood a vast collection of coloured glass bottles, jugs, decanters, vases and vials. With the bright lamps above and with the sun still offering a restless light through the mullion-paned window, the glassware appeared to tremble in a perpetual rainbow jive. Ruby reds flashed a shimmering radiance to their neighbouring snarly pinks. Further round, the dance was muted to purples, indigo blues, sea blues, aquamarines. Turn to the left and the entire wall shone bottle green, chartreuse green, silver and lemon. Go to the west-facing window and you were drawn into honeyed ambers and yellows ...

'My God,' said Lev. 'Fantastic ...'

Jasmina was pinching and plucking at her sari, to arrange it correctly. When she had it to her satisfaction, she smiled her transforming smile and said to Lev: 'I call it my "loneliness room". It's the kind of thing women do when they're alone for a long time: collect glass. I started with a few pieces, then, somehow, I just carried on.'

'It's lovely, though, Jas,' said Christy. 'It was worth those years.'

'No, it wasn't,' said Jasmina quickly, her smile vanishing. But Christy chose to ignore this.

'See, Lev,' he said, 'it's so nicely arranged, isn't it? With the little hot lights, an' all. And the way the see-through shelves reflect everything. I think it's a work of art.'

'Yes,' said Lev. 'I would say so. A work of art.'

'Well,' said Jasmina. 'I suppose so. But it all has to be dusted.

And once a month, I take every piece down and wash it and clean the shelves, top and bottom. It's insane.'

'I love it,' said Christy. 'I utterly and completely love it. Told Lev about it, didn't I, fella? Told you about the room of coloured glass.'

'Yes, you did. And I never saw anything like this.'

'Oh well,' said Jasmina, 'in the sunlight, I suppose it looks quite pretty. Now, sit down, please. I shall bring us some nibbles.'

Christy and Lev didn't sit, but stood in the middle of the room, still staring at the glass, shifting position now and then, like visitors at an exhibition. They didn't speak. Lev was trying to imagine all the individual transactions that had led to a collection of this incredible size. It seemed to him that they must have taken up an entire lifetime. Felt astonishment at the idea of that much leisure, that much spare cash flying away into bottles and vials. Remembered a solitary blue glass jar he'd bought for Marina at the Baryn market and which had stood – still stood – on a table in their bedroom. Remembered Marina's long-fingered hands, shining it up with a rag, sometimes sticking flowers into it. Remembered her saying to him: 'There's something about that blue jar, Lev, that I love.'

Jasmina came back into the room and set down a pewter tray on the coffee-table. On the tray was arranged a collection of small white dishes, filled with food. Between the dishes, on the shined-up pewter, Jasmina had sprinkled white rose petals. Her plump hands rippled tenderly over the food, making her bangles clink.

'Cocktail *koftas*,' she said. 'Spicy cashews, quick-fried prawns, cucumber dip, spinach and ricotta *samosas*. Please help yourselves. I will get the vodka.'

She went out again, and Christy contemplated the white dishes and the strewn petals. 'She got vodka for you,' he whispered. 'I told her you liked a shot.'

Jasmina wanted to serve the supper at the back of the house, on the patio, but Christy said, no, he liked to eat in here, watch the sun go down on all the restless colours. So they sat on the floor on bright cushions and Jasmina came and went with more and more dishes – enough food for ten people.

Though she drank only water, she served cold Indian beer in a tall jug and Lev felt his mind fill up again with the sweetness of the present. He'd never tasted home-cooked Indian food before. He liked the way, as you ate, the *perfume* of it still visited your nostrils, the way you *inhaled* it as you swallowed and felt its transforming properties slide into your blood. After only a few mouthfuls, he fancied his hair was scented with coconut, his skin radiant with cumin and ginger.

The shimmering glassware sparkled at the edge of his vision. Jasmina's voice was melodious, her vowels idiosyncratically perfect, as though she'd learned her English from some old sequestered duchess. And Lev could see that, whatever she was talking about, Christy was entranced. For a while, as they ate a lemon chicken dish with *dahl* and cauliflower, what she actually talked about was her job as a mortgage adviser at the Hertford and Ware Building Society, but the look of rapture on Christy's face, the attentiveness of his gaze, never faltered.

'Jas does really important work,' he said. 'Helpin' people to get started on the property ladder. That's philanthropy, I think.'

Lev saw Jasmina stretch out a hand and lay it gently on Christy's wrist. 'It's not really,' she said. 'I saw it like that when I started, but now I think mortgages are quite bad in many ways, especially very large ones.'

She turned to Lev and said: 'We have a mountain of personal debt in this country. An Everest of debt. And every day, the Hertford and Ware adds to the sum of it. I'm less and less comfortable with that, and more sympathetic towards the Muslims, whose law forbids them paying interest on loans, so they don't go down the traditional mortgage route. I mean, on Friday, I had a white couple in, trying to borrow *twenty-nine times* their salary. Where will it end?'

'It won't end,' said Christy. 'People will always long for things, and you help them to realise their longings, that's all.'

'"Loans for dreams", that's what I call it,' said Jasmina. 'The way I was brought up, you worked a lifetime to realise a dream. Then, at last, maybe you got it – like I've got this collection of glass. Now, in Britain, everybody wants it now, hurry-scurry: new house, new car, new fridge, new kitchen …'

'That's where I come in,' said Christy proudly, pouring more beer. 'I could get a year's worth of work out of this one road, couldn't I, Jas?'

Jasmina stroked Christy's forehead, as she might have stroked the forehead of a feverish child. 'Yes,' she said, 'but not if you start drinking too much beer again …'

'Look, you provided the feckin' beer, Jas. I'm just being a polite guest and drinkin' what you're offering.'

'And I hate it when you swear, Christy. You know I do.'

Christy seized Jasmina's hand and pressed it to his mouth and kissed the palm. 'Sorry,' he mumbled, between kisses. 'I take it back. I unsay it. We're having such a lovely time. And will you look at all the glass now, with just that last bit of sun on it, that *sunbeam*? Eh, Lev?'

'Yes, I see it. Very beautiful, Jasmina.'

'Only the mind of someone as exceptional as Jas could have contrived those colours.'

Now Lev saw Jasmina relax and the lovely smile returned. She let Christy hold her hand next to his heart and keep it there while he tried to guide another spoonful of *dahl* to his mouth. Lev noticed that, behind her glasses, Jasmina's eyes were moist.

'You're such a baby, Christy. Such a romantic. Isn't he, Lev?'

'Yes. A romantic. Yes.'

'Who cares?' said Christy. 'Does anybody care here? I mean, does anybody here care?'

'I care,' said Jasmina. 'I don't want you to change.'

'Listen to that,' said Christy, with a beatific grin on his face. 'Isn't that a pure peach of a thing to say? God Almighty. Will you marry me, Jasmina? Soon as my divorce becomes absolute, will you do me the honour of becoming my wife?'

Now there was a sudden silence in the room. Outside, there came the sound of kids riding skateboards up and down the street: the clatter of worn wheels, echoing laughter. Lev looked from Christy to Jasmina, saw her staring at him with her mouth open. Christy still held her hand against his narrow chest.

'Is that just something you're saying, Christy?' asked Jasmina quietly.

'No,' said Christy. 'Or at least, I am *saying it*. But it's not a *just saying it* kind of thing. I'm saying it, Jasmina, and I mean it. I'd like you to marry me. I mean, if you'd like to, too …'

She turned her profile towards the window, where the last yellow flares of the sun were sinking through the dazzling lemon and amber spectrum of the glass. Then she turned back to Christy.

'Yes,' she said gravely. 'I'd like to, too.'

Lev put down his fork. He held himself very still as he watched Jasmina and Christy lean in towards each other and cling together. The sight of Christy's scorched hand clutching to his thin, white frame Jasmina's plump, golden midriff moved Lev more than he could express, and when the couple kissed, he looked away. He let his gaze wander, once again, round Jasmina's solitary accumulation of coloured bottles. In any collector's existence, he thought, there must come a moment when he or she says, 'That's it. It's complete.' And he felt that such a moment had probably arrived.

20

Loans for Dreams

Lev was on his way home from Panno's at about one in the morning when he got a call on his mobile from Lora. He was by the gates to Highgate cemetery, where he noticed that someone had ditched a mound of rubbish in supermarket carrier-bags. Ahead of him lay the darkness of Swains Lane.

Lora asked him to send more money. Her voice sounded far away. She said she was in despair about Rudi. Rudi's depression now seemed to have got a hold on his body, making his bones ache and his muscles cramp and his feet sweat. She said he cried in his sleep.

Lev couldn't stand to picture this. When he thought about his friend, he liked to imagine him laughing, arguing, drinking, slapping people's shoulders with his huge paw of a hand. 'I'll send more,' he said, right away.

'I hate to ask you, Lev. You've been generous to everybody,' said Lora. 'But what I'm hoping, what I'm banking on, is if Rudi can get the Tchevi back on the road, he'll stop feeling that everything's over. Because that's all he keeps saying to me: that our lives are *kaput*, like the car.'

Lev stood in the dark road, staring at the dim light shining in a window of one of the camper vans. He longed to tell Lora that his plan for the restaurant in Baryn was going to rescue them all, that Rudi would have an important role in it, but he didn't dare say this, not yet, because he knew that his Great Idea had acquired no more real substance than when he'd first thought it up.

Lora now told Lev that she'd got a price on new tyres and repair of the cooling system. If he could send £200, then the Tchevi could be back on the road within a week.

Two hundred pounds.

Already Lev was a week behind with Christy's rent, two weeks behind with money to Ina. He began to walk down Swains Lane. He told Lora he could send the money after his next pay day, wondering as he said this how he'd live once it was gone.

He was level with the vans now. Saw, at the corner of his eye, two kids – one black and one white – come out from the dark space behind one of them, thought, It's late for them to be on the street, thought they couldn't be older than twelve, watched them go running down the road on the cemetery side.

' ... he refuses to look out of the window,' Lora was saying. 'He says he wishes someone would steal the Tchevi, so that he didn't have to see it parked there ...'

Into Lev's mind streamed the memory of the Tchevi bumping down the sandy paths that led to Lake Essel and Rudi describing how he was going to stun the fish with its powerful headlights, and how the stunned fish had turned that odd electric blue – a poisonous blue?

'Lora, listen,' said Lev. 'Make Rudi go to the hospital. He could be ill, not just depressed. Muscle cramps could be serious. It could be contamination from that trip we made to the lake.'

Lev heard Lora sigh. 'He won't see anybody. I wish you were home. You'd be able to help him, I know you would. But all I can think of at the moment is to try to fix the car.'

'Make him see a doctor.'

'Did you ever in your life *make* Rudi do anything?'

'OK. OK. But just remind him about the blue fish.'

'You know what I keep thinking, Lev? I keep thinking, if only we had a child. Then Rudi would *have* to keep going, wouldn't he, for the sake of the child, just like you had to keep going for Maya's sake?'

Lev began to remind Lora how long his own decline had lasted, then he paused as he saw the two kids running back up the lane towards him, running fast. He looked at their faces, the whiteness and the blackness of them emphasised by the shadowy light. He kept talking to Lora, but he heard his voice falter. He noticed that the white kid wore round specs, was shorter than the black boy, who had longer legs and could run faster. And now he understood, in a whirling, infinitely small moment of time, as the black kid slowed to let the other one catch up, so that they were running level, that the boys were going to charge into him, that he was their target, him and his phone ...

He had time to brace himself, only that, then he felt a stinging slap on the left side of his face and a blow to his right shoulder. He staggered, tried to lunge at the black kid, who'd slapped him, then realised he was still clutching his phone as the boys sped on past him up the hill.

He turned, saw them pounding towards the cemetery gates, got the phone back to his ear, heard Lora saying: 'What's happening, Lev? What's going on?'

'Kids,' he said. 'Kids ...' Heard his breath laboured, like his father's had been. 'Tried to steal my phone. Jesus Christ!'

'You OK, Lev?'

'Yeah ...'

He began to walk faster, wished he were nearer Belisha Road. At his back, he heard laughter, turned again, saw the boys grabbing bags of rubbish from the pile near the gates, saw them hurling the stinking bags into the air. Knew it wasn't over.

He told Lora he had to go, told her to tell Rudi the money would soon be on its way, told her to go ahead and get the tyres ordered, and the parts for the cooling system ...

Thuk! A bag of garbage hit him in the small of his back. Almost winded him. He wanted to run, but knew twelve-year-olds could outpace him. Better to keep calm, go on with a firm step, get his phone safe in a pocket. Because perhaps it was just a game, one they liked to play late at night on strangers who chose this dark road? Perhaps they'd spurn his ordinary cheap mobile, probably stole iPods and BlackBerrys and God-knows-what all the time and wouldn't think it worth their while to hurt him for this?

Thuk! Another bag. His shoulder now, the bag bursting and spilling as it hit him. And the bags were heavy, sharp-edged with empty tins and bottles, which clattered onto the pavement. Wouldn't be a game any longer if one found its target on his head.

Anger welled in him as he heard the boys begin to run back down the hill towards him. Because just exactly what did kids like these – of whatever colour – have as their excuse for attacking strangers?

What, for instance, did they know about disadvantage and pain? Did their fathers work for starvation wages nine hours a day at some stinking sawmill? Had their mothers died of leukaemia at the age of thirty-six? Were their homes threatened with obliteration? He turned again, but too late; they slammed into him and he lost his balance and lurched and went down, and now they were over him like carrion, pushing his face into the gutter, pecking at his clothes, gouging out the phone, tearing his shirt ...

He tried to kick out at their legs, their skinny arses, their feet in stinking sneakers, but connected with nothing. Began yelling at them in his own language, as Rudi would have yelled, felt their scavenging hands pause just for a second as they registered the unfamiliar words, then a tide of abuse shouted into his ear: 'Fuckin' foreign shi'head!'

'Immigrant fuckin' scum!'

Another slap on his face – just like the flat-hand blow of a school bully, petty, ignominious, stinging with insult, then everything being torn from him: keys, wallet, change, cigarettes, everything.

He thrashed out again and his foot collided with something, and a hand cuffed his head and the swearing resumed: 'Asylum-fuckin'-seeker!'

'Terrorist!'

'Cunt!'

Then he tasted dust in his mouth, heard the scuff of the rubber-soled trainers as the boys got to their feet and ran away into the darkness.

He waited until he heard the running footsteps grow faint, then got up. He wasn't hurt, but his face stung and his legs were trembling. He looked up and down the road, saw it deserted. The light in the van had gone out.

He staggered over to the cemetery railings and leaned against them. Felt in all his pockets to see what they'd left him, hoped at least to find his cigarettes. But there was nothing in the pockets. *Nothing.* No key to Belisha Road – and he knew Christy was at Palmers Green with Jasmina. No money for a night bus to anywhere ...

He attempted to run back up the hill, but his heart began to pound so hard he felt it almost stall. He slowed, tried to hold himself up, to still his anger, tried to remember those little English punks were no worse than the under-age petty criminals of Baryn, who hung about the market, nabbing small change, who nicked ice skates from the decaying old open-air skating rink, sold them back for cash in some market bric-à-brac stall and bought drugs wherever they could find them. They were just poor kids, that was all. Poor kids from poor homes, silted up with prejudice and misery. Poor kids whose parents were smashed or stoned or full of rage – or all of these. Poor kids who were already screwing up their own future.

He managed to run the last block to Panno's. Saw a light still on in the kitchen, began hammering on the door.

Panno appeared, his melancholy face lit up with alarm.

Panno agreed to advance Lev some money against next week's wages. He told him he was lucky, relatively lucky: his skull could have been broken by a bottle. And Lev knew Panno was right about the luck, yet he was still jittery. He felt that some part of himself had been broken.

He acquired a new phone. When he held it in his hand, he didn't know now how he'd managed to exist in the world for so long without a mobile. Then, moments later, it rang and it was GK.

'Got preliminary costings for you,' he said. 'Come at two-thirty tomorrow.'

Set out on the familiar table, where the air still smelled faintly of the previous night's crostini, was a single page of figures. This time GK offered Lev fresh lemonade.

'I typed the figures,' said GK, 'so you can see everything clearly. Take a look.'

Lev held the paper with hands that trembled. He began to read:

> *six-burner professional cuisinières (2) with double ovens: min £2,200 each new, or ex-restaurant second-hand £400 each (?)*
> *salamanders (2): £500 each*
> *steam extraction system: min £1,000*
> *professional gas grill: £650*
> *dishwasher and sinks: £900*
> *storage and worktops: min £3,000*
> *knives and blocks: £300*

> *pans, cutters, strainers, bowls, boards, etc., etc.: £300*
> *tables and chairs for 40 covers: second-hand? Price unknown*
> *cutlery and glassware: £500?*
> *linen ...*

Lev got to the end of the list and didn't dare look up. He started again at the top, saw in his mind one of the beautiful six-burner cuisinières with its obedient blue flames, and longed, *longed*, to be standing there in front of it. But when he'd read down the schedule a second time, he stopped when he got to *storage and worktops*. He just couldn't bear to have to take it in again, such a shocking accumulation of expense.

Lev felt GK's sympathetic gaze on him. 'That's only the *matériel*,' said GK. 'I really don't know how much it will cost you to fit out the premises. D'you know tame carpenters and electricians? Will those people still work for packets of Marlboro or shipments of panty-hose? Or is it going to be an hourly rate?'

'Hourly rate,' said Lev. 'But quite low.'

'OK. Well, I still can't estimate how that's going to come out. Depends on the premises you find and what's in place already.'

Lev was silent, staring at the bottom-line figure: *£14,000.*

Now he saw his Great Idea for what it was: a wild imagining, a thing of no substance. As a boy, he'd been a perpetual dreamer. 'Concentrate, concentrate!' his mother and father had often had to bleat, as he'd stumbled on the way to school or down the path to the river. 'Stop staring at clouds.' And now he'd been dreaming again, gawping at shadows again, that was all. Except that, this time, his future and that of the people he loved most in the world depended on the dream. Now he felt sick with fear.

'Have some lemonade,' said GK.

Lev drank. Loved the tang and sweetness of it. Thought how, if you were a real chef, you could anticipate and provide the tastes and textures that people would find consoling, even if only for moments at a time. Reflected that, in the end, life – and the memory of life that ran with you hand in hand – was made up of such fugitive spots of time.

'You have to remember, Lev,' he heard GK say, 'that I have no idea what stuff costs in Baryn. This figure is the minimum figure you'd need to equip a working kitchen here, assuming you can get a few items second-hand, but in your country, it would certainly be less. If you lower it to, say, 10K, to take account of the differential, you might be about right.'

Ten thousand pounds.

The whole enterprise was a pure fantasy. Even after his next pay cheque, Lev was stuck with less than £40 in his pocket once he'd sent something to Ina and the £200 to Lora for the Tchevi. And he owed Christy £180 ...

He wanted to laugh at himself. *Ten thousand pounds*! He saw a foolish person who once believed he could advance human happiness with a few poinsettia plants, a pathetic figure who, toiling home with stolen bits of wood, had been knocked off his bicycle by a hay bale and lain in the ditch like a crucified man. He was forty-three and his plan – his Great Idea – was a farce. In a year's time, his home would be under water. There would be no restaurant named *Marina*.

And what would happen to Ina? On his way back from *GK Ashe* this worry, above all the others, began to torment Lev once again. Because he understood at last that his mother was immovable. Auror *was* her life. If Auror was going to be drowned, then she would go to the bottom of the reservoir with it.

'Mamma,' he'd pleaded on the telephone, 'the flats in Baryn may be quite nice. They will have electric heating. I've heard some of them will look out on the river and we're going to try to get one of those.'

'I don't care what they look out on. I'm seventy years old. I intend to die in my village.'

'Mamma, think of Maya, how she needs you.'

'No. *You* think of Maya. She's your child. Come home and be a father to her and let everybody leave me in peace.'

'Mamma, please ...'

'I'm tired, Lev. Too tired to listen to you. Just let me be.'

She could break him with this kind of talk. She knew it only too well. But he asked himself: why did she *want* to break him? Why was she so angry with him?

Because he was a FAILURE. This was the word with which, as Lev got on his Northern Line train to Tufnell Park, he answered the question. He imagined it printed on some Tube-station poster, grafittied on some soot-laden wall: an assertion visible to all.

*

The following morning he did what he always did when he reached an impasse: he called Lydia's mobile.

Lydia was in New York, at the Ritz Carlton Hotel, and it was five in the morning. Maestro Greszler was lying asleep beside her.

'I'm sorry, Lydia,' said Lev, 'I didn't know you were in the States. I thought you'd be in daytime somewhere.'

He heard her pad out of the room and into another of those echoey, light-filled bathrooms that so gladdened her heart. She told him to hang on while she put on her complimentary towelling robe over her silk pyjamas.

He wanted to start by telling her about the attack in Swains Lane and how this had shaken him, but now he decided against it. He knew Lydia would remind him there was really nothing special about this kind of mugging, that these things happened every day, in every city across the world.

'Well,' she said, 'what did you want, Lev? I'm very tired.'

He began talking about the thing that pressed hardest on his heart: his mother's hints at suicide. As he talked, he could hear something clinking, and he sensed that Lydia's attention was wandering, probably towards whatever the clinking sound might be.

'What's that noise, Lydia?'

'Nothing. I'm just making up some Alka-Seltzer. Go on.'

'Are you ill?'

'No. But you know, in America, the food portions are very large. I ordered a simple grilled Dover sole – my favourite dish – for dinner, but it was a huge fish and already I'd eaten some crayfish tails with tomato relish as an appetiser, and that was after the salad they always bring you when you sit down, and some ciabatta dipped in olive oil, and of course Pyotor ordered some lovely Sancerre to go with my sole and I drank quite a lot of it. Just let me take the Alka-Seltzer and then you can go on about your mother. But you know, as I've already told you, Lev, that woman is engaging in emotional blackmail. You should stand up to her.'

He heard Lydia drink and belch.

'OK,' he said, when the bout of belching seemed to be over, 'I didn't really call to talk about Ina.'

'So why did you call?'

Lev had never heard Lydia sound more weary or reproachful.

He took a breath, cursed himself for stumbling upon the middle of her night. 'I called to tell you,' he said, 'that I've made a plan for the future.'

'Yes? You have? What plan?'

'Well ... I think it's quite a good plan. But it won't work without money.'

'Nothing works without money, Lev. I thought you'd know *that* by now.'

'I do know it. That's why I'm calling.'

'OK. So what is this "plan"? You'd better tell me.'

He heard her yawn and this silenced him. He saw the whole restaurant scheme as she would see it – as an absurd, arrogant fantasy. Yet he ploughed on, hoping to touch her heart. 'D'you remember,' he said, in a quiet and serious voice, 'on the bus, you told me about Elgar and the piano shop?'

'What? What are you talking about, Lev?'

'Don't you remember? You told me about Elgar—'

'No, no. You're absolutely wrong there. That was later. On the night of the concert. I told you about Elgar then, before you walked out on me. I think your memory is very bad.'

The night of the concert. That shameful night.

But she was right. Perhaps he was losing his memory as well as losing everything else.

'I'm like Elgar now,' he went on. 'I'm in that sad piano shop.'

'Lev, I'm sorry, but I really don't understand a word you've been saying. Are you drunk?'

'No. I just need help. I have to get to the next bit of my life, like Elgar did when he heard those sounds on the river, or wherever it was. I need to get to where I can be of some use to everybody back home.'

'So you've made a plan. But you haven't told me what it is. You've just been sidetracked onto Elgar, for no reason that I can possibly follow. So I think I'll go back to bed now. Why don't you call me tomorrow – tomorrow US time – when you're sober?'

'No, Lydia! I'm not drunk. Don't go. I'll get to the heart of it.'

He heard her sigh. She said wearily: 'What is the "heart" of it, then?'

He swallowed, took a breath and said: 'The heart of it is I need ten thousand pounds.'

'What?'

'I need ten thousand pounds.'

There was a silence, into which Lydia released another quiet belch. Then she said: 'Ten thousand pounds? Lev, what in the world is going on? Are you under threat from the Mafia?'

'No. There isn't a Mafia here, as far as I know.'

'I expect there's some kind of Mafia everywhere. But anyway, let's not discuss that. Please just kindly tell me what is happening to you. Because I simply do not understand a word.'

He slid into it then, like a man may slide sideways, rather than head-on, into a confession: the narrative of his Great Idea. He summoned it back to him, told her he could see it, smell it, touch it, his restaurant in Baryn, a place where everybody would want to come, the first place of its kind to serve beautiful food, *his* place, dreamed out of his work in the kitchen of a famous chef, out of the lanes of Suffolk, out of all his joys and sufferings in England, the *Restaurant Marina* ...

Lydia listened quietly to him. Down the phone, Lev could hear a police siren shrieking its way though the New York night. Then, when he paused in his 'confession' and the siren had passed and gone, silence fell between them. There seemed to be something absolute about this silence, as though the connection between them had been broken. Yet he could hear her breathing.

'Say something, Lydia.'

'Well. I just can't think of what to say. It's completely, utterly crazy.'

'You don't think my restaurant will succeed?'

'I have no idea. Maybe if you work hard enough. If you learn to be a good chef. But, really, Lev, you didn't need to call me in the middle of the night to tell me about this wild scheme. A restaurant in Baryn! I don't know where you dreamed up that plan.'

'I told you, it just came to me, I saw the logic of it.'

'Logic? Well, I have to say I don't see any logic in it. Our people don't care about good food. They never have.'

'Only because they haven't had the chance, but I'm going to give them the chance.'

'All right, Lev. Sure. But, look, it really is very late, and we've got a heavy schedule tomorrow, with a concert at Lincoln Centre. And I'm looking out of the bathroom window now and I can see dawn coming up. I have to go back to bed and try to get some sleep.'

'OK. But will you think about it, about my plan, and see whether it might be something you could mention—'

'*What*? What did you say?'

'I only wondered if you might be able to mention the scheme to—'

'To Pyotor?'

'Yes.'

'My God. Is this what you're proposing? Is that why you called me, to ask me to ask Pyotor to lend you ten thousand pounds?'

'I only thought ... what seems so much to you and me might not seem ... important to him.'

'Lev,' said Lydia, with a long sigh, 'I have to admit that you disappoint me. More than that. In fact, really, I think this is just atrocious. It's despicable! That, after all that I've done for you, you have the audacity to ask for this absurd sum.'

She was right. It was absurd. The whole thing was absurd.

'I only wondered,' Lev stammered, 'whether it might be something Maestro Greszler would be interested to fund. Then, when he came to Baryn—'

'He never comes to Baryn. It's not a place he likes at all.'

'No. But if he ever came ... and—'

'Lev, I'm sorry, but I have to go now.'

'Don't go, Lydia. Don't be angry.'

'*No*? You don't see what a wretched thing you've just done? I'm sorry, I really am, but I'm hanging up now. And I shall certainly *not* mention your request to Pyotor. I wouldn't want him to despise you. Goodbye, Lev.'

The line was cut. Downstairs, in the garden, the dog was yelping in the hot morning. Lev stood very still, staring at the pale sky. He thought, Jasmina was right. Dreams make you reckless, pitch you down roads you'd never normally take.

But what was there to cling to apart from this dream?

He put it to Christy: 'I don't know how else to think about the future.'

'I see the dilemma,' said Christy.

They were cleaning the flat for Jasmina, who was going to

come and stay for the first time. They were on to the kitchen: two 'nurses' shining everything up before Lev embarked on making the meal. But Christy kept being distracted by opening cupboards and finding things in them he didn't remember he'd ever possessed.

'Will you look at this?' he said, hauling out a tarnished copper fondue set with six meat skewers. 'Never been used. Probably a wedding present. That's what doomed it.' Later, he found a silver toast rack, also blackened by time. 'Heirloom!' he said, plonking it down on a worktop. 'Gift to me ma from some snooty Limerick auntie. Straight outa the pawn shop.'

Christy looked at this toast rack for a long time and then said that he was going to get rid of every material possession that belonged to his past, 'every last stitch of it', so that he could feel he was beginning his life all over again.

They worked until it was time for Lev to walk to Panno's.

Before leaving, he surveyed the clean kitchen, stood for a moment admiring the glistening surfaces, inhaling the scent of bleach. Then he set off. These days, he took another route, up Junction Road to Archway and left to Highgate, avoiding Swains Lane and the cemetery. The weather was warm. As respite from his anxiety about the future, he sometimes let his thoughts circle back to the days of the asparagus picking and the violets growing in the rough grass and the unstoppable laughter of Jimmy and Sonny Ming.

Hor-hor. Winna bar birriards, Rev!
Hor-hor-hor-hor!

He decided to cook *kleftiko* for Jasmina. He bought the lamb shanks cheap from the Greek butcher on the corner of Belisha Road, seared them in oil, then made a pungent tomato and rosemary sauce to simmer them in, let them sit in it for hours in a low oven – exactly as Panno had shown him – till they were as tender as veal. He'd serve the shanks with saffron rice and a Greek salad with olives and feta cheese. For pudding, because Christy had told him Jasmina adored sweet things, he was going to make a rich chocolate tart.

Rolling pastry, stirring melted chocolate and cream, on the quiet Sunday afternoon, he felt his mind suddenly at ease once more. He was sure the tart – one of Waldo's recipes – was going to be good. But he also knew now that the thing he'd chosen for his future was the right thing, right for him. Knew he could get to love cooking more than anything he'd ever done. Suddenly told himself that if you love a thing enough, then, somehow, you make it happen …

Next door, Christy was hovering nervously about, setting out scarlet paper napkins on the table, arranging and rearranging white carnations in an old crackle-glazed brown jar. He kept coming through to the kitchen and asking: 'How's it goin', fella?'

'Going good.'

'Should we have some little appetiser nibble things, like she made for us?'

'Yes. Don't worry, Christy. I make some baby cheese tartlets with my left-over pastry.'

Christy lingered and said: 'Next thing I have to do after tonight, if that goes all right, is to introduce Jasmina to Frankie.'

Lev threw more flour onto his shortcrust, rolled it thinner. 'Jasmina will like Frankie.'

'Yeah, but will Frankie like Jasmina? That's what I worry about more. Myerson-Hill could be a feckin' racist. That air of certainty the man has. That all-white loft. And it could've rubbed off on Frankie.'

'You don't know …'

'No, I don't know it, but some things you can just *surmise*.'

'Frankie will like Jasmina. She's a lovely woman, Christy.'

'Well, *I* know that. And so do you. But now I want everyone else to know it, too. I want the whole world, including me daughter, to worship at the hem of her garment.'

She arrived at seven, parking her old Renault Clio on the other side of the dusty street. Christy had put on a clean white linen shirt, above which his face looked anaemic with worry and excitement. The small flat smelled of furniture polish and chocolate.

Jasmina was dressed in a blue sari and she'd bought some new spectacles with blue frames. Lev thought, with her clear skin and her big eyes and the neatness of her hairline, she looked like an advertisement for those spectacles. Through them, she peered at the carnations in the crackle-glazed jar, at the red paper napkins now stuck into wine glasses.

'Very nice, Christy,' she said.

'It's a bit empty everywhere,' he apologised anxiously. 'Angela took a lot of stuff.'

'I think it's very nice.'

'See the rest of it, will you?'

'If I'm allowed.'

'You show her, Lev. I'll open the wine.'

Lev guided her from room to room. She didn't cross the threshold of Christy's bedroom, or of the bathroom, only peered through the doorways and nodded her quiet approval. But when they reached Lev's room – Frankie's room – Jasmina tiptoed in, almost as though there might have been a child asleep in the bunk bed. She stood very still at the window, looking out at the sky, then picked up one of the soft toys that still sat on the window-sill. It was a tiger. Jasmina stared at this tiger and said: 'You know, I've no idea how to be any kind of mother or step-mother to a child. But I hope I'm going to get the chance to try.'

'You will,' said Lev. 'For sure you will.'

'I comfort myself that Frankie's a girl. With a boy, I think I might be all at sea.'

Everything was eaten, including most of the rich chocolate tart. Jasmina sat back in her chair, with her neat hands folded on her stomach and commented: 'My God, I'm stuffed. You're a good cook, Lev. You'll make your restaurant project work, for sure.'

Silence followed this remark. The newly washed net curtains at the window moved gently in the night breeze. Christy poured out more white wine and took a hefty swig.

'If the project were UK-based,' Jasmina went on calmly, 'you might qualify for a small-business loan. The Hertford and Ware might even be able to help you. We've diversified, now, beyond mortgage-style funding. I could become your business adviser!'

'That would be nice, Jasmina.'

'Yes, it would be jolly good fun, wouldn't it? But the H & W won't touch anything outside Britain. That I know for sure. So you have to look at the structure of what's here for you officially.'

Lev was lost now. What did she mean by 'the structure of what's here'?

'OK,' said Jasmina. 'I'm talking about capital incentive schemes originating in your country: basically subsidy for new inward invest-ment. The Eastern-bloc countries are hungry for all Western-style business projects, even small-scale ones, so they presumably like to fund individual enterprise where they can. Do you understand what I'm talking about?'

'Yes.'

'OK, here's my thought. Why not go to your embassy and ask whether any loan system exists that you could qualify for?'

'Go to the embassy?'

'It's the logical place to start. Explain your project and the likely cost of your start-up. See what reaction you get. See if they know about any kind of scheme that could help you.'

'"Loans for dreams",' said Lev.

'Sure,' said Jasmina, letting her features break into that transforming smile of hers. 'But it's an OK dream. Isn't it, Christy?'

'Definitely,' said Christy. 'It definitely is. I'm totally in favour.'

Lev looked at Christy, whose head was lolling comfortably against the back of his chair. But Lev felt sure that Christy's mind had sped far off the subject of loans and subsidies, far off any subject at all, in fact, except the thought of the approaching night and the body of Jasmina beside him, at last, in his own bed.

21

Looking at Photographs

The embassy occupied a tall, white-stuccoed house not far from Earls Court Road, where Lev had once worked for Ahmed. Though the exterior paintwork of the house was fresh, the entrance hall overwhelmed Lev with its unaccountable darkness, its scent of things neglected. This darkness and neglect seemed both unnervingly familiar and yet shockingly out of place in an ambassadorial building.

Lev saw that a yellowing notice on the wall instructed visitors to report at Reception, located in a room to the left of the hall, where a young woman sat behind a steel desk, shaped like a kidney, beneath a portrait, blood-coloured in tone, of the country's President Podrorsky. The desk squatted on a faded old Afghan carpet, its heaviness mauling the carpet's shape. The drapes at the tall windows matched the blood-tone of the portrait and were partially drawn across the bright summer day.

At the other end of the room was a bar. Lev stared at it, saw a huddle of dark-suited men leaning there, drinking vodka and smoking. It was ten thirty in the morning. The bartender stood with his arms spread out, as if measuring fabric along the counter, his head inclined into the arena of smoke. As Lev came in, the bartender's eyes flicked upwards and all the heads turned and looked at Lev and immediately looked away. The drinkers were able to decide at once, it seemed, that here was a person of no account.

Lev hadn't prepared what he was going to say. Wished now that he could remember better what Jasmina had told him about loan systems and start-up capital. As he approached the desk and the cold stare of its occupant, inhaled the smell of dusty furnishings pomaded with smoke, he thought how all of this reminded him of Procurator Rivas's office in the Public Works building in Baryn, and resurrected in him the hatred of Rivas he'd never been able to conquer. Part of him wanted to turn straight round and walk out again.

The young woman said in English: 'How may I help you, sir?'

Her ultra-correct pronunciation made Lev think of Lydia – which he would have preferred not to have to do at this moment. He stood at the desk, made mute by memory and guilt. His stomach felt uncomfortable. He wondered whether the only thing he was going to utter was some enquiry about the location of the lavatory.

The woman stared up at him. Her hair was strangled back into a tight bun. Her skin was bone white, her lips a slash of glossy carmine. Despite the brightness outside, it felt cold in the room, as though sunlight had never entered there.

Lev cleared his throat. He thrust his hands into the pockets of his leather jacket. 'I came to ask …' he began.

The young woman screwed up her eyes, as if in pain.

'I came to ask … is there a … *department* … in this embassy that deals with commercial enterprises?'

'I beg your pardon?' said the young woman.

'It's just an enquiry. I was advised to come here … to see whether the embassy might be able to give me any help.'

'Yes. Help with what?'

'Well. With a commercial venture.'

The eyes didn't relax. The woman remained in pain, her skin stretched to such an excruciating pallor that it looked, to Lev, as though it had been nailed to her skull behind her ears.

'I don't understand you. What is the precise nature of the help you need, sir?'

'I just wanted to ask whether – at any level, in any department, the embassy is sometimes able to help with … matters of business.'

'I'm sorry,' said the young woman. 'You are going to have to make yourself understood better. Would you prefer to speak in English?'

Lev allowed a thin smile to touch his lips. 'No,' he said. 'I would not prefer to speak in English. All I wish to ask is, is there someone I can talk to about applying for funding to set up a commercial business in Baryn?'

'In Baryn?'

'Yes.'

'This is the London embassy.'

'I know it's the London embassy.'

'We're here to help our citizens in cases of personal or diplomatic difficulty. Are you in diplomatic difficulty?'

'Well,' said Lev, 'I seem to be in diplomatic difficulty right now, in this room, in that I'm not making myself clear to you. Perhaps I could make an appointment to see somebody a little higher up, somebody who might be able to answer my questions.'

'I can answer your questions. What is it you wish to know?'

Lev sat down on a leather chair – very like the chairs in Rivas's office – and pulled out his cigarettes.

'No, no, sorry,' said the woman, shaking a finger at him. 'You can't smoke here.'

Lev gestured to the suited men. 'Everybody there is smoking.'

'That is the bar.'

'It's all part of the same room.'

'No. This is Reception and that is the bar.'

Lev was familiar with this kind of illogic, knew that all you could do was resign yourself to it, that people in authority would never yield, so he put the cigarettes away. He looked towards the shrouded windows and the street. At this moment, a telephone on the young woman's desk rang and she snatched up the receiver: 'Embassy Reception, good afternoon.'

Lev held himself still. Ten thirty and she says 'good afternoon'. He tried not to let exasperation with the girl get its hold on him. He heard laughter begin to spill from the bar area. Heard the *snicker-snicker-snicker* of an unreliable, flint-worn cigarette lighter.

The phone conversation now absorbed the young woman. She turned her head away from Lev, spoke quietly, but with sudden, flirtatious animation: '… I didn't recognise your voice, Karli. I think you disguise your voice when you phone up, just to tease me … No, I really think you do. You sound like a Russian … Yeah. A Russian businessman or something … What? … No, I've never dated a Russian! Why would I date a Russian? … What? … I never heard that. Who says their dicks are big? You just invented that to … Wait a minute.'

She turned back to Lev. 'Will you wait over there, please,' she said, indicating a leather sofa under the window. 'I have to take this important call.'

Lev fixed her hazel eyes with a hard stare. 'No,' he said. 'I'm not able to wait. I would like to fix an appointment. With the ambassador.'

'No, no,' said the girl, holding the telephone a few centimetres away from her ear and shaking the bun violently. 'That is impossible. I'm not able to make appointments with the ambassador's office. You must apply in writing, stating your business and your credentials ... Hold on, Karli. I'm just sorting something out here ... What? ... No, he wasn't a stupid Russian. He was a Finn ... OK, sir? You must make your application in writing, stating the nature of your business, your name, home address, occupation, address in the UK, occupation in the UK, and all other data relevant to the meeting you are requesting. Please remember that all applications must be made *in writing*, not via email. We do not accept email applications under any circumstances.'

'Is that because you're not connected to the Internet?' said Lev.

'No. Of course we're connected to the Internet, but email applications have been deemed unacceptable.'

'Why?'

The girl now looked at Lev with undisguised animosity. 'It's embassy policy,' she said. 'That is all I can tell you.'

'Embassy policy. I see,' said Lev. 'But you say I can write to the ambassador?'

'Stating the nature of your business, your name, home address, address in the UK—'

'And the time of day, I presume,' said Lev, 'to help you distinguish morning from afternoon.'

'Sorry, sir? ... No, don't go, Karli, I need to talk to you about last night. ... What did you say, sir?'

'Never mind,' said Lev. 'Never mind.'

He got up and walked out. The front door was heavy and the sound of it closing behind him brought him a moment of unexpected satisfaction. He stood in the sunshine, smoking. The flag of his country hung lifeless from a white pole above him, with no breeze to move it.

*

He began to walk. He knew exactly where he was going to go. He wanted, suddenly, to feel it again, that long-ago moment of arrival in this city, in the hot sun, trudging round with his carrier-bag full of Ahmed's leaflets. As though remembering this *in situ*, remembering it all through his being, could reassure him that, if he'd survived this far, he was surely capable of realising the great dream of his future.

And here was Ahmed now: standing in his brightly lit kebab shop, cleaning the meat spit, his beard bushy and full of shine, his girth still impressive, his forearms glistening.

'Ahmed.'

The Arab turned. Lev smiled, and saw recognition arrive a few seconds later, as Ahmed wiped his huge hand on his apron and held it out across the counter.

'Hey!' he said. 'One of my leaflet men, right?'

'That's right. Lev.'

'Lev. Sure. I remember. Howya doin'? You look smart. Got a good job now, right?'

'Yes. I work in Highgate. Greek restaurant.'

'Greek? *Allah!* Beware Greeks! You know the saying? But it's better than working for Ahmed, eh? Better money?'

'Yeh. It's OK. But I worked for GK Ashe for a while and that was—'

'GK Ashe? That rich punk? You serious?'

'Yeh.'

'Why you leave him? Don't tell me. He tried to pan-fry your liver?'

'No. I had … what you call … woman problems.'

Ahmed raised his brown eyes to his ever-vigilant Heaven, then set up two saucers on the bar. 'Better have a coffee, then, to sober up,' he said. 'Woman problems make a man crazy.'

Lev looked round at the small space, empty in mid-morning, but hot and blinding on the eye, just as it had been the previous summer. He saw, though, that the floor needed cleaning and that the drinks fridge, from which he'd once drunk water in a green can, had a notice strung across it saying, *Sorry broken. Mended soon. Allah willing.*

'How are things going for you, Ahmed?' he asked.

Ahmed manipulated his Gaggia machine with his habitual

panache and set two espressos delicately on the saucers. Then Lev saw his eyes flicker with sudden sadness.

'I can tell you, my friend – because you're like me, you don't belong to this country – these days my business is down. And I know why.'

Lev waited. Ahmed pushed a sugar bowl towards him. 'You take sugar, or you sweet enough? GK Ashe grill your arse into a *brûlée* crust?' Ahmed chuckled, then he rubbed his beard and looked downcast again. 'Yeah,' he said. 'They're down because people in this country got a prejudice now against Arabs. It's crept up on us. Now, no matter what country you from, these days, they just look at you and think, Shitty Arab, suicide-bomber, Muslim scum. I'm not joking, Lev. That's where we are right now. Got us all pigeon-holed.'

'Yes. I've seen this.'

'I'm from Qatar, right? I got nothin' to do with Osama Bin Laden or none of those fuckin' fanatics. I'm even more nice and gentle than the Baghdad Blogger. You know this, because I think I was good to you, yes? I treated you fair.'

'Yes, Ahmed. You did.'

'Right. But British people – young an' old – look at me like I'm going to poison them. Some nights I got no business at all. Shit pizza joint next door is overflowing with customers, and I got no one. Pub closing time and my doner spit's sizzling with fresh meat and I got nice salads lined up in the chiller and there's no one in my fuckin' joint! I tell you, I just wanna stand here and weep.'

'I'm sorry, Ahmed.'

'Yeah. Weep. Like you wept in my toilet. And I notice something: I don't invent no proverbs any more. Like my mind is exhausted.'

Lev nodded gravely. The two men stood close to each other, leaning on the counter. Outside, on Earls Court Road, the crowds of people surged on by, blinking and scowling in the sun's brightness.

'Perhaps,' said Lev, after a while, 'this will pass. This way people think of you. Perhaps it's just part of the time now and it will end.'

'Sure,' said Ahmed. 'You may be right. Provided there are no more bombs. But the thing is, how am I going to hang on? Can't afford to get my chiller fixed, Lev. Can't even afford to print any fuckin' leaflets! I got a wife and kid. I can survive maybe two, three months like this. Then it's over. And it was my dream, this. To have my own place. To have my name on the window.'

Lev sipped his coffee, then he said quietly: 'It's my dream, too.'

'What you mean, leaflet man?'

'Got this crazy idea, Ahmed. Go home to my country, start a restaurant in a town called Baryn.'

Ahmed's eyes were huge with alarm. 'Yeah? You serious?'

'Serious in my mind – you know? But GK did some costings for me ...'

'OK. Don't tell me. Everything in the world comes down to money. That's why people love religion all over again. They're sick of the sound of the abacus.'

Lev went down the basement steps, saw the yellow front door and the cat dozing by the blue hydrangea bush. He stood still and stared at these things and the cat didn't move. The sun glanced down on the bushy hydrangea flowers and the sculpted bay trees. A tin watering-can stood under the tap on the wall.

He was in Kowalski's yard. The place was as silent and peaceful as it had ever been. Were Shepard and Kowalski at home? Was Lev going to ring their doorbell and announce to them he'd once trespassed all night on their land, slept tucked away under the road, relieved himself beside the tap? Something in him wanted to do just this, to say that he owed them a double debt, because that was when he'd first caught it, the scent of happiness in this city ... But he didn't move, just stayed where he was, half-way down the steps, watchful and calm. The cat slept on.

When his phone began to ring, he turned and walked back up into the street. He stood by the railings with the sun on his face.

'Lev,' said a woman's voice. 'Am I talking to Lev?'

'Yes.'

'Oh, good. Now I hope you don't mind my telephoning your mobile number. I got it from Sophie.'

'Who is this, please?'

'It's Mrs McNaughton, from Ferndale Heights care home. And I'm ringing to ask you a favour. Is this a good moment to speak to you, or are you busy?'

He remembered her now, the director of Ferndale Heights, efficient and severe, yet with a kindly face. 'I'm not busy.'

'Good. Well, now, this is our dilemma, Lev. I expect you remember Mrs Viggers and her daughter Jane, who worked in the kitchen here?'

'Yes.'

'Well, I'm afraid we've been very badly let down. They walked out yesterday, absolutely without warning. No notice. Nothing. Out they march and that's it. How people can behave like that is quite beyond me, but there you are. The thing is, I'm having a devil of a job finding a replacement. All I have at the moment is piecemeal help. The daughter of Captain Brotherton's former cleaning lady is doing sterling service, but she's extremely young and inexperienced and I can't leave her to cope on her own, can I?'

'No. I guess not.'

'Of course, I myself am pitching in. Needs must. But on Sunday, I simply have to go to visit my sister, who has shingles in Kent, so I was wondering ... would you be available to help out with lunch? I do recall that the kitchen work you did here was much appreciated. I know it's wretchedly short notice, but—'

'Yes,' said Lev. 'Sure I will.'

'Oh, will you *really*? That is so kind of you. We shall pay you properly, of course. I really am so grateful.'

'It's fine. How many for lunch, Mrs McNaughton?'

'Well. Let me see. Sixteen residents. We lost Mrs Hollander. So very sad. Such a ... leading light. D'you remember her, Minty Hollander?'

'Yes. The Christmas-cracker game.'

'That's it. Always loved to monopolise the games here. But nobody really minded. And we lost her so suddenly. I know everybody misses her.'

'Yes. I think so.'

'But there we are. *Let her paint an inch thick, to this favour she must come.*'

'What did you say?' said Lev.

'Oh, just quoting from *Hamlet*.'

'Hamlet is talking to the grave-maker, yes?'

'Yes. Absolutely. Where did you learn that, Lev?'

Lev, standing in the sunlight, knew there was a smile on his face. Not only had he recognised the line, but now he felt as if he'd suddenly understood why Lydia had given him the play to read: she wanted to show him that words written long, long ago could travel beside you and help you at moments when you could no longer see the road.

'A friend taught me,' he said.

'Well. Very good. Anyway, Lev, I'm so relieved you can do Sunday. I immediately thought of dear Sophie, but unfortunately she's busy with some art exhibition.'

'Yes?'

'Yes. I didn't think art shows happened on Sundays. They never used to, but I suppose times have changed.'

'I think so.'

'Well, Lev, if you get here at about nine thirty, that should do well. The residents like to eat at one. Then, if you can come to see me during next week, we'll settle your fee. Does that sound fair?'

'Yes,' said Lev. 'Quite fair. One more thing, Mrs McNaughton. What am I going to cook?'

'Right. Well, a roast of some kind. That's what we always have on Sundays. Lamb?'

'OK. Lamb. I'll bring some herbs.'

'Herbs? Oh, yes. Fine. But they like things plain. Don't forget this is England, Lev.'

'No. I never forget.'

Lev put his phone away, turned and looked down one more time at Kowalski's yard, imprinting it for ever on his mind. Then he walked away.

The kitchen at Ferndale Heights stank of burned-on grease, of the familiar turd-smell of boiled cabbage.

Lev opened all the windows, cleaned the cooker hob, tugged out a roasting pan and scoured this till his fingers bled. Then he began peeling potatoes.

His young, black helper arrived silently and stood at the door, clutching a clean folded apron to her body. Lev turned and saw her. She was sixteen or seventeen, with a frosting of acne across her cheeks and hair straightened into a wiry halo.

'I'm Simone,' she said.

He shook her hand, saw she was suspicious of him, of his *foreign-ness*, so he began straight away – as GK would have done – to give her tasks, telling her to finish the potatoes, wash and save the peelings for stock, then start on the carrots. Then, in front of her startled eyes, he took down all the packets of gravy granules, stock cubes and instant mash and threw them into the trash bin.

'In this kitchen, we make real food,' he said. 'You agree, Simone?'

'Wha'ever,' said Simone. 'You're in charge, man.'

'Today, I'm chef. So here's what we make to go with the roast lamb: a potato and onion gratin, a nice *jus*, peas, a carrot purée ...'

'Wha' I call you then? Chef?'

'Yes,' he said. Couldn't resist it. 'You call me Chef.'

The joint was huge, blood-smeared, slippery from its vacuum pack. Lev rinsed and dried it. Went to the bag he'd brought with him, containing a bundle of rhubarb, and took out a head of garlic and some fresh rosemary. Saw Simone turn and watch him as he conjured up these new ingredients.

'You got, like, a *kit* there? A chef's kit?'

'Yes. I know this kitchen.'

'Shi', innit?'

'It's shit. But today, we make it better.'

Lev produced the rhubarb, then a nutmeg, cloves, butter and cream from his bag. Simone shook her head. 'Ma Vig didn't know nuvvin' about cookin',' she said. 'Dunno why she *got* this job because she didn't deserve it.'

'No. Lucky for everybody she's gone.'

The worn white space soon began to smell of the fragrant lamb, the pungent gratin. Lev began squaring off butter and flour for a crumble, while Simone washed and chopped the rhubarb. He saw that the girl worked slowly, but with care. When he showed her how to caramelise an onion, then put the stock, made from the odds and ends of vegetables, in the onion pan to make a *jus*, he got from her a snuffling, delighted laugh. 'Wicked!' she said. 'I'm gonna show my mum this.'

Lev paused in his work, went to the door to smoke and looked out onto the Ferndale grass. Pigeons had colonised it and waddled over it, clucking and murmuring. Straight into Lev's heart came his old longing for Sophie. He imagined her sitting right there among the birds, arms round her knees, the sun on her hair, smiling at him. Then remembered her singing on Christmas Day,

> *Somewhere over the rainbow,*
> *Way up high …*

and all the residents of Ferndale stilled by her voice, soothed into dreams of the past, breaking into clapping and cheering when the song ended.

Lev stubbed out the cigarette, came back into the kitchen and asked Simone: 'Did you ever work Sundays with a chef called Sophie?'

'Yeah?' She said it like a question: '*Yeah?*' Then she added: 'She was nice, right? But she don't come 'ere any more. She got, like, some famous boyfriend, innit?'

Lev recognised most of the Ferndale residents: Berkeley Brotherton, Pansy Adeane, Douglas, Joan, the trembling and jerking Parkinsonian contingent, some of the wheelchair brigade … There were three or four new faces. But Minty Hollander was gone. She'd been their star, their diamond-dripping duchess, who'd once worked with Leslie Caron, who bossed them all into obedience with her silvery vowels and her obstinate, flirtatious charm, and now she'd left them.

Perhaps it was a relief to them that she'd died. They were certainly quieter without her, less quarrelsome, it seemed to Lev. And when he and Simone began to serve up the lunch, they fell into silence, staring down at their plates, taking their glasses on or off to squint at the unfamiliar-looking food. Then they began to eat and after a moment Pansy Adeane said, with her mouth full: 'Who made this potato thing?'

'Chef made it, Mrs Adeane,' said Simone.

'Well, it's lovely. Tell the chef, dear. Far better than our usual muck.'

There was no sign of Ruby Constad. Her place had been laid at the table, but the chair was vacant. When Lev asked Berkeley Brotherton where she was, he replied: 'No idea. Moping in her room, I wouldn't wonder. Bloody children never visit her, selfish creatures.' Then one of the day nurses, tying a napkin round Berkeley's ancient but proud neck, interrupted and said: 'Mrs Constad's not taking lunch today. Lunch is not obligatory.'

Lev and Simone circled the table, helping the two day nurses to cut food for those who couldn't manage to do it, sometimes lifting a shaking hand holding a spoon towards a gaping mouth or a tongue held out, as though to receive a communion wafer. Lev knew that some of the residents remembered him and some had no idea who he was. During the complicated High Mass of their Sunday meal, conversation was muted until the topic of Mrs Viggers and Jane began to surface.

'If you ask me, Jane Viggers was mental,' said Pansy.

'She had a scream on 'er, all right,' said Douglas. 'Like a scream out of ruddy *Psycho*.'

'Mrs Vig was no better,' said a faded, mousy woman, whose name was Hermione. 'She once wrenched my arm.'

'Wrenched your *arm*?' said Berkeley.

'Yes. Wrenched it out of its socket. She was a Marxist.'

'Sadist, don't you mean?' said Pansy.

Laughter round the table.

Lev wondered what it was they were all laughing at: the thought of colossal Mrs Viggers advancing on Hermione's meagre arm? Misuse of the word 'Marxist'?

'The Viggers used to jack stuff from the kitchen ...' This was Simone, who was going round with second helpings of rhubarb crumble.

'"Jack"?' said Joan. 'What's that?'

'Tell you're not streetwise, eh?' said Douglas. 'It means nick. *Steal*.'

A respectful quiet greeted these delicious words.

'Really? Oh, tell us, Simone, go on.'

Simone spooned out crumble. Several pudding plates had been scraped clean. 'Yeah,' she said. 'I was gonna, like, *mention it* to Mrs McNaughton, but I thought I'd be garrotted, or somevin'.'

'Garrotted! Oh, I like that. What did they steal, dear?'

'Loadsa stuff. Used to be an electric whisk an' a fruit press in that kitchen, but the Viggers jacked 'em. Same fing wiv the scales. And, like, small stuff as well: cutlery, cruets, parin' knives ...'

'Knives!'

'Did you see them *do* it, Simone?'

'Well, I didn't, like, *see* 'em right in front of me eyes. But I know they did it. Know wha' I mean? Mrs Vig had a hold-all type thing she brought wiv her. And I know that bag was stuffed wiv, like, *goods*. I'm not jokin'.'

'Well, all we can say,' said Berkeley Brotherton, 'is good riddance to them. In the Navy, they'd've been drummed out a long time ago. Because they couldn't bloody cook!' He brayed with laughter – *hack-hack-hack-hack!* – the laugh turning quickly to a wheezing cough. He spat phlegm into a handkerchief.

'Food'll be better now, dear, will it?' said Joan, plaintively, to Lev.

'Call 'im "Chef",' giggled Simone.

'Oh, Chef, yes, sorry, love. Chef. Will it get better now, like it was today?'

Lev was standing at the end of the table. He saw many faces turn to him. Silence in the room. 'I don't know,' he said quietly.

'You mean, you're not staying on?' said Berkeley.

Lev shook his head. 'Just helping out, today.'

'Damned shame,' wheezed Berkeley.

'Hear, hear,' said Douglas. 'For once I agree with the captain.'

When lunch was over and the nurses had helped the residents out into the sunshine or back into their rooms, Lev left Simone to load the dishwasher and made his way to Ruby Constad's room.

The voice that answered his knock was subdued. He found Ruby sitting in her armchair with a photograph album on her knees. She clutched it to her chest as Lev came in, as though he might have come to take it away from her.

'It's Lev, Mrs Constad,' he said. 'I used to come here with Sophie.'

She peered at him. '*Who* is it?'

He came closer to her. Saw her face very thin and drawn, where, only a few months ago, it had been fleshy. Her once-beautiful eyes looked startled.

'It's Lev,' he said gently. 'I was here at Christmas. And one other time. I helped to cook the meals.'

Her look softened. She held out a frail hand. He put it to his lips and kissed it, saw Ruby smile.

'I remember you,' she said. 'Always so *galant.*'

'I came to say, would you like me to bring you some lunch? I made a nice gratin ... and a rhubarb crumble.'

'No, thank you, dear. I'm not hungry. I live on Matchsticks now. Would you like one?'

She picked up a box of chocolate twigs from beside her chair and offered it to Lev. He accepted a twig. Ruby said: 'Pull up that stool. I'll show you some old snaps.'

He sat beside her and she lifted the heavy photograph album towards him. 'India,' she said. 'Just before the war. That's me here. It was a welcome pageant we made at our convent school for the Viceroy.'

Lev saw a faded picture of young girls wearing ankle-length dresses, lined up across a stage, bending their bodies in strange contortions. Remembered now what she'd told him and Sophie: 'We made the word WELCOME in girls.'

'See the O? I'm one half of it. The left half, there. My hair was dark then.'

Lev looked from the girl in the picture – so willowy and strong, so intent on being one half of a beautiful O – to Ruby, beside him, lined and emaciated in her heavy chair. He told her she looked lovely, that the welcome tableau was very clever.

She turned the page, pointed to a photograph of a smiling nun. 'Sister Benedicta,' she said. 'She was my favourite nun. She taught me about books. We used to read the poetry of Thomas Hardy and A. E. Housman in her room. Her spirit was wonderfully gentle.'

'Did you see her again?'

'No. I don't know what became of her. I did go back to India in the late 1970s, after my husband died, but the convent school was closed. The buildings had become what they called a garment factory. I went in, even though I wasn't supposed to. I shall never forget the noise of that place, and the sight of so many women working at wretched sewing-machines. As though *one* sewing-machine isn't terrifying enough! And God knows how many hours they had to put in, poor souls. I remember thinking, I am never going to buy a *garment* again!'

Ruby closed the album and asked Lev to tell her how he was getting on without Sophie. He lit a cigarette. No way could he tell the old lady that he still had erotic dreams about Sophie, could still get hard just thinking about the plump softness of her arms. So he took a different tack. He began to explain that the loss of Sophie had been buried underneath another loss – the coming disappearance of his village under the waters of the Auror dam.

'Oh, Lev,' she said, 'I never heard of such a frightful thing. To drown people's homes! Goodness me, it almost makes one long for a viceroy, or somebody of that ilk, to sit those unfeeling, petty bureaucrats down and say, "No. That is completely beyond the pale!"'

Lev smiled. He told her quietly that the coming of the dam had led him on to his wild idea of starting a restaurant – 'The first one in my country where the food will be truly good.'

'Oh, a restaurant!' exclaimed Ruby. 'How excellent. You must definitely do it. What kind of restaurant will it be?'

'Well,' said Lev, 'not so large. Fifty covers or so. What I imagine is: everything very clean and simple. Wooden floor. White table-cloths. Nice simple glassware. Perhaps a small bar. Some leather chairs here, in the bar area. Maybe a fire in winter ...'

'Oh, yes, a fire. Because your winters are cold. Good idea.'

'On the walls, some nice colour. Maybe ochre colour. And old photographs – like yours in your book – of our country in the past.'

'Photographs. Very good. To remember the past. It's important for us all. But also, Lev, I've just thought, if a customer's waiting for somebody to arrive, who's late or something, she can just swivel around and have a look at the photographs, instead of sitting and staring at nothing and feeling like a self-conscious twit.'

'Yes. I didn't think of that.'

'What about your staff? You must pick carefully. No Mrs Viggers!'

'No, no. I want all my staff and especially my waiters very smart. You know? Efficient and polite – not like in old Communist restaurants. Everybody happy to work there, to be part of my dream ...'

'I think it's brilliant, Lev,' said Ruby. 'I can already imagine it. I can imagine everything.'

She was smiling and Lev noticed that a thread of colour had returned to her sunken cheeks. He put out his cigarette and said: 'Ruby, now let me go and get you some food. You must eat.'

'I know,' she said, with a sigh. 'But I just don't feel like eating any more. I'm sorry. I would if I could. Perhaps when I'm better – if I ever am better – I'll go on a wild adventure to your country and come and have a meal in your restaurant and look at all the pictures on the yellow walls, while I'm waiting for my food to arrive.'

22

The Last Bivouac

An envelope arrived, addressed in Ina's writing, but containing no letter or message of thanks for the money Lev kept sending, only a crayoned picture, made by Maya. It was a drawing of water, coloured blue-green, with bright fishes swimming along and sea horses nodding in a line. At the top of the page, where the water ended and a blank white sky began, sailed a houseboat like Noah's Ark, but the ark was smaller than the sea horses and its decks were empty. Bare words were scribbled badly in one corner of the blue-green sea: '*To Pappa from Maya*'. Nothing more. No love, no kisses.

Lev showed the picture to Christy and Jasmina. Christy said: 'Look how nicely she's done the fishes.' Jasmina said: 'Perhaps that's what your mother's told her – that you're going to live in an ark when the flood arrives?'

Lev propped up the picture on his window-sill. Stared at it. Tried to imagine what was in his daughter's mind. Remembered the way she had talked to the chickens and goats and the sparrows bathing in the dust and thought, desolately, Who or what will she talk to in an apartment in Baryn?

Then he went to see Mrs McNaughton to collect the money she owed him, but instead of leaving when she handed him the cheque, he told her he'd be willing to work full time at Ferndale Heights, if she hadn't yet found a replacement for the Viggers. Mrs McNaughton put her hands together in an ardent prayer steeple and said: 'Oh, my goodness, Lev. How wonderful. That's exactly what I was going to beg you to do!'

He'd worked it out. He'd go in to Ferndale at nine in the morning and stay till three or four, after serving a hot lunch and preparing the cold suppers. Then he'd get to Panno's at five. Work till twelve or one. Be home and in bed by two. Get up at seven. Be out at Ferndale again by nine. The hours were long, sure, but that's all they were: hours. He could get through them. He told himself that none of them would be as arduous as a single hour in winter at the Baryn lumber yard. And he'd survived those for almost twenty years ...

Mrs McNaughton said Ferndale could pay him £17 an hour. With his heart pounding, he refused this offer. Reminded her this was a head chef's job and asked for £20. Watched her hesitate, then relax and agree. With her efficiency-conscious smile, she told him she knew Ferndale was lucky to get him.

He'd done the sums. If he worked six hours at Ferndale Heights seven days a week at £20 an hour, he could earn £840: £650 after tax. The money he made at Panno's – about £216 a week in cash – would, if he was careful, be enough for him to live on and pay rent to Christy. Getting £20 an hour at Ferndale, he could save in the region of £2,500 per month. He had only to work for four or five months to save the impossible-seeming £10,000.

The thrill of this – the realisation that, after all, he needed no government help, no expensive loan, no benefactor, but could make the money himself by balancing two jobs instead of one – made him breathless.

His first and only impulsive purchase was a set of chef's whites. He put them on and looked at himself. He put on the toque. Didn't care that a toque was, of itself, a ridiculous thing, that he'd once heard GK Ashe deride it as 'wanker-wear'. He paraded himself for Christy and Jasmina, and caught them smiling.

'We're not laughing,' said Jasmina.

'No, not at all.' said Christy. 'We wouldn't laugh. We're just dazzled by the sheer snow-whiteness.'

Lev tried to explain to them that he thought the elderly residents of Ferndale Heights might like to see their chef dressed in this old, elegant way, that theirs was a shrunken, altered world, but now, in his white-clad being, he was going to remind them they were being cared for.

'I see it,' said Christy. 'I think that's capital, don't you, Jas?'

'Yes,' said Jasmina. 'They'll think they're at the Ritz. Shame Miss Minto, or whatever her name was, isn't there to appreciate you.'

The ache in his back sometimes reminded him of the time when he'd been knocked into the ditch by the hay-cart. It got him late at night, when, trudging the tables at Panno's, he found himself longing for heat and sleep. But this was nothing. Only an inevitable part of the decision he'd made. He swallowed painkillers and carried on. And, slowly, the kitchen at Ferndale Heights was being transformed. Lev and Simone had cleaned out every cupboard and drawer, scoured away all the smears and detritus of the Viggers' long habitation.

'You know, they was, like, *sluts*, wasn't they?' commented Simone, as she soaked and chafed pans, scraped grease off shelves, bagged up stale packets of custard powder and soup granules. 'They could of *infected* the whole place.'

It was infected. This was what Lev felt. Infected with neglect, with indifference. It reminded him of the shabby restaurants where he and Marina had gone, vainly hoping for a good meal and finding only this residue of past things, this same absence of care.

'What I'd like,' Lev told Simone, after a couple of weeks, 'is to introduce *choice* into the lunch menu. Two main courses. Two puddings. Everyone can choose. Don't you think?'

'Yeah,' said Simone. 'But tell that to Ma McNaughton, she'll have a seizure.'

'Why?'

'Cost, Chef. Know wha' I mean? Choice is too whatsit – too wasteful.'

'No,' said Lev. 'Not if we make menus. Give out the menus one, two days before. Everybody decides. Tells us their choice. Then we know how many chickens, how many fish and so on for the suppliers. Should be no waste.'

'Yeah?'

'Yeah. Why not?'

'Yeah? Dunno why not. But she'll say no.'

Mrs McNaughton didn't say no. She said she'd run what she called 'a limited experiment for one month'. She cautioned Lev to balance the more expensive ingredients with cheaper ones each day.

When he told Simone, she said: 'Right. Well, I'd better write out the menus, man. Your spellin's atrocious, innit?'

'Yes,' agreed Lev. 'You write. You give them to Mrs McNaughton for the computer. Make every choice sound nice.'

Simone took the task home, came back with a formula she'd said she'd worked on with her mum and written out in a slow, careful hand. She showed it proudly to Lev.

YOUR MENU FOR WEDNESDAY

Wickedly lovely free-range chicken breasts stuffed with mushrooms, shallots and herbs, served with a totally brilliant jus
or
Chef's fantastic fish gratin with zero bones and non-crap crumb
and
Choice of non-frozen broccoli or beans or both if you want
–
Crème brûlée jacked by Chef from a recipe at GK Ashe
or
Watermelon sorbet with no black seeds or rubbish in it

Lev changed nothing before he took Simone's menu to Mrs McNaughton. Mrs McNaughton put on her glasses. Lev saw a smile spread across her face. 'Well,' she said, 'I'll let it go. We'll explain to everybody that Simone wrote it. There may be a few rumblings, but in the main I think it'll amuse them. And everything that amuses them I see as moments of light in their darkness.'

So then it became one of the highlights of the residents' day: reading out the lunch menus. The more extreme the language, the more the ancient occupants of Ferndale Heights liked it. It was as if the language already gave the dishes savour. As the weeks passed (and the costs remained stable and the month's 'experiment' was conveniently forgotten) the wording became wilder. At lunchtime, Lev might hear Berkeley Brotherton announce: 'I'm having the "bloody delicious vegetarian sausages with the non-packet-shit mash"', or Pansy Adeane say sweetly: 'Oh, Lord, I can't remember what I was havin', Lev, love. I think it was the "totally non-bull-shitting Guinness-marinated Irish stew", or was that Thursday?'

Lunchtime was noisier now. People ate more, talked more,

lingered longer at the table. 'If you ask me, it's a ruddy miracle,' Lev heard Douglas observe one early afternoon. 'We eat better here now than down the pub.'

'We do,' said Joan, 'but you can bet it won't last.'

'Why won't it last?'

'Nothing does. Nothing good does.'

'Well,' said Douglas, 'sufficient unto the day. The non-packet-shit mash might well outlive us.'

Only Ruby Constad played no part in any of this. Word went round Ferndale Heights that she had stomach cancer and would soon have to be moved out.

'Moved out where?' asked Lev.

'To a . . . whatever it is they call those damn places,' said Berkeley Brotherton. 'The last bivouac.'

Ruby lay in her bed, staring at her furniture. Sometimes, she listened to an old tape of Gregorian chant. Her frail hand would hold out the box of Matchsticks towards Lev, but he noticed that even these she couldn't eat any more.

One day, he found two middle-aged people sitting silently beside her. 'These are my children,' said Ruby, quietly. 'This is Noel and this is Alexandra.'

They didn't move from their chairs or hold out their hands, only nodded at him. It was hot in the room but he noticed that the son, Noel, was still wearing his lightweight overcoat. The daughter, Alexandra, had a grey waterfall of hair and wore a long denim skirt and sandals. The flesh of her legs was pale and dry.

'Do you work here?' she asked Lev.

'Lev is our chef,' said Ruby proudly.

'Oh, right,' said Alexandra.

'Ma can't eat proper food any more, can you, Ma?' said Noel.

'No,' said Ruby. 'I can't. But I know the meals have become wonderful since Lev took over. Tell about the menus, Lev. It will amuse my guests.'

My guests. This was how she referred to her son and daughter. Lev hovered by the door, noted a bunch of cheap carnations, still in their paper, resting on one of the Indian tables. 'Well,' he began, 'it's silly, really. In our new menus we try to describe how everything is fresh—'

'Yes, but you're not saying it right,' said Ruby. 'You see, Simone, the girl who helps Lev in the kitchen, writes the menus and she deliberately puts in outrageous words, so we get, say, "non-crap home-made crumble" or "sorbet recipe jacked from a famous chef" and lots more fun like that.'

The 'guests' smiled weakly, wearily. Ruby's face on the pillow was the colour of suet. 'Don't you think that's funny?' she asked her children.

'Not really,' said Noel. 'Not if you can't eat any of it.'

'That doesn't matter,' said Ruby. 'It's cheered everybody up. That's what matters.'

Ruby lay back on her pillow. She'd told Lev that talking tired her, that she liked to lie there, dreaming about the past, feeling that she wasn't anywhere solid or real – certainly not at Ferndale Heights – but in a land of her own imaginings, where the sky could be any colour she chose. 'I see wonderful things,' she'd said. 'I see white vestments blowing about on a washing-line; I see elephants being sprayed with water by their mahouts; I see vultures perching on enormous rocks ...'

Lev knew that the 'guests' were waiting for him to leave. He offered to find a vase for the carnations, but Ruby said: 'No, no, I've got plenty of vases. Alex will do it. Won't you, darling?'

'Sure,' said the daughter, Alexandra.

But she didn't move from her chair. It was, thought Lev, as though standing up on her pale, dry legs was a private act, something she refused to let a stranger witness.

Now, Lev and Marina were in a large room, and the sun fell in rectangles on a scented floor that was carpeted with sawdust. Together, they were brushing away this sawdust to reveal some solid parquet blocks underneath. 'This is the space,' Marina kept saying. 'This is the space.'

Then she told him that the sunlit room had once been a piano shop. Until recently it had been crammed with musical instruments and cases full of sheet music. 'Elgar used to live here,' she said, 'before he was famous.'

The dream was pleasant, with no sad edge to it. Little by little, the sawdust was swept away into a far corner and the wood underneath it began to shine. And Marina kept extolling the virtues of the empty piano shop. 'It's full of light,' she said, 'and there's a fireplace – look, Lev. I think you can get fifteen or sixteen tables in here and still have room for your bar.'

Lev wanted to ask her where his kitchen was going to be.

He understood that there was another room, behind the piano shop, where Elgar had once lain in a narrow bed, hearing music stir in his brain, but Lev dreaded to find this room dark and cramped, with the composer's coffin in it, so he let the door to it remain shut and never mentioned the kitchen. But the sweeping of the beautiful room went on and the *snick-snick* of the brooms was a gentle sound ...

Lev woke up from this dream feeling comfortable and happy, but as he stood making tea in the kitchen he began to realise that the dream had come as a reminder – a reminder that, back in Auror, nothing had moved forward. Although – thanks to the money he'd managed to send – the Tchevi was back on the road, Rudi was still in a silent, angry mood. He'd told Lev his days as a driver were numbered, that he wasn't prepared to tangle with 'the fucking taxi Mafia in Baryn and their crap cars'. Had said it was beneath the Tchevi's dignity. Said he'd rather lie down and die.

Then there was the tormenting question of the flats in Baryn. Lora had been given an appointment with an official at the Office of Rehousing, who hadn't hesitated a moment before taking her £50 bribe, but had said he couldn't promise anything with a view of the river and suggested she return in a month's time. As she'd gone out of the door, he'd made a gesture with his hand, rubbing his thumb against the pads of his fingers.

'He's *grey* as a rat, then?'

'I guess.'

'I'll send another fifty,' said Lev.

Lora told him she'd been out to the site and that nothing was being started yet, no sign of any building work where the flats were meant to be. She said the land was being used as 'garbage facility', with gulls and foxes scavenging there.

'Maybe that means the Auror dam's postponed?'

'No, Lev. Not at all. Surveyors and engineers are up and down the river all the time. We've been told they're starting work this winter. We'll find ourselves homeless and nobody will care.'

He longed to tell her that he had it all worked out, that if he could just keep working till January or February, he'd have made the money he needed to get his great enterprise started, but somehow he couldn't lay the plan before them, didn't dare to, felt afraid they wouldn't see it as he saw it – as salvation. What he dreaded most was that Rudi would laugh at it. 'A posh restaurant in Baryn! Well, that's a pig's testicle of an idea, comrade. Who's your fucking clientele? You think the citizens of that poor dump of a town can afford to pay for capitalist food?'

Lev told himself that when he was back there, face to face with Rudi, when he *had* the money, when he'd found premises that he liked, then it would become real to everybody. Then they wouldn't laugh. But his dream about the piano shop now indicated to him that the things he'd let himself imagine – the wholesome fire, the *automatic* success of the venture – were still only that: empty imaginings. The beauty of the sunlight, the scented room with its wooden floor, the presence of Marina in the dream – all these had consoled him, but what did they really express except a longing to snatch back the life he'd lost?

Late one night, as Lev shuffled in, aching, hurting, almost *bent* from his day at Ferndale and his stint at Panno's, his phone rang and it was Rudi.

'OK,' said Rudi. 'Lora says you got a "scheme". So what is the fucking scheme? Why aren't you *saying*?'

Rudi had been drinking. His speech was nasal, punctuated with flying spit. Lev sat down on his bed, kicked off his shoes, brought his feet up and let his back rest against the giraffe pillows. 'I'm not saying,' he said, as calmly as he could, 'because the scheme depends on a sum of money I don't yet have.'

'So why bother mentioning it to Lora? Arsehole! Why get her hopes up?'

'Why are you calling me an arsehole? Because you've got hold of some vodka for sterilisation?'

He hoped the old joke would soften Rudi's mood, but it didn't.

'I drink,' Rudi said, 'because my life is shit and because you're making everything *worse*, tantalising us all with your so-called "scheme".'

'Well, perhaps I shouldn't have mentioned it. I only wanted to reassure Lora—'

'No, you shouldn't have fucking mentioned it. But you didn't think, did you? You're so fired up with your life in fucking London, you don't remember any more what it's like here, do you?'

Lev sighed. He wished he wasn't so dog tired. 'I remember what it's like,' he said. 'That's why I'm trying to come up with something to change it.'

'Come up with *what*? Why you spin some fuckin' mystery around it? You planning to build Buckingham Palace in the Baryn municipal square? Or what?'

'Rudi,' said Lev, 'listen to me. All I'm saying is, you've just got to have faith.'

'Know what?' said Rudi. 'That's exactly what I don't have. I *don't* have faith in you any more. None! In fact, I was saying to Lora, I agree with Ina now, I don't think you're ever coming back. Sure, you'll send us money from time to time – a few handouts for the poor suckers left behind – but you don't care about any of us, not about me or Lora, not even about Maya.'

'Take that back, Rudi!'

'Why? It's what I believe. You're like everybody who goes to the West: you've turned into a selfish bastard. You used to be a good man, a good friend—'

'I am *still* a good friend. Who helped you get the Tchevi mended?'

'Sure. I bow down. I kiss your arse. But it's just money, comrade. And that's easy for you now. Send money, send money, send money! Easy as farting. In fact, I expect you've got money dribbling out of all your orifices now. But the day of reckoning's coming – or haven't you understood?'

'What "day of reckoning"? Why are you doing this, Rudi?'

'Doin' what?'

'Getting this mad at me.'

'Because you've left it too late! Too fucking *late*! I don't believe in the future any more. Nor does your mother, in case you hadn't noticed. So you keep your precious "scheme". You stay and have a nice life in England. Screw a few more English girls, why don't you? Forget about us because, I'm telling you, we've all *forgotten about you*!'

Rudi hung up. Lev lay there, cradling the phone. Told himself again that Rudi was drunk, that none of what he was saying counted for much. Yet he couldn't help but feel this, feel the terror of this in the cavity of his soul – that he should be *forgotten*. He put out an arm, wanting to hold something, clutch something to his exhausted body, but there was nothing on the bed, only his own frame, laid out there, with his feet in old, worn socks.

Now he felt it all around him, this forgetting. Everybody from home had turned away from him. Even Lydia.

He'd sent another cheque to her parents' address in Yarbl, but it had never been cashed. He'd called her mobile five or six times, but she had never answered it. He suspected, now, that when she saw his name appear on the display, she just switched off her phone. He'd left messages apologising for asking for money that night of the mugging, told her he hadn't been in his right mind after what had happened on Swains Lane, begged her to call back. But no return call had ever come.

He tried one more time, on a Sunday morning. Heard the number ringing. Imagined some spacious hotel room in Brussels or Amsterdam. Longed to hear her telling him excitedly about yet another glorious marbled bathroom, another robe, soft as velvet.

But it clicked in, her familiar voicemail:

> *You've reached Lydia, personal assistant to Maestro Pyotor Greszler. I'm sorry that I'm not able to take this call. Please call back later or leave a message.*

Lev sighed. He spoke softly into the phone. 'Lydia,' he said, 'it's Lev. I've left a lot of messages. I don't want to pester you. I'm sure you have a busy schedule, but I want to know that you've forgiven me.'

He paused here. Then he said: 'I'd really like to talk to you. I'd like to know how you are … That's all, I guess. Except I feel … I don't know how to put this. I feel as though everybody from home has just … let me go. And this is … well, it feels unbearable.'

He was about to hang up here, but then he added: 'Oh, yes, and I have a question for you. Did you ever finish that "jumper" you were knitting on the bus? Because I never saw you wearing it. I'd love to know if you ever made the sleeves.'

He waited. Part of him hoped – expected – that she'd call back straight away, if only to tell him about the jumper. He sat with his mobile on his knee, smoking and looking out at Belisha Road, where sleet was falling. 'Call,' he begged her silently. But time drifted on and no call came.

He got up and made tea. He knew he shouldn't be surprised that now, finally, Lydia didn't want to be connected to him any more. And yet he *was* surprised. He'd always assumed that Lydia and Pyotor Greszler were going to play some part in his future life, but perhaps, after all, this wasn't going to happen. Perhaps, from now on, there would be only her accusing silence.

He was tempted to dial her mobile again, but he was afraid, suddenly, to trespass into a different time zone, afraid to wake her.

One morning, when Lev arrived at Ferndale Heights, Mrs McNaughton called him into her office. 'Mrs Constad was moved to St John's last night,' she said. 'I promised I'd ask you to go and see her.'

'St John's?'

'St John's Hospice. Not far from here. Go today. I'll help Simone prepare the suppers so you can get away after lunch.'

Lev sat silently on the hard chair he'd been offered. Mrs McNaughton said: 'St John's is a good place. Run by Catholic nuns. Mrs Constad was brought up a Roman Catholic, in a convent in India, so I expect she'll feel quite at home. But, of course, for you, it's bound to be upsetting.'

Lev nodded. He thought of the sullen middle-aged children, sitting immovable by the bed and hoped they wouldn't be there.

'Did you know,' said Lev, 'that Mrs Constad was part of a welcome pageant the convent gave for the Viceroy?'

'No. I didn't know that.'

'Yes, she was. She was one half of the O in "Welcome".'

St John's Hospice was dark, with curtains drawn against the bright day. It smelled of incense candles and of something else: the old, familiar stench of the cancer ward.

Lev gave his name to a nun, wearing a plastic apron over her habit. He was told to wait on a chair in the small entrance lobby. An old man opposite him also waited, carrying a bunch of lilac wrapped in newspaper, and this made Lev conscious of the absence of any gift for Ruby Constad. And then he remembered the things he used to take to Marina when she was dying: wild flowers sometimes, but more often objects she'd been attached to and now missed, family photographs, Maya's first drawings, a Mickey Mouse clock, a green magnifying-glass, a wooden bird ...

'Come with me, sir. You can see Mrs Constad now. But as you're not family please don't stay more than a few minutes. We're trying to keep her very peaceful.'

Lev followed the nun down a corridor deliberately kept dark and lit only with pools of flickering tea-lights. It was so silent that his own footsteps sounded loud and heavy, the footsteps of someone who wasn't supposed to be there. He felt breathless, slightly sick. He thought longingly of the fresh breeze outside in the street.

Ruby's room was very small – a cell. The bed was high and the body in it kept from falling out by metal bars. A dim lamp was on and by the bed were a small night-table and a worn, rush-seated chair. Above it, on the white wall, a wooden cross.

Ruby lay on her back, with her nose pointing sternly into the air. Her hands were folded over her chest, as though arranged there by one of the sisters. Just perceptible beneath the hands was the slow rise and fall of her breath.

Lev stood and looked down at her. Dying had never seemed – in his presence, at least – to pitch Ruby Constad into the kind of agony suffered by Marina. It was as though she'd sat quietly with death as her companion, refusing food, turning the pages of her photograph album, and when the last page was turned, she'd come here, to St John's, to the semi-darkness that preceded the final and absolute one.

Lev said her name and the hands stirred, but her head didn't move.

'Who is it?' The voice was high, almost squeaky, like a child's voice.

'It's Lev.'

Now the head turned and Ruby looked up. Lev wondered

whether, in the low light, she could see him. He sat on the chair, and brought his face nearer to hers.

'Oh, yes ...' she said at last. 'I told the sisters: he's the one with the beautiful grey hair.'

There was a smile on her lips. Her breath was sour.

'Now ...' she said. 'Now ...'

Her hands clutched the metal bars and she tried to pull herself up in the bed, but her breathing immediately became stifled and she began to retch. On the night-table there was a kidney bowl and Lev held it under her chin as she spat a thread of foul-smelling phlegm into it. She sank back onto the pillows.

'*Old age is not for sissies*,' she said. 'Who said that? I can't remember. But they were right.'

Lev wiped her mouth and set the bowl aside. He wished he'd brought fat branches of lilac so that they could bury their faces in its scent.

He waited. With the back of his hand, he gently stroked Ruby's temple. After a while, she said: 'On that night-table thing ... by the water glass ... is an envelope, Lev. It's for you. Can you see it?'

He sensed that the stroking consoled her, was reluctant therefore to take his hand away, but he could see the envelope and he picked it up. On it, in wispy writing, were the words 'For Lev'.

'I've found it,' he said.

'Well, it's for you. It's a cheque. Only a small one. It's to help you set up your restaurant in ... whatever that town is called ...'

'Baryn.'

'Baryn. That's it. Don't open the envelope now. Otherwise you may start arguing with me and I'm too weak to argue. So this is what you must do. Are you listening?'

'Yes.'

'Go to the bank with it straight away. You do have a bank account, don't you?'

'Yes. Clerkenwell branch.'

'Right. Go now and pay the cheque in. When I die, my bank account will be frozen, so you must present the cheque before then. D'you understand, Lev?'

Lev looked down at the envelope. It weighed almost nothing, yet felt heavy in his hands. He couldn't now recall what he'd done – if anything – to earn this gift. He was about to say that he couldn't accept it, that it wasn't right for Ruby to give cheques to people she hardly knew, when the door of the cell opened and the nun wearing the plastic apron came in. The scented, flickering light from the passage made a timid entrance into the room and Lev felt this as a kind of relief, as though, in the yellow candles, the essence of life itself were burning.

'I'm sorry,' said the sister, 'but you must go now. You must let Mrs Constad rest.'

Lev nodded. He felt choked, unable to speak. He got up slowly, took Ruby's hand and kissed it, felt his own tears fall and moisten the fragile hand. 'Thank you,' he stammered.

'Lev dear,' she said, and he saw the shadow of a smile touch her face. 'Always so *galant*. I hope the restaurant is a grand success.'

He arrived early at Panno's for his evening stint and found the *patron* cleaning out his charcoal fire to re-lay it.

'Hey!' said Panno, when he saw Lev. 'Just the man. Got an offer for you. Nice offer, my friend. Vacancy in the kitchen from next week. You want?'

Lev stared stupidly at Panno. Even yesterday, he would have leaped at this offer, but now he hesitated, wondering: Can I do it? Thirteen or fourteen hours a day, six days a week, at the stoves. Will I survive this?

'What's the matter?' said Panno, seeing him falter. 'You're a chef, aren't you? With a nice reference from GK Ashe! You've been wasted on front-of-house. Come and learn Greek food in my kitchen.'

Lev nodded, stammered out his thanks to Panno, and said he'd do it.

'Good,' said Panno. '£17 an hour. OK? That way, you make ninety or hundred pound a night. And I keep paying you cash, so no National Insurance bullshit and no tax, right? It's a chance for you to get on your feet.'

'Thank you, Panno.'

'No, it's good for me, too. Shake on it, eh?'

The two men shook hands, Lev's hand cool from his walk, Panno's warm and dusty from his charcoal ash. Then Lev went to the sink, drew himself a glass of water and drank. His mind was already doing wild sums. Now, he'd be making about £1,400 a week. Already, by juggling his jobs at Ferndale Heights and Panno's, he'd saved almost £2,000. And today, he'd banked a cheque from Ruby Constad for £3,000. He was half-way to his target.

He put on his blue-and-white apron and began laying up tables.

He thought that he should have been walking on air, but his legs felt sluggish, his brain feverish with anxiety. And he knew this wasn't just tiredness or even sadness at Ruby's dying. It was because his dream, his heart's desire, his Great Idea was sailing closer, ever closer to him now, but there was one terrifying, insurmountable problem: far off in Baryn, where it would have its existence, no one waited for it. In his own country, where he longed to return, it wasn't even the empty piano shop of his sentimental reveries; it was nothing. It was nothing because no one trusted him any more.

23

Communist Food

Lev flew home in the middle of winter, mild and damp in London, but ice-cold in Auror.

He'd told nobody he was coming, preferred to arrive like this, a stranger in a world newly strange to him, make his own way, slowly, by bus, from the airport at Glic to Baryn and then on to his village.

On the first of the familiar, worn-out buses, belching heat from some blackened part of its engineering, Lev chose a window-seat and kept wiping the condensation from the steamed-up glass so that he could stare out at his country – at the abandoned farms and silent factories, at the deserted coal depots and lumber yards, at the new high-rise flats and the bright, flickering heartbeats of American franchises, at a world slipping and sliding on a precipice between the dark rockface of Communism and the seductive, light-filled void of the liberal market.

Lev was glad of the snow-shroud that softened the ugliness of the town suburbs, made the low village houses look picturesque, gave beauty to a straggle of mules being led through the purple afternoon, carrying bundles of reeds on their scrawny backs. He even found himself half hoping that, beyond Baryn, the road would be pronounced impassable so that he could postpone his arrival in Auror.

It was dark by the time the bus drew into the depot at Baryn, and the darkness gave Lev the excuse he needed to go no further that night. After all, no one was expecting him. No meal was being prepared, no lamp or fire lit. It would be better, he told himself, to arrive in Auror in the morning, with hoped-for sunlight making the snow look clean, when Maya was at school, when Ina was working in her shed, when Rudi was out on his taxi round. Better to arrive under a blue sky.

He found a room in the two-star Hotel Kreis, with a double bed and an old TV on a plastic console that was buckling under the television's weight. In the hotel dining room, Lev was served a meal of tinned soup and unidentifiable stew. He noticed that the tablecloth was stained and the tines of the forks tarnished. He drank a carafe of inky red wine and fell asleep with the trams grinding and clanking outside his bedroom window and the surge of the hotel plumbing above and beneath him, as though some unmapped inland sea were slowly filling the cavities of the walls. He slept a dreamless, exhausted sleep.

The morning brought sunlight and the beginnings of a thaw.

Lev got off the bus outside Auror, and looked towards his village, then up at the hills behind it. He stood silently on the empty road. He listened to the quietness of everything. Thought how, all the years he'd lived here, he'd never seen clearly how lonely, how far from all thriving worldly habitation Auror actually was. Nothing moved in the snowscape, only the glimmering droplets of the thaw among the hedgerows, silently falling.

Then Lev heard a low rumbling noise start up, like the sound of a generator. He couldn't see the river from here, but he looked over to where it was, saw the top of a steel crane rising above the trees. Now, added to the rumbling, came the muffled *wump-wump-wump-wump* of a pile-driver. So then Lev understood that it had begun: work on the Project of Outstanding Public Utility (POPU) known as Dam No. 917, adjacent to the village of Auror.

Lev picked up his bag. He could feel his heart beating loudly, as if in time to the *wump-wump* of the machinery pounding shafts into the riverbed. When the first houses came into view, he faltered and stopped. Why was it so excruciating, this moment of return? For such a long time he'd imagined it differently, with all the familiar faces smiling at him from behind the barrier in the airport arrivals hall, Maya rushing forward to fling her arms round him ... but now here he was, moving silently into his village like a ghost, as though he or the village – or both – were guilty of some terrible dereliction.

Who's there?
Nay, answer me. Stand and unfold yourself!

Lev remembered suddenly that it was Saturday. This made everything worse. Because now he had no idea where everybody was going to be; and he didn't know how best to imagine anyone. Would Ina be working in her shed? Would Maya be playing with her friends in the snow? Or would he have to walk into his own front room and find them both there beside the wood stove, see them turn to him with a terrified look?

He found himself wishing, irrationally, that he had Christy Slane with him, a comrade, a true stranger to whom everybody would have to be polite and welcoming, a shield behind which feelings could be hidden. Because alone like this, in the vacant white landscape, he felt a kind of sordid nakedness, as though his family had never before seen him, seen him as he truly was, and now they would, and when they saw what he was, they'd turn away in disgust.

He walked on. He was at the brow of a familiar incline. Any moment now his own house would come into view. The *wump-wump-wump* of the pile-driver was louder, closer ... Then he heard the sound of a vehicle and saw, as he reached the top of the incline, the unmistakable blue-and-white shape of the Tchevi moving slowly towards him. Lev stared at the approaching car. On it lumbered, its low centre of gravity as impressive as always, its chrome still gleaming in the morning light, and at the wheel ... well, it could be one person and one only. No passenger beside him. Rudi alone, probably setting out on an early taxi run to Baryn.

Lev put down his bag. The Tchevi didn't slow, but came gently on up the hill, its old American engine still throbbing and gurgling, like a big outboard motor on a boat. Now Lev could see that Rudi was wearing dark glasses against the snow's glare. Lev was about to raise an arm in greeting, but his arm felt heavy at his side, so he just stayed where he was and waited for the moment when Rudi would recognise him.

Now, the car slowed a little, but it was only a tiny diminution of its speed, a mark of courtesy to a stranger passed on the road. It didn't stop, but drove on by. Lev could hear the car radio playing.

Wump-wump-wump … *Wump-wump-wump* … *Wump-wumpwump* … The pile-driver, the beat of the car's music, the pounding of Lev's heart: all combined to isolate him inside a cold cavern of sorrow. His friend had seen him and driven on, driven away!

Lev turned in the direction of the Tchevi, raised both his arms in a gesture of despair, saw the car's brake-lights come on, saw it slide to a halt on the downward slope of the hill.

He waited. All around him, the snow was melting and shimmering.

Abandoning his bag, he began to walk towards the Tchevi, saw the driver's door open with its habitual, violent swing and the hunched figure of Rudi climb out into the road. He was wearing the worn Canadian lumber coat he'd exchanged for two spare tyres at the Baryn market. His hair was grey and wild.

'Hey!' he called. 'Lev! What the fuck … ?'

He stood by the open car door, holding onto it as though for support.

And Lev found himself wondering, What's the matter with him? Is he ill, is he lame, or what? Why doesn't he move?

But then, as Lev approached him, Rudi began to walk towards him, and the walk turned into a run or, rather, a familiar lop-sided jog, the only expression of speed Rudi's body had been capable of since the long-ago days of his youth.

'Hey!' he called again. 'Hey, comrade!'

Then the two men reached each other and clung together, in a slumped, exhausted embrace, like heavyweight boxers nearing the end of a bout. Lev wanted to say Rudi's name, tried to say it, but found that he was unable to speak.

Now Lev was sitting in Rudi's kitchen. Lora sat beside him, holding onto his arm, and Rudi was opposite them, staring at his friend with a kind of awe.

'It's like,' he said, 'I'm some heartbroken old apostle, come to visit your tomb, and then you walk out of it with holes in your fucking feet.'

They were drinking coffee, eating cinnamon cakes. The small

house smelled of cigarette smoke and wood fumes. Lev noticed that the ceiling above the stove was black with grime. The feel of Lora's hand on his arm was warm and comforting.

'So, what now?' said Rudi, after a while. 'What happens next?'

Lev reached for another cake, took a sip of his coffee. Felt the weight of the moment.

What happens next?

'OK,' he began. 'This is what happens next. I've been saving money. Quite a lot of money. More than you or I ever earned in our years at the mill. And this is what we're going to do with it ...'

Strangely, he felt calm as he talked. He laid out his vision of the restaurant in Baryn like a man describing some perfectly recollected memory that hadn't dimmed with time, but only gathered colour and clarity as the months had passed. He talked about the piano shop and the open fire and the wood floor and the white tablecloths and the bar. He said he was going to begin the search for premises in Baryn as soon as possible. He told Rudi and Lora how much he now knew about cooking and how it had become his belief that, in any human existence, good food might make a crucial difference to a person's day-to-day ability to go on and not give in to despair. He described the changes he'd made at Ferndale Heights and the way the residents had been cheered by them, even in their last months on earth. He boasted that he was going to try to ameliorate the lives of every citizen in Baryn.

After a while, as, in the hall, the broken cuckoo clock blurted out some hour or other and the telephone rang a couple of times and was ignored, Rudi began to ask questions.

'What's the "we" in all this, my friend? How do we fit in?'

'Right,' said Lev. 'This is how I see it. The thing I want is that everybody gets to do what they're best at.'

'What am I best at?' said Rudi. 'Getting plastered. Driving a twenty-five-year-old car. Pissing into engine coolers. What use am I going to be?'

'Maître d',' announced Lev, snapping his fingers for emphasis. 'Restaurant manager. Front-of-house. You run the dining room.'

'You're joking.'

'No. Why? You take drinks orders. Make everyone feel welcome. You'll be fantastic at this. Keep the waiters in line. Crack jokes. You're the face-of-the-place.'

Lora burst out laughing. 'Beautiful!' she said. 'The face-of-the-place! I never thought of anything so perfect for Rudi.'

'Why's it perfect for me?' said Rudi. 'My fucking face ain't so handsome any more. And my jokes are pathetic these days. There's nothing worth joking about.'

'Now there will be,' said Lora. 'Think of this, Rudi: your own bar area, a cellar full of wine.'

'These I like. But I'll be no good, my friend. I'll drink too much. I'll say some fucking rude thing to a customer by mistake. I'll be too clumsy.'

'Maybe,' said Lev. 'I was clumsy when I started at *GK Ashe*. But you'll learn.'

Rudi now rubbed his eyes and it was as though he was shining them up, because when he turned Lev could see them sparkling.

'Jesus,' Rudi said. 'God damn you, Lev! Why've you kept this secret so long?'

'Because I couldn't tell you till I had the money. And I wanted to be here, to present it to you, face to face.'

'Well, now you've got it, buddy, face to face with the face-of-the-fucking-place!'

Their laughter chimed out, ravishing the morning quiet.

'What's Lora going to do?' asked Rudi, when the laughter sub-sided. 'How's she going to get involved? I'm not bossing my wife around as a waitress.'

'I know,' said Lev.

'It's OK,' said Lora. 'I can just keep on with my horoscopes.'

'Those fucking horoscopes!' said Rudi. 'If I hear the word "Jupiter" one more fucking time, I'm going to start shooting at the night sky.'

'Well, this is what I wondered,' said Lev. 'I wondered whether Lora would like to work with me in the kitchen.'

'I'm not a chef, Lev.'

'Hey, but wait a minute, you make nice meals, babe,' said Rudi. 'That's a start. Isn't it? And sometimes she has to make them out of heels of sausage and stale bread and God knows what kind of bitter leaves. Eh?'

'Exactly,' said Lev. 'Now, I can get you good ingredients, Lora, and teach you everything GK Ashe and Panno the Greek taught me.'

Lora leaned against Lev and put a tender kiss on his cheek. 'We missed you so,' she said. 'Didn't we, Rudi?'

'Yes, we fucking did. Especially when we thought you were never coming back. Oh, shit, I know it's eleven in the morning, or whatever, but let's have some drinks to celebrate. Vodka for sterilisation!'

Rudi got up to fetch the glasses and the *vodichka*.

Lev looked round at the familiar room and thought that he could sit there for ever with his friends: let time drift and pass and never want to move from their side.

He reached for the vodka.

The next morning, Lev woke on Rudi's sofa. The world was encased in ice. Droplets of the thaw had petrified into a million glinting pieces of glass. As the sun rose, the dazzle of this glass world was breathtaking to see.

Lev sat with Rudi and Lora at the kitchen table, nursing his hangover, drinking Fanta, munching stale rice cakes. Beyond the window, the ice-trees tinkled in the northerly breeze, like a forest of chandeliers.

It was tempting to stay there, by the wood stove, not move for another whole day, to doze in the afternoon, to talk on and on with Rudi and Lora until a second night fell. But Lev was now longing to see his daughter.

This was the day when he would finally arrive home.

'Listen,' said Rudi, 'let me go ahead, prepare Ina. Otherwise when she sees you, she's going to fall over into the fucking wood-pile. You follow along.'

'No,' said Lev. 'I know where Mamma will be on a Sunday morning: church. I'll wait for her outside. She'll be full of sanctity so, with any luck, she won't yell at me.'

'Yeah, but her heart may stop.'

Lev sighed. 'Then it's a good end. She dies in front of her church, knowing her Prodigal Son has come back after all.'

Lev took a shower, then repacked his bag and set out. He walked slowly through the village. From behind closed windows, from behind lace curtains, he saw one or two people stare at him, a figure they almost recognised, wandering alone through the empty morning.

Now he stood in front of his house and looked at it. Nothing moved here: no sound at all. Even the machinery at the river had fallen silent. The boards of the wooden veranda were bleached grey-white with the passing of the seasons. A small purple bicycle was propped up against the wall beside the front door.

Lev found himself shivering. He wasn't used to the cold of Auror. Found himself wondering how he'd ever survived all those winters at the lumber yard. This work now had in his mind something inhuman about it, as though it had been a form of unspoken punishment all along – punishment for the simple crime of being alive in a complicated age.

He went up the steps to his front door. At his back, he could imagine it, the floodwater rising, already swallowing whatever had been left lying on the ground – broken tools, sacks of rotted potatoes, plastic buckets, chicken bones left by the dogs – then beginning to wash round the walls of the houses, beginning to seem deep, beginning to look green and dark ... And he thought, as he stood shivering outside his door, that it didn't matter, that Auror was a place so lonely, so abandoned by time, it was right to drown it, right to force its inhabitants to leave behind their dirt roads, their spirit rags, and join the twenty-first-century world.

Instead of walking down to the church, Lev went into the house and crouched by the wood stove, trying to get warm. The room smelled of damp wool. On a wooden clothes-horse, some of Maya's little clothes were drying. The doll she'd named Lili sat in a chair with her eyes rolled shut. Lev went to his bag and took out the presents he had brought for his mother and daughter and laid them out on the table, beside some plastic flowers Ina had stuck into a glass vase. He lit a cigarette and waited.

After what felt like a long time, he heard their voices, Maya's light as an elf's in the frozen air, Ina's a low, anxious growl. He went to the door and opened it and saw them walking up the path. Ina let out a shriek, and clutched her chest, wrapped in its black shawl. Maya stood still and stared at him. He didn't know what else to do or say except smile and hold out his arms. Then Maya began a delirious shouting: 'Pappa! Pappa! PAPPA! PAPPA!' And she came pelting towards him and he lifted her up and whirled her round, kissed her face, her head in its knitted bobble hat, then held her tightly, tightly against his heart, and told her he was home, home for good, and that everything, now, was going to be all right.

Ina regarded him from a distance, hugging her shawl round her, binding her arms, so that she could remain separate and aloof from him, keeping her anger intact. Lev saw that her face looked older and her eyes smaller. He saw, too, that she was trembling.

'You've put on weight,' she said.

Rudi and Lev drove to Baryn and put up at the Hotel Kreis. Lev had plans for a three-day visit. 'In the daytime we look for premises,' he said. 'In the evenings and at lunchtime we go round the restaurants and cafés, see what's happening to the food.'

On the Baryn road, Rudi drove like a man rushing to a longed-for date. He played the radio loud, talked through the din, told Lev that as well as being the face-of-the-place he could 'gun the suppliers into line', fill the Tchevi's trunk with crates of guinea fowl and boxes of lettuce.

'They're gonna fear the sight of this car!' he said. 'If they're not ready with their fucking tomatoes or whatever, they're gonna wish they'd died in a salt mine.'

Lev suggested they buy a second-hand pickup, for hauling in the bulky items, but Rudi said: 'I'm not driving a lousy pickup. Not as long as the Tchevi's alive.'

'OK,' said Lev. 'I'll drive the truck.'

'You don't know how to drive,' said Rudi.

'I'll learn,' said Lev. 'Same way as you did.'

On the first evening, they decided to have dinner in the Café Boris, a familiar restaurant on Market Square.

When they got there, they saw that the Café Boris had been renamed the Brasserie Baryn, and Rudi said: 'Uuh-uuh. I don't like the look of that, Lev. Did some smart-arse chef already get a hold on this town?'

They went in. The interior had been repainted blue. A blue neon sign advertised German lager. In the four corners of the square room stood shiny potted palms. But the smell from the kitchen was immediately familiar to Lev, the smell of beetroot soup, nameless stews, seaweed ravioli. 'I think we're all right,' he said to Rudi. 'I'm getting a whiff of Communist food. I can second-guess the menu already.'

The place was almost empty. They ordered two beers from a middle-aged maître d' so tired of his job, so tired of the world, it seemed, that he dragged himself about the place holding onto the backs of chairs, as though the building were tilting like a train. The backs of his trousers looked varnished, his shoes were filmed with dust.

'Stupendous,' said Rudi. 'What an advertisement he is! What a face-of-the-place!'

They began giggling like boys. Couldn't stop once they'd started. And it was like this, hunched over with laughter, that Eva found them.

She walked like a dancer, carrying the beers on a wooden tray. She wore a black dress and a white apron, with a name-badge pinned to it. Her dark hair was tied back with a velvet ribbon. Her hands, setting down the beers, were white and slim.

Lev and Rudi looked up at her and she smiled, watching them struggle to recover from their laughter. And they both had the one thought: she reminded them of Marina.

She went away and came back with menus encased in oily laminate. Her presence at the table was charged. Rudi and Lev took the menus in silence. Eva produced a piece of paper out of her apron pocket and said: 'Would you like to hear what the special orders are this evening?'

'Yes,' said Lev. 'We'd like to hear.'

'Well,' said Eva, 'I'm sorry but there are only two specials tonight. There's rabbit cooked with juniper berries or there's cold venison, served with boiled egg. Hard-boiled egg, I should say.'

'Thank you,' said Lev. Then he added quickly: 'Could you bring us the wine list while we decide on our food?'

'Yes, sir.'

'Oh, and tell us what you would recommend. Would you? The rabbit, perhaps?'

She blushed, feeling the eyes of the two men on her face, then flickering down, just for one irresistible moment, to her slim body in its waitress's uniform.

'I think the rabbit is nice,' she said.

She went away and Lev and Rudi began to drink the German beers. They said nothing for a while. Their laughter was gone. They studied the plastic menus and looked about them at the empty room and the handful of other diners and the mâitre d' now standing motionless by the bar counter. The neon sign kept lighting and relighting his face with a ghostly flare of blue.

Rudi said: 'D'you remember Lake Essel?'

'Yeah,' said Lev. 'Of course I remember Lake Essel. We've probably been dying all this time.'

'We *have* been dying all this time,' said Rudi. 'That's what I feel. But now we're going to recover.'

Eva came back with the wine list and Lev took it. He saw that half the wines listed had been crossed out. 'What happened to all these?' he asked.

Again, he saw her blush. 'I don't exactly know,' she said. 'I think maybe the French wines dried up. Sorry, I don't mean literally dried up but just didn't get as far as here.'

Lev nodded. Out of the corner of his eye he caught Rudi smiling. Suddenly he turned and said to Eva: 'Have you heard about the dam at Auror?'

'The dam at Auror? Yes. Everybody knows about the dam. I guess you're not from round here. They say the Auror Dam is going to change our lives.'

'Do you think it will?'

'I hope so.' She looked round the empty brasserie. 'I hope it'll bring more people, more prosperity. In time ...'

She was standing very near to Lev, her hips level with his shoulder. There was a lovely scent about her – something astringent yet seductive.

They'd planned to spend the dinner discussing their itinerary for the following day. They had three premises to see – all shops that had closed. They'd brought along a map of the city so that Rudi could work out the route. But silence had somehow fallen. Neither of them could say Marina's name, speak the thought about Eva's resemblance to her, but it was understood between them that something disturbing had happened, like an old piece of music suddenly starting up in a place where no music had ever been heard. Only later, lying wide awake on hard twin beds, listening to the night trams, Rudi said: 'She was a good waitress, Lev. Perhaps that's something we should do while we're here: take the contact numbers of people you might employ later on.'

In the morning, with a light snow falling, they drove back and forth along the narrow streets of Baryn, parking the Tchevi wherever it could fit, often with two of its wheels mounted on the pavement.

'I hate to see her like that,' said Rudi. 'She looks like a tart-car hitching up her fucking skirts, or like a dog pissing in the gutter. It's demeaning for her. So, listen, comrade, it's no use getting premises where the parking's crap.'

The three shops they were shown, empty since the summer or since the previous year, felt damp and dark. None of them bore any resemblance to the piano shop of Lev's dreams. The only thing that cheered him was that rents were low. He'd begun to hope that the money he had – almost £12,000 – would go a long way in this city.

They were heading back to the Hotel Kreis, in late afternoon, when Lev said: 'I've just remembered something. Lydia told me about a real piano shop, somewhere off Market Square. Let's try to find it.'

'Lev,' said Rudi, 'I thought you said you'd stopped being a dreamer.'

'No. I never said that. Dreams are what's got me by.'

They parked on the square, outside the Brasserie Baryn, and asked a man who resembled the former Tchevi owner, the professor of mathematics, if he knew of a music shop in this bit of town.

'Yes,' he said. 'It's right there, on the corner.'

They went in through a heavy door, whose movement set off a jangling bell above. The place was small and old and cramped, fitted with tilting shelves from floor to ceiling. These were stacked with sheet music, ancient 33 r.p.m. records and what looked like religious books or hymnals. On a central oak table, two violins and a tarnished saxophone were displayed on a velvet cloth. The elderly proprietor of the shop sat silent on a wooden chair.

Lev looked around, then back at the proprietor, who hadn't moved a muscle. He thought, If Pyotor Greszler made an appearance in this shop, this man would get up from his chair and come forward, amazed and flattered, transformed by sudden, ardent emotion.

'Lev,' Rudi whispered, 'wrong place, eh? Let's go.'

'Yup,' said Lev. But then, embarrassed, he turned to the

proprietor and said: 'Sorry. We made a mistake. We heard there were some premises to let here.'

The old man took up a home-rolled cigarette and reached for a box of matches. His hand shook. 'Come again next year,' he said, in a scratchy, smoke-afflicted voice. 'I'll be dead by then.'

Lev gaped.

'Meanwhile, ask next door. Number 43. The garage is closing down. They used to sell East German cars. But no one wants those pieces of tin any more.'

Lev thanked the proprietor of the piano shop, and they came out into the windy street.

'Shit,' said Rudi. 'Hadn't we better give up smoking? I don't want to get like him.'

They stood outside Number 43 Podrorsky Street – a road named for the president in his own lifetime. Then they went in and found two mechanics working underneath a ramp, servicing an ancient Citroën Déesse. The smell of engine oil woke Rudi from his late-afternoon torpor and he began to look around eagerly. 'Hey,' he said, after a few moments, 'lots of space here, Lev. And no problems with parking or access …'

The building was old. Had probably been a dozen different things in its time, just as the street might have had a dozen dif-ferent names. Bits of it – half of the first floor – had been ripped out to accommodate the garage, but the building had retained a kind of worn-out grandeur. Steel girders now held up the high roof.

On the left-hand wall there was a bulky brick structure and Lev walked towards this. It was, as he'd thought, a chimney-breast, and he began to caress the cold brickwork with his hands. The two mechanics ignored him. But Rudi, seeing Lev lost in his love affair with an imaginary fire, approached the men. Lev heard him tell them he owned a Chevrolet Phoenix, and ask whether the garage could get parts for the car.

'No, sorry, comrade,' said one of the men. 'We're closing down next month. What's a Chevrolet Phoenix, anyway?'

'Tchevi,' said Rudi. 'Big American car. Never seen one of them?'

'Nah,' said the man. 'How'd it get here? Fly?'

*

They decided to go back to the Brasserie Baryn for dinner.

Eva smiled her shy smile. They ordered beers and when Eva brought them, she said again: 'Would you like me to tell you about the specials?'

'Let me guess,' said Lev. 'Rabbit cooked with juniper, and cold venison.'

'Well,' she said, 'the rabbit is cooked with mustard seeds to-night.'

'Right. So what would you recommend?' Lev asked.

'Well ...'

'We had rabbit yesterday evening. It was a bit ... stringy.'

'I don't know, really. The seaweed ravioli is nice.'

'Yes?'

'Although my mother makes it better.'

Rudi lifted his brimming tankard of beer. 'Here's to your mother!'

'Right,' said Lev, taking up his own tankard. 'To your mother!'

Eva giggled, and looked sideways to see whether the maître d' was watching her.

Then Lev said: 'Do you also like cooking, Eva?'

'Yes,' she said. 'But I'm lazy. I live with my mother, so I let her cook for me – or I eat here.'

'How long have you worked here?'

'About a year.'

'D'you like this job?'

'It's OK. But I'm looking forward to the New Baryn, when there'll be more work for everybody.'

'The New Baryn?'

'Yes. When the dam's been built, they're going to change the city's name. It will be officially named "New Baryn".'

When they'd eaten their meal of beetroot soup and seaweed ravioli, and they were the only customers left in the brasserie, they invited Eva to have a drink with them. She sat down and sipped the white wine they had ordered and Lev found it difficult not to stare at her. He longed to ask her to undo the velvet ribbon that held back her hair.

After some moments of small-talk, Rudi began telling Eva that they were from Auror.

She stared at them, suddenly dismayed. 'I'm sorry,' she said, 'oh, I'm so sorry. I shouldn't have said what I said about the dam …'

Lev took this opportunity to reach out and lightly touch her arm. 'It's all right,' he said. 'We've got plans. Big plans. We're going to be part of the New Baryn.'

'Yes?'

'Yeah. Aren't we, Rudi?'

'We're going to *be* the New Baryn! We're going to embody its new spirit.'

'Yes? How?'

Lev's hand was still resting on Eva's arm. He kept it there and Eva didn't pull her arm away. The mâitre d', blue-lit at his post, stared at her. Rudi said: 'Our plans are secret at the moment. But, hey, would you like to come for a ride with us, in my big American car, and we can whisper them in your ear?'

Now she blushed. She lifted her arm from Lev's touch. 'I can't,' she said. 'I have to get home to my mother, or she worries about me. But perhaps you'll come here again and … try the cold venison?'

'Yes,' said Lev. 'Tomorrow night?'

It was late when Lev and Rudi left the brasserie but, on a whim, Rudi drove them out to the Perimeter Zone, on the north bank of the river.

They parked the Tchevi and got out into the light snow that was falling. They saw that the garbage dump had been cleared away and that five apartment buildings were going up.

They stared at the building works and at the water of the river, lit by the icy moon. And both of them had the same thought: that, despite all their ardour for the restaurant plan, it was difficult to believe their lives were going to be lived here, on the decrepit edge of the city, in a place that still stank of its waste. Lev looked around him at the mounds of earth and debris, at the puddles choked with yellow silt, at the rusty cranes and the stockpiles of flimsy cinderblocks. 'Hard to imagine this as home,' he said.

'Yup,' said Rudi.

They stood there in silence, letting the snow fall on them. And Lev felt his heart brim with sadness for Auror, for their old, dilapidated, care-worn village.

24

Number 43 Podrorsky Street

On the day they left Auror for ever, Ina, dressed in her widow's black, walked out of her house, past Lev and Rudi, who were loading the last of the furniture into Lev's second-hand pickup, and lay down in the dusty road. The two men stared at her, but neither of them moved.

'Is she saying some kind of prayer or what?' said Rudi.

'I don't know,' said Lev. 'I never know what she's doing or thinking.'

They went on with the loading. They saw Ina's hands scrabbling at the earth, gathering up dirt and letting it fall and scatter on her shoulders and on her head. Then she began to wail.

Lev stood still, leaning on the truck. He'd seen it coming, known it in his heart, in spite of Lydia's reassurances – that his mother was going to be the one to wreck the future. He pounded his fist on the truck roof, and the sound echoed in his head like an explosion. Anger welled up in him, an anger bitter enough to taste. He felt, at this moment, that he wanted to trample on Ina's outstretched form till he heard her neck snap. When Rudi said: 'Shall I go and help her up?' he replied: 'No. Leave her there.'

Maya came out of the house, clutching the doll, Lili. When she saw her grandmother lying in the road, she began a strange little gyrating dance of agony. Lev went to her and held her and said: 'It's all right. Everything's going to be all right.'

But Maya was rigid, pale as ash. How could everything be 'all right' when Ina had fallen into the dust?

'Hey,' said Lev, to his daughter, 'shall we get Lili settled in the truck? Make a nice comfortable space for her?'

But Maya just stuck her face into Lev's side, couldn't look at anything, couldn't speak. He stroked her hair, which she wore, these days, scrunched back into a funny little knot, secured with some vivid lime-green elastic thing. This knot was troubling to Lev. He felt it made Maya's face seem too wide, too vulnerable and unprotected. And what he did now was to unwind the green elastic and let Maya's dark hair fall forwards over her ears. Soon, it was damp and sticky with her tears.

Exhaustion hit him. He'd been working fifteen, sixteen hours a day, trying to get the restaurant up and running, either sleeping there, at 43 Podrorsky Street, on a mattress among the builders' rubble, or driving back to Auror in the early hours, making lists in his head, lists and more lists of all that was still to be done, of all that had not yet been sorted or acquired. And worried all the time that he was neglecting the prime thing: his cooking. When, at last, the restaurant was ready to open – if his money didn't run out, if it wasn't eaten away by all the *grey* sweeteners he was being forced to find – his mind might be a blank. He might be unable to remember one single recipe. The part of him that had yearned to become a chef might be dead.

He managed to keep talking gently to Maya, reminding her that tomorrow they were going skating and that Ina would be there at the rink-side, watching her perform her loops and jumps. 'She'll be happy again by then,' he said, without conviction. 'She'll be smiling all over her face.'

When he next looked at Ina lying in the road, Rudi was kneeling beside her. He heard himself sigh. 'Yeah,' he said, under this long, agonised release of his breath, 'help me now, comrade. Save the show for me now.'

Rudi got Ina into Lev's truck at last and Maya sat on her lap and clung to her, and they drove away. In the rear of the pickup, covered with a faded tarpaulin, their furniture jolted around.

Nobody looked back at Auror. Lev kept his eyes fixed on the steep road. Maya stuck her thumb into her mouth and went to sleep with her head resting on Ina's breast. Ina's hair was still matted with the road's grime, but she didn't seem to have noticed this, didn't seem to want to notice anything, but sat petrified in the worn old seat, never moving, never blinking.

'Listen to me, Mamma,' said Lev, when they were out of the village and going fast along the Baryn road. 'I'll say this once, but I'm not going to keep on repeating it. I'm sorry for everything that's happened. I know it's broken your heart. But it isn't my fault. The world's changed. And all I've done is to try to adapt. Because somebody had to. Right?'

He glanced sideways at her. It was as though she hadn't heard him. Her mouth was a map-maker's thin line.

Her silence endured. She acknowledged no words spoken to her by anyone, except Maya. She made no comment upon anything in the new flat – not even upon the electricity that never faltered. When Lev unpacked her jewellery-making tools and laid them out on a shelf in the small white room she was to share with Maya, she silently gathered them up, one by one, and hurled them into the ancient wardrobe she'd insisted on carting with them from Auror.

Lev didn't know what to do. Just prayed she'd speak to him at last when he showed her the work going on inside 43 Podrorsky Street. 'It's starting to look beautiful,' he ventured to Rudi. 'Don't beautiful places make people want to say things?'

'Yup,' said Rudi. 'Normally. But I guess this isn't normal.'

A month later, Rudi and Lev led Ina into the half-completed restaurant, through the heavy glass doors that had replaced the rusting louvres of the old garage. Lev watched his mother's gaze sweep past the ochre-coloured walls, the floor of pale wood, the brick hearth and the bright spotlights, and fly up to the workmen painting the ceiling, as though it were they and not the place she was being invited to admire.

She began to move slowly, anxiously towards the men. They turned to stare down at her – so thin, so wan in her black weeds – and one of them said a polite 'Good afternoon,' from his high perch on an aluminium ladder. But Ina didn't reply. She turned away from the workmen, turned back towards the light coming in from the street and shielded her eyes.

'What do you think, Mamma?' said Lev. 'D'you like the wall colour? Did you notice the fireplace?'

But she just ignored him, as she always did now. She walked slowly to a chair and sat down with her arms resting on one of the new tables. Lev watched as her hands began to explore the fibreboard surface of the table. Then she examined her palm, as if for splinters, or for dust.

'Inferior quality,' she said, in a whisper.

Lev looked at Rudi who, to his mild dismay, was already wearing the new suit Lev had bought him for his coming role as the face-of-the-place.

'She made a comment,' hissed Rudi. 'Didn't she?'

Lev nodded.

Rudi bounded immediately to Ina's side and said: 'Hey Ina, never mind the tables. What d'you think of my suit? Armani, eh? You know Giorgio Armani? First good suit I've ever owned. This certainly isn't "inferior quality". Want to feel the texture?'

He offered the suit cuff to Ina and Ina's gnarled and veined hands slowly rose up from the table top to pinch the soft, dark blue fabric that now enveloped Rudi's hirsute arms.

'Eh?' said Rudi. 'Lovely, isn't it? See the silk lining? Now just let me remind you that your son bought me this suit. With money he earned in England. This place, this suit – everything – has been made possible by him. And I hope, Ina, that this fact is making some headway into your mind.'

Ina took her hand away from Rudi's Armani sleeve. Then she turned her head very slowly towards Lev. 'I'm half-starved,' she said, in a quavering voice. 'If this is a restaurant, bring me some food.'

Lev gaped. He was still weeks away from being able to cook anything in the kitchen. The ovens and burners he'd ordered from Glic hadn't arrived. His contract for the gas supply had yet to be confirmed because *grey* money was still being demanded. 'Mamma …' he began. 'I'm sorry. But I'm not ready yet …'

'No, no, no, wait!' interrupted Rudi. 'Food is no problem. I'll get you something, Ina. Wait there. Unpack some china and lay the table, Lev.'

Rudi raced for the door and ran out. Lev didn't go to find plates and cutlery: he just sat down opposite Ina. He knew where Rudi was heading: to *Fat Sam's American Burger Bar* recently opened on Market Square. Here, on Friday and Saturday evenings, queues of people trailed half-way round the block, waiting for a table or to buy take-outs. Mostly, Lev tried not to think about this place, which the residents of New Baryn seemed to love so much, but he knew that Rudi and Lora were often among the customers, that Rudi's belly was already expanding with the greasy meat and relishes and baps he liked to gorge on there. If this went on, he'd soon be too fat for his Armani suit.

Lev looked at his mother. Her fingers had once more begun their exploration of the fibreboard table-top. Back and forth went her hands, as though they were laying out some imaginary game of cards.

'You're right, Mamma,' he said, as gently as he could. 'The tables are quite cheap, but I'm going to put white cloths on them. They're really going to look very nice.'

She turned away from him – as if to check whether her food was on its way. She behaved as though Lev were talking a foreign language she couldn't possibly be expected to understand.

Rudi came back with five polystyrene boxes of burgers – one for everybody, including the decorators.

Lev wasn't hungry. His burger stayed in its box, but he laid out a white china plate for Ina and set hers on it and she bent her head low and looked at it. Rudi reached over and tore open her little sachet of tomato ketchup, then opened her bap and squeezed the ketchup onto the meat.

'Eat,' he said. 'Like this.'

He picked up his own burger in his large hands and took an enormous bite. The smell of onions fouled the air and reminded Lev of riding on the London Underground. He wanted to walk away – from Rudi and from Ina. Weariness and frustration made his flesh feel shivery, yet peculiarly aroused. He yearned to be lying in a dark room in bed with a woman.

He watched Ina take up her burger. He saw her thin mouth open and a tiny corner of the burger disappear inside it.

'Nice, uhn?' said Rudi. 'Succulent, uhn?'

She went on eating, nibbling like a sheep. Grease began to glimmer on her chin and Lev wanted to wipe it away, but he didn't. He sat without moving and into his tired mind came images of Sophie, which he tried unsuccessfully to banish.

Rudi finished his own burger, then began on Lev's. Giving up on conversation with Ina, he turned to Lev and said: 'Just noticed something when I went out: they've unveiled the new place next door.'

Lev felt his heart lurch. Everything that was going on in New Baryn would affect him. He knew his enterprise would succeed or fail not only according to how good a chef he turned out to be, but also according to what happened round him in the city. He knew he was at the start of another complex and arduous road.

'No sign of any hymnals or corroded old oboes,' Rudi went on. 'I guess that's all under the earth with the former chain-smoking proprietor. But you'll never guess what the place is now.'

'Don't tell me,' said Lev wearily. 'Another restaurant?'

'No,' said Rudi, 'Wait for it. It's an art gallery.'

At these unfamiliar words, Ina looked up. She belched quietly.

Lev went to Eva's bed.

She lived separately from her mother now, in a rented room not far from Podrorsky Street. This room was high up, in the eaves of an old brick building. Pigeons, traipsing around on the roof tiles, performing vigils and courtships, made it noisy – as though rats were skittering about up there – and Lev slept badly.

In the light of early morning, he looked at Eva. A tilted nose. Dark hair strewn across the pillow. Small breasts, white and soft. He was reminding himself that, yes, Eva was beautiful, that, yes, he was lucky that she wanted him. And yet each time he went to her he felt guilty. Sometimes he found himself impotent, right there in her arms.

'Why?' said Rudi. 'I don't get it. She's thirty-one years old. She's got a smile like the Mona Lisa. And she adores you. What's wrong with you?'

'Dunno,' Lev said. 'It's just like that.'

'Like what? Explain it to me, buddy. Because it's not making any sense to me.'

It made sense to Lev, but it embarrassed him, made him feel slightly ashamed, so he couldn't talk about it – not even to Rudi. At first, after he'd met Eva, he'd thought he might be able to love her. He'd wondered whether they might not have a future together. One night, with a full moon shining in through her tilted attic window, she whispered to him that she'd like to have his child.

'Lev,' she said, 'wouldn't you like that? To be a father again?'

He lay by her side and smoked a cigarette. The words he knew he had to find felt heavy and sour in him, like rye bread. He told Eva that being a father to Maya was difficult enough: he couldn't imagine beginning the process all over again. He said that all he wanted to be a father to now was his restaurant, that this was the only thing that gave his life meaning. And when he'd admitted this, he felt light and flooded with sudden happiness, because he'd spoken the truth.

Eva began to cry. Lev watched her get out of bed and tug on her robe and stand at her window. Her flesh looked ghostly in the moonlight, and Lev thought, Yes, that's part of the problem: making love to her is like making love to a ghost.

But there was another factor. Between losing Marina and finding Eva, there had been Sophie. What had happened had happened. Sophie had healed him and then wounded him again. And the truth, in Lev's mind and in his dreams, was that she was still there, laughing, screeching, beating him with her fists. He could still taste her mouth on his, feel her skull pressing against his, bone on bone.

'I'm sorry, Eva,' he said. 'I'm sorry ...'

'So,' she said, 'what am I meant to do? Leave Baryn?'

'You must do what you want,' said Lev. 'You must do what feels right for you.'

Eva didn't leave. She told Rudi that she thought Lev was still in mourning for Marina, but would come to love her – over time.

'But is she right?' Rudi asked him, one morning, as they came out into Podrorsky Street to inspect the restaurant sign that was going up.

'No,' said Lev.

'Yet it's not over, my friend, is it? Because I know you still spend nights in her bed.'

'Yes,' said Lev. 'I do. But that has to end. I'm not going to go there any more.'

'But remember when we met her?' said Rudi. 'That night at the old Café Boris. Remember?'

'That's all I am, Rudi – memory,' said Lev. 'I don't need reminding of one single other thing.'

Now they were looking up at the sign: *Marina*. The lettering was silver on a dark blue ground. Two workmen were bolting it to the wall.

'Looks nice,' said Rudi.

Lev stared at the sign. And he thought how, day after day, year after year, this word, this ghostly name *Marina*, would be kept alive on the breath of the city, and how, for him, this was too melancholy to be borne.

'Take it down,' he instructed the workmen. 'I've changed my mind.'

Rudi dragged him to a new Italian coffee bar on the square where, in this mild autumn, people still lingered outside on metal chairs, drinking latte and cappuccino. When Lev sat in this place, it wasn't difficult for him to believe he was still in London.

'So, what's going on?' said Rudi, when they were settled with their coffee.

Lev rubbed his eyes. 'Rudi,' he said. 'Just be my friend, OK? Just be that.'

'What d'you mean? I am your fucking friend.'

'Don't be this ... inquisitor any more. Just stay with the friend-ship.'

'You doubting my friendship – after all this time? After all the shit we've shared?'

'No.'

'Then what? What?'

'You know *what*. I need to move forwards, not back.'

Rudi ladled up cappuccino foam into his mouth, spoonful after spoonful, till all the messy froth was gone. His eyes were heavy with – what? Fury? Incomprehension? He swallowed the rest of the coffee, slammed down money on the café table and stood up. 'I don't get you,' he said. 'It was always going to be *Marina*. You said you had the name before you had anything else. And now you're betraying the name.'

'No,' said Lev. 'I'm trying not to betray my future.'

'You talk in riddles,' said Rudi. 'You think you're some kind of philosophical genius, or what?'

He pounded off across the square and Lev followed slowly.

He caught up with Rudi in Podrorsky Street, where he found him planted in front of the art gallery that had replaced the old music shop. He was staring in at the window where a brightly lit sculpture, resembling a human torso sliced in half, turned slowly on a circular, mechanised dais.

'Look at that shit!' said Rudi. 'Look at that bit of waste. You recognise what they've made it with?'

'Metal,' said Lev.

'Auto-parts!' exploded Rudi. 'See that gut area: those are radiator hoses. Fuck them! Those "arteries" are spark-plug leads. That "heart" is a fucking distributor. Degenerate arseholes!'

As Lev stared, he saw the gallery owner, dressed in a well-cut suit, move towards the window and stand there, smiling, as though Lev and Rudi might be potential purchasers of the installation in his window.

Rudi saw him too and said: 'He can get out of my sight! I spent half my fucking life going in search of auto-parts. I lay awake at night worrying myself to death. And now what? Some arsehole sculptor just squanders them – as though they had no value. As though nothing had any value any more.'

Lev stood very still. He watched the gallery owner disappear back into the shadow.

'How has anyone ever been able to calculate value?' he said. 'Only by the price people are prepared to pay.'

Lev's restaurant opened in deep winter.

It had no sign, no real name. People just came to know it as Number 43 Podrorsky Street.

Sometimes, as he inspected the table settings, examining the glassware for cleanliness and shine, Lev would see people staring through the doors in the middle of the afternoon, as darkness was falling. 'The gawpers', Lora called them. But in time, it seemed, most of the gawpers became diners. This was still a small town, despite all the new building going on, despite the new enterprises obliterating the old, and rumours about the good food you could eat at Number 43 Podrorsky Street, for reasonable prices, swept round New Baryn like a long series of favourable weather forecasts. By the end of the winter season, bookings were running two or three weeks ahead.

Rudi – who nightly pirouetted from dining room to bar to kitchen and back with an air of seductive authority, like a conjuror, and whose interpretation of his role as the face-of-the-place led him to frequent, startling fits of generosity with free drinks – quickly commented that the place should have been larger, but Lev said no, this was right, this was what he'd wanted: this number of tables, this menu, this consistent adherence to fresh produce, this feeling of intimacy and light ...

In Lev's kitchen – his adored domain – the gas flames burned an obedient blue, leaped to yellow on sudden, triumphant command; the salamanders glowed and shimmered to violent vulcan red. And the sight of all this rainbow heat could often wake in Lev a feeling of joy as absolute as anything he'd ever felt. Because he'd *mastered* it. At long last in his life, these roaring, unquantifiable wonders had become obedient to his will.

He slept only a few hours each night, rose early and went out to the markets. He remembered GK saying: 'You'll have to *delegate*, Lev. You won't be able to prep and cook *and* collect poultry and listen to game-hunters' reminiscences all in the space of the same day.' But delegation wasn't always possible. Rudi, who was drinking and eating a lot each night, liked to sleep late. And not even he – happy as he was in his role as maître d' – shared Lev's ardour for the enterprise. No one else shared it. And so it was often Lev himself who drove into the mountains to pick up game from isolated homesteads, or made long, arduous journeys to Jor, to buy wine. Yet, he didn't mind. He was still on fire for his Great Idea. He still felt in his heart its hot, scintillating thrill.

On the road, he sometimes passed long-distance coaches, going south towards Glic and the border. Catching the reek of their black exhaust, he allowed himself to remember his long-ago journey across Europe, staring at a British twenty-pound note under dim lights, drinking vodka from his flask, eating eggs and chocolate with Lydia at his side.

Lydia.

He'd written a letter to her parents' house, telling her about the restaurant, enclosing a menu, offering her and Pyotor Greszler a free dinner any time they chose. In his dreams, she appeared at the door of 43 Podrorsky Street. She walked in, on the arm of the maestro. The clientele stood up and applauded as Greszler and Lydia were shown to their table by Rudi. Then Lev came out from his kitchen to greet them, and he held Lydia close and she whispered some words to him, always the same words. *I forgive you, Lev. I forgive you.*

But, in fact, they never came. And when Lev told Rudi the whole, awkward saga of his friendship with Lydia, Rudi said at the end of it: 'The thing that amazes me, comrade, is that you *expect* her to turn up.'

'I know,' said Lev. 'When I asked her for ten thousand pounds, I guess that was the last straw.'

'Yeah,' said Rudi, 'it must have peeved her. But that's not why she doesn't come. She doesn't come because she's afraid of what she still feels for you. So you just have to accept it and forget her.'

Lev thought about this. Across so much of his past life, he had attempted to lay some kind of enshrouding darkness. But the people and places underneath this darkness had an obstinate vibrancy. They kept calling to him. They were robed in bright colours. On them, the seasons still cast their alternating light.

One of those who called to Lev was Christy Slane.

Christy had married Jasmina in a registry-office service in Camden Town, and Jasmina had worn a white-and-gold sari and Frankie had been her bridesmaid, dressed also in a little sari that she kept winding and unwinding as the long day of feasting went on.

Christy wrote that his wedding to Jasmina had been 'the most thrilling day of my life' and told Lev that he was replanting the garden at Palmers Green and going to yoga classes. The flat in Belisha Road was let. Christy was done with North London: he was suburban-man now, specialising in kitchen fitting. He was getting fat on Jasmina's chicken *korma*.

Then, in the early summer of the year that Number 43 Podrorsky Street opened, Christy called to say that he and Jasmina had decided to take a holiday in Eastern Europe and they wanted to include in their itinerary a visit to Baryn. On the telephone, Christy said: 'Jasmina knows that one of the few people I miss, Lev, is you.'

They arrived in Baryn one Friday morning in August, driving a rented car. When Christy walked into Number 43 Podrorsky Street, he said: 'Holy shit! Looks like you did somethin' special here, fella.'

The two men embraced. The old tar smell of Christy's nicotine habit was gone and not a trace of eczema remained on his pink face.

Jasmina threw her arms around Lev's neck. 'Congratulate me, hey?' she laughed. 'I'm the new Mrs Slane.'

'Welcome, Mrs Slane,' said Lev. 'Welcome to my shop of dreams.'

When they'd toured the restaurant, admiring the cornflowers in slim vases on each table, and the glinting cutlery and the leather chairs by the fire and the well-stocked bar, Lev led them to the back table and Rudi opened champagne.

To Rudi, Christy said: 'It's hard for me to believe you're a living being. You have mythic status in my mind.'

Lev served lunch. A rabbit terrine on a bed of salad leaves with a herb mayonnaise; duck breasts with a juniper sauce and a potato gratin; a chocolate tart, almost identical to the one he'd made in Belisha Road when Jasmina had first come to supper, long ago, but with a shortcrust so perfected, so astonishingly short, it melted on the tongue like fudge.

'Jesus,' said Christy, when the last mouthful was eaten, 'you've made advances in the food department, fella. I can certainly say that.'

Ina and Maya were invited to this meal. While the grown-ups drank coffee, Maya climbed onto Jasmina's lap and Jasmina smiled and let the little girl examine her earrings and caress her lustrous hair.

As for Ina, this was the first time she'd ever been known to comment on Lev's cooking. Of the chocolate tart, she suddenly said: 'I liked the taste of that. It reminded me of sleep.'

Christy and Jasmina planned to stay three days in Baryn.

'The thing we truly want to see while we're here,' Christy said to Lev, 'is where Auror was. We want to see those hills you described and the new reservoir. We want to take all this back with us to England in our minds.'

Lev hesitated. He seldom went up to the reservoir. Seldom had the time or the inclination. The vastness of the dam itself, the roar of the falling water and the hydro-electric turbines created in him a stubborn kind of awe that pushed out sentiment. But driving the steep road above the dam, to where the water spread out in its vale of hills above the drowned village, made him melancholy. The thing he hated most – more than the loss of the old houses – was that the bodies in the quiet, rural graveyard, including Stefan's body, had been dug up and reburied in the municipal graveyard at Baryn, past which construction traffic now constantly churned and growled. Often, he had dreams of the wild marguerites that used to grow near Stefan's plot. In his imagination, these had been the scent of spring, and now the scent was gone.

But he gave way to Christy's request. He asked Rudi to drive them in the Tchevi, so that whatever feelings might overwhelm him, his friend would be there to understand them.

They made the journey on the Sunday morning, which dawned fair and warm. Rudi and Lev sat in the front of the car, on the newly polished upholstery, with Christy and Jasmina in the back.

The Tchevi's enormous gas-guzzling engine bore them effortlessly away from the town and out onto the old road to Auror. They passed the deserted lumber yard and the grey slopes above it, still bare of trees. Long before they reached the dam, they could hear its roar.

They fell silent as this noise grew in intensity. Lev saw Christy's face looking anxiously out of the window, as though the sound might have been the first rumble of an earthquake or some other catastrophe from which there would never be any retreat.

At the dam's edge, they got out of the car to marvel. Jasmina took photographs with a disposable camera. The August sun spread its hot, flat light across the extraordinary scene. Spray from the cataract was hurled upwards and flattened their hair, like rain.

'My God,' said Christy. 'The things man dreams up! It could make you horribly afraid.'

They drove on. Upriver from the dam, where the reservoir pooled to a depth of several hundred feet, an almost-silence returned and the sound of birds and tiny insects was audible once more. Here, Rudi parked the Tchevi in the shade of some tall pines and the four of them got out and walked down to the water's edge. Small ripples broke near their feet.

'Plenty of fish now,' said Rudi. 'Eh, Lev?'

Yes, thought Lev, concentrate on this, on the fish in the lake, on the way the sunlight on the water dazzles the eye. Don't think about Auror down there in the darkness. Don't think about the past.

He stood without moving. He lit a cigarette, then disliked the taste of it and threw it away. After a moment or two, he was aware of Christy's hand on his arm. 'We won't stay here long,' said Christy quietly, 'because I can imagine what you're feeling. I surely can, because you know what? There's something about it reminds me of Ireland. Something extreme. Eh, fella? Know what I'm sayin'? Something wild and beautiful and full of woe.'

Acknowledgements

My grateful thanks to Jack Rosenthal for showing me how to pick asparagus properly, and for the introductions to his Polish field-workers, who told me true and invaluable tales from Eastern Europe. Thanks equally to Alan Judd, whose impressive knowledge of cars and how their engines work enabled me to run with the 'Tchevi' saga. My thanks to Susan Hill for introducing me to her helpful and courteous police contacts. Also to David Lightbody, Vivien Green, Caroline Michel and Alison Samuel for their useful interventions. Abiding love and thanks to Richard Holmes, to El and Johnny Lightbody, and to my dedicatees, Brenda and David Reid. And lastly, and as always, love and thanks to my editor, Penelope Hoare, to whom my debt of gratitude is now of historic proportions.

R. T.

www.vintage-books.co.uk